WEEP NOT FOR ME

WEEP NOT
FOR ME

Patricia Rowe

A Deirdre McDonald Book
London

First published in 1995
by Deirdre McDonald Books
128 Lower Richmond Road
London SW15 1LN

ISBN 1 898094 06 3 cased edition

ISBN 1 898094 07 1 paperback edition

Designed by Mick Keates

Phototypeset by Intype, London

Printed and bound in Great Britain
by Hartnolls Ltd

I pray that in setting down this story
God will forgive me for intruding into the past.

Also I give the work to my dear lord and husband
to do with as is his pleasure,
for he has set at peace my troubled soul.

P. R. 1994

Preface

Among a profusion of wild flowers, I sit on a bench in the churchyard. It is springtime and I have been drawn back to this place. All around me, set at crazy angles, the old lichen-covered gravestones are peeling, the names almost unreadable. Yet it's not the gravestones which I see that haunt me, but those graves of my kin who have come before me and have no memorial, whose restless souls must drift upon the wind. A patchwork of fields slopes gently away from me and I am moved by the timeless beauty of the Estuary beyond.

I remember the tales of witchcraft and sorcery my grand-mother told me, the presence of Satan woven into the blighted lives of generations of women in my family. I dream that one day my sons will have children who will be interested enough to sit on my knee and listen to tales of a time when, in a different, almost unimaginable world, women toiled to overcome the superstition which was their inheritance.

But I have lost touch; the make-up of the village is changing and commuters occupy the old houses. Yet even today I see young men who look uncannily like my sons. Now, the symbols have all gone, lost for ever in the brown muddy waters. I have borne no daughters and after me there is no one left to inherit the evil. The little girls who stand on the Sea Bank, letting the wind and the past blow through them, have nothing to fear, for they are descended through the males of the line. It is all over, but I owe it to my forebears that their sacrifice shall not go unrecorded.

Patricia Rowe

Prologue

A gaping hole lay in front of me. My little boots, covered with mud, slipped on the edge and earth fell away, down into the abyss. I was overcome by terror. Men in black coats held ropes and fought to keep the coffin level as they lowered my mother into her grave.

I could not bear to look and turned away, clinging to the hand of a lady. The priest in long white robes held a black wooden Cross before him. I looked up at him, but he raised the Cross and would not look back at me. I was only four years old.

The churchyard was overgrown and I could see no path away from the grave. Tall elms, bare of leaves, gaunt against a grey sky, surrounded me. From where I stood, nothing obscured my view. Peaceful countryside spread out below me in all directions. Looking one way, in the far distance was another church. In the other, meadows swept down towards a great river, light reflecting on its calm waters as they flowed into the sea. Desperate with cold and grief, I felt the desolation that only a small child alone can feel. As prayers were said for my mother's Soul, a gentle wind that smelt of the sea blew right through me. On my own, I threw a clod of wet earth into the grave and with a dull thud it struck the coffin. The gentleman my mother knew stood apart, but then quietly came to me. Pressing something into my hand, he closed my fingers over it and motioned me to silence. Just as quietly he was gone. I never saw him again.

CHAPTER I

The Journey

My mother's funeral was long ago. I have always kept safe the simple blue brooch the gentleman gave me that day and often wondered who he was. The brooch has a plait of yellow hair at the centre and a circlet of old gold around its rim. I hope it is my mother's hair, for there is little else I have to remember her by, other than my name, Mary Cheyne. I was born, her love child, in the year of Our Lord 1841.

I have been the ward of the Rev. Thomas Stroat, Vicar of All Hallows, Kingswood, for as many of my sixteen years as I can recall. Kingswood is a fearsome place where few respectable people come. There are coal workings all over this part of Gloucestershire and the colliers are said to be mostly of the Gypsy race. When they come up from the coalface there are boys much younger than I, with vacant stares, filthy black faces and blooded hands and knees. Full-grown men, old before their time, ragged and dishevelled, caked with coal dust, are too tired to be angry.

My guardian has dared me to go out among the common village people. He despises me, saying I am no better than the colliers, being of the same race. I cannot deny the terrible slur, though feel he has to be wrong, for surely my mother was not a gypsy. I fear he would commit me to the workhouse if he knew I listen to the Wesleyans preach, but occasionally I have crept away to join their meetings which give me hope for a different life. My guardian hates the Wesleyans with a ferocity all his own. I ache for the day I can be free and leave this loveless house. I pray for freedom, as the wild and desperate men who toil in the pits pray for freedom from their eternal servitude.

One day in the early spring of the year 1859 my prayers were answered. I knew my guardian was expecting guests when he summoned me, sending word I should dress in my silk gown. In my cold attic room I looked at the gown, limp on its hanger. It had belonged to my guardian's sister. She had been kind to me in this austere place and I grieved when he kept me from her as she coughed her poor life away. I was forced now to put on the gown she wore before she died. Though it distressed me, there was no choice, for my guardian told me often enough that I should count myself fortunate he had educated me and not put me to work in his household. He insisted I should be grateful to him for his mercy. I smoothed down the dull black dress and put my hands to my head to check that my hair, drawn into a bun, was tidy. Considering me vain, my guardian did not allow me a looking glass, vanity being a sin. He reminded me constantly that my mother had been a sinner.

I was just eighteen years old, not very tall, but straight and unbowed: I had long ago learned to control my fear of this place. The dress fitted my slender figure, for I had not yet grown to full womanhood. The stays I wore were tight about my waist and I still wondered why I must be so constrained. The house-keeper had made me cast off my warm woollen vest when my maidenhood flowered and that day I felt for the first time the vice-like clasp of whalebone. The light was fading as I opened the door and, with one hand resting against the wall, descended the narrow staircase into the lamplight below.

The fire in the drawing room was banked up high. My guardian was given free coal before each winter. Perhaps the pit owner hoped for forgiveness and a head start at the Gates of Heaven. The fire spat and the acrid smoke which billowed occasionally from under the chimneypiece made my eyes burn. Standing with his back to me was the bent figure of my guardian and with him, warming themselves in front of the fire, trying to dry out their wet leggings, were two gentlemen I had not seen previously. Peggy, the maid, her hands red from the scullery, was busying herself with glasses on a silver tray.

My guardian turned and scowled at me as I dropped a curtsy to these strangers. The younger gentleman bade me sit down at the table. I felt the stays dig into my abdomen and a feeling of nausea welled up in my throat. The older of the two men was dribbling slightly and he made me want to laugh with an hysteria that came over me in waves. I looked from one to the other and at last the younger man smiled at me, took my hand and sat beside me. On the table was a parchment with a giant seal.

'My dear Miss Cheyne,' the older gentleman said. 'We have something for you which may answer questions you have regarding your pedigree.'

He looked down at the floor, seeming for inspiration. What a strange way to begin, I thought. What could he mean?

'You may remember your mother's death, maybe not. I cannot tell how much children of such a young age remember.'

He coughed.

'We are come here with instructions from your late father's solicitors in Bristol to inform you of your inheritance.'

My mouth was dry. In all the years in this house, no mention had been made of my father. The old gentleman continued and, opening the parchment, proceeded to read the codicil to a Will.

Mary Cheyne, child of my love for Mistress Hannah Cheyne, at the age of eighteen years shall receive the deeds to land and property bordering the Great River that flows through Gloucestershire. She shall also receive the salmon fishing rights and accrued income pertaining to her land. At the age of eighteen years Mary Cheyne shall inherit the box entrusted to lawyers, that was the property of the late Mistress Hannah Cheyne.

It was only then that I saw the small silver jewel box my

guardian was holding. With shaking hands, I took it from him. So my mother's name was Hannah. I was an heiress.

My guardian could not wait to be rid of me and agreed at once that I should make plans to leave. I longed for the interview to end so that I could return to my room and think. There, away from prying eyes, I could touch the precious contents of my mother's jewel box.

One brooch especially caught my eye, for it was ugly in the extreme, being a curled-up serpent with a heart suspended from its mouth. The serpent's eyes burned red and bright out of its jet-black head. I turned it over in my hand and gasped as the pin rammed into my finger, making it bleed. Shaken, I put the brooch back and covered it with pretty beads.

There was also a small silver pill box with the head of a lady painted on it. I cannot know why I rubbed the painting, but, as I did, it seemed to come to life and she smiled gently on me, as a mother would to a child. I wondered who she was.

Within three days I was ready to travel and felt a great surge of joy to be leaving the vicarage at last. I had had to be grateful to my guardian for long enough and was weary of his scorn. The lawyers had told me he was well paid for sheltering me and I no longer need be under any obligation to him. I was free and a pauper no more.

The weather was still bitterly cold for March. I pulled my shawl round me tightly, but shivered in the early morning air. The sky was fiery red to the east and clouds with broken, flaring edges skudded across it. Tiny raindrops stung my face. Shielding my eyes, I tried to see if the cart coming up the track from Warmley was the one ordered by my guardian to stop off for me on its journey carrying coal to the Netham. Steam rose from their backs as two huge carthorses toiled up the hill with their heavy load, the feathers on their feet dancing in the wind. What beautiful, gentle creatures they were and how sorely tried.

The driver looked down on me and took my precious bundle of possessions, putting them safely on the seat beside him. He had a kind face and, as though I were drowning, I grasped his outstretched hand. Suddenly I had begun to fear the long journey I must undertake alone. He told me his name was John Southey and under his breath he muttered, for he failed to understand why my guardian had not accompanied me. But he need not have worried, for I felt perfectly safe in his care. He had orders to see me on my way to the Broad Quay in Bristol. Sitting snugly next to old Mr Southey, I was secure and drank in the comforting smell of his pipe. He whistled a little tune to the horses. They whinnied, pulling themselves up to their full height, and we set off for the Netham.

I had thought Kingswood a harsh place, but it had ill prepared me for the sights to come. Great plumes of black smoke rose up into the sky ahead of us. The Netham seemed a furnace from Hell. The cobblestones shook my teeth in my head as we clattered through the miserable streets of Barton Regis. Mean houses were smothered with thick grey dust. Small ragged children, loaded with smoking bags of spent fuel, returned from the furnaces. Mr Southey said it was the only way their mothers had to heat their homes and keep the worst of the cold at bay.

I saw men toiling naked to the waist in the great iron foundry. All were in rags and the signs of deprivation were everywhere. Now and then Mr Southey hailed people he knew. There was one woman on her hands and knees scrubbing her step, her eyes vacuous, resigned to her drudgery. I thought how futile her life must be. John Southey found a carter who would take me through the Temple Meadows and past the great railway station to the Quay.

I was not his only passenger, for on the cart I met a girl called Rosie. I assumed she was about my age, but she seemed old for her years. She had reddened lips and ash all round her eyes, which made her look tired. Her bodice left bare the most alarming amount of bosom and she seemed to know all the men, who laughed at her and said things I did not understand. She told me she was going to the Hippodrome Theatre on the Quay and that she was an actress, but, shrugging her shoulders, she said if all else failed there was a clipper in from Australia. Rosie chatted all the way until we had crossed the river and together we were put down on the Quay. By now the sun was low in the sky. I said goodbye to Rosie and thanked her, for she had kept my spirits up all the way.

Stepping over ropes which snaked across my path, I was careful not to trip. The smell of the dock and a pungent aroma of tar filled my nostrils. In each direction, ships lined the wharf and pulleys lifted sacks through holes high in the fronts of the buildings. I felt out of place and, keeping my head down, followed instructions to a lodging house next to St Stephen's church.

Over the door of the house was a sign in faded blue paint. It read 'Home from Home'. I pulled hard on the door bell to make it ring. A tall, thin woman opened the door. She looked down at me with cold dispassionate eyes. Yes, she was expecting a Miss Cheyne and if I would follow her please. She led me through a long dark hall that smelt of beeswax. My boots squeaked embarrassingly on the polished floor. But from behind the many closed doors there was no sound. She escorted me up and up the stairs, until at last she opened the door to an attic room. It was not unlike the room I had left, but that seemed an age ago. Against one wall was a small bed and, against another, a washstand with a piece of rough towelling to dry myself on. A cracked blue chamber pot was under the bed and the room smelled of sulphur. The thin woman counted my coins for the overnight bed.

For the first time all day I was alone. My body ached from the journey and I lay down for a while. I did not bother to examine the bed, a straw palliasse, too carefully, for there was nowhere else to stay that night. When it was getting dark I lit the single candle, which flickered in a draught from the curtainless window. The grime that was ingrained would not brush off my skirts, but I was too tired to care. After washing my face and running my hands over my hair, I picked up the candle and went down to dinner. The house might once have been rather grand, but it had decayed. The walls of the dining room were covered with old green baize, except where lifeless portraits stared down on me. A young man, a cadet by his uniform, and an old lady were there before me, as was a middle-aged, well-dressed man.

He stood up and held a chair for me, bowing. I felt a flush creep into my face as he stared hard at me.

I barely noticed the meagre rations and, once I had eaten, retraced my steps to the attic. There I prayed that Almighty God would not neglect me this night.

Next morning, waking early to a cacophony of sounds, my head in a whirl, I went to the window. Looking out over the rooftops to the Quay I could see tips of tall masts that were level with my gaze. But there was little time to stare for I could not wait to see my inheritance and was anxious to be on my way. After a scanty breakfast I crossed the Quay to the carriage company office and bought a ticket. The waiting room was stuffy and filled with smoke, but on the wall was a map. A pin showed our destination, Milbury. Excitement overwhelmed me, but I was a little apprehensive too. The coach stood waiting and with much shouting two ostlers backed a pair of horses between the shafts. The bus, for coach was hardly the word for the covered cart we were to travel on, was full. There were rough wooden seats bolted to the floor and a tarpaulin to keep out the weather. The clouds of the previous day had blown away and today was sunny and bright. My fellow passengers came and went, but, as the sun rose in the sky, slowly we left behind the grand houses men were building on the fringe of Bristol.

The green fields of Gloucestershire, dotted with trees, were spread out before us. Already the air had changed and my excitement had not abated. The driver called out the stops and by the time we got to Almsbury the bus was less full, but from here it carried goods as well as passengers and the poor horses sweated under their extra burden.

For many miles we travelled on a ridge. By now the sun, like a great fireball, hung low in the sky until it disappeared behind the far hills. I doubted we should reach our destination before dark, for the strain on the horses had proved too much and one was lame. We proceeded more slowly until we reached the Inn at Veston where the horse was changed. The moment he was ready to go on, the driver hurried us back on to the bus, for it seemed he was no more anxious than his passengers to be on the road once darkness had fallen.

But it was long after dark when we finally arrived, exhausted, at The Swan in Milbury. Out of the cold and dark, we were welcomed into the warmth of a comfortable room where a fire of scented apple wood roared up the chimney. At last I was here in my new land and felt my old life fall away from me, as though it were a coat dropped, forgotten, on the floor. My new life had begun and I did not doubt everything that had happened to me until now was but a preparation for the future that awaited me here. Content, I went to bed and slept right through until it was morning and I was woken by the brilliant sun.

Refreshed, I set off in search of my inheritance and my destiny. With me was an old man, whose name was Jesse. I had not met him before, yet somehow it seemed as if I had always known him. He spoke my name so as it sounded different from any way I had heard it said before. For the first time I listened to the accent of the people hereabouts and knew that in centuries it had not changed. It held me spellbound. Though the sound was strange to me, in some way it was familiar and I was happy to be here.

It must have been by God's grace that Jesse became my guide. Perhaps he was an angel sent by The Lord to watch over me.

Jesse introduced me to Dolly, his willing little pony. She inhaled the sweet spring air and Jesse handed me up into the trap. I took turns with him to guide Dolly over the uneven ground. She seemed less certain of herself as we drove through the countryside, for we were going a long way for a small pony. Old hawthorn hedges, sometimes leaving only enough room for Dolly and the trap to pass, invaded the road. I prayed that the wheels would not fall off, for as we descended towards the Estuary where the Great River flowed into the sea the potholes became bigger. We passed dense fields of reeds. In some parts the reeds had been cleared and deep clay pits were revealed. Men as brown as berries were shaping grey slime into bricks and I thought of the great houses that were being built in Bristol some twenty miles distant.

Hedges slipped away and the lane became wider, with grass to one side and, to the other, a deep stream, which Jesse called a rhene. He said the rhenes were full of eels.

He stopped at a farmhouse that sheltered in the lee of a hill. The door of the house was opened wide to the bright spring sunshine. The sound of crackling wood came floating over the still air. I wondered who lived in this lovely welcoming place. Jesse took my hand and led me forward. A little way from the house a fire, smoke billowing in huge white clouds, obscured the entrance to a long low barn.

Jesse called out.

'Is anyone at home?'

'My father will be with thee now.'

The smoke was less dense and for a fleeting moment I could see a young man standing beside the fire. He was tying pieces of twig together. I wondered what he was doing. Then, it seemed from nowhere, a gentle breeze blew the smoke away. For the first time I set eyes on Decimus, tenth issue of Decimus Hillyer, and my heart beat so fast I could scarely breathe. The young man's father appeared through the haze. He strode from the barn towards Jesse and had about him a commanding presence. Jesse stood with his cap at his side and I made a curtsy to this farmer who towered over me. He was not really that tall, but had massive shoulders and his bulk cut out the sunlight. Involuntarily I stepped back and had to blink to look up into his face. He must have been very handsome when he was young.

I dared to look again at Decimus. He enjoyed the same huge frame as his father, but was considerably taller. He looked straight back at me, his eyes twinkling as though in some way I was funny.

I felt a sudden stab of annoyance. Who was he to think me funny? But what if my petticoats were showing or a button undone? I looked down at my feet again, but could not contain the flush that threatened my composure. What if I should appear immodest? Trying hard, I listened to what Jesse was saying.

'May we rest a while, Sir? We have come from Milbury to see the young lady's inheritance and the pony is tired.'

To be dazed because a strange young man had looked at me was the most foolish thing, but my mind would not concentrate, for I could feel his eyes had not left me.

The farmer's wife came to the door, preceded by two dogs running out to see who had arrived with the pony and trap. She was very small and wore a black silk dress that showed off her tiny waist. In her hair, that shone like silver, was a beautiful tortoiseshell comb. Tied at her throat was a narrow band of black velvet ribbon. I bowed my head and made a low curtsy to this elegant lady. She acknowledged me most kindly and welcomed me into her home.

Meekly I followed her into the parlour and looked around. Lavish furnishings surrounded me. The vicarage at Kingswood had been very comfortably furnished in a slightly faded way, but I was quite unprepared for the luxury displayed. Later, I would learn that Decimus's father had left the village a mile or so up river to be bailiff to a local landowner. The landowner had died and his widow, Decimus's mother, had married her husband's bailiff. The furnishings of the home she had shared with her first husband were bequeathed to her.

Time was pressing and Jesse wanted to move on so that I should see my inheritance before the cool evening wind blew up the Estuary. We had sated our appetites on fried eels with bread and butter. Jesse had washed his down with a flagon of cider, but I drank water from the cool spring. Dolly parted reluctantly from her bag of oats and we set off up the hill. As we neared the top, we could see green meadows that swept down to the Sea Bank of the Great River. Shaped like a sabre, the river sparkled in the sun. Beyond, just visible through the haze, were distant mountains. At the topmost point of the hill stood a church. Jesse seemed unsurprised when I turned to him, requesting he wait just a moment for me, for the beauty of it beckoned me.

The kissing gate opened to my touch and I followed a path strewn with daffodils and a multitude of wild flowers. To each side of me were old gravestones, some at crazy angles, seeming to grow out of the long grass. I walked on up until the walls of the church were behind me and I could see across fields to where far away in the distance rose another church. Turning my head, I looked towards the magnificent river.

Suddenly I was a small child again, clutching my mother's brooch, blue with a circlet of gold. I had been here before. How long did I stand there? I cannot tell, but dear Jesse knew I was grieving, for he let me dream after I had come back to him.

The lane led down to the village. At the foot of the hill was a barn where from behind closed doors came the piteous cries of an animal going to slaughter. Dolly, her ears set back, quickened her pace, needing no urging. To the right of us was an alehouse with a sign outside that proclaimed its clean beds. We crossed a bridge that spanned a little river; Jesse called it the Pill. Now the water ran in a tiny trickle, but he said that soon the tide would turn and the grey mud of its wide banks would be covered, before the waters receded again. The road forked, giving us a choice, but Jesse set the little pony straight on. The stone road we had trodden had become little more than a rutted track and Jesse struggled to keep the wheels in the ruts so as to save his springs. Then even the track was lost, but in the distance we could see a house and we drove straight on until we reached it.

So this was my inheritance. My heart sank, for the house had been abandoned many years. I climbed down from the trap and went to the front door that was swinging from its hinges. When I pushed it open, the door fell away in front of me revealing a dirt floor that was bare of covering. The outside walls had great gouges in them, letting the evening wind howl in melancholy through the house, as though the souls of the people who had lived here were lost and in torment. Only the sheep would find shelter in this sad place. I wondered if these walls could echo to children's laughter again. My shoulders were beginning to droop, and in spite of my foreboding Jesse led me to the path that would take me up on to the Sea Bank that kept the Great River from flooding the Vale. What other disappointments could my father's Will bring?

I can scarcely describe the glorious scene that opened before me. How infinitely small and insignificant we are in God's great firmament. Intoxicated by the vast expanse of sky, water and land, I stared in awe. Beyond the high Sea Bank, grass stretched for some hundred yards or so before giving way to glistening mud. The waters of the Estuary were fully three miles wide and on the far bank behind the foothills, through a mist, the mountains of Wales rose before my wondering eyes.

To the north, the bank followed the broad sweep of the river. It would not be bridged until it reached Gloucester some twenty miles or so upstream. South of me, the bank extended as far as I could see, until it turned inland where the Pill spilled out its waters to be swallowed in the power of the Great River.

The sun, that was soon to set behind the dark hills, shimmered through the haze. The reds and golds of the sunset cut a broad swathe across the timeless water that would become the sparkling silver ocean I would for ever call the Severn Sea.

My spirits lifted and soared with the gulls. Truly this was my land and one day it would be a happy place again. I knew then that the power of this great and wondrous river was with me and my kin as it always had been.

Jesse put his hand gently in mine. He understood and for a while we were silent. Then he advised me with words I would never forget.

'Whenever you despair and feel you are alone, my child, look into your heart and know that this land is where you belong and it will give you strength to accept God's will. No man can rob you of it.'

In the twilight, Jesse turned Dolly for home. It was well dark by the time we returned to The Swan in Milbury.

Jesse bade me sleep well and I obeyed him.

CHAPTER II

Given Away

During these first heady weeks of freedom Jesse is a constant companion. I have written several times to my guardian thanking him for the protection he afforded me and advising details of my changed circumstances. But I fear he has truly lost interest and forgotten me, for in all of four weeks I have received no reply to my letters.

But I am not downhearted for I relish my new-found ability to make my own decisions and have resolved to restore the house my father left me. It is my intention, for the time being, to enjoy the income from letting my land and fishing rights which will be more than sufficient to support me.

Meanwhile I must find somewhere to live, although Jesse has counselled me against judgements made rashly. He says I am unworldly and should stay at the Inn for a while and become accustomed to handling a way of life that is so remote from my experience.

Milbury is a respectable country town. Livestock going to or coming from market fills the High Street each Thursday. At that time the Inn is a bustling place, where farmers and dealers congregate. I believe my position to be something of a curiosity, for a young woman on her own cannot help but cause comment.

I have searched for my mother's resting place, but can find no headstone and wonder if she is buried in a pauper's grave. I have vowed not to let her name die with her.

My thoughts, though, keep returning to Decimus. I cannot forget him and dream that soon he will come for me. Jesse is looking forward to Whitsuntide when the weather will be set warm and his rheum will heal.

On a day when the heavens opened and sudden rain fell in torrents, I hurried back to the Inn to escape the deluge. It was market day and I had been shopping. Under my arm I carried a box; in it a new gown. I hated the dark sombre colours of the cast-offs I had been forced to wear.

Jesse was waiting for me.

'You have a visitor, my dear.'

He moved aside. Standing behind him was Decimus. In the open he had looked large like his father, but, confined, the room would not contain him. His hair was dark, above a rugged complexion. I was shocked; he seemed older than I remembered, his face already bearing deep furrows. He bowed, but his eyes did not leave mine. I averted my gaze, not able to look at him, for to do so rendered me helpless. His voice too was different, the dialect all but gone.

'My dear Miss Cheyne, you look surprised. Did you not expect me to call?'

He was mocking me. I could not fight him; I had no skill.

'I am pleased to see you, Sir.'

'May I sit, or would you rather I stand and wait for the inclement weather to pass?'

I flushed, in my confusion forgetting all my manners, and sat down, somewhat hesitantly indicating the chair opposite. His eyes still mocked.

'Will you take tea, Sir?'

Another shock awaited me. Decimus's manners were culti-vated. He was completely at ease in his surroundings, not at all the young man of my first impression. He sought to question me and I would gladly have told him what little I knew about myself had not Jesse, in the most casual way, interrupted me.

But Jesse did not stop me when I informed him I had been

16

the ward of a reverend gentleman. I could not allow Decimus to harbour illusions about me.

'Sir, I bear my mother's name and know not my father's.'

There, it was out, and his stare was more than I could tolerate.

'That is no reflection on you, Mary.'

He no longer mocked me and I hardly noticed his familiarity, for my heart near burst of love for him.

Within a week Decimus returned. He did not ride this time but drove a governess cart. He asked Jesse if I might accompany him with Jesse as chaperon. I was a little vexed he should not ask me directly, but it was only a passing thought. On that day, as we drove through sheltered lanes, Decimus was kind to me and gave me all his attention. He asked Jesse if he might have my hand in marriage and, swept away, I was overwhelmed with love for him. Jesse smiled and said that if I was willing he could see no objection.

During a glorious spring and early summer Decimus showed me the beautiful Vale of Hartley, where nearly everyone seemed in some way related to him. It made my head spin to try to remember all his cousins, uncles, aunts, great aunts, and second cousins twice removed. We laughed together as we counted them, for we rejoiced that we had found one another. Three months after I came into my inheritance, before the Altar of St Mark's in Milbury, Decimus and I were wed and I gave my life and my love to him.

Later, with the summer sun to warm us, in the corner of a quiet meadow, he took my maidenhood. I had promised to honour and obey him, but knew nothing of the ways of men and was awed by the power my vows had given him. He owned me now and suddenly I was in fear of him.

His wise hands pulled me down and we lay together in the soft grass. Willow trees, their branches rustling in a gentle breeze, protected our secret bower. The sun's rays played on us through the dapple of their leaves. Decimus kissed my lips and caressed me, seeming aware of the fear that welled inside me. I knew my duty was to pleasure him but knew not how. He took the pins from my hair, letting the heavy dark tresses tumble down my back; then raised my face to the sun. I closed my eyes.

'Open your eyes, Mary,' he said. 'You may close them later when I tell you to. Perhaps if you cannot see what I shall do, you may be less afraid.'

He unbuttoned my boots and slipped them from my feet. Raising myself, I gazed up into the branches above me, my mind transported by the warmth and the fragrance of my bed of grass. Lost in my love for him, his voice interrupted my dreams. He told me I must stand, for he wished to undress me. No one, not even my guardian's housekeeper, had seen me naked and shaking my head I tried to make him understand. He tilted my chin. I looked up at his face and into eyes that laughed gently at me.

'You can have no secrets from me, my dear. Now you will let me look at you.'

Trembling and mute I stood. I would endure it, whatever it must be, for I loved Decimus and was now his wife. He took off all my clothes and I could not bear to look at him. He unlaced my stays. I had always detested whalebone and now he freed me and the fresh country air bathed my skin for the very first time. He drew me back into the grass.

As I lay there naked, he was watching me. I looked up and trusted him. Decimus smiled and his hands were balm as gently he touched each of my breasts. Strange new sensations swept through me. I tried to raise myself again but could not, for he held me firmly. I dared not engage him in conversation, guessing he would not welcome it. I was caught in a web, my will not my own.

He set my legs apart and the cool air touched my secret places. His eyes travelled over me. Time had no place as we lay together that magical day. He turned me over and drew a long grass down my spine and between my buttocks. Sighing with pleasure, I felt faint, as though sleep would come upon me. He placed one hand carefully under me and his fingers touched me. My heart was pounding. I could not think what he intended to do.

Without warning, with both his hands he pulled me apart and in pain, feeling my skin torn, I cried out. Shaming me, he made me sit up and watch as my maiden's blood seeped into the grass. My hands tried to cover where he had injured me, but he held both of them in one of his and would not let me touch myself. I knew then in whatever life God gave me I would be in subjection to him, as was Sarah to Abraham all those centuries ago.

He told me to wash in the stream and come back when I was clean. When I returned, Decimus showed me the bare earth where I was to lie. No grass grew on the place he chose and the ground was hard to my bones. He spread my limbs to their extremity and kissed the parts he had so cruelly broken. Then he left me defenceless to wait for him and I lay in the dirt, subdued and fearful. He removed all his clothes. I had not seen a man naked before. He stood over me and I was desperately afraid. As he lowered himself, I tried to pull away and threw up my hands to protect myself from him. Shaking, I could not control my fear and bewilderment.

'Put your hands down, Mary, and close your eyes.' His voice was urgent and harsh.

Rigid with terror, I obeyed him. He penetrated me, the feel of his great horn deep inside me invading my very soul and stealing from me the being that was me. Again and again he thrust himself into me, his strength overwhelming my love for him. In his passion, he seemed to have forgotten me and I wept as he took what I knew was his right and his great hands bent me to his need.

Then for reasons I know not, my terror ebbed and my deflowering ceased to distress me. I put my arms about him, that he should know I did not mind his loving, whatever he must do to me. He fertilised me with his seed, that I might bear his first child, and, my girlhood gone, I became a woman. He helped me to dress. Weary but content, I put my arms about his neck and he carried me home to his father's house.

Decimus bade me call his mother 'Granny' as his brothers' children did. He instructed me that I must learn from her the crafts I would need to become a good wife.

Summer that year was still and warm and the water ran low in the rhenes. Grass grew lush and we gathered sweet-smelling hay during those long sunny days. Some evenings when supper had been cleared away, with a smile that was just for me, Decimus held my hand and together we escaped his father's house. We took off our shoes and, laughing, with naked feet trod the dew-drenched grass. Even in the dark, Decimus needed no light to guide him to the secret bower we shared. Giant stars stared down out of a black sky, so close we could almost touch them, and the air was soft like velvet.

Yet at the end of a long day I was often tired from the tasks he had set me, for my hands were not allowed idleness. Decimus seemed not to notice my pallor and in his passion made no allowance, his pleasure nearly always hurting me. Though nothing could diminish my love for him, fear of my husband grew, for not even my scent was my own now. My body smelled of him, its identity lost.

I have much to learn about the ancient way of life hereabouts, especially the fishing for salmon. Men wade far out at low tide into the mud of the river where they set cones of woven willow they call putchers. On the full tide, silver salmon returning to the sea are trapped in the gaping cone and stranded as the waters recede.

Decimus now owned land and fishery as far north of the village as the Old Inn that stands on the Sea Bank. He showed me how to handle the majestic and valuable salmon. We laid them in rows on a marble slab to keep them fresh until they could be taken to market. There were eels too, that were caught in the rhenes in nets and I watched horrified when Decimus chopped off their heads and skinned them, still wriggling in his hands.

Harvest time came and all the village, even small children, toiled under a full moon to bring in God's bounty. When the last of the corn had been gathered in, the farmers' wives laid out a celebration supper and everyone was there. Tables groaned with the produce of this beautiful land and the gypsies, who camped nearby, entertained us with their music and dancing.

Dear Jesse came and sat beside me. He knew I was with child though I was far from sure myself. Cupping his gnarled old hands about mine he held me, knowing my imprisoned soul would not lie still, and understanding too the rebellion in my heart, that even to myself I could not admit.

'Marriage can be a hard bed to lie on, my child, especially for one raised without a mother's guiding hand, but you must have faith. Give your husband your will and obey him above all things. Keep nothing from him and you will find joy, that I promise you.'

I remembered my wedding day. It was Jesse who had given me to Decimus and, despite my fears, my resolve to wed him had not faltered, for my love parched me with a thirst that would never be quenched. I had left everything at the altar to become my husband's chattel. The deeds to my land, my money and all I possessed were now his and lost to me. The freedom I had so craved, by my marriage vows I had given away, and it was too late now to change my mind.

Jesse let go my hands and, my duty made plain to me, my daydream ended. Through the throng of laughing faces, Decimus approached and stood over me. Fearing him, I bowed my head and dropped to my knees for all to see my quiet obeisance.

Darker evenings brought cool autumn winds that rose off the river and our first summer together became but a memory. The skies, an unremitting grey, were full of menace for the winter to come. The child in my womb grew and my husband ordered me to leave off my stays. My hands were chapped and my knees sore. Exhausted, I toiled without respite from dawn to dusk and had not in all my life experienced such labour. I wondered why Decimus was so unkind to me, but dared not question his authority. Granny observed the discipline he imposed, but made no comment, for had she not been moulded by two men?

When I felt a quickening in my womb, Decimus insisted I see

an old crone in the village. Her name was Mistress Morgan and he told me I must obey her as though her commands were his very own. She would examine me and tell him if I was to bear a male child.

Following Granny's directions, I found her house. It was old and dilapidated, its walls almost hidden by ivy. Smoke from the chimney was carried away in the stiff cool breeze.

My numbed fingers knocked on her door and it yielded to my touch. Before me was a darkened room. Old velvet curtains over tiny windows shut out all but the merest shaft of light. The door swung behind me and closed itself. My eyes quite soon became accustomed to the gloom and I could make out rag rugs strewn on a dirt floor. A very old lady was sitting in a high-backed chair with a cat on her lap. She was crocheting a shawl. Her deep-set eyes looked out of a face dark and lined, like old wood.

Into her hands I placed a basket of provisions Granny had given me to take to her.

'Mistress Morgan? I am the wife of Decimus Hillyer. My husband has sent me to see you.'

'I know who you are, my dear. I am expecting you. You must thank your husband's mother for the provisions.'

To understand her speech, I had to listen hard, for her accent was very strong. She set the basket down on the table beside her, the cat not troubling to move.

'This shawl is for your firstborn, my dear. Now lie down on my bed behind that settle and let me feel your belly.'

She put down her crocheting and the cat stretched, leaving her. The bed I was to lie on was raised and covered with a quilt of knitted squares. Mistress Morgan got up from her chair and came towards me, leaning heavily on two sticks. I wondered whether it pained her dreadfully to walk. The feeling of doom I had harboured these past many weeks threatened to engulf me, but I lay down as she commanded and let her lift my petticoats. I would have stopped her, but was reminded that Decimus had said I must submit to her probing. She pulled my drawers down and it was all I could do not to push her away when she touched the parts that were seen only by my husband.

From her pocket she drew out a watch on a long chain which flashed in the single shaft of light that fell on me. Dangling it above my belly, she stared at it intently. I could not tell if it swung in circles or backwards and forwards, but she seemed pleased and I chided myself for my unreasoning fear.

'You will give your husband a son, my dear. Tell him you doubted me, so he should name the babe Thomas.'

She laughed, though barely a sound came from her, and I felt uneasy. I hoped to leave and sat up, but into my hand was put an empty glass, cracked and smeared with dirt. She uncorked a stone pot that seemed too heavy for her old hands to lift and poured out a thick black liquid until the glass was full.

'Now to help your husband's child, my dear, you must take this cordial. It will taste bitter, but I want you to drink every drop.'

Drinking deep, nausea swept over me, but I had to obey her and finish it. My insides heaved and my senses reeled. I drank once more, gagging on the bitter brew, but drained the glass. The room swam before my eyes as she took the glass from me and pushed me back on to her bed. Before sleep overcame me and through a thick haze, I could see in her hand a knife, yet, even as I saw it, there was no escape for me and I knew little of what she did.

My head ached. The shaft of light was gone, the room almost dark. She brought her candle to me and when I looked down at my swelling abdomen I saw she had marked me and was thankful I had not endured her bloody trace without that fitful sleep.

Mistress Morgan wiped her knife that still lay on the bed and returned it to its scabbard. In deepest shock my feet found the floor. I pulled up my drawers and smoothed my petticoats. Her voice came to me through the fog that filled my head.

'Come sit with me a while, my dear, so that you are recovered sufficient to make your journey home.'

The cuts into my belly burned hot. Blood was seeping through my petticoats. I wondered, why? What had I done that I should bear this stigma which Decimus had seen fit to be placed on me?

But old Mistress Morgan knew the reason and reached up for her Bible. She opened it and selected a page, then placed the Book into my hands, instructing me to read it out loud to her. By the light of her single candle, I read the lines:

> . . . she took of the fruit thereof, and did eat, and gave also unto her husband . . . And the eyes of them both were opened, and they knew that they were naked . . .
>
> And the Lord God . . . said, Who told thee that thou wast naked? Hast thou eaten of the tree . . .
>
> And the woman said, The serpent beguiled me, and I did eat.
>
> And the Lord God said unto the serpent . . . thou art cursed . . . ; upon thy belly shalt thou go, and dust shalt thou eat all the days of thy life: And I will put enmity between thee and the woman . . .
>
> Unto the woman he said, I will greatly multiply thy sorrow and thy conception; in sorrow thou shalt bring forth children; and thy desire shall be to thy husband, and he shall rule over thee.

Struck dumb, I had no words. Mistress Morgan took the Book from my hands that could not hold it for trembling.

Fear consumed me. Had not my mother given me a serpent with a heart hanging from its mouth? Who was my mother and what had she done? What more sorrowing was there to come? I tried to speak but Mistress Morgan cautioned me.

'Your mother was not wed, nor her mother before her. There is a well just yonder where they threw your grandmother, for she was cursed. She was a Daughter of Satan. The men of the village attacked her with whips and flung her into its depths, leaving her to die.

'Now you, my dear, have returned to this Vale and will make reparation for the sins of your forebears. By his mark on your belly, I pray your husband and his child will be protected from you.'

Night had fallen when I left Mistress Morgan. In the pitch-black dark, blinded with tears, I could not see. In my grief, I whispered.

'Oh Decimus, why have you forsaken me and left me to endure this terrible penance alone?'

My underclothing, soaked with blood, stuck to my skin, each movement paining me. The path beneath my feet was slippery and I fell many times. A wind raced through the trees, roaring its defiance, tearing the shawl from my head. I thought to die. The clouds separated. The moon was rising and by its silvery light I could see the track ahead.

Decimus was waiting for me when I fell out of the night and into his presence. But his look was stern and forbidding as his gaze turned to my burning belly. Granny was silent.

I thought to question him.

'But why, Decimus?'

He ignored me.

'Put down your shawl and lift your petticoats.'

I did as he ordered and waited, while he pulled down my blood-soaked drawers and examined me.

'Mistress Morgan has marked you well, now go ye to bed and sleep.'

Granny rose from her chair, lit a candle and took my hand, leading me to bed. She wept when she saw my husband's mark that had been cut into me.

'I am so sorry, my child, but it had to be done.'

'But why, Granny? How can Decimus do this to me if he loves me?'

'Mary, my dear, do not ask me why. The potion you were given, though you cannot know it, has blunted the pain and you will sleep.'

Granny's kind hands undressed me for I was so weak I could not do it myself. She fetched fresh linen to dress my wounds. Then binding me tight, she closed the cuts and the bleeding was stopped. Gently Granny pulled my nightgown over my head, the folds covering my swollen belly. She released my hair and her soothing hands brushed it for me. For a moment Granny looked to say something more, but stopped herself and just held me, consoling me with her love. She kissed my forehead and put me to bed to sleep.

In the light of morning Decimus undid the bandage and looked at the mark I bore. He touched the place that was broken and his great hands could not cover it. I did not question him again. He brought a warm damp cloth and wiped away the blood that had congealed, opening the cuts. From the shelf he took down a small blue bottle and emptied the contents, a powder of darkest green, on to my naked skin. As he spread it over the wounds, I feared to die from the pain and wept, for it was more than I could bear. My back arched as he opened each cut, for none could be left untreated. My heart beat against my chest and I could hardly breathe.

He bathed the dreadful brand in cool water and as the powder was washed away I saw that on my belly and down into my secret parts he had revealed a delicate web of the utmost intricacy carved into my skin. He was well satisfied.

Decimus left me and, still in shock, slowly I dressed myself. Mistress Morgan's words rang in my ears and I wondered what torment my mother had endured and would in turn be mine, to atone for the sins our forebears had visited upon us.

Pulling my shawl about me, I left my father-in-law's house. The path to the church was steep and I was faint from my punishment. Clouds tore across the sky and rain lashed my face. My skin burned like fire and the pain obsessed me. The child within me would not be still. Despairing, I dragged myself up the steps, gravestones on either side of me. I thought of my poor mother and resolved to look no more for her grave. The church was empty and silent. I sank to my knees before the altar and prayed to Almighty God to forgive me. Lost in misery, I fell down on my face and stretched out my arms, begging for pardon.

I cannot know how long I lay alone in the biting cold before I felt Jesse come to me and by his presence he released me from my penance.

CHAPTER III

Thomas

The first Sunday in Advent has passed and the family is preparing for the coming feast of Christmas. Decimus has ordered my isolation from all who come to his father's house. He insists too that some part of each day be spent alone in quiet contemplation to purge my mind and body of impurities. Winter is hard upon us, darkness descending by four in the afternoon. During the long, silent hours of reflection the intensity of the quiet is all I can bear.

No hill stands between these low-lying lands and the Cotswold escarpment some many miles distant. As the prevailing winds change direction and blow from the east, the cold has found its way into the marrow of my bones and I begin to understand why the people of this beautiful Vale dread winter's onset. Willows, which they call withy in these parts, their branches bare above sturdy trunks, stand like sentinels; mists swirl across the sleeping meadows. All around, the ground yields, sodden, and no one dares tread except on the duckboards marking the track to the village.

But even in winter's depths, this haunting landscape holds me in rapture. From the window of the room I share with Decimus, I look out on clouds of plovers that sweep across the fields and honking geese that fill the sky.

My learning in Granny's hands continues. She has taught me how to turn golden cheeses that are stacked on shelves in the dairy to help mature them evenly, ready for market. Granny has described how we shall make clotted cream when the grass grows again in the spring and our cows give us milk in abundance. Above the range hang gleaming shallow pans which will be filled with the topmost milk from each churn. The milk will be left to settle, then be warmed gently, until a thick yellow crust is formed to be ladled out and set aside. When there is no more crust to be skimmed, the thin milk that is left is fed to the pigs.

Granny has a giant red earthenware pot that she has filled with waterglass. Stacked layer upon layer are eggs, laid down and preserved. Separately, to keep for a short while, other eggs have been covered with goose grease. Granny has given me a pot of the pure white fat to rub into my belly and help ease the tension where my skin is stretched by the child growing inside me. Thin silvery lines have joined the tracery of deep blue-green which is my husband's mark. Slowly, it is healing.

During these short winter days I have come to love Granny and dare confide to her my fears. Decimus has not made love to me since I saw Mistress Morgan and I feel sure I have offended him. Though I pray each day to Almighty God to forgive me the sins I have inherited, I fear Decimus will not forgive me and no longer wants me. Granny has tried to set my fears to rest, saying Decimus is anxious not to hurt his son and will not make love to me again until after I have given birth.

She has encouraged me to talk of my girlhood, to recall memories all but lost. We have talked too of her own childhood, about her father who could trace his line back to Good Queen Bess; of her ancestor who was the Queen's favourite courtier.

When she was widowed, Granny's father was dismayed that she should wish to marry her dead husband's bailiff, for he was just a common man, while Granny's family were gentry. But eventually her father had relented and settled land on the bailiff, Decimus's father, who was himself Decimus, the tenth child his mother raised. When Granny talked of her husband, her voice was lowered and reverent. I wondered how difficult it had been for a lady like Granny to become the wife of a yeoman farmer.

Mr Hillyer was such an intimidating man, yet I could see in Granny's eyes her abiding love for him.

We talked too of my husband. When he was born, Granny feared he would not survive, but through her prayers and piety the Lord had spared her babe and Decimus was always special to her. Granny had nurtured him and as the years went by he had grown a powerful frame and, by his disposition, an inner strength and bearing, which set him apart from other men. I did not doubt that should Granny outlive her own dear husband she would, when the time came, give her consent to the authority this son would wield over her, as would others who sheltered under his protection.

I cannot tell at what point a cloud crossed Granny's face, as though a long-dead memory had stirred, but it seemed of little consequence, for she quietly continued to reminisce.

When Decimus reached his majority, Granny's father had given him a farm, which by chance abutted my inheritance. Granny told me that after our child is baptised and I am churched to cleanse me of my labours, Decimus will take me there to live.

But Granny is emphatic there are many more lessons I must learn before that day comes. She has cautioned me most severely to concentrate my mind and follow only the path my husband determines for me. I cannot know what trials there are to come, but without Granny's love I fear I may falter.

Over countless generations, faith in God has sustained the people of this Vale against the adversity of flooding from the Great River. Each Sunday evening Mr Hillyer (I cannot bring myself to call him other than by his formal name, fearing that to do so would be construed as familiar) reads aloud from the Bible.

In the quiet of a December evening just a week before Christmas, Decimus placed the Holy Book into my hands, directing me to the words of St Paul to Timothy '. . . but the woman being deceived was in the transgression . . .' Decimus spoke sternly to me, saying I should mark it well upon my consciousness. He also directed me to the Gospel of St Peter and his instructions on the duties and status of wives. I understood the holy words and in my prayers asked God for guidance to accept the will of my dear husband with humility and joy.

Throughout those long dark months, Decimus confined me without remission, except for one precious hour when he allowed me the company of his brothers and their families who called on Christmas Day. He wished them to see that I was carrying his son and for such a little while the contract to which I had set my hand just six months previously was less onerous.

Granny has advised me all she can about the labour I must bear. She says the lessons I have learned so far are but a preparation for the watershed that is to come, when Decimus will test my disposition and strength for the road he has chosen for me to travel. The evenings are getting lighter and my time is drawing near.

It was late in the afternoon and I was helping to bake bread, the tasks Decimus set me being less rigorous now. Granny kept me company. Looking down at my swollen belly, she touched where her grandchild lay, then told me more about her favourite son.

'Had Decimus not admired your will and fortitude when first he saw you, Mary, he would not have wed you. He could not tolerate a weak woman and sought a wife with a will as strong as his own. But you cannot enjoy a will of your own any more, my dear, and I still sense the mutiny that is in your heart that you try so hard to conquer. Perhaps it will be easier for you to give way when the agonies of birth are behind you. Do not make your husband take your will by force, Mary.'

I thought that Granny would cry.

'When he discovered that wretched brooch and guessed you were your mother's daughter, you were already carrying his child. He had no choice but to shield his son and order Mistress Morgan to cut his mark into you, so that the babe might rest safe in the cradle of its protection. But Decimus will not let your soul be lost to Satan, Mary.

'Your life together is only just beginning and one day you will look back and wonder how you found such joy and love, the like of which few women are privileged to experience. You will become confident in the refuge my son will create for you and he will give you the courage to let him mould you into the woman you are destined to be. I see a family come forth from your union who, despite your heritage, will be respected in this Vale for more than a hundred years.'

A first small stab of pain floated through my body and, instinctively, I knew my labours were about to start. With both my hands I supported the precious burden that would soon burst free. He lay low and the weight of him pressed hard down on my abdomen. The day was fading fast and I prayed this child would see the morning light.

Granny held my hand and led me into the scullery, calling to her maid to lift down the copper bath and fill it with scalding water. Granny unlaced each of my boots and took them off. She released me from the shapeless gown, of which I have grown so tired. I let my petticoats drop to the floor and stood on them so that the stones would not strike cold, then undid my camisole. Without it, my breasts, that were so full now, were heavy and I crossed my arms to reduce their discomfort. Granny pulled down my drawers and eased my stockings from my feet. Now that the day I had looked forward to had arrived, in trepidation I shivered and waited for the bath to fill sufficiently.

The water was hotter than I could bear but Granny made me lie in it, saying the warmth would help relieve the pain I must endure. But it was so hot, perspiration poured down my face, my heartbeats deafening me. When she was satisfied I had soaked long enough, she bade me stand, but had to stop me from falling, for I was faint. Her maid soaped me, then ran cool water all over me. When I was dried, Granny rubbed scented oil into my skin. The perfume wafting about me lulled my fears. My cruel latticework stood raised on my belly and I noticed that her maid was staring in astonishment, but with a look from Granny she dared not speak of it. I still fear to contemplate what has been done to me and cannot bear to look, but in truth do not wish it otherwise. Decimus would not have marked me had there been any other way to protect his son from the evil in me.

Granny took my garments and, lifting a stove plate on the

range, placed them one at a time into the fire that roared beneath. I watched as all my clothes were destroyed but could not find the words to ask her why. Granny wrapped a blanket of fine wool around me and, clutching at the folds, I followed her upstairs. The bedroom fire threw warmth across the room. The counterpane had been folded away and except for layers of sheets and a pillow for my head the bed was bare. Granny took away my blanket and helped me to lie down. I lay there and waited while she hurried to fetch Decimus.

His great presence stood over me and my body trembled with fear. His eyes scanned me.

'I must leave you now, Mary, for this is woman's work. When they have done with you, I will take my son. You will not touch him until I bring him back to you to suckle.'

Decimus's fingers traced the brightness of his mark and I caught his smile that of late was rare indeed. Supporting himself on the bed that would see my suffering, tenderly he kissed my cheek. It was only then that I saw he was weeping.

My joyous heart reached out to him and I kissed his hand, for he loved me. He left me with Granny. The pain was more urgent now as my body prepared for its impending task. The bed on which I lay was hard to my bones, for the feather underlay had been taken away. Only the linen-covered board supported me. Humility and cold overcame me and I asked if I might have a quilt to cover my nakedness. Granny was not persuaded and I did not question her decision, for Decimus had instructed me that upon my childbed I should heed his mother's words as though they were his own.

The French clock, that was a gift to Decimus when he wed me, quietly chimed the quarters and the pains which had come but twice in each quarter when my labours first began came now five times as fast. As each pain became almost as one, nothing released me from my torment. But still the pain I must endure held me tighter in its grip until I could bear it no more. Granny smoothed my aching back to comfort me and lit a nightlight by my bed. Then she left me alone in the silence with my anguish. Turning down her lamp's wick, she dozed as my labouring continued and the quiet house slept. No matter where I turned, my forsaken body screamed and still the pain seized me more. There was no yesterday and no tomorrow. My being ceased to be. It was a trivial passing thought that even should I die, it mattered not. This sublime affliction that was upon me took me in its maw and I surrendered to my fate, which only God could know.

The clock struck many times, the sound of its chimes coming from far away, such was my concentration on this terrible journey. Suddenly and without warning, my waters ruptured and, bathing me in their warmth, they surrounded me.

Granny turned up her lamp and its light glowed bright. She took the wet draw sheet from under me.

Weeping, I turned to her.

'Granny, I hurt so much.'

'Mary, my child, you have withstood your ordeal well, but now you will learn why a woman must labour on her childbed, for your work is just beginning and only by your efforts will this child be born. Though your suffering will be far worse yet, the pain will not grieve you as you grieve now, for by each contraction the child within your womb will be pushed closer to his birth. My dear, I pray your agonies will be at an end before this night is over.'

Granny ordered me to turn on to my side and the reason for my nakedness became apparent. There was work she must do to make ready for the birth and a quilt would have hampered her. Nor would she permit me to hide from my responsibilities. Granny put one hand on my swollen belly and with the other, reached into my opening and parted me. I gasped as she slid her fingers deep inside me, but she smiled and looked down at me.

'You must not be discouraged, Mary, for though you see no progress you are doing well and when you are overcome by the urge to push you must bear down hard on your abdomen.'

Each pain was more intense and I pushed with all my strength. Fever burned in my body that had been cold as ice and Granny bathed my face in cool water. I feared my body would withstand no more, yet still my labouring continued. When each

33

contraction had faded, Granny bade me rest awhile during this too short respite, but my body would not let me rest. She turned me on to my back. Pushing my legs up, she bent my knees, so that the soles of my feet lay flat on the surface of the bed, then spread my legs wide. She gave me a knotted piece of linen to bite into. Taking away my pillow, Granny told me to hold on to the rail behind my head and as I felt the cold brass my sweating hands grasped it. With her scissors, though I could not feel it for the pain was at its height, she cut me, so that my dear child would be assured of an easier passage.

As though to give me strength, I gripped the rail and pushed. With each shattering effort, I bit hard on the gag, smothering my cries, for Granny said I must under no circumstance let Decimus hear me in my weakness.

Then quite suddenly Granny smiled again. She directed my hand to where I parted and there I felt the wrinkled head of my precious child and knew my labouring had been worthwhile. Bearing down, with all my might I pushed and his head, forcing a way, opened me. My mind obsessed with its task cared not for the agony my body endured. Granny's voice bade me blow a feather so as now I should not push too hard and tear. Then, in just a little while my child burst free and his dear sweet body warmed my innermost thighs. Granny held him up for me to see. He was attached by a long white cord which carefully she cut, separating him from me.

She called her maid to attend me for Granny's work was nearly done. Departing, she took the child to his father for approval. I lay quietly, deep in thought, for I knew a truth had been revealed. By his birth, the life in our child would surely carry me and my beloved Decimus to eternity.

With a final seizure, the afterbirth was free and while I waited for Granny to return to make one last reparation, her maid washed me. Granny carried with her a needle threaded with fine silk. I lay still as she stitched me inside where I was cut, pulling the skin up tight so that my condition should not hinder my husband's pleasure. Granny then took a porcelain dish and I watched her slice a sliver of afterbirth. She said I must swallow it. I fell back in horror, for I had not heard of this custom, but Granny said it would help my womb to heal and assist the milk to flow. So I did as she told me. The bed was stripped around me and when it was remade, the feathers puffed high and new linen brought, Granny let me lie down again. She covered me with a shawl of softest wool, which warmed my tired limbs. In this peaceful state, I watched the sun break through and waited in fear and humility for Decimus to bring his son for me to suckle.

My body drew strength in the warmth of my blissful bed and I thanked God for my child's safe deliverance. Waiting for Decimus, I touched my breasts which soon would suckle his son. I longed to hold the babe in my arms, but knew Decimus would bring him to me only when he thought fit. The shawl that covered me was Mistress Morgan's work. It was crocheted in the same intricate pattern that was on my belly. Running the shawl through my fingers, I marvelled that her cruel old hands could have made something so beautiful. Just to think of it all made me weep. Lying there safe in my father-in-law's house, pictures of Decimus flitted across my mind. At the Inn, he had looked so different from the young man who had laughed at my discomfiture. Yet it had not mattered. He had come for me, as I prayed he would. Dwelling on my wedding day, I reflected on what had happened to me since that moment not a year ago when by my own hand I had condemned myself in plenitude to the man who was now my master.

Granny disturbed my quiet reverie. She brushed my hair, spreading it about my shoulders, the tresses reaching below my waist, so long I could sit on them. Then she changed the pad in the open wound that was for my beloved child his entry into a mortal life. With bowed head, I awaited my lord.

Holding him as though he might break, Decimus came to me and, with just a fleeting frown on his bemused face, settled his son into my waiting arms and I touched him for the very first time.

'My dear wife, I could not ask more of you. Take my son and guard him well, for he is all the world to me. You will give me many sons, Mary, but none will be so precious as this first sweet child.'

My heart ached with joy that I should receive such praise. Decimus caught hold of the shawl and so very gently peeled it back, that he should see the place from where I had laboured. He touched my breasts and, taking one in his great hand, guided it into his son's parted lips. I closed my eyes, overcome with love for my babe as his tongue closed around my nipple and he sucked.

Decimus sat on the bed beside me and watched those first fumbling steps I took into the craft of motherhood. He saw I had much to learn and, putting his arm about my shoulders, he reassured me. When his son had finished this first clear liquid which would soon be gone, Decimus laid him in the cradle. Holding both my breasts, he gently squeezed them. Blue milk veins came to the surface as he increased his hold and I began to weep, for his new pain was too much to bear after my recent suffering.

I awoke with the clock's chimes. My babe still slept and I gazed in wonder at his tiny body, his head covered with golden down, his little eyelids smudged with grey. How perfect he was, swaddled and peaceful in his cradle, recovering from his hazardous journey. I tried to raise myself to touch him, but was too weak to move. Decimus was standing with his back to the window, his dark outline blotting out the light that was fading as another night drew near. When he saw I was awake, he brought a chair and sat with me. Before two more days were through, my milk would flow and Decimus told me that before then he must prepare me to nurse his son. He removed the shawl that covered me and held my hands in his.

'My darling, you have given me a fine son. By your labours, your commitment to me is absolute now, Mary, as is a Bride of Christ to God when she abandons all that has gone before and takes her final vows. What you owned, I took when I wed you. What is left I have burned. Now you will abandon your will to me too, Mary. Are you listening to what I am saying to you?'

36

I nodded, not able to raise my eyes. So this was the watershed Granny had warned me was to come. Decimus weighed his words before he continued.

'You will obey me, Mary, as though my wishes are your very own and slowly your mind will come to accept its servitude.'

Decimus called Granny's maid to bring the copper bath from the scullery and told her to make haste and fill it with hot water.

'Get out of bed, Mary,' he said.

I tried so hard, but he had to help me, for my body shook from exhaustion and I fell on my knees at his feet. He ran his fingers through my hair and kissed the tresses, whispering to me to be still. I felt the coldness of his shears touch my skin and heard their crunch as they cut through my hair. With the long strands falling about me, I feared what he would do to me. When I saw the razor in his hand, I wept, but was powerless to stop him and closed my eyes, letting him tilt my head so that he could more easily shave it. Decimus picked up the tresses and threw my hair into the fire, where the flames devoured it, until it was gone. A horrible smell filled the room.

He cradled me in his arms. When Granny's maid had completed her task, he carried me over to the bath and gently lowered me into the water, then bathed me with a tenderness which, until now, I had not seen in him. He dried my aching body and dressed me in a robe of pure white wool that covered all of me, except for where the bodice was cut away.

'Your breasts will not be covered, Mary, whilst you are nursing my son. Do not look so worried, my darling. You will become used to it.'

He carried me to bed, for I was too frail from my labours to walk and my weight was as nothing to him. He made me comfortable and sat with me, holding me close.

I asked him, why had he taken my hair? He ignored my question, but from his pocket withdrew a bonnet and gave it to me to cover my cold naked head.

I could not stop from weeping, for Decimus warned me he must hurt me now. Holding one breast firmly in his hand, with his other hand he twisted my nipple between his fingers, pulling it until I despaired, fearing it would tear. Then, undeterred by my weeping, he treated the other nipple, until both were hard and raised against my breasts. He covered me with Mistress Morgan's shawl and let me sleep.

I spread my arms wide on the cool linen and was resigned to the pain of my engorged breasts. Granny put pillows under me to ease my discomfort. Thick blue veins pulsed with life and I felt my skin would burst. For one long hour I waited for my child to waken and relieve me.

Decimus sat with me and caressed my nipples that craved the task they were set to do. When his son awoke, he gave the child my breast. With such surprising force the babe drew the nipple deep into his throat and drank. Uplifted, I watched him take my sustenance. Then Decimus gave his son my other breast, where the milk poured down in a running stream into the folds of my nursing gown. When the babe had taken all he wanted, Decimus gave him to Granny and, empty now, I could rest until he would have need of me again. I had proved to my lord that I could suckle his son.

Then, in fear and humility, I touched his face and whispered my gratitude, for I had never been so happy and content. I could not say his name, Decimus, to his face, for fear he would scold me for my familiarity.

CHAPTER IV

Penance

For the past three weeks I have spent my days in quiet joy nursing our dear son whom Decimus has named Thomas, as was Mistress Morgan's wish. Decimus has ordered my confinement shall continue and I have not queried his decision, for I must learn to accept the control he wields over me.

Barely a year has gone by since Jesse first brought me here. The course of my life has irretrievably changed. The freedom I yearned for, exhilarating but so transient, has been snuffed out, suddenly and without compromise, but I have no regrets. My body that a year ago had yet to reach full womanhood has survived the trauma of childbirth and is rounded and soft. I pray that it pleases my husband. When I sit in the window I see that the scene from Decimus's room has changed since he sent me to Mistress Morgan and my confinement began. Skeins of geese no longer fill the sky and their honking has been replaced by the raucous call of rooks colonising the tall elms. The promise of spring is everywhere. The willows are in bud; silky pearls and catkins soften their winter branches and illuminate the hedgerows.

As always Decimus was early to rise, but this morning he has advised me I should stay in bed for a while and rest all I can. When he returns from milking the cows, he says he will prepare me, for today I am to be churched. We have not entered a church together since that momentous day when he wed me in

Milbury. I have climbed the hill but once to seek sanctuary, where I prayed alone in the empty silence, my belly on fire and my mind tortured by Mistress Morgan's words. But whatever Decimus has done to me, I will always love him and he knows that.

I awoke with his kisses and pulled him close, his hard leather waistcoat rough against my skin. He smiled gently at me, and bade me stand to let him remove my nursing gown. He took off the bonnet that covered my shame and I knelt before him. His fingers lifted my chin and I looked up into his eyes. My lord was strangely affected.

'Never forget, my darling, that I love you.'

His words swept over me and my body was suffused with love for him. He bade me sit in the window, the wooden chair quite cold to my skin. Thomas, disturbed from his sleep, yawned, still content from his last feed. Decimus brought him to me, ordering me to put him to my breast so that he would be happy with Granny until I returned from Church.

When Thomas had taken from me, Decimus laid him in his cradle. Not troubling to cover my nakedness, he grasped my hand, leading me down the stairs and through to the scullery. The door was open to the air. There was no one about and suddenly, trembling with cold, I felt afraid. What would he ask of me? Skylarks had returned, their song shrill as, singing on the wing, they soared in the clear air. Daffodils once more lifted their yellow heads.

Decimus carried me in his arms to the barn where, it seemed an eternity ago, he had laughed at me through a haze of withy smoke. He put me down on the dirt floor and told me to kneel for him. He did not engage me in conversation and I had not the courage to ask what he intended. Feeling once more the sharp blade of his razor, despairing, I closed my eyes while my hair, which was but stubble, was shaved away again. Without explanation, Decimus told me to lie down. He shaved every part of me where I grew hair and even my eyelashes were not exempt from his shears.

He gave me a thin sleeveless shift into which horse-hair had been woven and pulled it over my head. It hung stiff, down to my knees. The harshness irritated my skin and my mark, newly healed, was sensitive to its touch.

Into my hand Decimus placed a scourge with several leather thongs and, instructing me as to its use, admonished me to be diligent in its application.

'I will leave you now, Mary, while you contemplate how you will demean yourself today. When I return, we will climb the hill together and give thanks to God for your safe deliverance.'

He closed the heavy door behind him and slid a great wooden beam across it, shutting me in. Except for a ray of light which crept under the door, I was alone in the darkness.

Taking the scourge as Decimus had instructed, I closed my eyes and began to thrash myself, first with one hand and then with the other. With all my strength I punished myself, until, weeping and exhausted, I sank to the ground. Decimus took the scourge from my hand. I had not heard the door open, nor did I notice the light.

He held me close, my body battered from my penance. He covered me with a huge warm cloak and over my head pulled the hood. With my feet still naked, he led me from the barn and together we climbed the hill to church. I cleaved to him, drawing on his strength, and though he would not touch me his love supported me. The final steps were very steep and, still weak from my labours, I dragged myself toward sanctuary. My feet bled, for they were unused to such harsh treatment. A gentle wind that came from the sea, as if I were not there, blew into my soul. Lifting my eyes, I saw written in front of me the name of the Blessed St Allwen.

A priest stood in my path barring my way. His arm was raised against me. Decimus spoke with him and took off my hood to show him my head was shaven. Then he removed my cloak, to reveal I wore horsehair and was lashed from the scourge. I waited, my head bowed, eyes downcast, feeling his scorn.

But the Blessed Saint must have guided him, for the priest

lifted his arm and let me pass. In front of the altar he railed at me.

'Your mother was an adulteress, your grandmother a witch. She was a Daughter of Satan. You have much to atone for, Mary. By God's mercy, your mother was buried in Hallowed Ground, for she repented of her sins before she died. Do not look for her grave, for you will not find it. It is not marked.

'Your husband has pleaded for you and I can see you are purged, but by the sins you have inherited you have fallen into transgression. The salvation you seek will be afforded you only if you obey God's law. Through your love and your sorrowing you may yet atone for the sins of your forebears. Remember, without love your soul will be lost.

'I pray your love for your husband will sustain you, Mary, though you will sorrow in his hands and without exception he will rule over you.'

My body was aching and cold. Kneeling, I bowed my head and my churching began.

'Forasmuch as it hath pleased Almighty God of his goodness to give you safe deliverance . . .'

The priest made the sign of the Cross and blessed me. I felt the reassuring presence of Jesse beside me and looked up. Sunlight shone on me, bathing me in its warmth. The Blessed Presence of the Saint was with me too and I thanked Almighty God for granting me sanctuary.

Decimus wrapped me in his cloak and led me away. His strong safe arms did not fatigue as he carried me home. We approached his father's house and it welcomed me. Decimus took me to the room we shared and setting me down, removed the cloak and released me from the horsehair vest. He brought me a bowl of clean water and waited while I washed my feet.

When I had dried them, he clasped my hand and I followed him to the looking glass. He insisted I should look at myself and swivelled it so that I could see all of me. Tears welled in my eyes and I could not contain my grief, for the apparition that confronted me was beyond my wildest imagining.

She stared at me with huge sobbing eyes set in a shaven head.

Her neck was very long and her shoulders, her arms, back, and even her oozing breasts, bled from the wicked weals of her self-inflicted wounds. Carved on her belly and into her private places was a web. The blue-green ribs of flesh, proud on her skin, were the mark her husband had made on her.

My hands touched the part most private of all that was shaven for all the world to see. Bereft, I looked up at Decimus.

'Lord, what have I done, that I must suffer so?'

I wept and wept, for I could not bear to hold the gaze of that poor creature who stared at me. Decimus silently watched me weep and when at last there were no more tears he stood over me. I sank down once more, humble before him, begging him to help me bear the sorrows that were to come. When he spoke, though he was firm, there was kindness in his voice.

'Your penance will come easier now, Mary. You are very young, my darling, but you have accepted your servitude and in your heart you know you do not seek its end.'

Decimus gave me a clean nursing gown and led me back to my childbed. He gave his son my breast and Thomas took from me. I was overcome by ecstasy as I fed my precious child. My husband's words were true and I no longer feared the torment I must bear. I touched my shaven head and looked down at my milk-stained breasts. Dark red weals burned into my flesh, but I knew tomorrow my body would heal and at last I yielded to the joy of my love for Decimus, the guardian of my soul.

Mary Cheyne Hillyer.
1860.

CHAPTER V

Thorn End Farm

The room I share with Decimus is bright with primroses Granny has gathered, so that spring can be a little closer for me and I shall not be dispirited by my continuing confinement. Following my churching, I have not worn a bonnet and am slowly becoming accustomed to the immodesty of the nursing gown that is my only apparel.

Today, not quite a week since that event, Thomas is to be baptised. I am stricken with panic and dread the moment when I must confront my husband's kin and they will see what has happened to me. I have begged Decimus to let me stay at home, fearing I shall bring shame on him but he will not hear of it. He has told me I must accompany him, for he has ignored advice, delaying Thomas's baptism, only in order that I may attend.

I can scarcely keep the tears from my eyes. Just for a moment Granny brought my babe to me, that I may see him in his christening robe. Thomas was so beautiful, sleeping in her arms. The heavy cream silk gown, edged with Honiton lace, cascaded almost to the floor and his little body, small and perfect, seemed lost in its folds. I longed to take him from Granny and hold him, but she said, while Thomas was dressed in his family's christening robe, Decimus would not permit me to touch his son. She allowed me just a kiss on the soft down of his dear sweet head.

Now the moment has come when I must meet my husband's

family and, waiting for Decimus, I have tried to compose myself. He will not let me ride, but insists I walk to church with him. Thomas is in Granny's care. She and Grandfather, whom I still think of as Mr Hillyer, will leave shortly in the governess cart that Decimus used when he courted me.

Decimus appeared in the doorway. How handsome he was in his black suit. Over his arm he carried the big warm cloak I had worn for my churching. He held out his hands to me and I ran to him. His strong arms encircled me and, breathing in his familiar smell, I was safe in his love. He wrapped me in his cloak, hiding my wounds.

But where was the hood? I stared up at him. Holding my hands over my poor naked head, I implored him to help me. Gently he lowered my hands to my sides and, when he spoke, the words he used chilled my heart.

'I am sorry, Mary dear, but your head will not be covered again until your hair has grown. All who see you must not doubt your penitence.'

Pleading with him to change his mind, humiliated, I begged him anew to let me stay at home. How could he be so cruel as to deny me a hood to hide my disgrace?

My feet were still sore and my body ached from its bruising. Decimus did not hurry me as together we climbed the hill to church.

Shame for my unwed mother and the sins of my grandmother, that I must atone for, lay heavy on my shoulders as I watched my babe baptised. But throughout it all, Decimus was with me. Not once leaving my side, he sustained me with his love. With eyes downcast, I prayed in the presence of the Blessed Saint for courage to tread the path my husband had chosen for me. Dear Granny understood my pain and when the service was over she brought her grandson to me and I cradled him tenderly in my arms.

Decimus had been making ready the house that was his grand-father's endowment and two days after Thomas was baptised my husband bade me say goodbye to Granny. I had come to love her so much and scarcely had time to make my farewells. I had only memories to take with me for I owned nothing else. Decimus handed me into the cart and, when I was settled, Granny gave Thomas to me. Mr Hillyer, standing behind her, said goodbye. How could I thank this unbending man for making me welcome in his house, when, in awe of him, I could not find words? I looked up and his eyes, the same colour as my own dear husband's, were smiling at me.

'God bless you, Mary,' he said.

Decimus set the horse towards the village. The weather, though bright, was changeable. My shaven head felt very cold, and pulling my cloak even tighter around me I still shivered. Decimus followed the road Jesse had taken when I had claimed my inheritance. I blessed my lord for not using the narrow track which avoided the hill and would have been a shorter way but passed Mistress Morgan's door. Once we had breasted the hill, the Great River was in view, its shining waters reflecting the early morning light. As we approached the village, we passed the alehouse I had noticed when I came this way before. There were people standing outside and all stared, aghast, when they saw me. I wept, my shame too much to bear.

At the farthest end of the village we came to a high crumbling brick wall, which in truth I could not recall from my previous journey. Behind it, hidden away, was Thorn End Farm. The house was old, seeming to grow out of the very ground it stood on, its walls matured over many years. Decimus opened the door from the yard and led me inside. He told me that this house, where I should live until my dying day, would be my haven, secure from the intolerant world outside.

In the scullery the air was cool. On the range a copper boiler gently hissed. Above it, hanging from the chimneypiece, were pans with long handles. Bolted to the stone flags of the floor was a pump, painted black, with a large white sink next to it. A scrubbed wooden table occupied most of the floor space and covering the walls were implements, many of which I could not recognise. Hung in a corner behind a settle was a large copper bath with little feet. Decimus, his hand on my elbow, propelled me up a step and into the kitchen. There, a dresser filled with blue and white plates, and cups suspended on hooks, took up one whole wall. The table, covered by a large white damask cloth, was already laid. Two rocking chairs were placed on either side of the hearth into which a bread oven had been set.

Foolishly, it had not crossed my mind that this house was already Decimus's home and he was but a guest in his father's house. I followed him through a long dark hall where he showed me two more rooms, one very formal with a deep red carpet, a piano and chairs with their backs and sides held together with silky golden tassels. The other room was a parlour. It was warm and comfortable and the tall window would catch the evening light. My eyes were drawn to the winged chair that had been Granny's, which Decimus had always wanted for his own, and, seeing it, I smiled up at my husband. He took Thomas from me, leaving me free. Elated, I rushed upstairs, to look in every room. Decimus laughed to see my pleasure and told me he had waited long enough and soon would make love to me again. Kissing his rough, farmer's hand, I whispered my gratitude that he should still want me, though I could not help but fear the pain, for in those first few months before he had sent me to Mistress Morgan his body had hurt me when he loved me.

He took his cloak away and, as I stood before him, my fear of him had not lessened and I was in awe of my lord. I thought of his words when he had shaved my head and prepared me to nurse his son and wondered what he would ask of me now. His eyes were serious as he addressed me.

'My dear sweet wife, I pray you will be happy and content in my house, for here I shall take you on a path that will help you bear a torment none can share. You will forgive me the sorrowing I cause you, Mary, for it is God's will that brought you to me and though I love you I shall not falter.'

Trusting my husband and caring not what he must do to me, I sank to my knees, abasing myself before him. I felt Jesse beside me and knew he had given me to this man that he should purify my soul. Now I gave my lord leave to carry through to its finish the task that had already commenced.

Decimus helped me from my prostration and gave Thomas back into my arms. He threw his cloak about my shoulders and told me to follow him. He led me back into the yard, where the scent of animals assailed my nostrils. Some of the workers he had hired were assembled in a line. He said I must choose a girl who would be my maid. I could not understand him at first and asked him why? But he cautioned me to be careful whom I picked. Though Granny had taught me well the crafts I should need to be a farmer's wife, that role was not to be mine.

There was one girl who would have been about my age. She could not speak, for her mother had been frightened by a hare when she was conceived. She was very ugly. Her mouth was twisted and her lips would not meet. She looked at me with my shaven head, bare feet and the babe in my arms. Hurt registered on her poor misshapen face. I drew her from the line, guessing her torment and knowing she would understand mine. When for the first time she saw me naked, she would not ridicule me behind her subservient eyes. Her name was Annie.

Decimus introduced me to his eldest sister, Ella, who was unmarried. He had installed her as his housekeeper and now I realised why the atmosphere in this house reminded me of Granny's. Ella's bearing was much like her mother's but she had none of Granny's grace or love. She was here before me and was mistress of her brother's house. Her attitude was contemptuous and I guessed she would enjoy watching my humility and fear of my lord. Decimus said I should not expect her tolerance. Dear Granny, the only woman who understood my love for Decimus, was not really far away, but it might as well have been an ocean that separated us.

Quiet months have slipped by as summer has turned to autumn. Decimus will not allow me to leave the confines of his farm, but as yet I am untroubled and content to let my body heal. My hair has begun to grow again, curling round my face, and from the twinkle in his eye I can tell my husband's delight. Thomas disciplines my days, for he must still be suckled and Decimus is overjoyed to see his son grow strong.

In early December, eight months after giving birth to Thomas, I rose one morning from my husband's bed. Between my thighs ran a trickle of pale blood and my belly ached. I was happy for Decimus, for my body was showing him it was ready to bear another child. But my husband saw a very different sign. From that moment, while the moon claimed me for its own, he barred Thomas from my breast. He said my milk was soured and must run to waste, for I was under the moon's baleful influence. Thomas was to have cow's milk in preference to mine. Decimus sent Annie to fetch a pan from the scullery and insisted I squeeze the milk from my breasts. When my milk had filled the pan and my breasts were empty, Decimus poured it away and I wept. Annie was told to bind my ribs with strips of linen as tight as I could bear. But all too soon my breasts began to fill and desperate hours went by before Decimus let Annie release me from the binds. About my breasts were deepest cleaves where they had struggled to be free. I milked the tender useless flesh and Annie was told to bind me again. For six long bitter days, until the moon had done with me, my body succumbed. When at last my womb had ceased to bleed, the milk was all but gone and I could give Thomas little more than a comforter.

Decimus ordered me to give up his son to sister Ella. On my knees, with all my heart I begged him to change his mind, but, no matter what I said, my pleading was all to no avail. He told me I was unable to mother his child and I could not refute the claim.

Ella's eyes softened as she took Thomas from me and cradled him in her arms. Beneath her cold disdainful exterior, I could see from the way she held him, she harboured a deep and abiding love for her youngest brother's son. But no matter how hard I tried, when I gave her my beautiful child I could not suppress the most terrible jealousy, for my babe was lost to me.

My heart grieved at my lord's cruel decision. The suckling was over and I had to be grateful that Thomas would be cared for by Ella, for in her hands he would know the love and tenderness I must deny him. From that day onward, I acknowledged my strange relationship with my husband's sister, accepting, too, my hurt was as my husband wished.

For two whole weeks I mourned my babe and Decimus did not trouble me for love. Late one afternoon, just before the feast of Christmas, he told me my grieving must end soon. Annie was ordered to bathe me. When she had finished, from the drawer she took out a razor and I could not stop from weeping. Holding my head in my hands, I tried to protect my hair, fearing she would have off what little I had. But Annie pulled my hands away and her gentle fingers brushed my face. Pointing to her lap, her eyes smiled at me and I understood the message, Her instructions were to shave the part that only my husband saw. As I submitted to her blade, silently I thanked my lord for allowing me a maid of my own choosing, for Annie did not mock me.

When she was satisfied her job was done, she gave me a warm blanket to go round my shoulders and on the tips of my toes, for the stone flags were cold, I hurried to the parlour where Decimus was waiting for me. The lamps were already lit and the room was warm. He asked Ella to leave us.

My husband stood over me. Coolly, he pushed me to my knees and, without ceremony, removed the blanket. Devoid of love, he looked at me and as my eyes filled with tears I stared at the floor. Cupping my face in his hands, he shook his head, for he saw I was weeping. Solemnly he affirmed to me what in my heart I should have known.

'In this life you own nothing and you never will. It is a harsh lesson for you, Mary, but Thomas is my son. He does not belong to you and you will not make that mistake again.'

I could not help but weep, for weeping came more easily than it had ever done. When at last Decimus raised me from the floor my spirit lay crushed and I was inconsolable. He scanned my body, now that my duties were done, and touched me where I was shaven and could not hide. When he had finished his examination, he gave me a gown to wear. It was beautiful; its material, like gossamer, shone in the soft light from the lamp. In a daze I let him dress me and when he tied the silken cord about my waist all the nooks and crannies of my body were outlined for him. Decimus sat in Granny's old wing-chair and pulled me down on to his lap. The robe hung open below my waist so that the warmth from the fire penetrated me. Slowly my weeping subsided as his great calloused hands, deceptive in their knowledge, parted me. Past where Annie had done her work, he caressed my lips and they began to swell. My lord's voice was soft, lulling me to sleep.

'Cease your sobbing, my dear, and be still for me. Hidden inside you is a key which will unlock a secret world you know nothing of. Give every part of yourself to me now, Mary, and together we will overcome the spirit of your forebears so it never invades your soul. I promise you, my darling, I shall always look after you. There is nothing in this world that will dissuade me and with God's help I will deliver you from the burden that fate has seen fit to lay on you.'

His probing hands explored deep into me. His fingers revealed a cleft that was thrilled by his measured touch. My body and I, we became alive, dancing with the flames of the fire. Held in a vice, we danced and danced to the music of every urgent stroke and, straining at the leash of consciousness, I prayed for the music not to stop. Still his strong hands held me in the dance, until at last, swaying with pleasure, I was in paradise.

Gently he kissed me, for he saw the key had turned, unlocking a passion that until this moment was hidden from me. From far away I heard his voice.

'Now I shall take you to a secret place, Mary. You will enter a new world I have made just for you, that I hope you will not leave. It will be a promised land and you will not have to pay again the penance your birth has inflicted on you.'

He pulled the thin silk from my shoulders and his fingers caressed my useless breasts. My body beat with life and my breasts grew firm under his touch as he kissed the nipples that were redundant now. I rested my head on his shoulder and my love for my lord overwhelmed me. He held both my hands firmly in one of his, then spread my legs so that they should feel more intensely the heat of the fire.

Taking a long wax taper, he held it above the lamp. A flame

51

appeared, took hold and glowed with life. As I watched his face, illuminated in its light, I wondered what he intended. He held the taper before my eyes, telling me to concentrate upon its flame. Then, dazzled by the flickering light, my eyes followed the flame as he held it to my breast.

Separating, the tongues danced around my nipple. With searing pain and sudden consciousness, I fell back, pulling away from him. But Decimus held my hands so tight I could not move and, helpless, I watched as slowly he scorched me on the other breast.

Consumed with pain, I lay in the arms of my lord. My mind struggled, defeated by a force beyond its control, as he destroyed my will for ever. He told me to open my eyes and look at the flame still dancing before me. I followed it and the flame became two, then many more, until in my world there were hundreds of flames dancing before my eyes. I cannot know how long I stared into their timelessness. For me there was no meaning to time any more.

Decimus put his fingers into my mouth. Then, wet with my spit, he washed my wounded nipples. Quietly he took another taper, held it over the lamp and again, as the flame took hold, he made me watch. This time, though, I did not flinch. The tongues of flame fondled me with their life, but the pain of it did not matter, for I was no longer there. My spirit had flown to that special place, the paradise Decimus had created only for me. The Mary I had been was dead and her penance was over.

Knowing I was chained to him with links which would never break, my lord held me safe in his arms. My child was lost to me, but now I did not mind. He carried me up to bed and, hardly conscious, with love I offered my body into my husband's hard uncompromising hands. When he had taken all I could give, I promised him I would strive, so as one day my soul might become but a mirror of his own.

As sleep overcame me, Decimus murmured that soon he would let me leave his house and together we should go to the Great River where I might see for myself a way of life which for centuries had sustained his kin.

CHAPTER VI

The Great River

Tonight will be the Eve of Christmas, that very special night when the air is stilled and, with reverence, a hushed world looks forward to the Nativity. Our preparations for the feast day tomorrow have been mostly made and Ella, her face flushed from her cooking, is a little less formidable.

This morning Annie has dressed me with careful hands, for not since I laboured with Thomas has Decimus allowed me more than a nursing gown and today, for the first time in many months, my breasts are covered. They ache and will not withstand touching. My nipples are hard and blackened from the flame, but I heed not the pain, for today Decimus will take me to see the Great River, where my eyes will dwell again on the vista that is a part of my very soul. I have not seen the river's high Sea Bank since Jesse brought me to this Vale. So many changes have come upon me since that day not two years ago, though even now I have yet to reach my twentieth birthday.

Annie brought me a cloak of deepest green to wear over my new grey woollen gown. It had a hood trimmed with rabbit fur to keep out the wind. When I asked her if I should have boots, she nodded, showing me a box. Buried beneath layers of tissue paper I found the French boots Decimus wished me to wear. I had gone bare-footed for so long and now, with trembling fingers, I touched the beautiful boots. The uppers of pale grey were of fine calf skin, the skin as thin as a glove would be. The soles, a wafer of leather, had heels more than three inches high.

Sitting down, I was robbed of breath, for the stays Decimus had given me bit deep into my belly, reminding me how much I had always hated whalebone. But my waist had spread during these past months when my body had been free and had to be constrained again, for Decimus would not be satisfied until he could span my waist with his hands as he had done when first we were wed.

Nervously, I pulled on the boots and took the button hook which Annie handed me. With my fingers all thumbs, I fastened the tiny buttons at the outside of my ankle. The boots fitted tight as a second skin, but, standing, I could not walk and nearly fell. In all my life I had not worn boots like these before. Annie also gave me a pair of matching gloves made of the same pale grey calf. With me holding tight to her arm, for I could not manage unaided, she helped to the looking glass.

The woman who returned my gaze was not the poor demented creature who haunted my dreams. She was happy and compliant, her eyes a little wistful. Each day I prayed for strength to become the woman my husband intended me to be.

Annie helped me hobble downstairs to the yard, where Decimus was waiting with the trap. Smiling at my helplessness, he picked me up and carried me over the flagstones, not expecting me to walk. Winter had come in earnest, for there was ice in the air and flecks of snow stuck to the horse's back. When I was seated and comfortable in the trap, Decimus lay a sheepskin rug over my feet, that they should be warm despite their inadequate covering. He climbed up beside me and, sitting close, we shared the rug. I thanked him for my lovely boots and he laughed, for I could not disguise my happiness.

I waited until we approached the village before asking him, should we meet anyone, how he wished me to conduct myself. Decimus was robust in his reply and my anxiety lessened a little.

'Do not worry, Mary dear, there are many hereabouts who do not know you, who fear the spirit of your forebears, but I shall always protect you. No one will molest you when you are with me.'

I sat even closer to Decimus, his massive frame sheltering me from the wind, though I confess I was somewhat apprehensive now that our journey had begun. Decimus had shut me away for one whole year and I dreaded meeting strangers. While he busied himself with the reins, I stole a glance at my husband. He was seven years older than I, in fact a little more than that, for his birthday was in September. His face was weatherbeaten, his hard rugged features ageing him more than his twenty-seven years. The young man who had laughed at me when first I set eyes on him was all but a figment of my imagination. For one fleeting moment I wondered if Decimus might tell me some day where he had learned to love, but cast the thought aside, for it did not matter.

The road was deeply pitted. Mud sprayed up at us from the wheels as the trap lifted, bouncing over ruts, the springs lowering us again. My heart flew into my mouth when we reached the Pound, for there were many men gathered there. Decimus hailed them, but when they saw I accompanied him they turned their backs on us. Decimus, his mouth set hard at the corners, held my hand.

Viciously, he turned the horse. The poor creature felt the whip on his back and squealed with fright. I watched where Decimus was taking me. He deviated from the track Jesse had used when first I was brought this way. I feared Decimus's anger, but thanked God he was not angry with me. Through clenched teeth, he told me there was something he must show me now this very minute, before we had covered another mile.

The lane was narrow and sheltered, for it was below the Sea Bank of the Great River. Though the wind was strong, here it had quietly died away. Unexpectedly, the lane opened out on to a broad sweeping drive edged with magnificent elms. At the end of the drive was an elegant house with many gables, a carriage waiting at the door.

I asked my husband, 'What is our business here?'

'This is your father's house!'

Shocked, my heart pounded against my chest. I would rather not have known, but Decimus was remorseless.

'You, my dear, are the product of your father's infidelity. You pay penance for your mother's sins, and the village people revile you for being a bastard. Had you been your father's legitimate daughter, they would not treat you so.'

I looked up at my husband and saw he was hurt that I should be so excluded.

'Your father was squire of this village and a respected man, but he loved your mother. He could not marry her, she being of the gypsy race and carrying the curse of her forebears in her veins. Had he wed your mother, his family would have disinherited him.'

With a shrug Decimus dismissed the thought.

'Anyway, he was married already.'

So my mother really had been a gypsy after all. My guardian's slur was the truth. Decimus cut into my thoughts.

'Your father, Mary dear, was higher born than mine, but believe me when I tell you, my sons will be as respected as any legitimate heir to this house.'

I touched Decimus's troubled face. He cared what others thought of me, though I truly did not mind their scorn, so long as he loved me.

'My life is in your hands, lord. It matters not to me the route I have travelled to find you.'

I thought of the small child burying her mother, when a gentleman had come to her. I wondered what agonies my father had suffered because he had abandoned me after my mother died. He was not a bad man and had I known him I would have loved him.

Decimus said nothing more, but turned the trap round, retracing our steps. When we reached the Pound, Decimus set the horse straight at the crowd of men. They scattered, cowering as they realised he did not intend to alter course to avoid them. His countenance bore a chilling look I had not seen before and I knew he cared not if he ran them down.

I recognised the path that Decimus was following, for we were back on the track Jesse had used when he brought me this way before. The path ended, but Decimus still urged the horse forward across the soft turf of the meadow to where the derelict house that was my inheritance stood, forlorn and alone. Nearing it, I saw that the roof had been made secure and the gaps in the walls mended, so that the wind no longer howled through the house like a lost soul in torment. Had not my boots hampered me, I should have jumped to the ground, but I had to wait for Decimus to remove them. The grass was cold and wet to my naked feet, but I did not care, I was so happy that Decimus was restoring the house that had been mine.

He would not let me venture inside, saying it was not finished yet and would keep for another day. I waited for Decimus to pull on his waders and then, holding his hand, walked with him along the path which led to the Great River. Together we climbed to the top of the steep bank and there before my eyes was the wondrous view I had waited so long to see.

Today the Estuary wore a coat of a very different hue. The far hills were lost in a cold, grey haze. Even the bank away on the Welsh side was shrouded in mist, so that the river looked for all the world just like the open sea. Beyond the broad Sea Bank where we stood, short grass spread out before us. Decimus pointed out putchers, stacked close by and safe from the highest tide, waiting for the next fishing season. I thought of the sticks he had been weaving when he had laughed at me through a cloud of withy smoke. Not until April would he set his putchers to catch the magnificent fish.

Taking hold of my hand, he led me across the grass towards the river. We walked until we came to a mark where the last tide had reached. Here, where thick grey mud began, the grass ended abruptly. At its edge, the mud was dry and crazed like old china, for it was not covered by every tide. Decimus pointed to the ocean, telling me that the nearest land was Labrador far away to the west and nothing lay in its path to rob the wind of its awesome power.

Clutching at his hand, I was led farther out into the mud. On and on for maybe half a mile we trudged and still the water seemed no nearer. The wind howled about us and birds took flight, swooping above our heads, for they were affronted by our presence. This was God's land and we were intruders.

The hood that had kept me warm was torn back from my head, but little did I care, for the wind was a friend and even the icy raindrops did not feel cold to me. The clouds, like the water, were an impenetrable grey. Decimus urged me on again, deeper and deeper. Sometimes we walked on sand but mostly it was mud. It oozed between my toes, came over my ankles and up my calves to my knees. Then I began to sink. Holding tight to Decimus, I looked all around me. We were a part of this bleak and beautiful panorama and the two of us were as nothing in a vast wilderness. Decimus pointed out paths that ran all the way to the distant water, but my poor eyes could not perceive them. He told me he could always find his way, but his knowledge was a secret passed only from father to son. Any outsider foolhardy enough to enter this watery kingdom would not survive the suck of the thick grey silt of the river's bed.

I could not move for the force that pulled me down and, inexplicably, as though someone had walked over my grave, I shivered. Then suddenly Decimus declared he had brought me far enough. Should he take me further, the presence of a woman beyond where we stood would bring him ill luck.

For my very life, I clung to Decimus and he helped me make the tortuous journey back to the land that I knew. At last, buffeted by the wind, our cheeks glowing, we gained the safety of the Sea Bank. Decimus held me at arm's length. He began to laugh and, as he looked at me, tears of mirth ran down his face.

'My dear sweet wife, you are a wayward woman. If only I had a glass to hold before you, then you too could see the picture that I see.'

I stared down at my mud-streaked cloak, then put my hands to my head. My cropped hair was tangled and the wind pulled it from my fingers. My naked feet were so numb I could not feel them. They were covered with mud. Standing before my lord, I was overcome by emotion and love for him. I owed him my very being and sank to my knees, as I had done so many times before. This time, though, I did not hang my head, but looked steadily up into his eyes, confident of his love for me. His words, dialect creeping into his voice, were approving.

'My dear, I cannot be lenient with you; you will always submit to me, you know that, but you and I have reached an understanding, haven't we?'

I perfectly understood my husband's words. He took me back to the trap and, cradling my new boots in my lap, I waited as he took off his waders and made ready the horse. I knew that each time I wore my boots, the day when Decimus had walked me into the Great River would be remembered, for their grey calf was the same colour as the silt that covered my naked feet.

I thought of tomorrow, Christmas Day. Decimus will take me to church and this time none will bar my way.

CHAPTER VII

Queenie

The spirit of Decimus grows steadily within me. Cocooned in the web of his love, I am not distressed by my fear of him. Within his severe tutoring, which could be but a cruel penance, I dance to the flame he holds before me. He encourages me to take long walks on the Sea Bank, allowing me Annie for company. He says the pure Atlantic air will cleanse me and give me courage to follow the path I am destined to tread. My isolation from all who call on him, which Decimus inflicted upon me as a punishment when first he learned I was my mother's daughter, is now a joy. My mind can think only of my husband, for he provides all my needs. In humility I toil at the tasks he sets me each day and in the many silent hours of solitude reflect on what I have learned.

In the spring of this year, 1863, Thomas was a little over three years old, and the tell-tale signs in my body informed me I was carrying a second child. With Annie, I walked on the Sea Bank of the Great River and was inspired by the beauty of the Estuary. I prayed that in November Decimus will take another son from my womb. Watching the majestic river flowing toward the ocean, I thought of the courage of the men who wade far out into the deep and treacherous mud. The pains of birth I so dread are little in comparison with their labours and I set my mind to accept with joy whatever agonies God thinks fit to visit on me.

Preoccupied by my dreams, my foot was caught in a rabbit hole. With my ankle swelling with pain, I could barely move. Dear Annie had not the strength to keep me on my feet and ran for help.

In the cool spring sunshine, watching the light playing games on the full waters, I waited for her to return with Decimus. The tide was just on the ebb and idly my eyes followed the waves as they broke, each one receding a little farther. A shadow crossed the sun and, startled, I looked up. Taking the light was a skewbald horse and astride his back sat a man. Reining him in, the man boldly set his horse to stand over me. Recoiling with shock and shielding my eyes, I stared up at him. Beneath a rough shaven face, he was swarthy, with a gold earring that glittered in the sun. His jet-black hair curled at his neck. His horse was without a saddle, the bridle no more than a rope halter. The man was a gypsy. He did not deign to leave his seat, but leaned down and, speaking in a tongue I did not recognise, offered me his dark brown hand.

In whatever direction I looked, there was no one to help me. At his mercy, I could not flee. No more could I ignore the outstretched hand and as I grasped it (for what choice had I?) he swept me up. I cried out as, without dignity, he threw me across his horse's withers, my feet to one side and my head to the other, my arms hanging all but a foot from the ground. Dear God, what had I done? As I felt the horse move away, nausea and fear for my unborn child welled in me.

Where was he taking me? It seemed we travelled for maybe a mile before we reached his encampment. I would never knowingly have trespassed there. The man had lost interest in me now. I was no more than baggage to him. The smell of woodsmoke and the incessant barking of dogs assailed my senses as noisy, shouting children surrounded me. He caught hold of my arm and, pulling me up, he pushed me, so that feet first I slid to the ground. Unable to save myself, gasping from the pain in my ankle, I fell in a heap. The rider gave his horse a command and without looking at me again he turned away and left. With hackles raised, the dogs sniffed at me, but then, as though I were a pariah, they too left me alone. I knew that here, in their encampment, in the hands of the gypsies, I should meet my fate. In my heart I called out to Decimus to come for me, but how would he know where to look?

Circling me with their ring, the children laughed at me. I could not bear it, but was helpless, unable to get away. Looking up, I saw an old woman, dressed all in black. She was leaning against the door of her waggon, watching me. Pointing her finger at me, she beckoned. Feeling compelled to obey her, I crawled on my knees across the open space until, my foot throbbing, I lay at the steps of her waggon. All the while the ragged children ran ever faster round and round me, mocking and laughing at me. Hopelessly I prayed for the nightmare to end.

Lifting my head, my eyes were drawn into her cold, black stare. She knew who I was. When she spoke, I had to listen hard, for the dialect was quite unlike that which I was used to.

'So you have come at last.'

My stomach churned as she continued.

'We do not want you here, but your presence in our encampment is meant to be. Your ancestor put a curse on us and for her sins, so long as each girl child in your belly grows, you too will never be free of it.'

Fear of her was rooted in my very bones and I could not move for terror. With downcast eyes, I dragged myself after her into the dark and musty confines where she reigned. Pulling the door shut behind me, she commanded me to sit at her feet. The only light now came from a skylight and, as though I were naked, I felt her eyes bore into me.

'Show me Mistress Morgan's work, then I can see for myself how far you have atoned for the sins that have been visited on us by your kin for so many generations.'

I forgot the pain in my foot and stood up. With hands I could scarcely control for their trembling, I lifted my petticoats for her to inspect my belly. Signalling I should raise my skirts even higher, she peered at me. But that was not good enough for her prying fingers. I could not take my eyes from her leathery old face as, with my knees made of jelly and my body immovable, in my horror and without resistance I let her undress me. My hands tried to cover my secret places, but she pulled them away and naked I stood in front of her. She could see I was just with child, but then she had known that before she took off my clothes. She kicked them behind her where I could not reach. There was no escape and, powerless to help myself, I wondered if I would leave this place alive.

Suddenly the old woman pushed open the door and cold air rushed in. Sunlight fell across the terrible mark that Decimus had ordered Mistress Morgan to carve into me. The old crone knew I was cold, for I could not stop from shivering. But she only smiled and I feared her even more.

'Mistress Morgan did indeed mark you well, my dear. One day you will have difficulty remembering your belly as it was before its mutilation.'

She fingered me with her cold old hands, touching the stigma I had borne for more than three years now. She must have known the affliction still frightened me. Her fingers ran over the weals of love my body wore. Nodding her head, she seemed to soften a little, but my eyes, like a rabbit's transfixed by a beam of light, could not leave her face and she continued to hold me fast.

'I see you have a husband, my dear, who loves you enough not only to mark you well, but is not afraid to purge you of the sins of your forebears. There are indeed few women who are given the courage to withstand such loving.'

Her fingers continued to touch me. No part of me was sacred. The muscles in my face were dead and my jaw dropped, hardly belonging to me. With lips I could scarce feel, I tried to plead with her.

'Please, Mistress, do not touch me. I cannot help but fear you.'

'I wish you no harm, my dear. I shall not hurt you. Only your husband can do that without causing you pain. Even so, he cannot protect his girl child from the curse you carry in your womb.'

Cradling my bare belly in my hands to protect my child from her, my terror intensified. Had not Mistress Morgan done her work well? I could not bear for it to be done again.

'This child will be another son,' she intoned.

Her voice had moderated.

'Dress yourself, my dear. Then when you are ready, I shall tell you about the flaxen-haired maiden our people stole and of the penance we still pay even today for our wrong-doing. You will learn, too, why each girl child born of your line will be vulnerable to the curse. Only when there is no female heir to carry it within her womb will future generations of your kin be free.'

She helped me to dress, pulling my stays tight so that my waist was the hourglass shape that pleased my husband. In a little while my body would be unconstrained so as to allow his dear child to grow.

In spite of my fear, now the old woman had begun, I had to listen, for only through her might I learn the terrible secrets my mother, by her death, had kept from me.

She indicated a bench where I should sit, then ordered me lift my foot for her.

'Before I tell you about yourself, my dear, let me see to you.'

Her voice had lost its threat. She held my injured ankle in her bony old hand and pressed my foot hard against her body. Stroking me from my knee to the tips of my toes, her warmth, like a gentle current, flowed through me. With each stroke, she wiped her hands in the air as though to rid them of some imaginary grime. The heat intensified as the pressure of her fingers increased until, tingling all over, the pain was drained from me. Smiling at me now, she rose and bade me join her. The pain had gone.

She took the lid from an earthenware pot, not unlike the one Granny used to preserve eggs, and ladled a cordial into a fine china bowl. At first I was cautious, but then drank it, lest she should think me ungrateful. I had not realised how parched my mouth had become. The taste was sweet, but I hesitated to ask her from what fruit the cordial was made, for it was spring time and what was there that was ripe?

I felt the spirit of Decimus rise up in me unbidden, and my uncontrollable fear lessened. He had not deserted me. The old woman continued to smile, for she understood. She had seen my body and knew I was shriven.

As yet I had not looked at the inside of her waggon, for my eyes had travelled no farther than her wizened old face. She indicated I should sit opposite her and, holding my hands in hers, she commenced her tale.

'Many years ago, one of our young men cast his eyes at a woman who was not of our race. He carried her back with him. She had just reached maidenhood and was beautiful, with flaxen hair. But as she grew to maturity she also grew to hate our people. She was cursed and the sons she bore all bled, so that even the smallest cut was fatal. Our men retaliated and used her for their pleasure, but she took her revenge and the seed carried to future generations. If any of our women gives birth to a fair-haired girl child, she must not suckle it, but put it out for the foxes, for it is a throwback.'

Oh no, I could not do that. The sheer horror of it all was too much and I tried to shut it out, but into my mind's eye came a blue stone with a circlet of old gold. A plait of yellow hair was at its centre. I had always hoped it was my mother's hair, for I could scarce remember her. Now I knew it was not, for she survived and must have had dark hair like mine. Whose hair had she given me that I had kept so safe? No, it could not possibly be . . . my thoughts had wandered, but the old woman drew me back.

'There was one, though, who inherited the curse, but she beguiled men. She had dark hair, like yours, yet none the less was a true Daughter of Satan. She was your grandmother.

'Your mother gave you a brooch with a serpent holding a heart in its mouth. It belonged to her mother before her. I know your husband has taken it now. Though he has left you with nothing save his love, my dear, you will not that easily be rid of its evil, for the brooch is merely a symbol of the curse you carry in your veins. Your daughter, for there will be just one who will live, will be dark and have a gypsy's bearing as you do, but beware of her, for only if she weds a man who, with love, will take her soul from her will she be free of the curse.'

My thoughts were whirling. I mused on what she had told me. The old woman seemed to have finished her tale, yet strangely I had no compulsion to leave her. Her spell was broken, for now I could look round at my surroundings. Though her home was but a waggon, it was spotlessly clean and filled with things that shone. Copper and brassware hung from the roof and glowed in the spring sunshine which poured in through the open door. Pendulous crystal caught the light, fractured and threw a kaleidoscope of colour across me. Heat radiated from an ancient black stove that stood, almost lost in shadow, in a far corner. A chimney poked through a hole in the roof, with smoke occasionally wafting back in the breeze. Every surface was covered with brilliant glass and china knick-knacks. As my eyes alighted on each pretty thing, the old gypsy's hands enclosed mine.

I looked more closely at her now and wondered by what name she was known, but hesitated to ask. Her hair, surprisingly still black, was pulled severely into the nape of her neck. Some escaped the heavy enamelled ring that held it and cascaded down her back. One nostril was pierced by a gold ring. Other heavy gold rings were in her ears, the holes in her lobes so big they stretched near to breaking. Woven into her shawl, dancing in the sunlight, were yet more gold rings and sovereigns too. With the door wide open, the strange musty smell that pervaded the air was not as strong. Why did I crave the sweet sickly scent?

Patting the seat next to her, she indicated I should sit closer. My fear of her was gone. Almost as if to herself, she began another tale. This time the strange old gypsy told me of her own past.

Her father was leader of the tribe and she was his first-born daughter. She was still a maiden when her mother died, but would always remember the day her father wed for a second time. Her true brothers, who were now alas all dead, were strong and able men. But the half-brothers her father's new wife bore him all died as infants. They bled to death, for there was no one who could staunch the flow. Her stepmother gave birth to a daughter. The daughter grew sturdy, but had a trait in her. When others were sad, she laughed. When others slept, she was awake. Others killed living things only to eat, but she killed for pleasure.

She had bad blood. Yet in spite of her wickedness, she had a way with her which charmed men, leading them astray.

It was not difficult to guess what the old gypsy would tell me now.

'My half-sister was your grandmother.'

Her eyes found mine and she held my hands even tighter.

'Your husband protects you, my dear, but, never forget, the girl child you will bear will be given absolution only if she is content and willing to give her soul to a husband who will consume her. Then, when she meets death, she will be fulfilled, as you will be when you die, my dear, after a lifetime of obedience and devotion to your husband.

'You are a gypsy through your mother's line. Though your life has been far removed from our way, you cannot escape your past.'

Suddenly my ears were tired of the truth. Desperate now, I could bear it no more and longed to be safe with my love. My heart cried out to Decimus.

'Lord, please find me!'

The old woman must have read my thoughts and, sensing she was losing her hold over me, her tones mellowed to a gentle lilt. In spite of my longing to leave this place, my resolve was lost. My mind, seeming not my own, was lulled by the enchantment of her voice and seduced, like a bird that is trapped and resigned to its cage. She held me in her power.

'My dear, you wanted to know my name. People who are not of our race call me Queenie, but when I was young my name was Parvatay, Daughter of the Highest Mountains.'

'May I call you Aunt, if that would not be familiar?'

I awaited her acceptance of my proposal. She squeezed my hand and curiously, sitting next to her, I felt I belonged.

'Now let me show you our encampment,' she said.

Until now I had not noticed how frail she was. Climbing down the steps, I took her arm, supporting her. The children who had mocked, silently stood aside. My Aunt had accepted me and they were not bold enough to abuse me now.

A young woman approached, a kinswoman, I guessed. I had

seen her previously when she had knocked on Decimus's door. Invariably she carried a basket of pegs and bunches of violets or dried flowers to sell. Ella saw her as nothing better than a beggar and sent her on her way, ignoring her offer:

'Cross my palm with silver, Lady, and I will tell you your fortune.'

How different she looked today. Here, she was not an outcast or a vagabond as the gypsies were always portrayed to be. Her body was graceful, her fragrance encircling her. Her gentleness caressing me reduced me almost to tears. Smiling, she placed the palms of her hands together. Pressing her fingers to her forehead and stooping slightly, she acknowledged me.

Propped against one of the waggons, his hands in his pockets, Decimus was watching. Reality was restored and, oblivious now to the scene that surrounded me, I ran to him and sank to my knees in gratitude. He had heard my prayers and, lifting me, gently he kissed my forehead.

'When Annie came home alone, I guessed the gypsies would find you. You had to meet your kin, Mary, but I hoped to postpone the day, until you had enough of my strength in you to withstand Queenie's inquisition.'

His gaze was quizzical.

'And from what I see, I am here not a moment too soon.'

Decimus, taking her hand in his, kissed the gnarled old bones and, his eyes laughing, elaborately he bowed.

The voice that had seduced me asked him to bring me again.

'I will, Queenie, and the new-born babe too.'

Decimus took me home.

CHAPTER VIII

Harry

Sleep was but a sham and my mind was in turmoil as I lay alone in my lord's bed. I rose, went to the window and opened it. In a still, black night, soft spring rain pattered quietly on the windowsill. Leaning out, I shivered and listened for his footsteps. How could he find his way with only a lamp and not even stars to guide him? I thought of the paths in the deep, sucking mud that my poor eyes could not perceive and prayed he would be home before the tide turned.

Queenie's words haunted me. Now I knew it was from the old gypsy that Decimus had learned I was my mother's daughter. In all this time he had known the awesome truth of the curse I had inherited but had kept it from me. How frightened I had been when I returned from Mistress Morgan, cut and faint from her knife. Yet how could Decimus have explained his reasons for sending me to her? Had I known what she intended to do, I would not have had the courage to let her mark me. Dear Granny must have realised what could happen to my child, yet she had not rejected me. What would I have done without her love? I miss her so much.

Racked with self-pity, I wept, for how could Decimus love me, knowing the sons I had yet to bear him might bleed and, helpless, he could only watch them die? Touching my belly, I spread my hands, feeling his mark under my fingers, and prayed that his new child, lying so small in my womb, would be protected from me.

Looking out at the night, into my mind came a picture. It was harvest supper. Jesse was sitting next to me. In the silence, I listened again to the words of the wise old man. I had kept nothing from my husband and without exception had obeyed him. But the voice in my head said, 'Have faith'.

On my knees, with my hands locked together, I vowed before God to rid my mind of the evil I had inherited and for the sake of my husband to dwell only on the new life he had planted in me.

During these past many months, Yasmin, the gypsy girl who is my kin, has knocked several times on Decimus's door. Ella, as always, remains aloof and declines to acknowledge her, but Decimus, who is not prejudiced against her people, allows me her company and I look forward to her visits. Though she is about my age, her life is very different from mine. While she is free, I am confined and subject to my husband's will, yet I do not envy her. Enthralled by tales of her travels, in my imagination I travel too.

The short, bleak days of November are drawing to a close and my time is near. These days and nights that lead up to my childbed are joyous, for Decimus is unstinting in his tenderness. Lying together before sleep, with the covers peeled back, he loves to touch the place that harbours his child. The babe is very active and my lord likens my belly to the swell of the sea, as waves sweep across a stormy ocean. Sometimes he rests his hand where he can feel the son he hopes for. When he is kicked, Decimus smiles and his face lights up. Then for a moment I see again the young man who laughed at my discomfiture. Though Decimus no longer loves me with his body, I better understand him now and know he fears his loving, which so often hurts me, might damage his unborn child.

Although I dread giving birth, during these final weeks the babe bears down so hard I can scarcely walk and I long to be released from my burden. Gradually my mind is stilled as I contemplate the work I must do, and pray that soon Decimus will receive his gift of me and will have another son in time for the feast of Christmas.

Just before dawn on the first Sunday in Advent, the pains began and my sorrowing, which was for me, as it is for all women, God's will, could be delayed no longer. I asked Decimus if he might allow Granny to attend me, but he would not agree to it, saying the time had come to test the strength he had given me. But he would allow Yasmin to be with me, for she is my kin and her people had schooled her well in the craft of birth.

Decimus told Annie to go at once to the encampment and bring Yasmin back with her. Annie shrank from her task, for she was sorely afraid of the gypsies. But no harm would come to her while they remained on her master's land.

Ella filled the copper bath with hot water and, wanting nothing to do with childbirth, made her excuses, leaving me alone in the scullery with Decimus. Poor Ella, who longed for the babe almost as much as I, could not overcome her revulsion for my condition. Decimus helped me undress, for I could not manage on my own. My body was clumsy, seeming to me grotesque. I could not see my feet for the vastness of my fullblown belly. Even his mark was partially obscured from my vision by the curve that held his child. I was so much bigger than I had been with Thomas and my breasts, always heavy since I had nursed him, were distended, etched with deep blue veins, the nipples dark and thick. Decimus held me in his arms, telling me he loved me, not caring how ugly I felt, for I carried his son. Silently I prayed to God that He would give me strength to endure the perilous hours ahead. The pains were coming faster now as Decimus helped me into the bath. The water was deep, lapping my chin, and I drew comfort from the warmth. When Decimus was satisfied I was clean, he dried me and led me upstairs, then helped me lie down on the hard bed that Annie had prepared.

The shawl Mistress Morgan had made for me lay folded on the chair next to my bed. I wrapped myself in it, insulating my body from the chill of the late November morning. Decimus

71

stood over me and removed it, leaving me cold and naked. He had not shared his thoughts with me and, trembling, I feared him, yet need not have done, for I had not offended my lord. He sat on the chair and his fingers traced the ribboned skin raised on my swollen belly. With hardly a sound, he hummed a tune, a shadow crossing his face.

'I have not sent you back to Mistress Morgan to have my mark cut deeper, Mary. I need protect neither myself nor my sons from you, my dear.'

I opened my mouth to protest. Despite my resolve, I was so frightened to give birth to a son who might bleed and would gladly have submitted to Mistress Morgan's knife had Decimus asked it of me.

'My dear, I know what is in your mind. Once was enough. In my hands you have received more loving sorrow than I could ever have instructed Mistress Morgan to inflict upon you. Your penance is over, my darling. Now set aside your fears and allow your mind to dwell on the joy your labours will bring me. I know I need not remind you that the product of your womb is mine and you labour for me alone.'

Looking up into Decimus's eyes, I recalled the day I had given up Thomas to sister Ella and my terrible jealousy that I could not quell. The memory no longer disturbed me and in spite of my growing discomfort I had to smile, for his stern warning could not disguise his fear for me. Reaching up, I touched his face, my fingers pressing against his lips.

'Hush, my love, could you doubt I understand you? I have only to look around me. All, save the air I breathe, is yours. Even this childbed that I lie on and is so hard to my bones is yours. I have learned my lesson well and am resigned. I know the child to be delivered of my womb, though flesh of my flesh, will be yours.'

His great arms that all his life had known heavy work encircled me and held me safe. He let me lie back and covered me again with the shawl, then piled more wood on the fire to keep the damp and cold at bay.

'Would you like me to stay with you for a little while, Mary dear?'

My heart racing, quite shocked by the suggestion, I turned my head so that I could more easily see his face. When I had laboured with Thomas he had left me with Granny, saying it was woman's work. Now I was taken aback by his quiet solicitation. Though I had no secrets from my husband, I had not anticipated he would want to watch my labours and unexpectedly was embarrassed.

'Lord, I cannot help that you will see and hear me in my weakness and Granny said that could not be.'

Decimus sat down with me again. Holding my hands, gently he explained what I had failed to comprehend.

'In my house, Mary, convention will not come between us. Neither your tears nor the sight of your labouring will trouble me, my dear. Though sometimes I care that others might scorn you, I care not what they make of me.'

The child was anxious to be born and my hurt came often and was very deep. As I struggled to give Decimus a son and my body descended into torment, I felt the flame of his love ignite. He must have had duties to attend, but he did not leave me. Holding hands, we were but two sides of the same coin, my love and I. I could hold back my tears no more, but he did not mind my weakness and nothing mattered to me, save my love for him. Should this sweet agony not end, it was of little consequence so long as Decimus was with me. He turned me on to my side and, smoothing my aching back, spoke words of love, encouraging me.

Yasmin entered my calm sea. I knew she had come, for her scent was all about her. Without demur, caring not for convention either, she accepted the presence of my husband. For hour upon endless hour my anguished body was seized, held in the grip of fate, but Decimus stayed with me, touching me and supporting me with his love.

Yasmin asked Annie to fetch a thick plate that would withstand the fire she must make. With worried eyes, Annie hesitated, but her master bade her hurry. Yasmin took small burned embers from the fire basket and laid them on the plate; then she drew a leather pouch from her pocket and deftly sprinkled its contents of dried leaves over the hot ashes. As the pale green leaves began to smoulder, tiny tendrils of smoke rose, curling in the draught. Leaving the plate next to me, Yasmin insisted I breathe in deeply, for, she said, the spirit of the leaves would help my womb to open and ease my lord's dear sweet child into this mortal life.

She blew the smoke, wafting it into my face, and, suffocated by the sickly, perfumed smell, a point inside my head began to dance. It was not Decimus's dance, but slow and ever slower were the waves that pulsed through my head. Now I lay quietly, relaxed by the bitter-sweet smoke, and watched my body, that belonged not to me, labouring to give Decimus his child.

Decimus made ready to leave, for the cows had to be milked and they would not make allowance for his absence. He lit a candle, that my mind should concentrate upon its flame. I kissed my dear love's hand and bade him farewell.

His flame burned with a steady light. My eyes were lured into its depths and my eyelids grew heavy. The ocean on which I travelled was stormy and sometimes I felt I might drown, but, through it all, Yasmin's gentle voice talked to me.

Decimus came back. Not comforting me now, he sat where he could take his child from my womb. He had helped many of God's creatures into this world and, unmoved by my fatigue, he watched my labouring. Truly, I did not mind his dispassion. It was God's will that I suffer on my childbed, for I was but the vessel who would give my lord his sons. My babe was nearly free now and gently, with loving hands, Decimus eased him from me, taking his gift.

The evening had drawn in and except for the candle's eternal flame the room was dark. I thanked God the long slow night of pain I had so dreaded was not to be. Decimus bade Annie light the lamp and lifting his son, he held him up for me to see. The infant cried. A thick white cord bound him to me, but about his body was a luminous grey caul. My husband smiled down on me as he freed his son from the enveloping skin.

'Thank you, Mary dear. A caul is a lucky omen. This son of mine will grow strong and be a credit to you.

'Now, Yasmin, free him from his mother so that I may take him to meet his elder brother, for Thomas has been waiting up for this moment.'

Yasmin took the child and with skilled fingers shredded the cord with her nails, separating my babe from me. Sitting beside me, Decimus put his arm around me as, weary beyond measure, I lay against him, his body warming me. I did not expect him to let me touch his son. Yasmin folded a length of soft lawn and carefully wrapped the child, swaddling him, then gave him back to Decimus. Telling me he would not leave me long, my lord departed, allowing me to finish in peace the work I had almost completed. Dear Annie had not seen a birth before and was quite overcome by emotion. Carefully she washed me in lavender water and made the bed around me, putting back the feather underlay and puffing up the pillows to make me comfortable. She gave me Mistress Morgan's shawl and, covering myself, I was warmed and could rest until Decimus brought his son back for me to suckle. Yasmin's knowledge and my husband's love had sustained me. Secure in his house, I had not been afraid.

When Decimus returned, he laid his child in my arms and, touching the sweet babe, I wept as my lord held him to my breast. How perfect he was. Dark brown hair covered his little head. Even the tops of his ears were coated with down. I unwrapped one arm and his hand found my breast, his little finger nails, so long, digging into me like tiny pins. Through his swaddling I felt his warmth. How heavy he was. Truly happy, in gratitude I kissed my dear lord's hand.

'This son I shall name Harry,' he said.

Decimus sat with me and I closed my eyes, resting my head on his shoulder as Harry took those first clear drops of sustenance my breasts had prepared for him.

Yasmin stayed but a few days more, until my milk began to flow. She could not stay longer, for Decimus said to be imprisoned in a house was a penance for Yasmin and he must let her go, for all her life she had known the freedom of God's open sky. Yasmin promised she would come back soon and in quiet prayer I put my hands together, copying her. Smiling, she held my two hands between hers, kissed me and was gone.

I lay in bed for three weeks, during which time Harry was baptised. Decimus wished my seclusion to be sustained and left me at home. I did not query his decision. On the fourth Sunday in Advent, I accompanied my lord to church and, kneeling before the altar, was cleansed of my labours.

At all times Decimus's new son took precedence and I again became accustomed to the nursing gown I wore. Sometimes I would notice Ella looking at Harry with benign interest, for she knew as I did that I should not enjoy him for too long.

Seven months have passed since I gave birth to Harry, who is with Ella now. It is June 1864 and I am twenty-three years old, yet often feel I am more than that and have been wed to my lord many years longer than five. My memory is fading and sometimes I fear its loss, when in a void I cannot remember who I am.

Annie assisted me as she had done so many times before. Now that my body was restored, Decimus had summoned me. Annie helped me into the bath of warm scented water and let me soak. I washed my hair, then waited while she sharpened her razor. Swiftly she drew the blade up and down the strop until the steel shone, its edge honed. I was always a little fearful when she shaved me, but should by now have become used to it. When I was soaped and sufficiently composed to submit to her, mindful of her master's instructions Annie shaved my body, leaving my skin smooth and clean.

She gave me Decimus's gossamer gown to wear and brushed my hair until it shone. The tresses had grown heavy and they spread over my shoulders. In the evening light of the parlour, the gown would be beautiful, the silk glowing as though it were on fire, and I hoped Decimus would be pleased with me.

Knocking on the parlour door, I waited, my hand on the latch, until Decimus bade me enter. Ella, more patient with me nowadays, left me alone with my lord. As I stood before him, at first he did not acknowledge me and my apprehension grew. Without looking up, his hand reached out and touched me. When he spoke, his voice was forgiving.

'Your mourning is natural, Mary. I know your heart is hurting. I have called you now because tonight I shall erase your sorrow, my dear, and make parting with Harry easier for you to bear.'

Tying tighter the silken cord at my waist, I went outside with Decimus. He led me well away from the house, to the barn on the far side of the first field. As we approached, the remains of a fire glowed in the fading light. New putchers, standing like skeletons, almost obscured the entrance to the barn and I shivered despite the warmth of the evening.

Decimus told me to take off the gown. Fearing to snag the delicate fabric with his rough hands, he would not touch it. As I removed it, a gentle wind blew soft on my skin. To examine my body closely, Decimus held my arms, stretching them wide. I did not ask my husband what he intended to do, for even had I done so I doubt he would have answered me.

Looking up at him I saw he was happy in my company, for he had the air of a man who is content within himself. His quiet confidence was not born of arrogance but from the knowledge that, at thirty years of age, he was old enough to know he was master of his destiny and of all the men who owed their living to him. My feet sank into the soft hay as, in the gloaming, I followed him farther towards the back of the barn. I was a little nervous now, but the familiar scent of woodsmoke calmed me. As my eyes became used to the gloom, I saw he had prepared the long high bench he used for his work. Not even in my heart would I confess to fear, for if he were to take my life it was his to do with as he pleased. But Decimus was not fooled by my demeanour and put his arm around me, turning my face so that my eyes met his.

'Are you ready, my darling, to travel again on the path of learning that I intend for you?'

I nodded, trembling a little, but he did not need a reply. He could not have missed the flame that burned bright within me.

Requesting I give him my hands, he bound each securely, though not so tightly as would have been uncomfortable. When I tried, but failed, to move my hands against the bondage of the soft white rope, my husband's smile was gentle. He led me to the wooden bench, which I noticed he had cleaned, and urged me to climb up on to it. It was difficult without my hands and he had to help me. I lay down on my back and relaxed as he told me. He said I should soon not feel the hardness of the bench that supported me. Taking my bound hands and holding them above my head, he pulled me so that my arms were outstretched behind me. I could not see where they were tethered, but the binds did not hurt. Carefully Decimus laid out my hair so that it fanned around my head. He ran his hands over my body, caressing the parts that no more I thought of as secret. From my ankle to my toes he wove a cradle for each foot. One at a time, he stretched my legs, pulling them. The tension ran through me and it hurt a little as he secured my feet to the extremity of the bench. The cool air brushed where my legs parted and my body was shaven. All the while Decimus's voice urged me to rest and, obeying him, my apprehension left me and I lay still, submissive and happy to please my lord. Across my abdomen to restrain me, he drew very tight a wide leather strap and now I could not move at all. He explained that the part of me which was his alone must not be injured by what he was to do to me. His voice was soft, concerned for my welfare.

'There, Mary, I've finished. Would it help you if I covered your eyes, my dear?'

I assured him I did not fear what he must do to me.

'I am always safe with you, my love. Your bonds that have made me secure restrain me no more than swaddling would do a babe.'

Gently Decimus kissed me. He said he must leave me alone for a while that I might become settled in my surroundings. My eyes grew used to the dimness of the light and, staring up, aimlessly I counted the rafters above me. Gradually my breathing became more shallow and I was less conscious of my heartbeats.

I forgot the hardness of the bench and the tightness of the strap that pinched my abdomen.

I turned my head, for it was the only part of me not lost to my control. Decimus's frame filled the doorway and in his hand he carried a large leather bucket, brimming full of water. Gently at first, for he did not wish to spoil my mood, he splashed it over me, the water cool on my skin.

Spreading the wetness, he touched me inside, where none but his hand had leave to pass. When I was completely wet and he was sure I was ready, from beneath the bench he retrieved a soft willow that had not been robbed of its leaves. Its touch was as light as a feather. From my face to the tips of my toes Decimus stroked me. The sensation was soothing and I closed my eyes to enjoy the feeling even more, not wanting it to stop. Gradually it seemed as though the feather had become heavier. Deliberately I dozed, so that I should not wake and by my anxiety be denied this pleasure.

Decimus understood, but he could not let me sleep. He said I must look only at him, for he would know when he saw pain behind my eyes and did not want me to hurt too much. Trusting him, I looked up at my husband and was not afraid. The willow he now held in his hand was leafless and much heavier. My senses were lulled and I lay quietly for him as he drew it across my body. To me, his soft leafy willow had not changed. The smoke from the fire entered my head and my mind began to sing. Decimus was unhurried as slowly his hand with every stroke increased its pressure. Time waited for me. My mind became obsessed by the rhythm, my brain absorbing the intensity of the song. Decimus released my feet and abdomen, though for a while I did not notice my freedom. I was tethered only by my hands now as Decimus turned me on to my belly to expose my back and buttocks. With each stroke the music played faster and faster, until lost in a new world I wept as my body pulsed to the willow's song and, overwhelmed, though I tried so hard, I could not keep my eyes from closing and had to sleep.

Abruptly the song died away. Decimus released me from my bonds and held me in his arms, wiping away my tears.

'You have done very well, Mary, but you have listened long enough to the music of the willow, my darling. You will always remember the first time you heard its song and soon it will sing to you again, then again and again until you are never free of it.'

My body was on fire, but I did not mind the pain. Decimus carried me into the cool night air and we lay in the grass together. He gathered dew and bathed the hurt that he had caused. I thought of the first time I had lain with my lord when he had taken my maidenhood. I guessed even then, and I knew nothing of men, that he would demand much of me. The old Gypsy Queen had seen the scars of love on my body and understood my husband's needs.

Looking up, I could see the stars were emerging from a blackening sky and I knew I should always belong, body and soul, to Decimus. Our love was of our own creation and I suspected few, save my dear lord and I, would ever understand it. He kissed me, taking all the hurt away, and I longed for him to love me with his body. As I touched his forearm, the muscles tensed under my fingers. That glorious night, I ached to give my love what he had not already taken, but sensed I must wait, for he would not forgive a brazen approach.

When at last he took off his clothes, together we lay under God's sky, as did Adam and Eve in the beautiful Garden of Eden before provoking God's wrath, when Eve was beguiled. I gave myself into my lord's loving arms. His skin cooled the fire that consumed me and I knew even if I were a Daughter of Satan I was secure in my husband's love and my soul was safe from the Devil.

CHAPTER IX

No Illusions

The pale dawn light casts barely a shadow as I lie quiet and happy in my lord's soft, cool bed. Though he has left me now, I still feel his arms about me as they hold me safe in his love. His fingers wandering over my body had wakened me and, opening my eyes, I had looked up at him. His smile was gentle. When I asked him why I ached so, leading my hand he let me touch the imprint of his love and I remembered then what he had done to me. Reaching up for his kisses, I could scarcely move and, concerned that I suffer too much, he has ordered me to stay in bed awhile and rest. Yet I, not heeding the pain, and with the song of his willow soaring in my head, am content to have pleased my husband; my mind is at peace.

This afternoon Decimus plans to take his sons to see my old Gypsy Aunt and Yasmin too. Though my strength is quite depleted, I know my indisposition will not cause him to change his mind and he will wish me to accompany him.

Annie helped me dress in a new cotton gown Decimus had brought me from the city. It was white, with sprigs of leaves and rosebuds. Lace petticoats peeped from beneath the hem and a red ribbon sash set off my waist. My hair was pulled back and on my head I wore a wide-brimmed hat, for Decimus was anxious my face should not catch the sun.

I was much relieved to see the pony and trap waiting in

the yard, for I had feared he would expect me to walk to the encampment. Though it was not far, my fatigue was such that to walk even a short distance would have been beyond me. Smiling down at me, Decimus took my arm and, shooing off the chickens, cleared a path for us. He had put a cushion on my seat. Thomas, holding Ella's hand, was excited to be coming too and needed no urging to climb up beside me. He was four years old now. Decimus must have looked very like him when he was small, for there was no mistaking this sturdy child's identity. I could not help the lump in my throat when Ella placed Harry into my arms, for he seemed so happy to be with his mother again.

Conflicting emotions raged in my heart as I contemplated where Decimus was taking me. For a while now, I had accepted the gypsies were my kin, yet I did not look forward to meeting Queenie again. Decimus saw my anxiety and was not a little irritated.

'Whatever ails thee now, Mary?' he asked of me.

Trying to explain my anxieties, I found it difficult to compose myself and my words came out in a headlong jumble.

'I think the old Gypsy gained my confidence too readily. My terror was so great, I feared for my life. When she spoke kindly, I was thankful and sought her approval. Please do not leave me alone with her, lord, for I fear she will put her spell on me again.'

I had expected Decimus to laugh and hung my head. He held my face up to the light and did not mock me.

'None but I will keep you under a spell, Mary. I shall not let her hurt you.'

Decimus took up the reins and guided the pony out on to the dry, uneven track. Hawthorn hedges overhung our path and the sun beat down on us out of a cloudless sky. Not far ahead a thin ribbon of smoke rose above the trees. The same sounds which had assailed my senses before were carried on the warm summer air. There was much activity. The gypsies were moving on. I asked Decimus where they were going, but he just shrugged. He said there were signs in the hedgerows they left on their way, but only the gypsies, not he, could read them. At our approach the young men who were preparing the waggons stopped work and doffed their caps to Decimus.

The old woman we had come to see was sitting on the step of her waggon. She was crocheting, but the hook moved stiffly across her work. She looked much frailer than when I had seen her last, over a year ago. With watery eyes, she watched us.

'So you have brought your sons to see me, young Sir.' Immediately I felt uneasy as the lilting voice that had seduced me before dulled my wits. I held Harry tight in my arms and did not stir from the trap.

'I can see you husband has beaten you, my dear. You look weary. Ask him if you may sit alone with me and make an old woman happy.'

Her wheedling plea was piteous. Before, when she had undressed me and I had stood naked before her, the voice even as it softened had been strong and I could not help but obey. Now its pitch rose unsteadily and though perplexed that she should want to see me alone I felt sorry for her. I could not help my weakness and looked to my lord to save me. But already it was too late. As though a lever had been pulled, I was dazed and in her power again. There was nothing I could do to help myself and, shivering, I wished Decimus had left me at home. Even so, I asked my husband if I might stay awhile. Decimus ignored my request.

'No, Queenie, my wife cannot sit alone with you. Her duty is to me.'

Though he laughed, there was no mirth in his voice. There was malice in hers. I listened as they haggled over me and it mattered not if I were there. Had I not gained her respect and had she not come to like me when I was here before, letting me call her Aunt? She did not like me now. All pretence was lost and I wondered, was this the first time insidiously she had tried to set my husband against me?

Now I understood; when my mother had died, the gypsies had wanted me back. How many years had Queenie harboured a grudge? Why did she still want to possess me? It was much too late now. Decimus had given me his strength and I drew myself up.

Looking straight at her, I asked of her, 'Why should you seek to deny me my lord, knowing only he can save me from damnation?'

Seeing his will was stronger than hers, her fury overflowed and with hatred in her tired old eyes, her tongue laden with vitriol, she turned on me. Wishing me dead, she called me a Daughter of Satan and, sickened, at last I learned the truth.

Had my father given me to Queenie when my mother died, she would surely have put me to death. For she knew that I alone now carried in my veins the curse that poor flaxen-haired maiden had visited on the gypsies. Protecting me, Decimus held me safe and I knew, no matter what she had told him, he would always love me.

The spell was broken. She had lost interest now. Turning her back on us, she resumed her crocheting. Slowly, on her haunches, she began to rock backwards and forwards, oblivious to the activity that surrounded her.

We saw Yasmin coming towards us from the far side of the camp. Her body seemed to float, such was her grace. About her flowed a long, loose robe, gay ribbons at the hem. The bodice was black and tightly laced so that from her waist she swayed as she walked. She greeted us, the movement of her hands fluid, her ringed fingers upturned at the tips. Her neck was long and her head quite still. Clinging to her was a sense of peace which enveloped me. I could hardly turn my eyes away, for she was so lovely. A shawl, partly covering her long black hair, was hung with fringe and glinting in the fringe was gold. She told us she had been chosen by the elders to hold the secrets of her people. Soon, when death claimed her grandmother, she would be Queen of the gypsies.

I asked Yasmin whither they were going. She said it was a most secret place, where even the birds did not sing. Many miles to the east at the foot of the Cotswold escarpment was a wide open common, but to reach it needed knowledge and skill. The lane leading down was narrow. Deep ruts could prise the wheel off a waggon and it was always dark under the thick green foliage where the sun never shone. There was no other way in or out, for the woods that hemmed the common were impenetrable, the face of the hills behind almost sheer. People would come from many miles distant to attend her grandmother's funeral, but Yasmin said they must make haste for the old woman's mind was fading. I should not take to heart her wounding words, for my Aunt was near to death and her brain had succumbed to dementia.

When the tribe assembled and the appointed hour was reached, every mortal thing which Queenie possessed would be piled on to her waggon. The men would collect kindling and the children would gather soft brown moss for a bed.

Yasmin's sad duty was the most onerous of all, for she had to ease her grandmother's path. The gold the old woman wore on her fingers, in her nostril and the lobes of her ears would all have been removed and when it was done, Yasmin would free her grandmother's nipples from the heavy rings that pierced them, and pour scented oil on to her naked body. Lastly she would wrap the old woman in a fine lawn shroud.

Yasmin showed me a potion she had made. It had taken many weeks to collect the sap of the poppy. When her grandmother was ready, Yasmin's last duty was to lay her on the bed of soft moss and administer the potion. Then the waggon would be set to the torch and, though she would feel the warmth of the flames, before they reached her the old Gypsy Queen would already be in the embrace of the Goddess of Death.

When the last spark of life in the fire had finally died, Yasmin would kneel before the elders of the tribe. She, too, would be permitted to take of the potion to lessen the pain when her breasts, in turn, were pierced with gold.

Decimus asked if we should see her again and whether her people would return to our Vale, but Yasmin shook her head, for she did not know where her destiny would take her.

We bade the gypsies farewell. Decimus gathered up the reins. With Thomas sitting between us and Harry in my lap, we returned home.

Standing in the yard was a large black horse. The saddle on his back bore a coat of arms. Ella rushed out to meet us, saying there was a messenger from the Castle waiting indoors. Decimus handed me down from the trap and I followed as he strode into the house. Ella had taken the messenger into the reception room we rarely used. He wore a livery of brilliant yellow. From a pouch he took papers, presenting them to Decimus. Decimus's grandfather was sick. He bade me hurry. Though the afternoon was well advanced, we were to go at once to the Castle. He had forgotten how tired I was, but seeing his distress I thought not to mention it.

I had not travelled to Milbury since Decimus took me for his bride. The church of St Mark, far to the east, where he had wed me, gradually came closer. The old battle-scarred walls of the Castle, which stood next to it, were also in view. The gaunt, crumbling ruin rose in front of us. Some of the battlements were broken completely away. This fortress had harboured Mary Tudor when her father had been rid of her mother, Catherine. Now the old place was at peace and sheep grazed unhindered. Granny's family had lived on this site for a thousand years, but her father, the old lord, was dying. We drove through to an inner courtyard, where Decimus helped me down from the trap. I straightened my new gown that I had worn all day. It was creased and looked a little sad. A liveried footman led us through an ivy-covered entrance into a cool, dark hall beyond. Granny, accompanied by a gentleman she introduced as her brother and whose features seemed vaguely familiar, was waiting for us in a vast panelled room. I had not seen Granny for such a long time. She kissed me and asked if I minded waiting alone for a while.

Gratefully I sat down, fearing I might faint. The chair was held together with thick tasselled ropes. It was the same pattern as the ones at home. A huge stone fireplace was surrounded by heraldic shields and almost covering the walls were paintings of the family. Aristocratic eyes looked down on me in the soft evening light. I doubted I should really be here in this fine place, but had noticed Decimus was not troubled at all by the grandeur.

I had not waited long when a thin little man, his shoulders

bent in deference, stood hovering in front of me. Avoiding my eyes and sniffing slightly, he requested me to follow him. My husband had summoned me to his lordship's apartment. The light was fading quickly and the wooden stairs, though wide and shallow, were cloaked in shadow. Holding up my skirts to see my feet, I followed the old servant. The first landing was large and furnished, a room in itself with an oriel window which caught the last of the sun's rays. From here, though, the stairs were stone and climbed round a central core. Somewhat surprised the bedchamber should be so inaccessible, I was shaking with fatigue when we reached the top.

The room was hung with tapestries, the air musty and stifling, for there were no windows open. An aged man was propped up on pillows, but he recognised no one. On his face lingered the vacant stare that comes before death. Granny was sitting beside her father, holding his hand. She looked up and smiled encouragingly at me. Decimus beckoned me nearer to his grandfather's bed. I felt uncomfortable, for the old man's unseeing eyes followed my every movement. It seemed the eyes flickered in recognition.

'Lydia,' he whispered.

My love met my astonished stare but quickly motioned me to silence. He ordered me to kiss his grandfather before I retired. I did as he said. The old gentleman's skin was cold and crêpe-like against my lips.

Decimus held my arm and led me away, helping me descend the dark stairs down to the long panelled gallery where I had been left on my own. I asked him why his grandfather had not been moved to a more convenient place, but Decimus said the old man had loved the river and from the topmost rooms on a clear day he could see the sparkling silver waters and beyond to the mountains of Wales.

Then, taking a deep breath, I asked my husband, 'Who was Lydia?'

Granny was at my elbow. Though my infirmity was obvious for her to see, she did not comment, but gently held my arm, telling me she would show me a portrait of Lydia. She guided me to the far end of the gallery. Decimus brought a lamp so that I should more clearly see the picture that hung in front of me.

A flaxen-haired girl played in a forest glade with a spaniel dog. To the left of the picture was a tall, haughty man. He had cruel eyes. In his hand he held an old-fashioned hat with curled feathers. His other hand rested on the little girl's head.

A dark-haired lady in a red velvet gown held the spaniel's lead. As I looked up into her haunting eyes, she seemed to smile down on me as a mother would do a child and I could scarcely draw my gaze away. I knew her well. Decimus caught me in his arms.

I still breathed, but with difficulty, as the terrible truth dawned. That night in Kingswood after the lawyers had left me, I had opened my mother's jewel case. The lady in the portrait smiled at me then and I had wondered who she was.

On the gilded frame was printed LORD JAMES 1737–1784 and LADY LYDIA 1748–1782. There was no mention of the young girl who played with her dog.

Granny was telling me about Lydia, yet I could not concentrate for it seemed her voice came from far away.

'Poor Lydia died of a broken heart, Mary. She bore her husband James two sons, but both died. Her only daughter, Jane, was lost and never found. Lydia went into a decline and none could console her. According to records, the child was just thirteen years old.'

Stricken, I turned to Granny, who, seeing my face, clasped my hand tightly and continued.

'Lord James died without leaving an heir. The title passed to his younger brother. He was my grandfather. My father is dying now and he sees only the past before his eyes. He thought you were a ghost, Mary.

'My dear, I must confess I too believed I had seen you before when you first came to the Vale with the old man you called Jesse. I do not understand, but I see in your eyes that this portrait has been a revelation for you. Some day I know you will tell me why.'

I could not speak for shock. Decimus held me close, knowing how terribly I was troubled. Leaving me with Granny just for a moment, he paid his final respects to his dying grandfather, then, waiting no longer, took me home.

My thoughts were in turmoil. I did not care for the deep ditches that had worried me on our way and they passed unnoticed. I asked Decimus if, when we reached home, he might let me see the pill box my mother had left me.

He said that maybe tomorrow if I were stronger we should examine it together, for I was far too tired tonight. My lord had not forgotten how much the pain of his loving had exhausted me and he let me sleep propped in his arms while the sure-footed pony carried us homeward.

Decimus made me wait, for he would not be hurried. It was nearly noon before he called me. He was sitting on the bed. Spread out in front of him were the contents of my mother's jewel box. He bade me sit down. Carefully avoiding the dreadful serpent which nestled under pretty glass beads, I drew out the blue oval brooch with the circlet of old gold my father had pressed into my hand so secretly. My eyes were drawn to the plait of golden hair and holding the brooch in my palm, thinking about Jane, I dreamed a little. I had no doubt she was the flaxen-haired maiden the gypsies had stolen and so reviled. What a terrible life Jane must have endured, with nothing to remind her of her family but her mother's portrait on the little pill box. I wondered, had she ever known love? What a long time ago it had been. Yet all this while generations of daughters had kept safe the brooch and the pill box too.

Decimus, impatient with my dreaming, would not wait longer and, grasping the little box, studied it intently. He ran his nail round the edge of the porcelain, then taking his knife, with care prised the lid from its silver mount. He turned it over and we could see revealed on the back was a date, 1779.

'She would have been thirty years old when this portrait was done.'

Decimus's voice was steady, but I sensed his excitement.

Under the date was a scroll. But examining it more closely, we could see it was not a scroll at all, but a curled-up serpent with a vile head, its tongue forked. When the porcelain caught the light, I swear the serpent smiled at me. Appalled, I froze.

So Lady Lydia had carried the curse. The room swam before me. Quickly Decimus replaced the porcelain in its mount. He put it aside and gathered me into his arms. The enormity of it all was just too much. I was so frightened. The curse was far older than Jane. It had been visited on me and my kin for over a hundred years. My confidence, so carefully nurtured by my husband, was destroyed. He must know my soul was beyond redemption. Surely, he would reject me now. How much penance could I do in my lifespan to let me atone for the sins I had inherited? Perhaps the Lady Lydia had paid her debt by dying young. I wished to die now, that the curse should die with me, for as yet there was no daughter with a trait in her to beguile men and bear sons who might bleed. An ancient fear had settled on me and I knew the serpent would never leave me in peace.

Condemned to its evil, not bearing to look at Decimus, I let go of him. I was not worthy of his love. His voice, sounding strange, ordered me to undress and, unquestioning, I took off my clothes. Crouching before him I was bereft of tears. His grip on my arm hurt me as he propelled me to the long glass. He made me look at my poor naked body.

I saw the bright mark Mistress Morgan had made on me, the thin silvery lines of stretching I had sustained with joy and the long weals of the willow where Decimus had imprinted his love. I was swollen all over and blue with bruising.

Decimus was standing behind me. His fingers traced the long painful streaks. His eyes had filled with tears.

'Does not my loving cause you sorrowing enough, Mary? Believe me, you will not pay penance again. We are kinsmen, you and I, as well as lovers. You have given me two fine sons and both live. You will not dissuade me from loving you, my dear, and whatever the future brings, we will face it together.'

In his arms, I wept until my tears had run dry. Though it was not long past noon, he gave me the gossamer robe, saying I should put it on now, for my clothes chafed me where my skin was broken.

Even Ella's disdain could not disturb me. My love had plucked me from the jaws of Hell and though in my heart I prayed the curse should die with me I knew that decision was not mine to take. It would be God's will.

Within a day, Decimus's grandfather was dead, having lived a full ninety-five years. On the day of his funeral Decimus took me to stay with Granny, for she was grieving. Apart from the few moments of her company at the Castle, I had seen her but twice since Decimus had taken me from his father's house, my head shaven and with Thomas in my arms. I had missed her so much when Harry was born.

The loving relationship had not withered, for she embraced me as though I were her own daughter. Both Granny and Grand-father Hillyer had aged considerably and I was shocked to see Mr Hillyer. I had not thought of him as old, but he looked not long for this world. Recalling that first year of marriage when Decimus and I had lived under his father's roof, I remembered how harsh my husband's discipline had seemed, when he had instructed me in my duties, and how supportive Granny had always been. I thought, too, of the conversations I had had with her.

She had said then that her father opposed her marriage to Mr Hillyer, considering him inferior. According to Decimus his grandfather had relented because Granny was spoiled. Though she had as yet borne her first husband no children, her virginity, that most precious possession, was lost. Now I learned there was far more to it than that. Only after Decimus had left us did Granny confide why she must stay at home and could not attend her father's funeral.

Quietly, in the peace of the orchard, Granny and I sat in the sun's dapple and she told me what even Decimus did not know. She opened her heart and I was grateful to her for granting me such privilege. Her story was so sad.

Granny's first marriage had been convenient to both families, devout Catholics. But her father had given her to a man she did not love. She was just seventeen and had no choice but to obey her father's wishes. When a dashing young bailiff, Decimus

Hillyer, came into her husband's employ, Granny dared to look at him with love in her heart. In the privacy of the confessional she admitted her sin and asked for forgiveness. She had been wed less than two years when her husband sickened and died. She could not mourn for him and, her sins compounded, Granny prayed again for remission. Paying penance for her wickedness, she returned to her father's house and fasted.

The bailiff, who was not of their faith, none the less asked Granny's father for the hand in marriage of his widowed daughter. Calling him a common adventurer, her father refused, dismissing him. But Decimus Hillyer was persistent and would not go away. Granny begged her father to change his mind. The only suitors he found for her were old men who had lost their wives. Desperate for love, Granny had fasted again, until fearing her death would be on his conscience her father relented. Giving the bailiff land and throwing money at him, telling him he had got what he came for, shaming Granny, he cast her out. But Granny was to pay an even more terrible price for love, for her faith as well as her family were taken from her. The priest barred her from his church, and the confessional was denied her. When she was wed in a Protestant church, none but her new husband's kin attended.

Though Granny had borne many children, ten of whom had lived, she was never free of guilt for the death of her first husband. Weeping quietly, Granny told me how much she loved her own dear Decimus, but accepted that without absolution when the dreadful Day of Judgement was upon her she would suffer eternal damnation to be consumed in the raging fires of Hell.

For some reason, known only to himself, her father had taken to her youngest son and she was consoled. Not until he lay on his death bed had the old gentleman pardoned his daughter.

I could not help dear, dear Granny, for I too was torn by the anguish of penance. She showed me the rosary she always wore, hidden beneath the folds of her gown, then led me into the house that was her haven.

'I will show you something now, Mary, that few, other than my dear sweet husband, have ever seen.'

In a secluded corner I saw the shrine where she prayed each day to the Blessed Virgin. Patting my hand, Granny remembered what was on my mind and, as if glad to put her own bitter-sweet memories behind her, she advised me more about Lydia.

'When I was a child, my mother told me a little about the beautiful lady in the red velvet gown. She was a cousin to James. Her father's house was near the great Roman road called Stane Street that forges north from the sea in the county of Sussex. They say the land where she came from is much like ours, flat and quiet, the smell of the sea and cries of birds being all around. Lydia was fifteen years old when she was taken from there and forced into a marriage of convenience with Cousin James. He was a cruel man and she could not love him.

'Bearing children was a torment for Lydia. Both sons bled and died in infancy. The soldiery searched the county for her only daughter, Jane, but could not find her. Lord James did not forgive Lydia her inability to give him an heir. When she lost her daughter, she could not survive in the harsh world James had created and gave up the will to live.'

The day went by and we hardly noticed its passing. Granny talked of her six sons but I knew her youngest son had a special place in her heart, for her love was so great, each time she spoke of Decimus, she shook her head and wept. I did not need to tell Granny about the flame he had lit in me, or the song the willow sang, for I believe she knew the song was in my head and I could scarce think for the sound of it.

By the time Decimus returned, I had repeated to Granny all that Queenie had told me about my mother's kin, and she understood.

Grandfather Hillyer did not see another harvest. Within a month, Granny had lost both her father and her beloved husband. Decimus made all the arrangements for his father's funeral. How odd it seemed that he, the youngest, should be looked to as head of the family.

We buried Mr Hillyer on a brilliant sunny day in July in the shadow of the north porch of the church of the Blessed Saint

Allwen. He was seventy-seven years old. Granny, her face drawn and eyes downcast, stood next to her youngest son. As the coffin was lowered she turned to him and, bending her knee, acknowledged his authority. Kissing his mother, Decimus steadied her, that she should not be embarrassed that his brothers observe her obeisance.

Afterwards, when Decimus's kin were assembled, his eldest brother, Luke, as convention dictated, read his father's Will.

Will the passing of Mr Hillyer, I had come to realise how old Decimus's family was. Indeed, Luke's eldest son was two years older than I. Though the farm was left to Luke, it was decided his son should take on the responsibility, letting Granny live out her days, as was her husband's wish, in the house where she had given birth to all her children and had been happy with her own dear Decimus.

CHAPTER X

Arcadia

The flame Decimus holds before me burns bright and ever brighter. My spirit lives in the willow's song. Many seasons have passed since Mr Hillyer died, yet as they slip by I do not count them. My husband holds me steady to the course he has set for my learning. His firm hand has taken away my fear of the curse that is my inheritance and his tutoring allows me to forget the shame of illegitimacy. My thinking is only as he wishes me to think. My mind is as though it has not known a will of its own. Memories of a life before I was wed have become hazy and died.

Though I kneel at his feet, my lord does not need me to inform him that the child he has planted grows inside me. It is more than four years since he delivered Harry of my womb and I pray my body will please him again, giving him another son. He has told me that after Easter I must see Mistress Morgan once more. I fear the encounter dreadfully, but it is my husband's will and pointless wishing it otherwise. I have no choice and doubt not that he owns me. I cannot expect him to change his mind.

Flooding that came during Lent cut off the village, but by Easter the waters had receded, leaving the ground marshy, fit only for geese to wade in, though most of the wildfowl had left us by then.

Decimus saw my anxiety, for I concealed nothing from him.

I could not remember the last time I had left his house and now must go alone to see Mistress Morgan. He pulled my shawl around me and I was consoled by the kindness of his words.

'Wife, she will not hurt you. I wish her only to tell me if you carry my son.'

The evening was still light as I set out across the duckboards towards Mistress Morgan's door. Consciously I pulled back my shoulders and held my head high, for Decimus had said I should be confident, my thoughts being his thoughts, fearing no one but him.

Mistress Morgan, older than ever, sat in her darkened room, her cat in her lap, its breathing heavy and rhythmic. An air of innocence exuded from her as, in time, her rocking chair creaked. On the last occasion I had seen her I had found her accent difficult to understand, but during the intervening years I had become accustomed to the dialect spoken hereabouts. I no longer had to strain to hear her words.

'Come in, my dear,' she said. 'So your husband has sent you to see me again. I knew he would. Now take off your things and lie on my bed.'

Shuddering, disturbed by an old terror, I looked around me. I saw no knife on the table and, conquering my fear, lay down on the bed behind her settle. I had not worn stays for several months and, resigned to endure her ministerings, I lifted my petticoats and lowered my drawers, uncovering my belly that was already swollen. She dragged herself from her chair, seeming not to notice her crippled feet, her face not registering pain. I looked down at the mark she had cut into me when I was last here. She hovered over me and I say still, battling with the torment in my mind, yet knowing I must obey her. Her pendulum swung, first one way, then the other. I could smell the fear on my body and guessed she could too. Smiling, she fingered the trace that was still bright and sensitive to her touch.

'Your belly carries your husband's mark well, my dear.'

The pendulum swung again. She had grown tense and I felt my flesh creep. Certain I carried a daughter, I asked of her,

'Please, Mistress, I beg of you, how can I protect the girl child in my womb from the curse my dear lord has lifted from me?'

She shook her head.

'There is nothing I can do to stop this child inheriting the curse you carry, my dear. The old gypsy, Queenie, told you no lies. Only if your daughter is purged of her sins by a man who loves her and will take her soul will she know peace. Now go home to your husband.'

Leaving Mistress Morgan, in tears I retraced my steps. She had not hurt me, but I would not have cared if she had. I wondered how to tell Decimus that I carried a daughter. Perhaps Mistress Morgan was wrong, but no, I knew in my heart she was not. Musing on the day I had walked on the Sea Bank of the Great River and the gypsies had found me to tell me about myself, I wondered how much longer than I Decimus had known the truth. I prayed that he could accept his daughter born of me. If she survived, would she find a husband she trusted as I trusted Decimus and could she love him enough to have the courage to let him free her of the curse in her blood, as my lord had freed me? Decimus was waiting, but as soon as he saw me, without need of words, he knew Mistress Morgan's prediction. Gratefully, sick with anxiety, I collapsed into his arms.

The child inside me grew. She would be born by June. My lord's loving hands did not spare me as he prepared my body for the torment to come. The infant in my belly was pressing hard on my abdomen when I asked him if I might have Granny with me for the birth. The gypsies had not returned and I had no idea if I should see Yasmin again. Annie would help me for she was always there.

Ella's spinster eyes glowed at the thought of her new charge and when my time came Granny was called. I laboured again but knew not whether it was night or day. This child was slow, sapping my strength. Two long nights had elapsed before she lay on the bed, delivered of me. I longed to touch her, but Granny comforted me, knowing I dared not until my husband had given his permission. Understanding, too, how very tired I was, she stayed with me, giving Annie the infant to take to Decimus for his approval.

As soon as my body had finished its work, I asked Granny if I might have a covering, for though it was mid June the weather was still cool. Refusing me, she insisted I lie unclothed with only a sheet under me. When she had delivered Thomas she had allowed me Mistress Morgan's shawl to warm my weary body. Yet Granny knew better than I that Decimus had every right to reject the child, and her mother too, if his daughter bore the mark of the Devil. I did not question her judgement. Shivering, in fear and humility, I waited for my lord.

Closing my eyes, exhausted, I had drifted into sleep, yet sensing his shadow I awoke with a start. Decimus stood over me. Fearing his decision, hesitantly I looked up into his face. He smiled and, seeing from his countenance the happiness my suffering had brought him, my heart leaped with joy.

Sitting on the bed with me, he said we should remember this day, for I had given him his pride and joy, a daughter. He would call her Lydia.

My face betraying my shock, I spoke before he could silence me.

'Oh no, Lord!'

'Mary, you will not influence my decision. I wish this child to bear the name Lydia. The unhappy Lady Lydia and her daughter were my kin too, remember?'

I held my dear husband's hand, putting it against my lips. How could I thank him for his generosity in accepting this daughter who may one day cause him pain. Giving me the child, he held her to my breast and her sucking was soft, for she, like me, had barely survived the trauma of birth. Until now I had not wept, having no strength for weeping, but as I looked at this beautiful babe who had inherited the curse from me my weeping knew no end.

Decimus's bulk filled the room and with his great presence sitting next to me he gave me courage to accept the challenge this daughter set before us. Covering me with Mistress Morgan's shawl, he watched the first suckling. His words, spoken softly, uplifted me.

'I understand all that troubles you, Mary. Soon your strength will return just a little, so I can love you again. In my hands you will forget and cease to worry. You know, my dear, there is nothing now you or I can do to protect our daughter, but I promise, when the time comes, I shall seek a husband for her who will love her as I love you.'

Suckling was not easy, for the moon claimed me very early. When Lydia was almost three months old, she was taken from me and given to a wet nurse. Decimus found a woman who was clean and knew well what she was employed to accomplish, but my heart was near to breaking as, with smothered breasts, I watched my little babe being suckled by another.

My strength was still depleted when Decimus sent for me. Even though weak, I craved my husband's embrace. It was as though my very weakness helped me offer myself into his stern but loving hands. My mind had long ceased to be my own and when my dear lord took what was his right the suffering my feeble body underwent had no relevance. It seemed as though the weaker my body became, the greater the burden my husband placed upon it. The greater the burden, the easier it was to carry, for my body, like my mind, was lost to me. Decimus's love knew no compromise and each day when I had accomplished the menial jobs that kept my hands from idleness Annie would prepare me so that, if he called, I was ready for him.

Our daughter became stronger as autumn turned to winter, but my ability to converse was lost and only Decimus's song occupied my head.

I have faint recall of those years when it seemed I dwelt in Arcadia. Decimus took a third son from my womb, whom he named Richard. Even the anguish of birth was blunted for my lord protected me and, like a moth, my spirit danced and died in his flame.

Richard, like his brothers, grew in the image of his father. My body was not allowed to regain the vigour it had enjoyed before the birth of Lydia. When I looked on the beauty of our daughter, my wanting in strength was unimportant, for within the loving seclusion Decimus created for me the frailty of my body was not irksome. Had not God sought to weaken me, then I do believe my husband would have undertaken the task himself.

I was thirty-two years old when I knelt before Decimus to advise him I was with child again. He was overjoyed by my news and did not mind if I gave him a son or a daughter. In Lydia he found boundless joy. He disciplined her very gently, unlike his sons, who would not seek his displeasure. Even so, Lydia acquiesced to her father's will.

I wondered how long Decimus would wait before he told her of the curse she had inherited. I dreaded that day, for how could I encourage her to take the tortuous path that might ease her sorrow? Her father looked often at Lydia's body for signs that the Devil knew her, but encountered only innocence and love.

Preparations for the birth of this fifth child were well practised. One day, when the babe in my belly was still, I knew something was wrong. The child had kicked until the eighth month, then lay silent. The great bulge pressed low down, but was inert. Decimus called a doctor from Milbury.

He put his hand on my belly, then inclined his ear, and sadly shook his head. He said I must be brave for the child inside me was not living and I should gather whatever strength I had to free my body of the death in my womb.

That night I lay awake and prayed the babe was only sleeping, but by early next day, awaiting the doctor's return, I was reconciled that my child was dead.

To help me during those desperate hours, Decimus sent for Granny, who was by now very old. Waiting for her, I cradled my belly where the poor mite lay, knowing I must give birth soon, before the terrible rot started inside me.

Granny understood better than I that my life could soon be ended, for her thoughts turned to a priest. Though it be a sin, Decimus was the only confessor I needed now. The doctor gave me a tumbler of evil yellow oil, saying I must drink it all, for the oil would lubricate the passage he must open. I was reminded of the thick black cordial Mistress Morgan had given me all those years ago, but this stuff seemed so much worse. I was retching, for it was too thick to swallow but I could not chew it. Between each horrible mouthful Annie gave me bread to ram between my teeth, that I should not bring it back again. Then, when I had emptied the tumbler, she helped me into the bath.

The day was thundery and humid, yet still I shivered in the blanket she wrapped me in. Decimus led me upstairs to the hard childbed Annie had prepared and, awkwardly, I lay down. Granny called out to the doctor, telling him I was ready. Annie held my hand and though she was but a servant her master did not mind. The doctor indicated that she should remove the blanket. All dignity lost, I lay naked for him to examine me and, overcome by shame, I turned my head away. I was ill-prepared. My body, as familiar to my husband and Annie, and to Granny too, as it was to me, for the first time was looked on by another man, albeit a doctor, and I could not bear it.

His eyes scanned my swollen belly and, seeing Mistress Morgan's work, he raised his eyebrows, but with Decimus beside me did not speak of it. As he placed his bag on the bed it fell open and there, confronting me, cold and glittering, were his instruments that in a little while would tear into me to free an unborn child of its mother's womb. The doctor cautioned me to be still, then nodded to Decimus. I clutched my husband's hand, but should have known he would not leave me. Even Granny, who valued convention, made no effort to persuade him to go. He held my gaze as the doctor's hands touched my body where only my husband's were welcome. Decimus told me he loved me and cradled my head. Slowly at first, the hard cold steel was pushed up inside me.

Overwhelming pain in great searing waves tore at my belly. The steel had stretched me inside, so far up even Decimus could not reach.

Held in a vice, belatedly my body tried to release its burden so that the doctor could go away. But he must have known my pathetic efforts were useless and quietly waited, drumming his fingers on the smooth brown leather of his bag, until my contractions had died. Then he stretched me again. Grabbing at my husband's hand, I could not move for fear the hard steel inside me would hurt me more. The doctor wiped the sweat from his brow and seeing beyond him, I looked into Granny's sombre face. She could not hide her fear and I knew my purgatory was only just beginning.

The passage the doctor had made accommodated his hand, and outlined against the skin of my belly was his hard cruel instrument that was inside me. Again he prised me open and my stretching had been as nothing compared with the agony I now endured. In terror I tried to pull away, but Decimus held me still. Raising my head a little, I saw blood etched against the whiteness of the sheet and panic gripped my heart.

In despair, I whispered to my own dear lord that more than life itself I loved him, but begged him to let me die. I had killed his child and did not expect him to forgive me.

My pain was too much to bear and I longed for sleep. But Decimus would not let me sleep. Convulsions took over my body and I tried to understand, why should my husband wish me to endure such Hell? I implored him to let me escape into the bliss of eternal sleep, but even sleep he refused me and harshly drew me back.

Compelled to give birth, from far away I heard my screams, yet they came not from me but from a wounded animal that was trapped in mortal combat and I knew not how to stop them. I entreated my lord to let me go to his paradise I so loved, but ignoring my plea he held me firm and I stayed in this terrible place where I suffered. As in a thick swirling fog, I saw the doctor, a rope around his arm. He was pulling on the rope and the thing inside me moved.

Darkness had fallen and Granny had lit the lamps, but the torture I endured eroded all sense of time and place. Through a weary sea of abject misery, Jesse came to me and stood over me. He wore a long white robe and about his head was a shining arc. He lifted me in his strong old arms, saying I should go with him if my suffering did not end soon. He would guide me and together we should enter the gates where St Peter was waiting to welcome me.

Jesse did not leave me and my terrible pain began to lessen, for sleep would not be kept from me. He held me safe and with my hand clasping his we started to ascend the steps. Peace and quietness were all about us.

But I remembered my love and could not go on. Dear Jesse understood and knew I had the strength to return. He let go my hand and I awoke from my slumber. Decimus still held me in his arms and I saw the child, a girl, was delivered of me. She lay between my legs with a thick black cord tight about her. The doctor released her from its deadly embrace but on her body was its imprint and it was as though a serpent had wrapped itself around her, squeezing her life away.

I cried out.

'Dear God, help us!'

Decimus could not console me. Though he had released me from my penance, this poor child by its death had paid for my absolution.

The sound of my sobbing scarcely reached me. Jesse was with me as, looking down, I saw the child placed unbaptised in her coffin. The afterbirth was pulled away from my womb and Annie, her poor face contorted with grief, washed my poor limp body. Decimus ordered that I sleep now and I obeyed him.

With Jesse for company, as in a tempest, I was adrift, not knowing where or who I was. When I awoke, the night had gone and the sun shone across my bed. In its rays, particles of dust sparkled and, illumined by the light, I could see the steps where Jesse still waited to take my hand.

Lost in a foreign land, sometimes I felt Jesse standing over me. At others my dear husband was beside me. The doctor came and examined my useless body, but it was of no consequence to me. I heard him tell Granny that he had staunched the bleeding, that my womb was torn and would bear no more children. Lost days went by. My unknowing body had not been told its child was dead. Decimus ordered Annie to bind me tight and my weeping breasts were encased, it seemed, in iron.

Jesse returned to my side. In my fever, I begged him to let me stay with my own dear lord, praying that he would let my agony continue if that were the price I must pay, for I could not bear to leave my beloved Decimus.

One day my bed was taken outside, for the air was still and hot. Swifts dived and screamed overhead and a curlew called. The scent of dog roses wafted over me in the warm breeze that came from the Great River and slowly my body was returned to me. I felt the pain in my bound and aching breasts and held up the shawl that covered me. My belly was flat now and, touching it, my hand felt the cotton wadding the doctor had stuffed inside me.

Sadness welled over and could not be contained. Decimus was watching me and saw my grief. Kneeling next to me, he took my hand in his and his action made even worse my grieving, for he had not knelt to me before.

I beseeched him. 'Lord, I ask so little.'

'Mary dear, you will not make me promise.'

That was true, but again I asked.

'I have killed your child, lord, and can give you no more. Please, I beg of you, my love, the wadding which holds back my life blood; take it away so that I may die, then you can seek a new wife, for I am useless to you now.'

I saw he was weeping.

'My dear sweet Mary, you have lived even in the shadow of death. I will do anything you ask, but not that. Do you not understand? You are my love. I would have died for you if it would ease your pain, but I had to watch you suffer and could do nothing to help. I could not let you sleep, or you would surely have slipped away. My darling, the babe you lost was innocent. I know your Jesse will have taken her and she is in Heaven now. I swear I shall not let the serpent touch you again. My love, I will not let you die. You have given me three fine sons and a daughter. My appetite for heirs is sated.'

He took off the shawl and looked at my naked body.

'Soon your breasts will be free again and the wadding taken from your womb. Let the sun warm and heal you, Mary dear, then we will find a reason for you to live. There is a new life waiting for us, where you will stand next to me. Your body, though you have little regard for it now, is still mine and together we will bring it back to life.'

I know I will heal, lying here in this beautiful place with the comfort of the sun and the warmth of my husband's love enveloping me.

Jesse has taken my poor dead child. With him, she has ascended the steps, to enter the gates that have not yet opened for me.

Mary Cheyne Hillyer.
1874.

CHAPTER XI

Granny

It is with some anxiety that I look towards the future, yet Decimus insists I must. Six unhappy weeks have gone by since my poor dead child was delivered of me. My breasts no longer crave to suckle her. The wadding that was inside me has been taken away and the doctor has ceased to visit. My belly pains me less and though my body is still weak I am no more perceived as an invalid. Even so, my hands are fit for nothing more strenuous than hem stitching, that most tedious of occupations. But I do not mind, knowing the Devil might find work for my hands if they are allowed idleness. In the very tedium of the task that is set me, my mind is allowed to wander, recalling days gone by before those hazy memories are extinguished for ever. When drawn back from my reverie, I am plagued with doubts, thinking of little other than my child lying dead in her coffin and wondering why God has let me live. I fear too that my useless body which can bear my husband no more children will not pleasure him in love.

Decimus is patient with me, but as a reminder that my life has changed irretrievably he has ordained that I wear only black. In fact, he has given all my clothes that are not black to Annie, in preparation for the regime he has promised me. Though I should look forward to the new path of learning I shall embark upon, being so lacking in vigour I cannot help but worry about my husband's intentions.

Harvest had been gathered in and Decimus suggested I go with him to harvest supper. I could barely control my panic as Annie helped me dress. Having long ago lost the art of conversation, I dreaded meeting our neighbours.

Sitting next to Decimus, I tried to recall the only occasion previously when I had accompanied him. It was so far back, all of fifteen years, and before he confined me to enforced solitude. A young wife, only eighteen years of age and just with child, watched the merriment. She loved the man she was wed to, but had come to realise she hardly knew him. As inexorably he erased her identity, her fear of him grew. How could she guess, then, that her husband would become her lord and slowly but surely he would take her soul from her. Jesse was sitting beside her, his old hands covering hers. He knew, but then Jesse had always known, from the day he stopped at a farmhouse, breaking their journey. He had let her set eyes on a young man who had laughed at her. Her duties made plain, Jesse calmed her and the young wife knelt in obeisance at the feet of her husband. Many years would pass before she grew used to her fear of him. Yet what joy she and Decimus had known.

The gypsies had returned to the Vale. After supper Yasmin came and sat with me, for I had not the strength to move far on my own. She was more ethereal than ever, for she carried a heavy burden. On her body was the wealth of her people. Gold bangles encircled her ankles and wrists. In the lobes of her ears were heavy gold rings. Soon the lobes would be stretched as were her grandmother's. Her beautiful fingers, upturned as I remembered, wore more gold rings. Her tunic was loose. She was with child and her time was very near. When she bent to kiss me, I could see her breasts too were pierced with gold. While the young girls flirted with the boys and we watched them dance to the music the gypsy fiddlers played, Yasmin and I talked. Though Decimus always made her people welcome on his land, I found myself wondering afterwards when, if at all, I should see Yasmin again, for her life now, like mine, was lost from her control.

★

In early November, when the first frosts made white the naked willows and soft mists clung to the ground, Decimus called for me. I trembled at the thought of what was to come, convinced he could not love me. He considered my body healed enough and gave Annie instructions to prepare me.

I do believe she loved her master, yet poor Annie was so ugly, I doubted any man could look at her with love in his heart. Maybe in making me ready for my husband and contemplating his pleasure she found joy.

The scullery was so cold, I could see the air from my breath and, after the warmth of the bath, I shivered, goose pimples rising on my arms. But Annie would not be hurried. Spreading all over me a soothing oil, an essence of sandalwood, carefully she rubbed it in, its soft sheen enhancing the colour of my skin. Scraping back my hair, Annie pulled it into a bun, its tightness so severe that if I turned my neck I felt the restriction. On my eyelids she brushed powder of palest blue and, bringing the faintest touch of colour to the pallor of my cheeks, dusted them with rouge. My nipples, too, she rouged. My breasts, though empty, were heavy and, as I supported them, I wanted to cry. Could Annie's efforts really make him want me, barren and ruined?

When she was satisfied she could do no more, Annie gave me a new shawl to wear. It, like everything else I was given, was black. Long silken fringes weighted it down, its open weave not hiding my nakedness. Still shivering, my bare feet making no sound on the stone flags, I made myself walk to the parlour. The moment I had dreaded for weeks had arrived and with a fluttering heart I knocked on the door. Decimus's voice called to me to enter and my hand froze on the latch. For a second, I wished my lord had let me die.

Decimus was alone, sitting as always in Granny's chair. The cool autumn air was excluded and a fire burned low in the hearth. He looked up and, putting down his book, smiled at me and held out his hands. Terrified his eyes might tell me what I begged not to see, I could not engage them and, my knees buckling, I fell prone at his feet.

Gently he took off my shawl. Trembling, my body was locked in its submissions, his critical gaze unbearable. Decimus shook his head.

'I know the thought of my loving torments you, Mary, but I have tried to understand and have waited long enough.'

I opened my mouth and a voice, hardly recognisable as my own, pleaded with him.

'How can you want to love me, lord?'

He could see my trepidation and, not touching me, let me weep at his feet, still cold, caring nothing for the warmth of the fire. He moved the lamp, turning it up. Bending down, he cupped my chin with his hands, raising me. His arms held me, his voice urgent in my ear.

'Tonight, my darling, you will put aside your mourning and know that I love you. I promise you, Mary, I will not hurt you. You have suffered more than enough and I swear, even in my passion, I will try to be gentle with you.'

If he could only find me a place in his heart, I did not mind how much he hurt me. Seeming preoccupied, he threw the shawl round my shoulders and ordered me to follow him.

In the bedroom a new fire blazed and I saw the counterpane was already turned back. He took away the shawl and told me to lie down. The linen was cold but it did not matter and waiting for his rejection, weeping, I turned away from him. Whispering words of love, he took me in his arms, kissing me. Sensing the tension in his body and disconsolate with love for him, I pressed myself against him, my fear easing just a little. Smiling, he asked that I hold my hands together and, beginning to dream, I obeyed, giving them to him. Through my tears I watched as he bound my wrists with a long silk scarf, securing them firmly against the brass head of the bed. Bathed in his kisses, I heard his words come from far away.

'I love you, Mary,' he whispered. 'Your hands are bound only so that you cannot help me. This way you will understand how much I need you. Your body belongs to me and we will bring it back to life just as I promised. You will see.'

He took off his clothes. Naked, his frame was outlined against the light of the fire. He was so beautiful. Overwhelmed, my heart began to race and I could scarcely breathe.

It seemed all my consciousness was centred in the slow progression of his hard, possessive hands. No part of me escaped their searching and I longed for the harshness of his kisses.

Passion had not died for us as, at his mercy, I cried out, begging him to take me. In paradise now, I felt his love flood into me, and the terrible fear that had corroded my mind melted away.

My body had pleased him and soon he would have need of me again. The flame of his love consumed me with its life and my head almost burst with the willow's song. I glowed once more in the warmth of his protection and at last could look forward to tomorrow.

Only days had passed when Decimus was informed that Granny was sick and dying. We took Ella with us to be at her side. Though Granny had been a widow for ten years, she still missed her own dear Decimus and, without his support, I do believe her lonely heart was so wounded by the birth of my dear dead child that she had not the will to recover.

Granny was eighty-two and the tide of her long and courageous life was ebbing fast. Alas, her eyes stared unseeing into the distance and she did not recognise us. I touched her hand that was cold and could not be warmed. Then I sought the rosary beneath her nightgown, knowing it to be there, and gave it to her. Holding it, she pressed the crucifix to her lips, then one by one ran the beads through her tired old fingers. Without comment, Decimus turned on his heel and left us.

I followed him into the yard, where he had saddled the hunter that as a foal had been the apple of his father's eye. Leaning down from the saddle, Decimus kissed my forehead. I wished him Godspeed as he rode the horse away, as fast as he dared, to Milbury. He had to find a priest while there was still time. Though another's religion was to him of little consequence, he understood how important was Granny's faith to her. When Decimus trod, God fearing, the secret paths into the Great River and was surrounded by the Lord's firmament, he had no need of a priest to show him His Glory, for it was all around him.

Within the day Decimus returned and with him brought a priest. When he had learned from Decimus that Granny had always kept the faith, the priest needed no persuading. Granny's eyes focused and a faint but fleeting smile lit her face as she watched him prepare for his sad ritual. With shaking hands, she touched his vestment, kissing it. We left Granny alone with her confessor. In a little while, with the rest of his family, I knelt with Decimus beside her bed and together we prayed for her Soul. Anointed and no longer fearing the raging fires of Hell, a terror that for most of her life had not left her, Granny was at peace with God and could leave us.

We watched her gradually slip away into unconsciousness and I remembered her stubborn old father. Knowing Decimus's respect for him, it was none the less still hard to quell my sinful and terrible anger. I had seen the old lord but once, on his deathbed, when he had called me Lydia. Dear Granny, the purest soul I had ever known, had paid penance all her life for flouting her father's wishes. Yet I had to believe her love for her husband was so great that, in all these years, she had not regretted her rebellion.

Later that night, when silence had descended on the old house, we were with Granny when she breathed her last. Silently I prayed that Jesse might know her and guide her, as he would have guided me, to the gates where St Peter waited and God would judge the quick and the dead.

Three days later we attended Granny's funeral. In death she was drawn back by the family that in life had driven her out. She could not lie in the warm forgiving earth next to her second husband in a Protestant grave, but was laid to rest with her ancestors in the cold wastes of the family vault. I wept, for Granny had been to me the mother I had never known. She understood as did no one else the infinite love I bore her youngest son.

When the ceremony was over, with utmost sadness we set out for home. Decimus stared straight ahead, his mouth set and downturned. Sitting behind us, Ella wept quietly. This visit, like the last to that gaunt and loveless castle, had ended on a bitter note. I would not forget Granny's generosity when she and Mr Hillyer had welcomed me, a stranger and a bastard too, into their home. I thought of her love and kindness to the children I had borne and my fingers touched her tenth child. With his free hand he clasped mine and we had no need of words between us.

That night when everyone was abed and his house was still, Decimus lit a nightlight and talked of the happy days of his youth. We held one another close and I cradled my love's head in my arms, stroking his coarse black hair that was turning grey. I marvelled that such a man should be born to one so small and gentle. My tears built up for the love of my dear husband's mother. One day we should meet again, but not this side of Heaven. The night crept by and we did not stir from each other's arms. An owl called in the distance. Decimus felt under his pillow and pulled out a long thin case. Without a word, he handed it to me. Slowly my hesitant fingers opened it. There, in the dim light and glowing softly against black velvet, was a graduated rope of pearls. I looked up at Decimus and saw his eyes were shining bright.

'She wanted you to have them, my darling.'

I touched the luminous milky pearls that lay, cool and incandescent, in the aura of the single flame. Holding the circlet in my hand, I longed to wear them.

'Please, my love, will you fasten them round my neck?'

I flushed, having presumed upon his tolerance. I had not meant to be disrespectful.

Decimus took his mother's pearls from my trembling fingers. Inclining my head, I felt him secure them. His voice was gentle.

'Go, look at your reflection, Mary.'

He had not thought me bold and, in gratitude, I kissed his hand and rose from his bed. Standing before the glass, I saw the radiance of Granny's pearls against the skin of my throat. To reassure myself they were truly there, I reached my hand up to touch them. My dear love was standing behind me and I looked up at his image.

'My mother rarely wore them, but you will wear them, Mary, in the new life I have planned for you.'

He undid my nightgown, letting it fall from my shoulders. Reflected in the soft light, the scars his willow had made and the burns from his flame had faded. Mistress Morgan's mark was still bright, indelible against the whiteness of my skin. With his hands clasping my waist, he turned me to face him.

'Mary, you satisfy all my needs, yet I have to believe you too exult in our love. My mother loved my father much as you love me, my dear, rejoicing in his passion. With God's mercy, Lydia too will find fulfilment and be freed by a love like ours. One day this curse you have inherited will have run its course and the terror will end. Now tell me you are content, my darling.'

'Lord, you know I am content. All I have ever needed from the moment I first saw you was to serve you and, even unto eternity, dwell only in the world you would create for me.'

Decimus carried me back to bed and his loving was gentle. I could bear him no more sons, yet bathed in his passion I knew my husband still loved me and his flame that lived in my heart would burn me for ever.

CHAPTER XII

Perry

The months following Granny's death have been spent in quiet contemplation, trying to adjust my mind to the changed life Decimus has decreed for me. We had thought we were prepared for Granny's passing. She was very old, yet strangely had not seemed so to us, for her brain had not addled with age. Whenever the family had need of her, she was always there. Now a void had opened. She had left us and we could not reconcile ourselves to her death. Ella grieved the worst of all and Decimus had to compound her sorrow, for in the New Year Harry joined Thomas at school in Milbury, leaving only Lydia and Richard for Ella to spoil. Richard is a happy child, given to dreaming, his disposition reflecting those uncounted years when my spirit lived in Arcadia. Lydia has the warm olive skin of her Romany ancestors. Each summer her dark hair is bleached by the sun. Decimus allows her to run wild with the gypsy children and Ella, who has always despised the gypsies, has acknowledged now that they are a part of our lives.

I am just thirty-four years of age in this April of 1875. Tomorrow I shall accompany my husband to the Spring Fair at Rockingham. Remembering nothing of the world that lies beyond the four walls of his house, I know myself to be naïve and pray my deportment will not displease him. In fifteen years, except for my walks on the Sea Bank with Annie and occasional attendance in church, I can count the number of times I have left Thorn End Farm on little more than the fingers of one hand. Anticipating the ordeal tomorrow, a bird in my throat flutters, my stomach churns and I know tonight I shall not sleep for worry.

Very early in the morning, though long after Decimus had risen, Annie laid out the clothes her master said I must wear. Though it was laborious, Decimus had insisted she carry the bath upstairs, that I might reflect upon my duties while I bathed and dressed in the little solitude that was left to me. Lying back in the hot scented water, I tried to relax, wondering if I should meet my husband's expectations.

To please my husband, with my hands gripping the bedpost for support and drawing in my breath, I begged Annie pull on the laces of my stays until they were truly tight. With her knee pressed into the small of my back, my discomfort unimportant, she helped me and, my confidence boosted, I put on my gown.

The black silk dress hugged my waist, its starched petticoats stiff under the billowing skirt. The bodice was cut low revealing the curve of my breasts, leaving my shoulders bare, not a country gown at all. But that was of little consequence, so long as I looked as my husband wished. Decimus had bought the gown to show off his mother's pearls to advantage, though fearing to lose them I did not wear them to the Fair. To lessen my confusion in the company of strangers and worried my chest might catch cold, Annie gave me a shawl to drape around my shoulders. I smiled to myself, for previously I had worn it only on those occasions when, naked, my duty was to pleasure my lord.

In the yard, the men had already loaded the cart. Round golden Gloucester cheeses, eggs and furmity, all would be sold at the Fair. Old wooden cider barrels, full now, but emptied many times before, would soon be emptied again. Noisy, squawking pullets, crammed into large closed boxes, brown beaks occasionally appearing through holes cut into the sides, they too would be sold.

Two farm horses, tossing their heads as if to rid themselves of imaginary flies, waited impatiently between the shafts, their brasses gleaming in the early morning light, long thin strands of mist escaping their nostrils. There was barely a cloud in the sky, but the air was cool. Standing in the doorway, nervously I awaited my husband's approval.

Decimus strode towards me. He was ready to leave. My eyes downcast, sinking to my knees I greeted him the only way I knew how. I had not meant to keep him waiting and, sensing his irritation, began to tremble. His hand brushed past my face and with a perfunctory greeting he set me on my feet. He was wearing his Sunday best suit, his boots shiny with new polish. He did not even look at me.

Climbing on to the carter's seat, he thrust out his hand. I grasped it, but I was flustered: my foot could not find the hub of the wheel. It was impossible to bend against the whalebone of my stays. My full skirts, though I held them gathered over my free arm, took my vision. Laughing, for he could not be angry with me for long, Decimus hoisted me up beside him. With the force of his pulling, I fell hard against him. My poise and breath lost, my eyes found his. He still laughed at me and I flushed, but my heart ached with love for him and I was grateful for his indulgence. I laughed too, my anxiety lessening. Decimus nodded to his man to release the horses and, as one, the pair set off into the morning sun in the direction of Hartley. Soon we left the village behind and I wondered how large the town of Hartley was, for this Vale bore its name. The hunt often crossed our land. Decimus said, if it took him a hundred years, he would not turn me into a country woman, for I feared too much for the fox. He found my squeamishness difficult to comprehend, for hunting was as natural to him as was his fishing.

Inexplicably, as I watched steam rise from the horses, thoughts flooded back across the chasm of my memory. The weather was colder, a little earlier in the year than April, certainly before Easter. A young woman, her life ahead of her, her body not yet grown to maturity, sat next to an old carter. He whistled a tune to the horses. For as long as she could remember, she had dreamed of the day when she would be free. I looked up at

116

Decimus. He too whistled a tune to the horses. A saying that Granny had often used flashed through my mind.

'You meet your fate by the road you take to avoid it.'

Once I had taken the road that led me to the Great River my fate was sealed. The freedom I had yearned for, exhilarating but so transient, was snuffed out, lost for ever. Would I have faltered and turned back the day Jesse had brought me to Decimus had I known the tortuous path to servitude that lay ahead of me? My husband held my hand. How could he have guessed my thoughts? Drawing his fingers to my lips and bowing my head, I kissed his hand.

We followed the track that ran almost north. It was raised above the marsh, that wet land covered with reeds and fit only for waders and web-footed birds. Some way ahead of us was a solitary hill. As we drew nearer we had to skirt it a mile or so to the west, for the land was private. Passing wrought-iron gates with a family crest set in an arch high above them, we could see at the end of a gravel driveway, surrounded by cedars, was a magnificent mansion. High railings with pointed tips to deter intruders marked the boundary of the deer park. Decimus said this estate had been Granny's home when she was wed to her first husband. Here she had met the bailiff, Decimus's father, her true love. What splendour we could see behind the railings. Yet Granny had not found happiness in this house. Though still low lying, the ground had risen slightly now. We could see the broad waters of the Great River and barges making their way up towards Gloucester.

Having paused by the hunt kennels where hounds were baying, it was ten o'clock before we reached Hartley. Decimus pointed out a grand white house with a high brick wall encircling it.

'This house is my cousin's, Mary. He is a friend of mine, a doctor and a well-respected man hereabouts.'

What high connections Decimus had. How little I knew of my husband other than what I had learned from Granny. The old castle, where a good king was killed, dominated the town. It was just as forbidding as the castle we knew. Suddenly I shivered in the wind that blew up from the Great River and drew my shawl tighter. Though our quickest way would be straight ahead, Decimus was anxious the heavy cart should not get bogged down. It was still early in the year and the ground as far as the eye could see was flat and, Decimus said, below sea level. So we turned the horses east for a while and crossed the bridge at Waveridge before heading north again.

Through the trees, the spokes of a giant wheel, chairs hanging from it, seeming suspended in the sky, rose before us. We were approaching the Fair. Children's screams and laughter assailed us. The noise was deafening and, quaking with fear, I held Decimus's hand. A barrel organ played, but not just one, there were two, competing with each other. A poor little monkey; I had quite forgotten what they looked like, clambered on to my lap. Decimus gave me three farthings to put in his hat. The organ grinder doffed his cap to us and picked up his monkey, before passing on to the next cart that followed behind us.

Half the world had come to Rockingham. Tall houses lined either side of a broad swathe of green. Crowds gathered outside an inn where men danced. On their arms and round the calves of their legs they wore tiny silver bells. Ribbons cascaded from their tall black hats. The sticks they carried crashed together in unison. Their dancing was aggressive. Sitting very close to Decimus, quite overwhelmed by the density of people, I could smell the sweat from their bodies. Decimus said maybe, if we had time, we would come back and watch the dancers when he had finished his business.

Stalls almost covered the grass. Two steam engines, belching black smoke, hissed, their fly wheels spinning. Thick bands of rubber, rotating ever faster, powered machinery for the round-abouts and the stench of hot oil mixed with steam filled the air. Decimus jumped down and held the horse's heads, for I guessed they were far more frightened than I.

A helter-skelter, its slide polished, was in demand and was the source of much screaming. The smell of toffee was in the air now. Abandoning my fears and feeling like a child again, hugging my knees, I tried not to behave like one. My eyes were dazzled, there was so much to see. In such an easy manner, Decimus greeted old friends. In all the years we had been wed my husband's acquaintances had not seen me before. In sudden trepidation, I shrank from them, knowing they thought me odd, not understanding why Decimus had waited this long before introducing me.

In those few hours at the Fair, watching him talk and witnessing the deference of his friends, I knew without doubt that my husband was very different from other men. Silently I thanked God for guiding me to him and knew, if I knew nothing else, that without him I should perish.

When Decimus had sold all our produce we walked together, mingling with the crowds, laughing at the gaily painted horses, nostrils flaring, dipping in tune with the music. Among them were unicorns and I longed to sit on one and hold tight its twisted golden horn. But it would have been unbecoming. I was too old and did not ask my husband's permission. Decimus gave me a heavy wooden ball and told me to knock Aunt Sally over, but, try as I might, I could not throw it far enough. He gave me pennies to buy pretty ribbons that he wove into my shawl, making bright bands of colour against the sombre black.

A fortune teller caught his arm. He shook her off, annoyed. Was he afraid she might unravel his secrets?

By the time we returned to the inn, the Morris Men, as Decimus called them, refreshed, were dancing again. Decimus drank ale but gave me thirst-quenching lemonade. Though he ate bread with crumbly ripe cheese, I abstained, my stays too tight for eating. We sat in the shade of an elm tree and watched the activity. Some men carried tambours, which they drummed with their fingers in time to their singing. Others had masks to conceal their identity. I felt uneasy and did not know why.

The afternoon wore on and the sun warmed us. I saw the way men looked at me, for my gown, though made modest by my shawl, was still lacking somewhat in decorum. I tried not to notice. Decimus showed me the sheep pens. These animals came from the Forest of Dean that was far away on the other side of the Great River. They had forded the river at a place called Newnham on the Welsh side and were destined for markets at

Dursley or Wotton. When I listened to the speech of the men who herded them, I noticed their accents were different, soft and melodious. Decimus said they were Forest men and their horses, strong and short-legged, with feathered feet, were descended from the ponies that lived wild in the hills of Wales. He called them Welsh Cobs.

There was one beast who stood apart from the others, as though he knew he was their leader. His head was held high, his heavy brown and white coat shining with health. His long mane and his tail blew away from him in the breeze. As if he were dancing, he picked up his great feathered feet just for me.

I was entranced. Decimus saw where I was looking.

'Do you like him, Mary?' he asked me. 'He would make a strange carriage pony, but then, neither you nor I care much what other folk think.'

I could not understand what Decimus meant.

'Oh my love, he is beautiful.'

'You shall have a governess cart and learn to drive, my darling. He will be part of your new life and will suit us well.'

Decimus pulled me close and I held my breath. Did he really intend to buy a horse just for me?'

That evening with the sun reluctant to set, we journeyed steadily homeward. The cart was loaded with ropes and implements which Decimus had bought for the farm. Tethered loosely behind us and walking quietly was the new horse. Long before we were home the stars came out, but I hardly noticed the night, I was so happy to be with my husband. I had not disappointed him and slept safe in the shelter of his protection.

The very next morning I rose early, my excitement uncontainable. Decimus had already milked the cows when I picked my way through the yard towards the first meadow.

There, standing alone in the middle of the field, was Decimus's new horse. I knew little of horses, but to my eyes he was the winged horse of the gods. Somewhat afraid, I stayed at the gate, looking at him. Throwing up his great head for me, he whinnied and came to my call. He was about fourteen hands or so high, Decimus had said, but he looked very big to me, watching me from one side of the gate as I stood on the other. His soft forgiving nose found the palm of my hand. Wishing so much I had brought him something, I stooped, gathering fresh grass, which though it be a humble offering he gladly took.

I wondered what name should we give this wonderful animal with courage to swim such treacherous waters. He was far from his native Wales, where buzzards and peregrine falcons roamed the skies. I left him then, for we were both subject to my lord's will and had to obey his instructions. As yet we both still awaited them. Later that day I asked Decimus if we might call his new horse Peregrine, for his wandering had ended. He had come home to us.

An idyllic summer has followed that memorable spring when Decimus first showed me a new life. Without his love I know the wounds in my heart would not have healed. A year has gone by since the stillbirth of our child. Though I have yet to leave my husband's shadow, steadily he is preparing me to face a world that I had thought never to re-enter. Thomas and Harry are at home for the long summer holiday and we are a whole family once more. Each day his two older sons help Decimus school the handsome new horse.

July had given way to August and I was helping Ella with her chores, for my hands were still not allowed idleness. My lord's will that was so harsh, I understood. Those hours not lost in quiet contemplation were spent in unremitting toil that freed my mind to wander in the world he had created, where my frailty did not matter and I could ignore the pain of servitude.

Thomas burst in on us with a message for me from his father. I took off my pinafore, smoothed down my hair and unrolled my sleeves that I should be tidy. With suppressed excitement, Thomas grabbed my hand and dragged me, protesting just a little, to the first meadow.

Standing fearlessly between the shafts of a spanking new trap was Peregrine. Smiling broadly, Decimus called me.

'Hurry, Mary. I cannot wait all day for you. See, Perry's burden could not be lighter.'

Harry helped me up into the trap. My heart beat faster as, taking the reins, I was on my own. From the middle of the field, yelling his instructions, Decimus encouraged me. Quite quickly I became used to the feel of the reins in my hands. How many years had passed since Jesse had let me guide his dear little Dolly? What a cherished memory that was, misty now as my husband intended. From that very first moment when I set eyes on Decimus, my life was his to do with as he pleased. Deep in concentration, I tried so hard to obey his commands.

Gradually I learned. Perry had not pulled a cart before, but instinctively he judged the width he must leave. When I made mistakes, he forgave me. Through the reins in my hands I felt his strength and knew he longed to fly. Climbing up beside me, Decimus shouted at Harry to open the gate. My heart in my mouth, I guided Perry out through the yard and on to the dry rutted track that led to the village.

Listening to his hooves beating their rhythmic pattern on the road, I was flushed with heat and happiness. Perry held his head high and picked up his great feathered feet. His mane and tail floating, he was every bit the dancer I had fallen in love with at Rockingham Fair. His movement was effortless and I held the reins steady, the way Decimus had shown me. For a passing moment as we left the Pound, I thought of the men who had scorned me so many years past. Decimus guided my hand and set Perry on the road to Milbury.

I dreamed of Boadicea, or perhaps one of the goddesses I had read of in days long gone by. Those memories too were lost, wrenched from me, but I did not want to remember the lonely, despairing days when I was schooled by my guardian. Staring only ahead, I pitied Boadicea, for she drove alone in her chariot and had not been as happy and free as I. Decimus understood my joy as I stood, pinned to the rail, my hair pulled by the wind, while in my hands Perry, like Pegasus, flew.

In a while Decimus bade me sit down and took the reins himself, for he feared I might tire. Though in my heart I knew

I should never tire, as always I obeyed him. He urged the great strong horse to even more valiant effort until Perry's canter had become a gallop. Holding tight to the side, for fear of falling, I watched as the wheels beside me turned faster and faster over the uneven ground. Exhilaration overwhelmed me, my fear soon lost and forgotten. Decimus gave me the reins again and we stood at the rail together. He held me close, his arm around my waist supporting me. Still the stout-hearted beast galloped on until Decimus called him to slow. Under his sweat-streaked coat Perry's muscles rippled. His nostrils flared and I was entranced all over again.

The tower of St Mark's and the walls of the gaunt old castle loomed ahead of us. We were nearly in Milbury. Touching my husband's hand that had taken the rein, suddenly I was serious, overcome by emotion.

'I have not the words to thank you, lord, for the new life you have set in train for me. I pray I shall not disappoint you, either by my demeanour or in my ability to accomplish the tasks you set me.'

Decimus hung up the reins, not chiding me for my solemnity. He spoke quietly.

'Your will is my will. Your soul is but a mirror of mine. I took your spirit long ago and it is lost to you for ever. You *are* me, my dear, and you will not disappoint me, Mary.'

My lord's words were no less than the truth. I could change nothing, yet even if I could I should not seek to try.

The dirt road gave way to cobbles. The street veered right and the broad, windswept Plain lay ahead of us. A sign on the wall said Back Street and Decimus drove Perry down a narrow alleyway. We passed a busy yard. It was behind the inn where I had stayed, still a maiden, waiting for Decimus to come for me, as I prayed he would. A coach stood awaiting new horses. Men shouted, tired from their labours in the heat of the day. I wondered where Decimus was taking us.

He read my thoughts.

'Perry must be well shod, my dear. His shoes are worn down and should be replaced.'

Concerned for poor Perry, I enquired, 'Will it hurt him, my love?'

He laughed and I felt rather foolish.

'My dear sweet wife, the horn is hard and insensitive. It is no more painful than cutting your nails. Would you like to watch?'

The smith was built like an ox. His leather apron, with tools of his trade hanging from his waist, covered all but his bare arms and shoulders. Strangely, Perry showed no fear of him and, unperturbed, was released from the traces. A young boy, an apprentice, I guessed, led Perry into the forge. I held back. From the doorway the smell of burning, the heat and the noise hit me like a blow. This was a man's world. My helplessness and frailty were out of keeping here. But it was too late now to change my mind and I shrank into a corner, propping myself against the wall. The smith shouted to his boy to pump the bellows. The heat was stifling. I need not look. No one would notice if I did not. The furnace glowed white hot. Staring up at the roof, I thought of the barn at home. How many times had my husband taken me there, where, in another world, I had learned to serve him. But I had left that world, my womb torn and useless. Interrupting my dream, Decimus put his arm about my shoulders. My stomach lurched with the stench from the forge. Smoke poured from poor Perry's hoof. The smith, his mouth full of nails, was hammering the still hot shoe on to Perry's naked foot.

'You have seen enough, Mary. We can't have you fainting. Maybe our next port of call will be more to your liking.'

Decimus was smiling at me and I took his arm, gratefully letting him lead me out into the sunlight. As we walked together he matched his steps to mine and we both laughed for he looked so funny. I began to feel better.

'You are woefully short of dresses, Mary, since I restricted you to black. Today we will make reparations.'

There was something vaguely familiar about the shop we entered. It was a little apart from the others, the upper storey overhanging the pavement to afford shelter from the rain. Inside all was dark and dusty. I held back a sneeze. An obsequious little man in a black suit that was threadbare with age, a chain across his chest, came forward. Looking more closely at him, I could see he was really rather tall, yet, conscious of his height and his inferior position, he stooped. Decimus ushered me past him, ignoring him, and it seemed he just melted away. A middle-aged woman, her stays holding her ramrod straight, appeared from the far recesses of the shop. She inclined her head while Decimus advised her of my needs. She seemed already prepared. Perhaps Decimus had done business with her before. With a smile set like stone, she asked me to follow her upstairs. I did not take to her.

Upstairs the light was stronger. She indicated a cane chair, the seat rotting a little. I sat down, hoping it would hold me. From a rail she took several dresses. All were black, conforming to Decimus's instructions. She expected me to undress. Showing me to a cubicle, with a swish she pulled a curtain behind me. Embarrassed in case she should catch me unawares, quickly I tried on each of the dresses. Somewhat surprised, I found they all fitted me. The curtain was pulled back again. Her cold eyes were ridiculing me. Making clucking noises, deftly she ran her tape measure over me, then left me alone.

The colour of the next gown she brought was of deepest, deepest black. Jet glittered on the bodice of stiff bombazine. A full skirt, watermarked, was heavy with lace. Had Decimus ordered this beautiful gown especially? She lay it across a chair and I could see buried beneath the folds was a corset. It was shaped like an hour glass, its contours rigid. At first glance the corset looked quite pretty. It was much shorter and quite different from the stays I had always worn.

Flushed with confusion that she should see me half clothed, my fingers fumbled with my laces and the wretched woman had to help me. She requested I remove my shift, for this corset, she said, must be worn next to my skin. As I took off my shift and my drawers, her hostile eyes swept over me, resting for a moment on my mark. Protruding from the wall was a peg and she told me to reach up and grasp it. Closing my eyes, I drew in my breath as under its satin cover the cold, hard iron gripped me.

Though I could not look down, for it would have widened my waist, I felt the corset tighten, until I was gasping. It was so tight it hurt me. The hinge clicked. There was no adjustment. I felt sick from my restriction, and she had to support me. In her hand she held a key. She had locked me in, imprisoning me. Her eyes gleamed in triumph.

I tried on the gown, its slender sleeves extending to my wrists. I was sure Decimus would be pleased with my waist; it was so small his hands would span it with ease. But I could not pull up the bodice. In all my life I had not seen a bodice cut so low. My shoulders were bare, my breasts just covered. Ignoring all modesty, my nipples, nearly visible, were concealed only by gauze that was ruched and gathered. The stiff-faced woman fussed over me, her smile not wavering.

She led me to a long looking glass, which she tilted until, with another behind me, from every angle I could see my reflection. Was the voluptuous woman who looked at me really me? In the mirror I saw Decimus's reflection. I felt faint and swiftly he caught me. The woman smirked, unable to conceal her contempt.

'Do you like the gown, Mary?'

'It is beautiful, but I cannot . . .'

'No buts, my darling, I ordered it for you and the corset too. Now let her help you take it off. Then when you are ready, wait for me at the smithy. See that Perry has been fed and watered. I shall not be long.'

I left him, knowing any protest to be useless, and was glad to see in her face that my tormentor too could not hide her anxiety at my husband's stern expression.

When Decimus returned to the forge he was laden with parcels. He did not speak to me, but threw his purchases into the trap. Taking the reins, he urged Perry forward. As Perry's new shoes clattered on the cobbles, I wished with all my heart that Decimus would forget about the new life he wanted for me and let me stay at home where I was safe and happy. When the sound from Perry's hooves changed, muffled by the dirt road, a mantle seemed to lift from my shoulders, such was my relief to be leaving town.

Decimus saw how distraught I was, though I tried not to weep, for what way was that to thank him for his generosity. Tenderly he put his arm around me.

'Mary dear, try to be patient. In time you will become used to strangers and they will not distress you, as that woman did.'

Still humiliated, I clung to him.

'Lord, please help me.'

Gently, his hand squeezed my shoulder.

'You know I will help you, Mary. You will always be secure in the world of our love, but my mind is made up. There is no choice for you. You will stand alongside me and you will not flinch when my acquaintances observe you.'

Confused, I tried to understand what I had to do to please him.

'How can I be secure in the world of our love, yet embark on a new life, lord? I fear our world is soon to be lost.'

In a small voice, no more than a whisper, I implored him.

'Do not make me change.'

'You will not change, Mary, though that will probably be the hardest lesson of all.'

Perhaps, though until now I had not guessed, there was yet more he must take from me. In panic, lest I had not the strength to satisfy him, I pleaded with him.

'I have not the courage to wear among strangers the beautiful gown you bought. Please, my love, do not force me.'

I could not stop from weeping and, almost as an afterthought, added.

'And the corset, it frightens me.'

Decimus fastened the reins loosely to the trap, allowing Perry his head. My lord's look defied dissent. Suddenly I was in awe of his wrath. In my mind I had given up and he knew it. Holding me at arm's length, the heaviness of his hands pressed into my shoulders, hurting me. Unresisting and humble, as the years of harsh tutelage had taught me, I crumpled. He commanded me to look at him and I could scarcely do so for the trembling that shook me. He did not raise his voice.

'Do not argue with me, Mary. You will do as I say.'

Fawning at him, I pleaded with my husband.

'Please, lord, how can I? I have not the fortitude.'

His hands still dug into me. He had not finished.

'I cannot alter what I have done to you, Mary, neither do I wish to. Nor can I permit your pride to interrupt your learning. But I promise you, you will take from me whatever strength you need to resist the taunts of the world outside.'

His tone was dismissive as he continued.

'The gown is little more revealing than your other gowns. You will become used to it, Mary.'

His voice had hardened still further.

'As for the corset, you will wear it because I wish you to wear it.'

He released me and my fingers tingled as I felt the blood surge back into my arms. I fell against the seat. Throwing myself across his lap, desperate for approval, I clung to him again. Gradually the warmth of his body next to mine stilled my panic and his strength seeped into my soul. Aloud, I prayed that God would not let me disappoint my husband. In a little while, Decimus could see I was quiet and reconciled to his decision. He helped me sit up and placed the reins into my hands. Perry, feeling their tension, threw up his head and thrust onward towards home.

Ella was shocked and offended, turning her eyes away, the first time I wore the special gown Decimus bought me. She has made me a chemisette of black velvet, which my lord has let her tack into the bodice to cover my nakedness. I dread wearing the corset, but without it my gown does not fit. Decimus has introduced me to many of his acquaintances and, drawing on his strength, gradually I am learning to ignore the reaction my humility promotes in others. I believe my lord is pleased with my progress.

Decimus takes me to Milbury and allows me to drive. Once he let me travel alone with only Perry for company. Then for a little while, with the wind in my hair and Perry's reins in my hands, it was as if my lord had set me free.

Sometimes at night though, lost and in purgatory, I dream I do not know my husband and have never met him. Each time I wake, so thankful the nightmare has ended, I kneel beside the bed until he senses my presence. He is always gentle with me then, holding me and murmuring words of love. He knows that without him my soul will be lost. He cannot doubt that I long to return to my life of seclusion, yet I dare not seek his indulgence.

We were well into autumn when Decimus noticed the moon had not claimed me. Knowing I longed for another babe, he sent me alone to church. Climbing the hill to sanctuary, with every step I prayed that God would favour me, that the doctor had been wrong and He would let my womb bring forth my husband's child. Decimus promised if I gave him a son, he would shut me away again and let me forget my new life. But our hopes were destroyed in the week that followed Christmas when my womb rejected the child my husband had given me. The moon's long shadow was cast across my benighted body for two whole weeks before I was freed of my burden. In tears, as I knelt at the feet of my beloved lord, I knew he would not reject me.

It is God's will that I obey my husband. By taking my child He has shown me the path I must follow. Now on my knees in prayer, I promise to tread, without looking back, only where Decimus leads me.

CHAPTER XIII

Hartley

Holding Decimus's hand, I watched the village children, and Lydia too, dance round the Maypole. It is May Day and I wonder when I shall see our daughter looking so happy again. This afternoon Lydia is to leave us. Decimus has decided she shall live with his cousin in Hartley. Though my lord loves to see her run wild and free with the gypsy children, he says Lydia's spirit must be tamed. Cousin Hector will discipline and educate her. Ella has pleaded for Lydia to be allowed to stay at home, but Decimus is adamant, acknowledging that in his cousin's house she will learn the skills and graces she will need for a good marriage. I fear terribly for our daughter, for little Lydia is not yet eight years old and is still such a baby. I dread not seeing her every day, yet I must acquiesce to my husband's wishes. Ella cannot contain her grief, but mindful of her place in her brother's household she too remains silent.

While we waited for Decimus to bring the new trap round to the yard, Lydia said her tearful farewells to Ella. Loaded with baggage, we set off. When I enquired of my husband why Perry was not between the shafts, he laughed with merriment.

'Cousin Hector would never live it down, my love, if a skewbald horse stood in his carriageway.'

By the time we reached Hartley, the sun hung low in the sky like a great fireball, throwing long spindly shadows ahead of us. Cousin Hector's white house, illuminated in its golden rays, looked even more impressive than when I had seen it on our way to Rockingham. I was nervous as the wheels crunched over the raked gravel drive. A footman hovered and held the pony steady, allowing Decimus to hand me down. Sweeping steps led up to a double front door, a polished crest with lions rampant above it. We should stay here overnight to see Lydia made comfortable in her new surroundings. My husband had told me how proper Hector FitzWarren was and I hoped my country manners would not let me down. Caring little for his own title of yeoman, Decimus knew he was as good as any man living and was completely unconcerned.

Hector and his wife Grace waited on the steps to receive us. Hector had been at our wedding. I could recall making my vows with ease, yet of the rest my memory had lost all trace and I could not remember my husband's cousin. He was a little older than Decimus. His bright blue eyes met mine and travelled over me, telling me they knew my secrets. He was tall with greying hair. His eyebrows, like my own dear husband's, curled, meeting in the middle. An impressive man, his every gesture carried authority. My heart warmed to him and I knew he would understand my position. Smiling down on me as I dropped him a curtsy, Hector took my hand, steadying me, and introduced me to Grace. Though she would have been no older than I, her fair hair had faded and was pulled back from her face, accentuating her small beady eyes that darted anywhere rather than look at me. Her lip curled, she was hostile and it was plain she did not look forward to my presence in her husband's house.

Suddenly we were surrounded by children. Four little girls, their pale yellow hair hanging in ringlets, their blue, china-doll eyes staring up at me in unison, were laughing and telling me their names: Lucy, Amelia, Martha and Kate. My heart turned over. How different from them was Lydia, with her cat-like eyes, her olive skin and her long dark hair. Standing behind them and smiling was a thin young woman wearing spectacles, her features slightly severe. She was introduced as Miss Harding, governess to Hector's children. With a quick kiss for her father and without a backward glance, Lydia left us. Decimus squeezed my hand,

131

understanding my anguish, yet knowing too it was by his actions that our daughter was scarcely acquainted with her mother. When would he let me see her again?

Leaving Decimus with his cousin, I followed the maid upstairs to the room that had been prepared for us. The ceiling was high, tall windows let in the last of the light, and long, pleated satin curtains matched the striped satin drapes that hung from the bed. A pale blue carpet covered the floor. The furniture was white with ornate gilded beading. In the closest I found a lavatory and a wash bowl with taps. I wished Decimus could be with me for I was quite overawed. I unpacked our clothes and took off my travelling gown, putting everything neatly away in the closet. I unloosed my stays and I washed my hands and face. Carefully I sat down on the edge of a satin-covered stool in front of the dressing table. I released my hair and, counting each stroke, began to brush it. Looking at my reflection, I asked myself, who was I, Mary Cheyne, a bastard and a gypsy, to be in this fine house? Would my husband have wed me had he known me to be a gypsy? He had left Perry at home because he looked like a gypsy horse. I wanted to weep. Would Cousin Hector regret taking Lydia now he had seen her?

I jumped. Decimus had opened the door, disturbing my thoughts. His hand brushed my shoulder and I bowed my head. Lighting the lamps and closing the curtains, he seemed unaffected by the luxury of his cousin's house.

With the same ease as if he were dressing at home, he donned formal dress. I had not seen him looking so grand and the tension that had racked me dissipated as we laughed together. He was such an elegant man, no one would guess, except for his hands, that he was a farmer. How different he looked from the Decimus I knew.

Gently he asked me if I was ready to be locked into my corset. I sought to postpone the moment, dreading its grip, yet knowing it could not be put off for long. Decimus let me coil my hair, securing it for me with a silver comb. I dusted my face with powder, then took off my underwear.

Standing naked and holding myself in, with my arms stretched above my head, I dared not breathe as he drew the corset tight around my waist. Without difficulty his strong hands closed it. I heard the lock click. As he secured the key to his watch chain, he smiled. Abashed, I asked him what he would say if his cousin should comment.

'I shall tell him the truth, Mary dear.'

Decimus helped me into my gown. The beaded jet glittered in a myriad points. The skirt, its petticoats stiff with starch, fell bell-shaped to the floor. My slippers were black and dainty, the heels giving me height. Decimus put his arm round me and his touch was loving.

'Come, Mary, see your reflection in the long glass before we join my cousin and his guests.'

I had thought to meet only the family, not a party. Standing before the mirror, I saw looking back at me a fey woman, her body soft, her spirit compliant. She was small-featured with a skin the colour of thick honey, her head barely reaching her husband's chest. Her waist was cinched so viciously that her body looked to break in two.

Fastening Granny's pearls, Decimus caressed my shoulders, then reaching into my bodice, without warning he ripped out Ella's inset, the tacks unresisting. When I saw what he had done, involuntarily my hands reached up to cover myself, but Decimus caught them, holding them firmly behind my back. Vulnerable, my pride torn from me, I looked up at his image, pleading with him.

'Oh no, lord, please do not shame me in this house.'

My breath, constrained by the vice that held me, almost failed. He told me to look at myself. Carefully arranging the gauze, he made me respectable. Strangely my appearance did not look coarse. The gown was beautiful, showing off Granny's pearls that glowed, lustrous, at my throat. My tiny waist and the frailty of my body, too, were enhanced. He released my hands and without being told I let them fall to my sides. My husband was smiling, pleased with me, as still faint I tried to concentrate on what he was saying.

'My dear, sweet wife, you are not shamed by your attire. Do

you not know you are a most beautiful woman? You have not aged, for your beauty is born of humility and it is rare indeed. When my cousin casts his eyes on you, my darling, remember you belong to me. Do not let his looks intimidate you.'

Fearing Cousin Hector might bar me from his table, I asked Decimus whether my gown was not too shocking. He laughed, assuring me that in society a lady would not hesitate to reveal the curve of her breasts. Hector would, in my lord's circumstances, expect nothing less of me. For a moment I thought to ask my husband what he meant by this remark, but was too concerned for the ordeal I perceived to be ahead of me to dwell on it. Whatever my dress, I knew Hector and his guests would be witness to my submissions. Turning to Decimus and fighting my panic, I sank to my knees, pleading with him.

'I am not worthy to be your lady. I fear your high-born friends will ridicule me, lord.'

His face swam before my eyes. My tears welled and nausea rose in my throat.

'You promised you would help me.'

Enveloping me in his arms, gently he kissed me, consoling me, his kisses stilling my torment until, lost in his love, I cared nothing for the extremity of my position. To show him I loved him with all my heart, I promised that no matter what he asked of me, until my dying breath my body and soul would always belong to him. When we were ready, he placed my hand on his arm and escorted me down the wide, shallow stairs.

There were two other guests, both gentlemen, much older than I, and friends of Hector. Neither spared me my blushes. In the magnificent dining room, sitting apart from my love, I watched his ease in the company of his cousin. There was so much I had yet to learn about my husband. The years when I had known nothing and cared little for the company he kept alas were over. He had shut me away for so long, I doubted I should ever be comfortable with him, other than at his feet.

Watching Grace, I noticed she showed her husband scant respect. She seemed unable to see that though he tolerated her silly laughter his eyes did not love her.

After we had dined, though I could eat very little, Grace requested me to follow her into the drawing room, leaving the gentlemen with their cigars and maderia. The lamps here were less bright and were kinder to Grace, for were she not careworn she would have been a pretty woman. Her gown was intricate and I imagined expensive. But the dress did not flatter her, its dull brown satin taking her colour, the high, lace-edged collar reaching almost to her ears. Without Decimus to give me confidence and knowing she did not like me, I felt uncomfortable. I wished so much she would stop staring at me, for my appearance could not be changed. We had no conversation. I noticed her hands were shaking. She was flushed and excusing her action, Grace took out her needlework. Quite sharply, as though her courage would wane if she did not immediately speak her mind, she put down her work and asked me.

'Mary dear, my husband tells me Decimus shut you away for nearly seventeen years because you are cursed and a Daughter of Satan.'

My head reeled; the floodgates had opened. It was clear now why she was loth to talk to me.

'Hector says your husband cut a terrible mark into your flesh to protect himself from the evil in you.'

Grace hesitated for a moment. Taking out her handkerchief, with her hand to her chest, surreptitiously, she crossed herself. She blew her nose hard, but could not quell the tears that threatened her composure.

'Oh Mary, do please tell me it is not true, for I am so frightened by you. I wish you had not come here. You can see Hector is besotted with you. He has threatened I shall be confined in this house and beaten, as he says Decimus beat you.'

Her voice trailed off. Grace did not mock me as I had feared she might, but in those few heartfelt words that came tumbling from her lips lay the terror which had followed my kin through centuries. The curse of my forebears lived on. Leaning towards her, I took her hands in mine, but her body stiffened as I touched her, so I let go.

'You cannot know, Grace, that Decimus is the guardian of my

soul. The gypsies say the curse is in my blood, but I can do nothing about it. I promise you, though, I have suffered in full the retribution demanded of me to assuage the sins that I inherited. My lord possesses me, body and soul. He has consumed my guilt and permits me to pay penance no more.'

I saw the look of consternation on her face, for now she must believe what until this moment she had hoped she would not have to. Trying to set her mind at rest, I continued.

'Yes, Grace, it is true that my husband ordered my belly be marked, so that his dear child in my womb was protected from me. Many years ago an old crone used her knife on me. The trace will always be there but I no longer fear it, though for years I dared not look at what had been done to me. Now I accept it is the will of my dear husband and am content.'

Making no effort to conceal her fear, Grace cringed. I could not help her, for it seemed with every word I uttered she was driven even further from me. Shaking her head, she put her hands to her own covered breasts.

'Whatever your inheritance, Mary, have you no pride? How can you let your husband treat you so?'

Her fingers found her mouth. Her tongue had run away with her. Yet still seeking to allay her fear of me, I did not mind.

'No, Grace, there is no place for pride. My husband has taken everything from me. I love him and live by his will. I cannot change my condition.'

How could I explain to Grace the depth of our love if the flame of her husband's passion had never burned her, nor had she heard the willow's song? How could Grace know that the pain of her husband's loving did not matter, when after it was done, lost in her memories, she dreamed of the night she lay in the cool, wet meadow, her body on fire, thinking of the Garden of Eden?

I longed for the evening to end, to be safe in bed with my lord, where with my body freed of restriction I could soak up the strength I needed to be as my husband wished. When eventually he came for me and we were all alone, we whispered to one another in the darkness. The Decimus I knew and loved held me close.

'My darling, a man like Hector desires you because his jealous eyes tell him how happy we are. Poor Grace has not the courage to give her life to him as you have given yours to me.'

Lying next to my husband, I knew I had become the woman he had worked so hard to make me and was as different from other women as my lord was from other men. In the morning we would return home and I resolved to ask him if we might walk soon on the Sea Bank of the Great River to feel in our hair the wind that blew all the way from the Americas. As our bodies knit together in sleep, in my prayers I delivered my soul into my lord's protection.

I blew Lydia a kiss as, holding her governess's hand, she waved us farewell and Decimus turned the pony for home. The heavy gates clanged shut behind us. Anxious to be on his way, Decimus set a cracking pace, fearing that left on their own too long the hired men would have slackened. The morning was dull and overcast; heavy clouds backed by a keening wind rolled up the channel. I hoped the rain would keep off until we were home. Would Lydia be happy in Cousin Hector's house? I prayed that Grace would be kind to her. Decimus's voice, snatched from the wind, interrupted my thoughts.

'Thomas will not go back to school after the summer, Mary. He will learn to be a farmer and when he reaches his majority, shall have your inheritance. It is fitting that our first-born should live in the house your father left you. Tomorrow I shall take you there, so you may see what has become of it.'

Touching his dear weatherbeaten face, my fingers placed a kiss. With all my heart, I loved him.

I hurried to make myself ready. Decimus had long since finished the milking and waited impatiently for me. Together, we set out to walk the Sea Bank that would take us north, in the direction of the old house. The weather had not really warmed yet and Decimus was concerned that the first cut of grass would be late this year. But the wind that had brought rain yesterday was balmy and all about us was the promise of summer. We walked for nearly two miles before we could glimpse the roof and chimneys of the old house between the trees. How many years had gone by since the momentous day when Decimus had brought me to look at my inheritance? That day he had not let me enter, but had taken me on to the Sea Bank and shown me putchers, stacked weathering and waiting for the next fishing season. My feet bare, icy raindrops stinging my face, Decimus had guided me deep into the silt of the Great River. Far out we had stood, just the two of us alone in that grey and beautiful wilderness.

Nearing the old house, I sensed Decimus's excitement. I was exhausted by the long walk and he helped me descend the steep bank. The short hard grass of the bank was replaced now by a long, lush growth. Elms, marking the boundaries to his land, spread their branches over us and only the tips of the trees, unprotected by the high bank, swayed, moaning in the gentle wind. Holding my hand, Decimus led me closer. The house had been transformed. Of the patched-up ruin there was no trace. The walls were sound, the slates on the roof, even. New paint gleamed and the windows that had been boarded up now boasted glass. Decimus laughed like a schoolboy, as throwing the door wide, he lifted me in his arms and carried me over the threshold. I felt like a bride again, except I loved him even more now than when he had wed me, though at the time I should probably have disputed it.

Decimus took my hand again, leading me from room to room. In wonderment I looked around me, for the ghosts had all left. Though it was empty, the house breathed with new life. One day this place would echo to the sound of our grandchildren's happy laughter and my fears of long ago must have been for some other time that I could not imagine. Until now, I had not thought to enquire of my husband by what name this house was called. Who had lived here before it was mine and how long ago had that been? What a flurry of questions I asked him.

'The place was always known as Cloudsmoor Farm, Mary, but

for as long as I can remember the house has been empty and derelict, the land let anonymously through an agent in Milbury.'

Cloudsmoor Farm, what a lovely name that was, but even now I knew little more of its history than when I had first seen it with Jesse. Perhaps my father had not intended me to know. When his lawyers had read the codicil to his Will, deliberately they had concealed his identity from me. I had learned only my mother's name, Hannah Cheyne, and that I was the child of my father's love for her. Decimus bent down and kissed me. Basking in his love, I threw my arms about him, my cheek brushing against the rough serge of his jacket, then remembering my position, lest he should think me bold, I lowered my eyes. Cupping my chin in his hand, he tilted my head so that I should look at him. Though he still smiled, his voice was serious.

'I am so proud of you, Mary. It was hard for you to wear your new gown as I intend you to wear it, my darling. It was hard, too, to defend our love in the company of Grace. I knew it would be. She is appalled by what I've done to you and it is too much to expect her to understand our happiness. But be confident, Mary, in time you will grow used to my friends. I want you to know, though, that whatever scorn Grace has heaped upon you, I'm pleased with you.'

My heart happy, I sought to tell him I did not mind how strict he must be and, more certain of myself now, I assured him. 'I understand what you expect of me, lord. I shall try never to disappoint you.'

He touched my lips and my words were silenced. Behind his eyes was a glow. In all the years we had been wed, not once had I hesitated when he called upon me. His eyes did not leave mine as, kneeling before him, with my fingers fumbling just a little, I unbuttoned my gown, to let it slip from my shoulders. Looking round, I saw nothing in the bare room that might ease the penetrating cold of the stone flagged floor. Seeing my predicament and reading my mind, my husband laughed.

'Are you so old that you need a feather mattress to lie on before you will let me love you, Mary? Quickly now, get up and take off your gown. You can rest on that.'

Carefully he laid my gown on the floor, then relieved me of my petticoats, placing them on top. He watched, not a little irritated, for, daring to tease him just once, I did not hurry as I rolled down my stockings, taking them off with my boots. The stones were cold to my feet and I shivered. He loosened the laces of my stays and I unhooked them, freeing my body, but I was too slow for his need and taking them from me, muttering an oath under his breath, he cast my stays into a corner. Standing quite still, I let him remove my shift and my drawers. Naked, the cool air brushing my skin, I stretched.

He took the pins from my hair, his eyes laughing as he released the tresses and shook them, spreading them about my shoulders. Once, my hair had been long enough to sit on but I could hardly recall those days. Since Decimus had shaved my head, it had not grown that long again.

Holding me at arm's length, his fingers dug into me, their message urgent, their imprint white on my skin. He lowered me, pressing me flat to the floor, and the gown under me was as nothing, such was the cold that soaked into my bones. His voice, its timbre resolute, told me to close my eyes. Forgetting my discomfort, as always I obeyed him, listening to what he was saying.

'Until the day this house belongs to Thomas, whenever I bring you here, Mary, I will let you forget your new life and will love you as I have always loved you. My loving will sustain you, my darling, and give you strength to withstand the perils that await you in the world outside.'

His soft kisses lulled me. When they became stronger, reflecting his passion, I was already lost, drowning in an ocean of pleasure. His teeth, not shielded by his lips, trembled on my skin, bruising me, but I hardly noticed, such was my contentment. The willow's song invaded my head and still he held me, my flesh sucked tight between his teeth. Acknowledging no boundaries, he covered my body with kisses, but the pain of it all belonged to another world that unheeded, I had left, caring not whether I returned.

I awoke, cradled in my lord's arms, still naked, recalling neither time nor place, his jacket about my shoulders, warming me. Seeing I had woken, Decimus set me on my feet and helped me with my dressing. Then, taking my hand and supporting me, he led me from the old house, along the path that ended at the Sea Bank of the Great River. With his arm around my waist, together we climbed the bank. Marvelling at the magnificent Estuary, we gazed at the beauty God had set out before us. A gentle wind that came all the way from the Americas touched me and I recalled Jesse's words.

'Whenever you despair and feel you are alone, my child, look into your heart and know that this land is where you belong and it will give you strength to accept God's will. No man can rob you of it.'

Long before I understood, Jesse had known who I was. It was God's will that my troubled soul would be stilled only if I trod with love an unending path to selflessness. Jesse had given me to Decimus, making me love him, knowing that only my husband would have the courage to take me on that journey.

Decimus has given me the strength to accept God's will. Now he is taking me on a new path of learning and I must not fail him. I know he will not rob me of this land, for this is his land too and here, standing next to him, is for all eternity where I truly belong.

CHAPTER XIV

The Fish Market

Last September Richard started school in the village. Although he was almost five years old, he would always be the baby of the family. With the last of her charges finally taken from her, Ella was lost and, like a broody hen, immersed herself in house cleaning and polishing. When eventually she buried herself in her sewing, we were all greatly relieved.

In this June of 1877 more than a year has passed since Lydia left us and gradually we have adapted to her absence. In a neat hand, her language correct, sometimes she writes to Ella, who shows me the letters. Even now though, it hurts to talk about Lydia and we leave the subject alone. Not once has Decimus allowed her to return home, saying the upheaval would be more hurtful for Lydia than it would be for the family. I fear in time she will forget us.

We are used now to seeing Thomas about the farm. Happiest with his head in a book he is not a natural farmer as is his father, yet nothing is ever said. Thomas will follow in Decimus's footsteps and work the land as his kin have done for generations before him.

Until the middle of August Decimus was preoccupied with the fishing season, taking the salmon twice a week to the wholesale fishmarket in Bristol. Some days I accompanied him and while waiting for him to finish his business with Bigwoods, the wholesalers, he allowed me to wander round the covered market. Under the high, vaulted roof, it was always cold, no matter what the weather outside. With familiarity I was sure, even blindfolded, I could find my way, for walking from one end to the other the smell of fish was slowly banished by the sweet fragrance of flowers.

The church of St Nicholas, its slender spire reaching for the heavens, stood guard over the market place. One unforgettable day when the noise of merchants haggling and the general mêlée were too much for my country ears, I opened the heavy bolt-encrusted door of the church, to find sanctuary. In the all-pervading silence, the door closed behind me with a gentle whoosh and the stillness enveloped me. From somewhere, I could not readily discern quite where, came the sound of quiet sobbing. Shadows cast from long candles flickered on the walls and my eyes could see only a short way, such was the dimness of the light. Looking all about me and straining to see, as I became accustomed to the darkness I could make out a figure. She was slight, huddled in a pew. Was this a child or a woman? I could not see past the tattered shawl. She knelt prostrate, crumpled and weeping.

Before I could go to her, a man I had not noticed, for he was obscured behind a pillar, bent over her. He muttered something. She cried out, cowering as he took her arm, yet overcoming her resistance he bundled her away. As he ushered her past me, I saw she was a grown woman. Her desperate eyes caught my uncomprehending stare and for a moment I thought I recognised her. But no, I could not possibly have seen her before. How foolish I was to have followed them. How much I wished afterwards I had not. But where had I seen her? My wretched memory so often played tricks on me.

Her companion led the woman back through the market towards a maze of narrow side streets behind it. This was a direction in which Decimus had forbidden me ever to wander. Realising I had gone too far and heeding his warning, I was about to turn back, when I saw the couple had stopped outside an alehouse. The man, at the top of his voice, began to shout.

'Meet my wife, Rosie!'

I crept into the shadow of a doorway, sheltering from their ribald laughter as a crowd of half-drunken men gathered. Oh dear God, what had I stumbled on? Flattening myself against the sheltering arch, I prayed not to be seen. Her husband pushed the poor woman forward and, still sobbing, she flinched, but he held her fast. The crowd was getting larger all the time: there were maybe twenty men, some shouting encouragement, some just standing there watching the sport. Her husband pushed her further into the crowd, shaking her, as if forcing her to participate. He was shouting again.

In her betrayal, the poor woman's eyes searched about her, but none pitied her. Laughing, beer spilling down his front, one man prodded her stomach with the end of a stick.

'Casn't see she've got a bun in 'er oven, ya fool?'

Holding close her shawl with one hand and spreading the fingers of her other hand to protect her belly, she pleaded with her husband, but like a half-filled sack, he held her, thrusting her in front of him.

Another tormentor yelled. 'Well, 'e won't get much for 'er like, will 'e.'

The crowd roared its approval. Rosie, I had known a Rosie. No, how could it possibly be? This woman was old, her hair sparse. She tried to hide behind her husband, but holding her even more firmly, with both his hands gripping her arms, he drew her into the crowd that was mocking her. Suddenly, he let her go. She lost her balance and tripped, the ragged shawl falling from her as she tried to save herself. Dragging her body across the filthy cobbles, she sought to get away, but with the crowd jeering at her, the disgusting man who was her husband caught hold of her hair, pulling her upright. The pathetic shawl lay in the dirt. I saw her chest and shoulders were covered in sores. She tried to retrieve the shawl but her husband, laughing, kicked it from her reach. I could not believe my eyes as he tore open her gown, revealing her naked breasts.

'Feel free to touch 'er, lads,' he bawled.

Her hands found her breasts, desperate to cover herself in front of the shaming mob. Suddenly her pleading eyes looked straight at me. I knew not how she saw me, pressed so tight to the wall, but with arms outstretched she begged me for help. As the men who had gathered turned to look at me, the clouds in my memory parted and I knew for certain where I had seen Rosie before. Her haggard and ruined face was a travesty of the face of a young and sparkling girl with her life ahead of her, who had kept me company on a journey away from a world that my memory had buried and long forgotten. Frozen to the spot, watching Rosie, I could not move. She was whimpering now, utterly degraded. In defeat, Rosie made no effort to cover herself. Her mouth had parted in a half smile as she gazed vacantly at the men who tormented her. Sinking into the gutter with the rubbish, she accepted her fate, her listless eyes looking up at the husband who auctioned her.

Some of the men still looked at me and, seeing their hunger, Rosie's terrible shame was suddenly mine. Creeping away so as not to attract more attention, I left the awful scene. Then in panic, decorum thrown to the winds, I picked up my skirts and ran, desperate to find my beloved Decimus.

He held me close. Breathless, I was safe in his loving arms. Tilting my face, he did not hide his concern.

'Whatever has happened, my darling, to distress you so?'

'My love, I went into church and heard a woman sobbing. Her husband came for her and dragged her out. I thought I recognised her and followed them where you have warned me not to go. Please do not be angry with me, lord. They reached an alehouse and he tried to sell her! When the woman looked at me, I knew she was Rosie, a girl who shared my journey all those years ago. She was desperate, covered in sores and with child. I was so shocked. Please help her.'

Decimus looked relieved.

'Poor Mary. Is that all that troubles you? By confining you at home, my darling, I've neglected your education. You have been protected from the harsh world. Now wait in the cart. I have almost finished here.'

'But, lord, the woman is in mortal danger. I beg of you, please, you must help her.'

At first he did not answer. When I opened my mouth to ask him again, Decimus put his fingers against my lips to seal them. I had displeased him! My breath was already spent and I had stitch in my side from running. Now my chest was constricted as I saw his eyes had narrowed. His tones were clipped, without a trace of dialect.

'You will not question my instructions, Mary. Do I make myself clear? Now, wait in the cart until I am ready to leave.'

He turned from me and I obeyed him. I could not remember him being so angry with me, not ever. I had provoked him and I feared him terribly. Rosie's face, abject in her degradation in front of the crowd, rose before me like a spectre. What misfortune must have befallen her since that day when we had talked of our dreams? Waiting for Decimus, my face and my body rigid, I could not weep. The noise of the city seemed blotted from my consciousness and I heard only my husband's words ringing in my ears.

Decimus climbed into his seat. With my head bowed, I dared not look up at him, such was my fear. Without a word, he took the reins. Perry lifted his head, always lively when he knew he was going home. With nausea rising from the pit of my stomach, I held on tight, as the cart without its load bounced over the cobbles. Decimus did not speak to me as we took our turn, following the High Street up towards the Cross. At the corner of Wine Street, set into the wall, little figures would soon strike the quarters, Usually we timed our approach so that I could watch them, but not today.

A sickening silence lay between us as we drove down Broad Street and through the narrow City Gate in the old City Wall. The church of St John that was built into the wall had offered a safe haven to travellers from time immemorial. In front of us and to our left were ships drawn up to the Quay. We turned right and soon came to an open space where a Horse Fair was held, old houses crammed in on three sides. This was the resting place for victims of the Great Plague. Some townspeople still hesitated to venture here for fear of infection.

Ignoring me, Decimus stared only ahead. I had transgressed and did not matter to him. What aberration had overtaken me? How could I have been so foolish as to question him? Now he had withdrawn his love and I knew not how to soften his wrath. I did not touch him, for fear he would push me away.

Gripping my seat I begged him, 'Please, my love, speak to me. I am so sorry, but the woman, she was sick and, surely, there but for the grace of God go I?'

His look was implacable. Dear God, what had I said that was so wrong? His voice was hard and impersonal.

'No, Mary, despite your lineage, you would not have become a whore. Men will always need women like Rosie who ply their trade in the market. But her life is worthless.'

He was damning. My heart despaired at his cruel words. He seemed not to notice my tears as I tried again to placate him.

'Lord, I have offended you. Please forgive me.'

He hitched the reins and held my unprotesting face, making me look up at him. His countenance was bleak.

'I understand you were distressed by what you saw, Mary. You not only ventured where I had forbidden you to go, but you ignored that offence and sought to question my instruction that you wait in the cart. I will not tolerate your disobedience.'

I remained silent. He did not look for a reply. As the country road wound like a brown ribbon ahead of us, I longed to be home. The surface, now the cobbles had ended, was more to Perry's liking and Decimus, with a flick of his whip, quickened the pace. We had travelled for many miles before Decimus deemed my punishment had lasted long enough and decided to engage me in quiet conversation.

'As I have broken you in love, Mary, the poor soul you called Rosie has been broken by the men who have used her. I can understand compassion was in your gentle heart, my dear, but the die was cast for Rosie long before the day you met her. Do not weep, for your tears can do nothing to help her.'

I thought my lord's mood had softened, but as he continued, I was sorely mistaken.

'Beware, Mary, by your behaviour you do not force me to reprove you. Until now I have struck you only in love. But be careful. Should you be the slightest changed by your new life and disappoint me after all, you will feel the weight of my displeasure.'

His voice was cold, his words harsh. Shaking, I took hold of his hand, kissing it. From between lips I could not keep from trembling, I asked him to pardon me, knowing should I transgress again I could not expect his mercy. He squeezed my hand and I prayed he had forgiven me.

The evening was turning chilly and he put a cloak around my shoulders. I was so tired I fell asleep. In the inky black of a moonless night, propped safe against his towering presence, I dreamed of Rosie and thanked God I belonged to Decimus, never to stand destitute and alone in the market place.

Though he could not doubt I was happiest if he left me at home, there were other occasions that summer when Decimus insisted I accompany him to Bristol. Gradually Rosie's face receded from my consciousness. In the company of my husband, without exception I bowed my head, that my humility should not go unnoticed. I had learned my lesson well and rarely conversed with him unless he requested it of me.

We are nearing Christmas and still Decimus has not allowed Lydia to come home. He has visited her in Hartley, but neither Ella nor I have set eyes on her since her departure on May Day of last year.

This Christmas Harry is just fourteen years old and one day will have the stature of his father. Unlike Thomas, who was loth to relinquish his studies, Harry is tiring of school. Decimus insists, though, that he stay another year, knowing in later life Harry will not regret his book learning.

Over the years my relationship with Ella has changed. We have become fond of one another. When Decimus first brought me here, Ella, already in residence, resented me, fearing I should threaten her position as mistress of this house, yet now she understands, as do I, that her status is unchallenged.

Though I have tried to adapt to the new life my husband wants for me, I am so apprehensive when Decimus is near me that I ache with fear. Sometimes, exasperated, Ella will chide me for my weakness, saying I should make a stand. After all these years of silent observation, watching my lord mould me to his will, still Ella finds my reverence disconcerting. But she adores the children I have borne her youngest brother and is mostly tolerant of me. I do believe in her own way Ella respects me. When, quite often, I am fatigued from the tasks she sets, for Decimus allows Ella responsibility for my labouring, she will sit me down, make a pot of tea, then finish the job herself.

As a spinster lady, who has never had a beau, Ella cannot comprehend the bond of love between my lord and me. She can know nothing of his passion. If she could understand, she would see why, in spite of the intensity of my fear, my duty is to serve him.

With the privations of Lent, hardly a day went by when Ella and I were not hungry and we were looking forward to Easter. Unexpectedly Decimus announced he was going to Hartley to fetch Lydia home for the holiday. Ella was overjoyed, as was Richard, who had missed his sister, his other two siblings being far too old to play with him. I, too, should have been happy, yet of late, like a dark cloak, depression had taken hold of me and I feared the confrontation, acknowledging that Lydia, who hardly knew her mother when she left us, would have little affection for me.

A serious child sat next to her father as he drove the trap into the yard. Watching him hand her down, I saw how much she had grown. Her eyes searched for Ella and with her arms outstretched, she ran to her and they embraced, both weeping. Turning to me, how graceful yet how formal was her curtsy.

My heart was heavy as I followed them indoors. Ella and I had worked so hard to make this a memorable home-coming and now, as I looked at the retreating figure of my daughter and guessed how altered she was by her experience, I feared this encounter would be a strain on us all.

Her new demeanour pleased her father, but I longed for the wayward spirit of the little girl who had run wild with the gypsy children. Though she was not yet ten years old, in his every action Decimus was preparing Lydia for marriage, making her quiet and docile. He feared the destiny that awaited her if she could not love the man he chose to be her husband.

The child was melancholy, seeming to accept without question the conventions her governess had imposed on her. I could have wept for Lydia as over the Easter season I saw her tender youth had drained away. But I could not forget the dire warning my lord had issued that comfortless day when I had seen Rosie, her life auctioned in the market place, and dared not voice my anxiety. To have disputed my husband's intentions was out of the question.

All too soon he took Lydia back to Cousin Hector and a part of me went with her.

One evening in May, not long after Lydia had returned to Hartley, Decimus took me to the old house. At thirty-seven years old, I was too young to be a matron, yet my childbearing years were over. We walked on the wide grassy bank, the still air heavy with the scent of blossom, the sun suspended, wrapped in a great ball of flame. The full waters on the high tide shimmered, a sparkling silver through the haze. Taking my hand, Decimus led me across the short springy turf to where at the mud line the tide had eroded a little cliff. Together we sat on the edge, our feet dangling. The rays of the sun cut a broad ribbon of gold and red across the water, almost to our feet.

Decimus stroked my hand and I looked up into his eyes. With the dying sun still warm on our faces, he suggested we should sit awhile and talk.

'You are troubled, Mary,' he said.

I sought to allay his anxiety, but could not in truth find words.

'I will not shut you away again, my dear. That is the easy way.

Believe me, Mary, in time you will become adjusted to the life I want for you.'

I stared down at my hands, then looked up at him, trying to make him understand.

'I try not to disappoint you, lord. You do not let me question you, yet you encourage my participation. I fear I may change and bring your wrath down on me. I dare not talk to you of my confusion, or you may consider me to be familiar.'

Such was my pleading, I took hold of his hands and pulled them to my face, smothering them with kisses.

'Lord, I beg of you, please shut me away safe at home where I cannot offend you. For four years since our dear dead child was delivered of me, I have tried to be the woman you want me to be and to adjust to a new way of life. But now I fear your anger more than I have ever done. You no longer seem to care if the willow sings or if the flame burns me. Truly, I am without hope.'

Fearing my outburst would anger him, in despair I threw myself across him.

Putting his arm around me and pulling me upright, he turned my face to his. He looked kindly on me and for one blessed moment I thought he would restore me to the seclusion I so longed for. But it was not to be.

'Mary, do not give up hope, for we have travelled such a long way together. Try to be patient with yourself. My dear, since you lost your child, I cannot bring my hand to cause you more suffering. Though I no longer burn you nor do I beat you with the willow, I thought the flame and the song remained in your heart.'

'Oh, my love, they do, but the flame grows dim and my heart will not listen to the song the willow sings. I am consumed by my dread of rejection.'

'Mary, my love, do not yearn for your old life, for it is gone. We can neither of us go back. You will not question me, you know that. Nor will you disobey me. But, my darling, where is your courage? You must be confident. I think maybe you forget that your will is but a mirror of mine.'

Decimus took me in his arms. Tenderly he comforted me, then gently helped me to my feet.

'Come, Mary, when we reach the old house I shall love you, my darling, and take every inch of you to paradise. I promise, you will not doubt that I worship you.'

Later that night after Decimus had brought me home and we lay in bed together between the cool clean sheets, judging my little question would not provoke his anger I asked him why he was not already wed, for he was no longer young, when first I came to see my inheritance.

He just laughed and said that no one would have him. Like his father, he enjoyed a reputation as a ruthless man.

'No man in these parts would give his daughter to the tenth issue of Decimus Hillyer, for fear he would be cruel to her. You, my love, came to me in ignorance of that reputation. You had no father to warn you against me, my little one, and I took advantage of you.'

In the dark I touched him, not caring if he mocked me.

'It would not have mattered, my love, for I could wed no one but you. I loved you from the moment I first saw you.'

As he turned over, Decimus sighed.

'I know, Mary, go to sleep now.'

My hips ached from the weight of him. Running my hands over his back, I dared not ask him where he had learned to love, though somehow guessed he had known dark days before Jesse had brought me to him.

CHAPTER XV

The Accident

We have had Perry for five years now and I am still entranced when he dances for me. Decimus allows me often to drive alone, to go shopping in Milbury. He laughs, knowing as I hold the reins in my hands and set Perry to a gallop, I dream and shall escape my shackles.

I have overcome the fear that my lord will withdraw his love and am used now to my place at his side. Submitting to his rigid discipline, I know it is God's will that I tread with humility the path Decimus has mapped for me. My lord will never compromise. I do not expect it. At times it is hard to tolerate the mockery I see in the eyes of others. When some days I am weary and feel I cannot go on, then Decimus will take me to the old house and, letting me forget the world outside, will love me as he has always done. His faith in me gives me confidence and under his authority I am free.

I try not to think too much of Lydia. I cannot change the pattern of the life Decimus dictates she shall follow, yet each time we see her I am close to despair. We shall not enjoy Richard's company either for many years more. He, like his brothers, will go to school in Milbury. Though I am a little apprehensive, I have not yet voiced my fears. Decimus is convinced Richard, who is still a dreamer, will benefit from leaving home.

Thomas has grown almost as tall as his father. He is muscular as are all the Hillyers, yet in his face is the sensitivity he inherits from Granny. He is just twenty years old and in these past two years has taken over the fishery, leaving Decimus with more time to indulge his ambition. My husband looks forward to increasing his herd. Already he had invested in new pedigree stock.

Harry is thrilled to be helping him. Like Decimus, he is a born farmer, at one with the elements, perceiving his own and others' mortality, a breed apart. I do believe Harry, when he is fully grown, may be physically larger than his father. Ella says he looks like me, yet I see only Decimus in his countenance, especially when he frowns and his eyebrows, almost joined at the middle, threaten to hide his eyes.

With the return of spring, life in the soil, that most precious spark, is renewed and seeing the cattle turned out to grass we thank God we have survived the winter.

Suddenly the quiet of an April morning was shattered. From the yard came shouts and the noise of splintering wood. Then there was silence, until ear-splitting screams followed the lull. Staring at one another from across the scullery, for a moment neither Annie nor I could move. Wiping my hands on my pinafore, I got up from my knees and ran to the yard door. Wrenching it open, before my eyes was a scene I cannot erase from my memory. Thomas and Harry, my precious sons, at either end of a long iron pole, were grappling with their father's prize bull. They were holding him with the pole rammed through the ring in his nose. The beast was bellowing, his huge head twisted and bent. The animal shook with rage, his feet gouging great holes in the ground.

A young stockman, of no more than Harry's age, writhed in the dirt, clutching his belly, blood oozing through his fingers. His screams would have woken the dead. Across the yard, my beloved Decimus, his face in the mud, lay quite, quite still. Two hired men looked on, transfixed by the horror.

Annie crept up behind me, grunting noises coming from her throat. Turning to her, I saw her eyes had clouded with fear and, like a half-wit, her tongue lolled out. I snapped at her.

154

'For God's sake, Annie, don't just stand there. Go fetch Mistress Ella and be quick.'

Though it be a sin, I had eyes only for Decimus, the noise and commotion being but a backdrop to his suffering. Kneeling beside him, I talked to him, pulling him to me, cradling his dear head in my arms. In profusion my tears fell on his dirt-stained face and, wiping away the grime, I could see beneath his rough, windburned complexion my husband's skin had the pallor of death. His shirt was ripped and, where it parted, a long red bruise ran down his side. All the while the boy screamed in his agony and, beside myself with terror, I prayed to Almighty God.

'Oh dear God, please show me what I must do.'

When I touched my love where he was hurt, for a moment his eyes had opened. Closing them again, he moaned. With all my heart, I prayed he should live.

Harry was beside me, telling me Thomas had made safe the bull in his pen. He was asking me, what should he do? Why ask me? How should I know? I could not think. Shaking with panic and near to dementia, I looked all around me. There was no one to help. Then, as though a hand had reached down from Heaven to guide me, no longer demented I had ceased to shake. The panic had receded. We were all in God's hands. Decimus had prepared me for this day. My head had cleared and I told Harry what he must do.

'Saddle your horse, Harry, and ride him as fast as you can to Milbury. Find Dr Mac and bring him back with you.'

My lord tried to move; so cold, yet beads of sweat formed on his brow. Thomas was with me, helping me. With a mighty effort he picked up his father, the heaviest of men, and carried him from the yard into the scullery. Decimus was barely conscious as Thomas lowered him into a chair. A thin trickle of blood ran from the side of his mouth, staining his shirt. The exertion had been too much. I bade Annie fetch a cushion for her master's head and a blanket to keep him warm.

Young Gabriel Meredith was near to death when the hired men carried him in. They laid him on the table and looking at his wound I nearly retched. His insides had spilled out; his blood was everywhere. He no longer screamed, but lay shivering and crying for his mother. By the time Harry returned with Dr Mac, Gabriel could well be dead. Fighting my nausea, I bade Annie fetch my work-basket. There was no other course; I must try to help him. Afraid for my husband and not daring to look at him, I washed my hands in the strongest carbolic. Then I took the longest needle and threaded it with embroidery silk while the two men held Gabriel still and Ella cut off his clothes, revealing his wound.

I asked Almighty God to guide my hand. Fearing I might touch him, the man next to me had distanced himself. My thoughts turned for a moment to Hector's wife, Grace. She could not bear me near her. After all these years that I had lived among them, the village people still reviled me. Sadness welled in my heart, but I put my emotions aside, for there were other things, so much more important, that must occupy my mind.

Carefully and trying not to hurry, I pushed Gabriel's warm innards back inside him. Drawing up his flesh to cover the hole, as though he were a fowl to be trussed, I sewed him together. Suddenly, overcome by my nausea, I was faint. Ella gently ushered me away, saying I had done enough. Grateful, I left her to bandage the wound.

Decimus, though battling for consciousness, had watched me. Kneeling at his feet, I held his hand in mine. Dear Annie – I had been so unkind to her – wiped away each droplet of blood that appeared when he coughed. Tears ran down her face and into her poor misshapen mouth. She loved her master, maybe as much as I. Thomas strode past us. I had not had the time to notice his absence. He took down his father's gun from above the range.

'I'm going to shoot him, Mother. No one will handle a bull that has gored a man.'

I stood up and my voice was clear and steady when I spoke to my son.

'No, Thomas, I cannot allow it. You must wait. Your father is still Master in this house and only he will decide whether his bull lives or dies.'

Such was his surprise, Thomas was stopped in his tracks. He did not demur, though he looked hard at me as he put back the gun. My dear love squeezed my hand. I had not imagined it; despite his pain, a ghost of a smile had crossed his face. Kissing his brow, his cold, wet sweat was salty on my lips. I wondered how we should move him and prayed that Harry would find Dr Mac.

Horses were in the yard. Surely Harry had not been to Milbury and back. Why had he returned so soon?

There, as large as life, was the answer. Dr Mac, his face grim, stood in the doorway, dwarfed by Harry standing behind him.

'They told me in the village, Doctor was expected at Squire's house, Mother, so I had not far to go.'

Covering my face, my hands stained with Gabriel's blood, caring not who saw me, on my knees, I sobbed. Our prayers had been answered. Knowing Satan had killed my child, only Decimus could truly understand my release. My fear, never far away, was that one day he would strike again to rob me of my family.

Gabriel Meredith is recovering from his wounds, but it is doubtful if he will walk upright. For the rest of his life, crutches will be his constant companion. Had Decimus not been there and driven off the bull, young Gabriel would not have lived. When the beast turned on him, my husband, no longer spritely, could not avoid the vicious horns. The doctor says he is lucky to be alive, for his ribs are broken and his poor body crushed inside. He fears my beloved husband may not regain his old vigour, but Decimus's strength has always been that of two men and, in the circumstances, we are thankful for his survival.

On my knees each night I pray to God that with His help and with my tender care, He will let my dear love recover from his injuries. Decimus is not an easy patient, for until now he has not experienced ill health. He has been confined to bed for nearly three weeks and is not in the best of temper.

With Harry's assistance, Thomas has taken over the every-day running of the farm. Decimus, though helpless, can find no release from his responsibilities and, cursing his plight, will not allow himself the luxury of peace.

We were nearing Whitsuntide. Ella and I had hoped, until his accident, that Decimus might have allowed Lydia home for the holiday. Now everything had changed. I stood at the foot of my husband's bed and began the speech I had rehearsed all morning.

'My love, I have been talking to Thomas.'

Decimus, propped up on pillows, looked up from the book he was pretending to read. Through lowered brows, he glowered at me. I had not expected the interview to be easy. He grimaced as I sat down on the bed next to him. Holding his hand in mine, I could not stop now.

'Lord, I seek your permission to go to Bristol.'

His eyebrows shot up.

'Thomas is quite capable, with Harry, of managing the farm, but they cannot make time to take the salmon to market.'

He put the book down.

'What are you trying to say to me, Mary?'

'My love, someone has to take the salmon to the wholesaler and whom would you trust other than me?'

Fearing his tongue, I lowered my eyes, waiting for his inevitable reaction. He would have none of it. He shook his head, for once in his life lost for words. His mouth set and downturned, he muttered but one word: 'No!'

His response was only as I had expected, but none the less my heart sank. I loved my husband more than I could bear and was deeply saddened to see him lying in bed, weaker than a babe.

Summoning my courage, I entreated him, 'Lord, do not concern yourself. Look at me. You see I am what you have made me. I know my will to be but a mirror of yours. My actions will be your actions. My heart is yours. You have given me confidence, my love. Please, I beg of you, do not betray that trust I have worked so hard to earn. Should I perish, you will always know I have wanted nothing better than to serve you since the moment I first saw you. You are the whole world and more to me. You have schooled me well and I will not fail you in this task. I love you so much and will do anything you ask of me to prove that love.'

His face had clouded. I could see his mind struggled. Surely he must know that without him I was nothing. I got up from the bed and quietly, without fuss, undid the buttons of my gown, letting it slip from my shoulders into a heap around me. His eyes did not stray from me. Undressing until I stood naked, that he should see well the indelible mark he had put on me, I took then his hand, placing it so that his fingers touched the blue-green web carved deep into my belly.

'You touch the mark which I shall endure for the rest of my life, lord. Am I not truly of your will and your mind? The fear I shall experience alone on the road will be no more onerous than was my fear of this affliction which you had Mistress Morgan cut into me.'

His eyes had filled with tears. As though he wished me to remember the pain of his love more intimately, his fingers pinched hard the ribs of flesh raised above my pitted skin. Holding his hand steady, I leaned closer to the bed so that he could more easily touch me, not flinching as he hurt me more. He turned his head away.

'Mary, I am putty in your hands. Go to Bristol if you must. You have my blessing. These past weeks I have tasted the confinement you have craved so long and must tell you, my dear, it is not to my liking. I cannot be out of this bed too soon.'

My heart leapt with relief and I sought to assure him.

'My love, you were moulded by a different hand.'

'Aye, Mary, I was too, and I tell you in truth I could not have sustained my sanity had my will been taken from me as I have taken yours.'

Listening to Decimus, his speech overtaken by dialect, I knew his conscience was stirred.

'That is why, lord, I was created woman. I seek no other life than the one you have made for me. My joy has always been to please you and love you.'

Decimus pulled my hands to his lips and kissed them.

'I know that, Mary, as did Jesse. I cannot delude myself it was chance that brought you to me, that I should be your master. Perhaps, that day, Jesse planted the seeds of my love for you, too.'

As he continued, my husband's look was wistful.

'Jesse knew long before either of us that deep in your veins ran the curse of your forebears.'

Decimus ran his fingers over my naked belly. His thoughts had wandered. As though he had not considered it before, he questioned me.

'Do you forgive me, Mary, for succumbing to superstition and placing this terrible brand on you? I'm no better than the rest of them, you know.'

That my dear love should be under no misapprehension, I hastened to reassure him.

'Oh my love, do you not yet understand? Every day I cannot help but touch myself. Sometimes when I have bathed and Annie is drying me, even now the mark burns. But I have not feared it for many years, knowing it is your will that my body shall bear it. There is nothing to forgive.'

In his mood of reflection, I asked Decimus, 'Please tell me, my love, for I have often wondered, but dared not ask. Did you regret our marriage when you found out who I was?'

For such a long moment Decimus did not reply, his thoughts chasing one another across his face. My heart beat faster, anticipating what he might say. I wished I had not mentioned it.

'In truth, I wished the circumstances were otherwise, Mary. But when Mistress Morgan put my mark on you, you withstood her knife bravely, my darling. In spite of your pain I saw you still loved me. I had hurt you so much, I did not believe you could. You cannot have forgotten the day when you lay naked on your childbed for the first time. You were hardly more than a child yourself and your belly was greatly swollen. The cradle that had protected my son was fresh. Your skin was stretched and, where she had cut you, you were still sore. The flesh beneath protruded, green and mutilated. Proud at what I had done to you, I stood over you and admonished you, then left, telling you your labouring was woman's work. But in that moment I feared I might lose you, Mary, and did not care what you had inherited.'

160

'I know, lord. I remember the tears in your eyes.'

'I have been a cruel master to you, Mary. Jesse knew the reputation I had. He told me not to spare you. He said you would find salvation only if I took your soul away from you. I did not ask him why, for it suited me very well.'

Tears ran down my husband's face, such was his sorrow.

'My love, do not look sad. If you were sound in body, you would not think to question what you have done to me. Remember God made woman from the rib of man. It is His will that man shall rule over her. I am truly happy being your woman. I cannot change what has happened to me even should I wish, but I do not wish it and never have done. It is difficult for my mind to recall the early days when my heart was close to despair and my soul in torment as I learned to obey you. But those days are well gone and I long to see you leave your bed with your health restored. Maybe my thoughts are selfish and I should not tell you, lord, but the weight of your discipline is so much easier to bear when you are standing over me and I feel the burden of your authority. But I shall not forget when I undertake this journey that my permission comes from you.'

I saw my love had exhausted what little strength he had and I was not distressed when he dismissed me.

'Go now, Mary. You will leave at dawn, my darling, but before this night is out I want you to love me. You will come to bed early and then I can show you how.'

Leaving him to shallow sleep, I picked up my clothes and crept away. His poor broken ribs, encased in webbing, were bound as tight as mine had been each time the moon deprived me of my babes.

It was barely dusk when I withdrew, leaving Ella alone in the parlour. Behind the settle in the scullery, Annie had filled the bath. After undressing me, she helped me lie down in the deep, scented water, then left me to soak, replenishing the water from time to time so that the constant heat should soften my skin. I washed my hair, letting it trail wet, in the water. Resting, I began to doze. How many times had I pleasured my

161

husband? I guessed this time would be different, though. Not that it mattered, God had given him my body to do with whatever he wished.

The pads of my fingers were wrinkled, as were the soles of my feet. Laughing, I told Annie she had cooked me well. I rose from the bath, and she wrapped me in warm towels while together we dried my body. Objectively I looked down at myself. Though it was six years since I had borne a child, my breasts were still full and heavy. My belly was flat and no bones protruded to disturb the roundness of my hips. My hair was still dark, though occasionally if I found a white one I would pull it out. Pouring oil on my body and rubbing me vigorously, Annie seemed to enjoy my preparations as much as I did. Sitting down, I drew the towel around me so that the oil should penetrate my skin, then let Annie dry my hair, leaving it free to fall about my shoulders. In the light from the lamp my skin would glow and, truly naked as my lord insisted, I should not hide my gender from him. Annie wanted to rouge my nipples and colour my face, but gauging his condition I thought not to do so. She gave me the black silk shawl and, draping it about me, I tiptoed over the cold flags, into the kitchen that was always warm and up the stairs to bed.

I knocked gently and Decimus bade me enter. Taking off my shawl, I opened the door. He was waiting for me, the lamp at his side just lit, a thin feather of smoke rising from the flame.

'Lock the door, Mary.'

My heart sang. His voice was strong and commanding.

By the side of his bed, where he could see me, I knelt, prostrating myself. His fingers found my hair, and he raised my head until my face was level with his. He nodded, satisfied with my obeisance.

'Stand up now, Mary, and let me look at you. Soon you will have work to do, my dear.'

His hand reached out, warm on the coolness of my skin.

'You are cold, Mary. Come to bed and warm yourself for a while.'

Lying next to him, the familiar odour of his body intoxicated me. To think that once I had been afraid because he had taken my scent. He told me to kiss him and raising myself I leaned over him, careful not to touch his poor wounded chest.

'Fold back the counterpane, Mary.'

I did as he said. Below his bandages he was naked too.

'Let me feel your kisses, my darling.'

Seeing his need, a little cautiously, I kissed him. Then as he instructed me, as I had never done before, I kissed him again. He sighed, his strength hidden from all but my lips. I could scarce catch my breath for the joy of it and, except for his love that filled me, my being was reduced to emptiness. Though he had left me no secrets, his fingers explored me, as if to check I had not changed. Then when he was ready, with both his hands, firmly he held my face, telling me to be still. Drowning in his love, I did not move as his strength flowed into me.

When he had released me from my duties I made him comfortable and doused the light. I climbed into bed beside my husband and lay there, listening to him sleep. Looking up into the blackness of the night, I wondered where he had learned to love, but was grateful to her, wherever she was now, for it truly did not matter to me that he had loved before.

CHAPTER XVI

The Highway

I woke with a start. Through a crack in the curtain dull light filtered into the room. Decimus still slumbered, his breathing laboured, as though even in sleep his poor body hurt him. Both hands on the clock pointed to four. By the time this day was out both my love and I would find out if my will, given to him so many years ago, really had become a mirror of his. Trying not to disturb him, I slid from his bed. Still naked from his loving, I shivered, shocked as my bare feet touched the cold linoleum. Washing my face in the bowl, the water too struck cold and all trace of sleep left me. I picked up my clothes that I had left on the chair and tiptoed to the door. Lest he should see my weakness, it would be better if my husband were not disturbed.

He was laughing. He had been watching me for some time.

'Draw back the curtains, Mary, so I can look at you.'

Dropping my clothes, I hurried to do as he asked, yet wished he still slept. The dawn invaded the room.

'You are a fine-looking wench, Mary.'

Did he flatter or mock me? I was not sure. It was pointless now to creep away and, making no effort to cover myself, I let him watch me dress. His eyes followed my every movement and to match his light-hearted mood I flirted with him just a little. But I could not manage it. How desperately I needed him. Half-clothed, I ran to my lord, falling to my knees at the side of the bed. What I most dreaded had happened. He had seen my cowardice. Instantly, though, he pulled me to him, kissing me.

'Come back to me safely, Mary. I shall not sleep again until you are home, my darling.'

I closed my eyes, feeling the touch of his hands. He understood my fear, but did not try to dissuade me from going. I felt secure in the warmth of his love and would not forget this precious moment.

'Bring something back that will remind me of your courage,' he said.

I did not feel brave. The cockerel was crowing from his vantage point. Sounds of activity came from the yard. Thomas and Harry were waiting for me and I could delay no longer.

Downstairs, in the warmth of the kitchen, I finished my dressing and drank the cup of tea that was left in the pot. It was too early for breakfast. I tied my bonnet and pulling my shawl tightly around me I opened the scullery door. The door to the yard stood ajar, letting in the cool early morning air. I shivered, but set square my shoulders and went out to greet my sons.

Clouds raced overhead. The sun had not yet escaped the Cotswold escarpment yet even when it rose, I doubted we should enjoy its warmth today. Perry stood, stamping his feet, harnessed between the shafts of the heavy cart. When he saw me, he tossed his head, impatient to be moving off. Harry was fixing down a tarpaulin to protect the load, while a wind gusted up the channel, trying to pull it from his fingers. He looked at me from under his eyebrows, his eyes wary. He did not want me to go. I tried to reassure him.

'Harry dear, your father would not let me leave if he considered the journey too hazardous. Save your worries and help Thomas all you can.'

I kissed my dear sweet son. He was so like Decimus. Maybe he understood better than I supposed the battle I had had with his father. Harry helped me put on oilskins but could not suppress his smile. They were far too large and smelt of linseed, not very pleasant, but the skins would keep me warm and dry. As he helped me on to the carter's seat, Thomas, his responsibilities weighing heavily on him, joined Harry to wave goodbye. The house still slumbered, but looking up I saw a small solemn face peering down at me. With my fingers to my lips, I blew my youngest child a kiss. Richard's face lit up and with his hands pressed to his mouth, excitedly he returned my greeting. Gathering the reins, I set Perry for the open road, my little boy waving after me, until at the bend in the lane he was hidden from my sight.

Perry was in a hurry and I had to restrain him. He could not know how far he must haul his load. Within my grasp was a long black leather whip. How cruel it was. I shuddered, yet there was no doubting I should use it if I must. All the while I was with him, though, dear Perry's broad back would not feel its sting. Leaving the village, we followed the road that would take us over Woolfords Common. Mostly flat, with the cart, it was an easier route to Milbury than the way we usually went. Farther inland, the warm wind that had blown up the Estuary was soon gone. Mist covered the empty fields and clouds that had threatened when first we left home were as one thick, low grey blanket, deadening all sound. In the stillness, alone in a world seeming devoid of life, with only the horse for company, I had to acknowledge the enormity of the task I must complete. When Perry's hooves clattered over the cobblestones, the good folk of Milbury were still abed. As we rattled over the Plain, a breeze blew the cobwebs away and, rounding the corner, I saw the High Street, deserted. Usually there were several horses waiting to drink at the trough that was set beside the pavement, but this morning we were far too early and there were none. Only the statues, painted white and set above the porches to the inns, seemed to live. Like ghosts in a sleeping world, a lion padding across some imaginary desert stalked an outsize swan that glided opposite him.

Leaving town, at the end of the incline, I saw smoke from a locomotive billowing above the railway station. Someone else had risen early too. I wondered if a time might come when the new train would take our catch to market. It had begun to rain and, turning round, I rummaged under the tarpaulin to find

Decimus's sou'wester. When I pulled it on it was so big it fitted over my bonnet. Fastening my collar tight up under it, I was prepared for the weather. Steam rose from Perry's wet back and water in tiny, silent streams ran down my oilskins, making puddles in my lap. As we approached the bends that preceded the long tortuous hill we must climb to reach Veston, the macadamed road became muddy. In the rain, what a long way it seemed to the Ship Inn where Perry could rest for a while. He splashed through the puddles, where unseen potholes, obscured by the wet, sent the cart lurching as the wheels made contact with the uneven surface. All too soon, rain found its way down my neck. Along the road's broad verge, droplets of water, like shimmering beads, clung to the grass. On the skyline ahead of us trees were lost in grey and endless cloud. The mist swirled now, as in the breeze, it blew down off the fields still warm from yesterday's sun. But I was not deterred and my spirits lifted as the smell of the warm, living earth told me this was God's land and, even without the sun's glow, there was no mistaking the beauty of the morning.

In a silent world, we started to climb the dreaded hill. Calling Perry to a halt, I held my skirts over my arm and stepped down on to the rain-soaked highway. Perry had weight enough to draw without mine. I thanked God that only the surface was wet, for being early in the day the stony road, though rutted, was still passable. Perry pricked his ears as I caught hold of his reins and held him. I blew gently up his nose as Decimus had taught me, and Perry rolled his eyes, showing me their whites, and snorted. Together we took up the load and walked on. Merciless rain beat down on us and I could scarcely look up for the torrent that ran into my face. My breath came in gasps and the stitch in my side would not go away. Perry, straining in a cloud of steam, battled his way over the slippery stones. Still there was no let up from the endless sheets of driving rain. Though I feared the cart would be bogged down, Perry was sure-footed on the treacherous ground. A carter hailed us as he passed, going in the opposite direction. His team, slipping in the slurry, panicked and I feared they would fall, yet, even so, the whip found their backs. His poor beasts would never escape the penance of their imprisoning shafts. Holding Perry's head, I whispered words of encouragement to him until, both of us exhausted, we had reached the brow of the hill. It was not by chance that the Inn had stood where it had for centuries. Dragging myself on to the cart again, I urged Perry towards the sanctuary of its welcoming yard.

An ostler came out, touching his cap.

'Well I'm blessed, Mistress, 'tis you. Fer moment thought 'twere a lad. Where's Master, then?'

Having explained my circumstances, I left Perry and the cart with him.

'Don'ee worry, Missus, I'll take good care of 'orse for 'ee. Thou'st better get them wet things off afore 'ee catch yer death o' cold. This 'un 'll not come to no 'arm with I.'

Opening the door to the Inn, I was met by the smell of woodsmoke and old tobacco. The walls were painted in yellow ochre. A banked up fire burned slowly; its smoke, wafting from beneath the chimneypiece, settled on the ceiling. I hung my oilskins on a hook as a pretty girl came forward and without self-consciousness dropped me a curtsy, bidding me follow her. She led me along several passages until the flagstones gave way to warm red rugs, and a smell of cabbage conquered the all-pervading aroma of woodsmoke. Having taken my shawl, she came back bringing a towel, with soap and a bowl of warm water. I took off my bonnet and gratefully washed off the dirt of the road while she waited. The hem of my gown was caked with mud, but otherwise the shawl had absorbed the water that trickled down my neck and the oilskins had mostly protected me. Smoothing my hair, I followed the girl into the breakfast room. I was hungry and the bacon smelled so inviting that for a moment I did not notice the eyes that stared at me, a woman alone. A little confused, I asked whether I might sit by a window in the corner where I could watch the rain and Perry did not seem so far away. Outside, a coach was preparing to leave, the coachman blowing his horn. The noise around me gradually ceased as the passengers got up and left. Looking round, I saw I was alone, save for two men engrossed in conversation on the far side of the room.

The bacon stopped short of my mouth. In shock, I gaped at them. One had mentioned my name. 'Mary Cheyne' was all I heard. But then again I caught my maiden name. Shrinking into the shadow, my cheeks burned like fire. What if they saw me; might not they guess who I was? I longed to be out of this place, but was curious too and questioned the maid when she took away my plate.

'Who are those gentlemen on the far side of the room? Should I know either of them?'

'All I can tell you, Mistress, is that one of them is Squire Thwaite.'

I could not swallow; nor could I breathe. My heart thudded against my chest. Now I was told, there was no doubting which of the gentlemen was my father's son. My darling Harry bore a striking resemblance to my legitimate half-brother. Holding my hands tightly together to stop them from trembling, I hid them under the tablecloth. All I knew of him was that my husband held him in contempt. He had left the village many years previously to live in Jamaica, deserting his wife and children. Now he was back.

The other man was speaking. The coach rumbled out of the yard in the quiet that ensued and I could hear every word he said.

'You know, he's let her out now. That arrogant bastard Decimus Hillyer thinks he's safe. Make a fine pair, I should say. She put her spell on him good and proper. Thinks he's beaten the Devil in her; well, we shall see.'

Squire Thwaite leaned back in his chair, his heavy watch chain straining across an ample stomach. His greasy black hair, thinning on top, curled about his collar that was almost hidden by his thick-set jowls. What a horrible man. Harry must not grow into that. Squire Thwaite sat forward with a jerk, his face contorted in anger.

'I swear I won't rest 'til I've despatched that witch as I despatched her wretched mother before her. The old fool of a father of mine: he was besotted with the whore. Now his bastard sits up there at Thorn End Farm as though butter wouldn't melt in her mouth. But I tell you, Desmond, here and now, I'll drive her out just like the rest of her ilk have been driven out of these parts.'

Oh dear God, when will it end? The other man was speaking now and I had to listen.

'They say, Squire, that she put her spell on young Gabriel Meredith. By all accounts he should be dead. Bull gored him real bad, but she sewed him up, you know. My man told me, the boy was close to death when she said peculiar words over his body, then he came to.'

No, no, it was not like that. How could he tell such awful untruths? I was mortified and prayed they would not look at me. His mouthful of toast not impeding his words, the Squire was speaking again.

'How interesting, Desmond. Pity I wasn't here when it happened. Maybe the poor fellow will snuff it yet. We can say she killed him. I hear Hillyer can't leave his bed. Maybe his indisposition will provide me the opportunity to put an end to her trouble-mongering once and for all.'

The appalling voice of my half-brother droned on.

'I had a letter from my wife on my return to Bristol. The witch's eldest whelp is to get Cloudsmoor Farm when he reaches his majority. What do you make of that, Desmond? The old bugger left it to her deliberately. He knew it should have come to me. God damn it, he was born there, did you know that? Christ, it makes her whelp look more legitimate than I. I'll never forgive my father for it. A curse on his Godamned memory.'

He looked up. As though he had only just noticed me, he rose from his table and approached. With a flourish, he bowed.

'Madam, pray forgive me, for I had not seen you. My language is perhaps a trifle colourful for such a delicate flower as you, but I am recently returned from the Indies and forget my manners.'

He did not know who I was, thank God. Lowering my eyes, I nodded. A man so long in the company of foreigners would not expect more. I could not have spoken to him anyway for I

170

was numb with shock. As he and the other man left, I wondered in which direction they were going and hoped I would not see them again.

Though the sky had lightened, rain still ran down the window. Looking up I could see the clouds had broken a little, tiny patches of blue separating them. There would be plenty of time on my long journey to dwell on the conversation I had overheard. Gabriel Meredith would not die, of that I was sure. Even if God alone knew what I had done, He would not deliver me into the hands of my evil half-brother. I had no doubt that God's mills ground slowly but they would grind exceeding fine and Squire Thwaite would on Judgement Day stand God fearing, at the Gates of Heaven.

My shawl harboured a slight smell of cabbage but had dried. As I left the Inn, with my oilskins draped over my arm, the rain had stopped. Carefully I avoided the puddles that covered the yard and found the stall where Perry was housed. Softly, I called to him and he raised his head, the hanging bundle of hay for a moment forgotten. He came to me and his soft warm muzzle found my neck, his teeth gently nibbling at my shawl. A voice from behind me spoke.

'If you be ready, Missus, I'll 'arness 'im up for 'ee. What a strange one 'e be, b'aint you, me 'andsome.'

Waiting for Perry, the fat supercilious face of my half-brother hovered like a mirage, blotting out my senses. If only it would go away. He knew nothing about me, yet he loathed me.

We had travelled some way and still I scanned the road ahead, praying I should not see that face again. While with one hand I held the reins, the knuckles of my other gleamed white and my nails dug into my palm. I opened my fist; an object lay there. It was just an ordinary little button. I had picked it up from the table where my half-brother had been sitting. It had popped from his waistcoat and, not heeding its loss, he had left without it. Bringing it to my nose, could I smell his sweat? Closing my hand over it again, I began to weep and listening to Perry's sure feet beat their rhythm on the hard stony road, as self-pity over-came me, I could not ignore what his hooves seemed to say.

'Please God, let him die. Please God, *make* him die.'

Suddenly Perry shied. His feathered feet danced. I had to hold him or he would have bolted. Whatever had upset him so? Through my tears, I saw standing by the side of the road an aged man. He stooped, his face almost hidden from me by the hood of the cloak he wore. Pulling up, innocently I felt it to be Jesse. In my distress, he had come to console me. Without a word, taking hold of the outstretched hand I helped him up, moving over for him. As he climbed on to the carter's seat beside me, the cart dipped gently, the springs hardly noticing his weight. He held my hand, his presence calming me, and I was glad of his company.

The hand that held mine was almost covered by the cloak he wore. Though he did not release me, I did not mind. Through my tears, I could not see the webbing of his fingers, or the thick horn of his nails, but glancing into the saintly face I was surprised and drew back. The face was longer than I remembered. For a second, did I see fire glowing behind those tired, bloodshot eyes? Unlike Jesse, he did not look benevolently on me. In the strengthening breeze, a gust of wind pulled at his hood, revealing his face and the outline of his head. I caught my breath; he had more the head of a goat than a man.

'Who are you, Sir? I cannot believe you are Jesse.'

'Sweet lady, I could be Jesse if that is your wish, for once I knew Jesse well. But he preferred the narrow way, so I parted company with him.'

'You try to deceive me, Sir. You are no more than a humble tramp. I would not have left you, old and weary, alone on the highway.'

'Mary.'

He said my name and I shivered, for how could he possibly know me?

'Do not fear me, my dear. Let me share your troubles.'

I tore my hand from his.

'Do not seek to reject me, Mary. You must listen to me, my

172

dear, for I understand you. I am a part of you. I have many daughters and your mother was one of them. Come back to me now, my angel, and let me protect you. Do not doubt that I, and not Decimus, am your true master.'

'No, Sir, you are wrong. Before God, my husband is my only master and I can serve no other.'

'But, Mary, did you not call out to me? I heard you praying in your anguish. In your heart, you know that only I can help you. Surely you recognise me, my dear?'

Desperately I looked all around, but there was no one to call on. Perry, his ears laid back, still trod the road, albeit more slowly. My eyes could not avoid the fiendish face and my body shook uncontrollably.

'Sir, you play games. I do not understand any of what you say.'

'Sweet lady, of course you do; I would not have come had you not willed it. The half-brother who detests you is well known to me. You must fight fire with fire, my little one. You will not destroy him without my help.'

I bit my lip, my teeth drawing blood.

'I think I know you after all, for you, Sir, are Satan himself. Get thee away from me. Please, I beg of you, do not beguile me, for I have lain in the Garden of Eden with my beloved lord and need no other discipline but his.'

'Sweet Mary, you cannot avoid me. I have come for you. Only I can set free your Soul that your husband dares to imprison. You will walk with me into the Fires of Hell to enjoy their warmth, just as I do. I have witnessed your obedience and sacrifice to Decimus and you have served him well, but I will not spare you pain as he spares you pain. With me you will find such a paradise as you could never have conceived. Your body will dance for ever to the song of my willow and you will burn unto all eternity. You will learn to obey me and, I promise you, whatever task I give you will be a joy to you. In time, you will come to love me, too.'

'No, never. You robbed me of my child. Oh dear God, what have I done that I am so alone?'

173

With my arms encircling my knees, I tried to protect myself. In despair, averting my eyes, I prayed to Almighty God.

'Dear God, help me close my ears to this obscenity. I will pay any penance you ask of me, but please, I beg of you, do not abandon me.'

'You try to be rid of me, Mary? He does not hear you. In your innermost being, you know you need me. Do not hesitate, my dear. Put your hand back into mine and say you will belong to me for ever, my darling.'

Staring down at his webbed fingers, watching them undo my gown, I could not move. Pulling the silk away from my breasts, he lay his hoof on my nakedness.

'Oh please, Sir. No, do not touch me!'

He smelt of rot. A filthy horned hand gripped me, holding me still as his eyes bored into my very being. In my palm, the button burned like fire and as I let go of it it fell at his feet.

'And what were you going to do with that, my dear? Put a spell on your half-brother?'

Laughing, he kicked the button away and I saw his foot was cloven. He touched my nipples that stood proud for him, as if they enjoyed his assault. I swooned. Consciousness almost left me.

'Sleep now, my angel. Though you are barren, the seed of my loins will reawaken your body as it awakened your mother's before you. When I have fertilised you, Mary, you will not belong to Decimus again.'

His foul-smelling breath made me vomit. The shroud-like cloak fell back, revealing a disembodied head. I pushed at the shroud and it fell empty about me, stifling me. Ivory horns butted my cheek, scoring my face. His disgusting spittle ran down my neck. I could fight him no more. His infernal strength was bending me backwards. I could do nothing to help myself and, blinded, felt my skirts pulled over my head. Silently, I prayed to Almighty God to save me.

Then in my passion, as if in a vision, my beloved Decimus stood over me, the true Jesse at his side. In his hand Jesse held a stave and as I watched he drove it deep into the evil head. In an instant the shroud took form and became a snake. Its coldness slithered over me and fell on to the verge. On its belly, the snake slid away and disappeared into the long grass.

Rain fell silently from the heavens, but I was oblivious to it. Perry's hooves rang on the stones. Very soon the place where the snake had gone was lost to my sight. To cover my nakedness, with shaking hands I snatched at my bodice. What did it matter if I were wet? In a daze, I pulled the oilskin over my head and put the sou'wester back on. Gripping my legs tight together and wrapping my skirts around me, I tried to comfort my ravished self. All the while the burn in my hand reminded me of my ordeal.

I asked of God, what had I done? But I knew what I had done. I had abused His name and called on Him to destroy my half-brother. In my wicked heart, I had wished him dead and prayed now that God would purge my blasphemy. I could not fight Squire Thwaite with Satan's fire, for, should I do so, Satan would surely consume me.

I thought of my poor disgraced mother. Was she truly a daughter of that vile and incestuous creature who had waylaid me? If, as Satan said, he had inseminated her and I was the progeny of his seed, then truly I was damned and without hope.

But what of Jesse? He had always been at my side whenever my soul was in danger. Had he not held my hand when Satan took my child and I was near to death? Had he not, just minutes ago, driven off the evil presence? Had he not given me to my beloved Decimus, knowing me to be my mother's daughter and knowing, too, that only my lord had the will and the fortitude to love me?

A voice deep inside me would not be stilled.

'Satan lies,' said the voice. 'Satan has always lied. What more is a lie than the dark side to the coin of truth?'

My heart sang out loud and screamed – Yes!

But my head would not listen to my heart. I prayed anew that God would guide Decimus's hand when he exacted of me the penance I had promised in my anguish.

As Perry followed the Ridgeway and we came under the lee

of the hill at Almsbury, away to the west, blue sky had banished the grey gloom of the land. Far across the valley, miles away, the Great River met the full waters of the Estuary. The sun's rays bathed them, its light reflected on the shining silver sea. The trees whispered their gratitude as the breeze picked up and became a wind that blew the clouds away.

The air from the distant sea immersed me in its gentle warmth, cleansing my lungs and body of the stench that clung to me. I wondered whether my mother had looked from this ridge with her mind in torment, fighting for her sanity.

Why should I know that Lydia would one day stand here and look towards the distant Estuary? She would be alone, lost in her torment and in the twilight of her years. Dragging my eyes away from the valley, I reached for the reins and, my sobbing unhindered, desperately clinging to reality, I urged on the strong skewbald horse who lengthened his stride.

Looking behind me, I was reminded of the task I had set out to accomplish and checked the cart. Once before, when I had faltered, my husband had asked of me, 'Where is your courage, my darling?'

Now, aloud I answered him.

'Lord, I will not give up.'

I would love my husband for ever and from the depths of my heart, thanked God I belonged to Decimus.

CHAPTER XVII

The Confession

Ahead lay a flat and desolate scene. The road wound its way south through miles and miles of scrub, where docks and nettles grew among the bracken. Small stunted trees and yellow gorse barely rebutted the wind as it swept across the untilled soil. Decimus called this place Gypsy Patch, because Romanies and Irish tinkers, too, camped alongside the road. Here they were safe from harrying, for there were few farmers like my own dear husband who would welcome gypsies on their land. All the people who made this inhospitable place their home were outcasts, and wayfarers hesitated to travel this way alone. But with Perry as my guide, why should I fear them, for was I not a Romany and an outcast?

It was eleven o'clock before we reached the Horfield barracks. Behind high iron railings I could see a splash of colour. Soldiers paraded; how young they looked with their fresh and beardless faces. Their mothers must have wept to see them go, for a soldier's life was short. Looking across the fields, I saw the city spread out before us in a wide shallow basin. On the horizon, like a low grey cloud, brooded the distant Mendip Hills. Before we went on, I let Perry drink. The Gloucester Road was downhill all the way from here and I felt a tingle of excitement as we left the fields behind us. The road had become busier and Perry sensed my impatience, for we must hold back, our pace dictated by others. Small boys ran beside us.

'Give us a lift, Missus,' they yelled.

Shooing them off, I found myself laughing. Whatever my fears, I must put them aside. I thought of Decimus, my love, lying strapped and helpless in his bed. I would not let him down. Once we had passed the Horsefair and St John's church in the City Wall, our progress up to the Cross was very slow. There was a commotion ahead. A horse had died between the shafts and lay prostrate. We had to wait for men to put a rope around its legs before they dragged it away. What a poor, puny creature it looked and how heavy its load of coal.

By the time I had guided Perry down the High Street and past St Nicholas's church, it was almost one o'clock when we arrived at Bigwoods. Charlie, the man Decimus had told me to seek out, was surprised to see me on my own. Though he was probably as honest as the next man, I waited until he had unloaded the cart and weighed the salmon. Everything tallied with Thomas's list. I did not like to leave Perry between the shafts, but he had to rest and seemed content enough with his head in a nosebag. Charlie promised faithfully he would look after him, so I left Perry there.

First tying my bonnet, I straightened my gown, hoping the mud would not show too much, then pulled on my gloves. Alas, the years of servitude had taken their toll. Though I rubbed in snowfire every night, my hands were rough and I could not pretend they were those of a lady. How shy and out of place I suddenly felt in the city. I did not belong here, but holding high my head and gritting my teeth I thought of my love and chided myself for my shortcomings.

From where I had left Perry, steep steps worn away by count- less feet led up to the flower market. I doubted I should see Rosie again, but there were several women like her. Between the flower stalls I noticed a young and pretty girl with an open face. She was about to accost a man. Foolishly I approached her, for how could she know the perils her life would bring? Before I could speak, she pushed her face into mine.

'Get off my pitch,' she spat.

The venom in her voice belied her prettiness and I could not draw breath to warn her. My husband's bleak and cruel words came flooding back to me; how naïve, to think that I could influence her. Leaving the market behind me, I crossed the High Street. A sign on the wall said Narrow Wine Street. A row of shops on either side enticed me, each vying for my custom, their windows brimming full of merchandise. Perhaps shopping might take my mind off the journey home and for a moment let me forget my worries. There were two big stores next to each other, Baker Baker and Jones. Which one should I choose?

The step was wide, tiled in tiny squares of black and white. The panelled door of painted glass yielded to my touch, closing noiselessly behind me. In the centre of the mat, stencilled in black in copperplate writing, was the name 'Jones'. How strange it felt to be here without Decimus. In my country clothes I must look odd to these townsfolk. How noisy the store was; perhaps it would be quieter upstairs.

At the top of the first flight of stairs, on a shelf, sitting all in a row, rag dolls fell against one another. One caught my eye. He was all of three feet high, his arms and legs gangling. He had a pigtail and a proper sailor's suit. How my little boy would love him, but Decimus would not approve, for Richard would be nine years old in October and his father considered him sensitive for his age. Dolls with white waxen faces stared at me with unseeing bright blue eyes. If only Lydia were just a little younger too.

She was nearly twelve years old and soon would reach maiden-hood. In just a few years from now Decimus must seek a husband for Lydia. There was nothing I could do to help my daughter and I wondered when Decimus would let me see her again. Yet daring not to dwell on her, panic threatening to overwhelm me and my composure very nearly lost, I dragged my thoughts away.

Up and up the stairs I trudged, until on the topmost floor I found a powder room where in privacy I could wash, at last ridding my hands of the stench that still clung to them. On the same floor was a tea-room. Maids in starched white pinafores and caps hurried in and out. In a corner an elderly lady played a piano. From the table I was given, through a wide window I looked down over the chimney pots to the River Avon far below. I sat and stared, unseeing, at the barges drifting silently by. A pot of tea and thin bread and butter were placed in front of me. But I was not really interested in food. My heart called out to my love.

'Decimus.'

It was only in my dreams that I had the courage to call him by his name.

'Decimus, my love, pray that God will guide me and let me return to you safe this night.'

Almost aloud I sobbed. I was so full of conflict, how could I sit here? I longed to be home, but dreaded the journey. This was the real world; had my tormentor been but a fantasy? Could I have imagined Lydia, an old woman, standing on the ridge and looking towards the distant Estuary, despair in her heart? The burn in my hand throbbed.

'Dear God, do not let Satan come for Lydia as he came for me.'

Through tear-filled eyes I surveyed the room, but no one noticed my distress. When I left the table, I determined to buy a present for the child who would always be my babe. Richard should have the little monkey on a stick that ran up and down as you pulled its chain. From my purse I took out two silver threepenny bits and handed them to the assistant. She put the monkey in a box that she tied with yellow string, leaving a little loop for me to carry it by. Forlorn eyes followed me, for I had left him on the shelf. Why had the sailor captured my heart? Before leaving the store, I bought ribbons for Lydia's hair and a stiff silk swathe of deepest heliotrope to decorate my hat.

Suddenly shopping had palled for me. My head ached and I felt so alone, jostled by strangers, hating this noisy and raucous world. A clock above the door pointed to a quarter past three. Gathering my purchases, I retraced my steps.

Walking towards the Bristol Bridge, I came upon a lane I had not noticed before. It ran steeply down to the river. Here the din was left behind. I doubted if anyone, other than lovers, came this way. At intervals were seats where for a little while I could sit in peace and watch the barges unload. My dear love was near me. Closing my eyes, I spread my hand on the seat beside me. There was nothing there, yet I felt his touch. As the hour approached when I must make the long journey home, terror threatened me again. Might Satan be lying in wait for me once more? I prayed that God would watch over me.

As, in unison, the City's church bells chimed four times, I judged Perry would be rested enough. He had heard me coming and whinnied a greeting. Pushing his soft warm nose into my face, he blew rolled oats down my neck. The deadening spell was broken and, in spite of my foreboding, my spirits rose. A bag heavy with gold sovereigns was put into my hand. At last we were going home. High under the springs Decimus had made a secret compartment to hide the bag away. No one would find it there. Homeward bound, Perry hardly needed encouragement and once away from the cobbles he chose his own pace. When the road twisted, I had to shield my eyes from the setting sun, but mostly we headed north.

Perry's hooves broke the silence. Smoke from many small fires hung on the evening air. Since he had shown me a new life I had come this way with Decimus on numerous occasions. Though I was on my own now, with Perry for company I did not feel threatened as we crossed the Gypsy Patch. Suddenly and without warning, a window in my memory that I had imagined closed for ever opened, and I recalled the first time that I had passed this way. I remembered my excitement at being free, and how impatient I had been to confront my destiny. At the Inn in Milbury, not really by chance I had met Jesse. From that day, whenever I felt I could not go on, he was always there to support me.

As we approached the Almsbury Ridge the sun was finally lost, setting behind the Welsh hills on the far side of the Estuary. Now all about us was dusk, the land lit only by pale yellow clouds, that even as I watched turned to grey. In the shadows, where the light had already faded, was blackness. As I urged him on, Perry seemed to understand, for neither of us would be at peace until we left this open and unprotected ridge. The welcoming lights of the Inn at Veston beckoned us and we rested there awhile. Perry drank his fill of the pure, sweet, country water. When we set off again, the very air we breathed had changed. A cool westerly breeze tugged at my hair that escaped my bonnet but I pulled my shawl closer around me and did not feel cold. I belonged in this land, for the woman who strayed from here was not really me but some impostor who wore my clothes. I had no doubt that, with Decimus beside me, not even my monstrous half-brother could deny me my birthright. A sliver of moon barely lit the way, but Perry did not need a moon to guide him and he brought me safely home. The village slept, but Thorn End Farm was still awake. They heard us coming. Thomas and Harry, with hurricane lamps held high, waited to greet me. Holding my precious sons one by one, I felt my heart would nearly burst with love for them.

From out of its secret hiding place I retrieved the bag of sovereigns, leaving Thomas and Harry to see to Perry. In trepidation though, my stomach fluttered as I ascended the stairs, suddenly fearing what I must tell my husband. The truth must not be kept from him. I dreaded the confession I must make, for now that moment had come upon me.

Decimus, propped up on pillows, looked much as I had left him. He sat waiting for me within the bright arc of the lamp. He did not greet me. My feet seemed to drag as slowly, not meeting his eyes, I approached the bed. Kneeling at his side, I bent my head and without looking up placed the bag of sovereigns in front of him. They spilled out, cascading over the counterpane. He ignored the coins.

'Turn your hands over, Mary, so I can see your palms.'

He knew! Taking my left hand, he traced the outline of the small round burn, which was raised and sore.

I looked up, meeting his gaze that was hard and critical.

'So, I have not dreamed it after all, Mary,' he said.

Tears welled as his unsmiling face swam before me. In blinding fear, the achievements of my day as nothing to me now, I wept.

'How can you forgive me, lord. I called on Satan's evil power.

He touched me! If you touch me, like pitch, you too will be defiled.'

In despair, my voice faded completely and only my lips moved.

'You asked me to bring home something to remind you of my courage, yet I bring you nothing but disgrace, lord.'

He still held my hand. As he put it to his lips, I felt the wetness of his cheek. He had heard my confession and seen my wretchedness, yet still said nothing.

My eyes averted, I begged him, 'Pray that God will guide your hand, lord, when you exact the penance that is the price of my deliverance from evil.'

His fingers were under my chin and with a jerk he made me look up at him. Tears coursed down his face. He did not seem to care that I see him weep. His voice was harsh and brittle.

'May God forgive me, Mary. I would not have let you go alone had I known before you set out the agony you would suffer this day. It is I, not you, who should pay penance.'

For a moment he turned his rough unshaven face away from me and wiped his tears on his sleeve. He was so weak, how could I take his hurt from him?

From between clenched teeth, he continued, 'I was told that debauched half-brother of yours had returned to the Vale and I should have warned you. My God, Mary, you have no need to prove your courage to me. You have achieved everything I asked of you and more besides. Now get off your knees and come to bed.'

Loosening my hair, he draped it about my shoulders. Gently I kissed him. He had not rejected me. Caring not for my exhaustion, though I ached from fatigue, I washed my body all over, cleansing it of the city grime. Pushing my nightgown under the pillow, my husband beckoned me. Still naked, careful not to hurt him, I slipped into bed beside my lord, and let his loving warmth surround me. He put out the light and in the darkness spoke to me again.

'The experiment is over, Mary. Though I shall not use force to shut you away, to protect you I cannot let you out on your own again. Tell me you do not mind, my dear.'

'Lord, as always I am content with whatever is your wish. You know I am happy at home, but had you wanted me to undertake the journey again I would gladly have done so.'

'No, Mary, you will not venture far without me. Those days are over.'

He squeezed my hand. The subject was closed, the freedom he had allowed me, withdrawn. As if in a deep warm pit, safe in my lord's protection, I fell asleep.

Mary Cheyne Hillyer,
1880.

CHAPTER XVIII

Cousins

Decimus's injuries have been slow to heal. In front of my eyes Thomas has grown in stature and become a man. Though he is just twenty years old, his quiet authority will not be denied. I feel in my heart he will not easily defer to his father's will, once Decimus is up and about again.

In nearly six months Decimus has not allowed me to leave the sanctuary of home and my fears for my half-brother's intentions have gradually receded. The conversation I overheard at the Inn is remembered as though it were a dream that had not really happened. Now it is late in October, the evenings have drawn in and the cold damp of winter is ahead of us. Decimus, though weak, has left his bed. He has told me our eldest son shall not wait until he reaches his majority before inheriting Cloudsmoor Farm, but intends Thomas to take it over as soon as the Christmas festivities have ended. I am hardly surprised my husband has foreseen that two masters under one roof will be intolerable. This morning I have to supervise the making ready of Thomas's inheritance and Decimus has ordered Annie to accompany me.

Stepping over the threshold with Annie, I contemplated that this might be the very last time I should come here before Decimus gave Thomas the old house. But not for one moment did I imagine that within only a few days Thomas would take possession of the farm. The cold stone floor beneath my feet had warmed to the love my dear lord and I had shared when in those secret hours away from prying eyes he had brought me here. Just to think of it was enough to make my head spin.

I tried to picture my father. What sort of man could he have been, to have given this house to me, his bastard, hoping that my son, though not his legitimate heir, would inherit the place where he himself was born? Though Decimus had assured me on countless occasions that there was nothing my half-brother could do to reverse his father's calculated slur, none the less, as Annie and I inspected each room, I thought of Squire Thwaite and a small stab of fear pierced my heart. Dreaming a little, I did not notice the door behind me had quietly opened. Startled, I looked up. Standing in the doorway with the sun behind him, for a second, I saw my beloved Decimus. But the figure that took the light was slighter.

Annie hovered behind me.

'Sit down, Annie dear. Your poor legs will not suffer for the rest.'

Loyal Annie had not managed a single intelligible word in all the years she had served me. She adored her master, as a spaniel would that had been beaten and craved forgiveness of whatever sin it had committed. Sometimes I was bemused when by her gestures she implied that maybe we were both servants of the same master and I was not really her mistress at all. It was hard to deny the truth. Because I was my husband's possession, Annie would care for me until my dying day. But she was a dear friend too and it did not occur to me to dismiss her now.

The figure I had mistaken for his father was Thomas.

'You startled me, my darling. Has your father spoken to you already of his wishes?'

Thomas looked surprised.

'No, Mother, I followed you here, for I have something I just have to tell you.'

Thomas could not hide his excitement.

'I cannot bear to wait, not even for one more day, Mother, before you know.'

'My darling, whatever can it be that you have to seek me

here? You know, Thomas, that I keep nothing from your father and must caution that your secret, if it be such, will not be safe with me.'

'I do not harbour a secret, Mother. I wish merely for your advice. You know as well as I that Father can be a most difficult man.'

Suddenly Thomas looked uncomfortable, not knowing what to say next. He shuffled his feet as though wishing he had not come.

'Oh Tom, you keep me waiting and I am on tenter-hooks hanging on your words.'

His countenance was so unhappy. Within the space of a moment, his confidence had waned. I caught his arm.

'Hush, my love, it cannot be that bad. We will decide together how best to tell your father. What ails you that is so terrible you have not the courage to stand before him?'

Drawing himself up, Thomas took a deep breath.

'Since they were at school together, Father and Squire have always hated one another. But I love Squire's daughter. Her name is Isobel. I warn you, Mother, I want her and will wed no other . . .'

The floor swayed as his words flowed over me. Holding tight to his arm, I feared I should faint.

'Oh Tom, you know nothing of the bitterness between your father and Squire Thwaite. Is there no one else you could love?'

As I spluttered forth the words, I regretted my foolishness.

'I cannot help you, my darling.'

His pleading eyes looked down on me, but I could not say more. How could he possibly understand the distress his news would cause?

'You know not what you ask of your mother, Thomas. Please go. Leave me now, for I can say nothing without your father's permission.'

That evening, once supper had been cleared away and the lamps were lit, Decimus summoned his family. He instructed me to present myself in the reception room that we used only on special occasions. With a dreadful sense of foreboding I smoothed down my gown and with an unsteady hand knocked on the door. Decimus bade me enter. I closed the door behind me; there was no escaping now. What an elegant room I had stepped into, not at all fitting for a farmhouse. Sitting uncomfortably in an ornate tasselled chair, Decimus faced me. Spinster Ella in the corner, busy with her crochet, glanced up, scarcely adjusting the rapid movement of her fingers. Thomas, with his back to me, sat opposite his father in an identical tasselled chair. He stared straight ahead, for he was apprehensive, as I was. A fire roared up the chimney, dispelling the musty air. Harry, on the piano stool, idly ran his fingers up and down the keys. He blew me a kiss, smiling his encouragement, as if he guessed my ordeal was about to begin. Decimus rose, one arm protecting his chest. The thick carpet muffled the sound of my shoes as I approached my lord. With his free hand he held me steady as I made my obeisance. For my ears only, he whispered.

'There is no shame accorded to you, my dear, in what I am about to tell my sons.'

He guided me to the chair he had vacated and nervously, for I was not usually permitted to sit while he stood, I sat down. With his back to the fire, not uttering a word, he looked in Harry's direction and Harry's fingers were stilled. Apart from the ticking of the grandmother clock in the alcove, there was no sound. Decimus, in spite of his disability, remained standing and addressed his eldest son.

'Thomas, your mother has told me that you wish to marry Isobel, Squire's daughter.'

Tom looked miserable. My lord did not wait for him to reply before he continued. Poor Tom, I wished with all my heart that this day had not come, but perhaps it had to eventually.

'It is incumbent on me to speak now of history that is buried and I hoped would not see light of day again. But, my son, that is not to be. I cannot allow you to present yourself to Jacob Thwaite without knowing the full truth.'

Decimus spared his sons nothing. He talked of Granny who was born the Hon. Mary FitzWarren, whose second marriage had been to Decimus's father, her dead husband's bailiff and a man socially her inferior. Granny's father, after giving her new husband land and fishing rights, had wiped his hands of her, abandoning her to her fate. Decimus told his sons how his grandfather, the late lord, had relented and given him, Granny's youngest child, Thorn End Farm, where he had brought me as a young woman with Thomas in my arms.

Decimus talked of his youth when he and Jacob Thwaite, the squire's son, had been at school together. Jacob had always hated Decimus. Because Decimus's father was of less than yeoman stock but his mother was high born, Decimus had not found a place within the rigid social pattern that sustained the village hierarchy. Consequently he had always been a threat to Jacob Thwaite's authority.

'Then, Thomas, when I was long past my twenty-fifth birthday, an old man brought your mother to me and my fate was sealed.'

Decimus stood behind my chair, placing his hand on my shoulder to steady himself.

'Your mother had inherited the old house we call Cloudsmoor Farm, its land and fishing rights. I pursued her, wanting to add her land to mine. For my sins, I married her for her money.'

Nothing moved. The eyes of my precious sons bore into my very soul. I thought, 'Oh Decimus, how could you?' and began to weep. Perhaps I should have known my husband had not loved me when he wed me, but I was blinded by my passion. I was so ashamed I could not look up, but Decimus had not finished his speech yet.

'Your mother was a spirited girl but innocent about worldly matters. I enjoyed the challenge and set out to take her spirit from her, binding her to me in servitude for the rest of her life.'

Decimus's voice broke as he remembered those early days, but he could not stop now. Reaching up, I covered his hand with mine, lest he forget I loved him. Through my tears I looked at Harry. His brows were knitted together and a look of loathing crossed his face as he watched his father.

'I took everything from your mother and gave her nothing in

exchange. Among the possessions I took from her was a hideous brooch. As soon as I saw it, I guessed who she was, though your mother had no idea of her identity. God knows, I was repaid for my selfishness and greed. I would not have wed your mother for a king's ransom had I known before I took my vows who she was.'

My heart screamed, alone in its silent anguish: 'Oh no, my love, do not say that. I have always loved you and always will, no matter how much you have taken from me.' Decimus's confession was relentless, for there was more to come.

'I have to tell you, Thomas, that your mother is the bastard of Jacob Thwaite's father, the old squire. Her mother was of the gypsy race. She was his whore. Her mother before her was whipped and drowned as a witch in a well on yonder side of the village.'

Was there no end to this? Sitting there in that handsome chair, my soul was naked.

'Your mother's legacy came from the old squire. He left Cloudsmoor Farm to her, his love child, slighting his legitimate son, Jacob. There are many hereabouts who say that my dear sweet wife has inherited the curse of her forebears, though I care not for their opinions.'

His hand, that rested in mine, shook and my heart went out to my love in his agony.

'The day your mother lay on her childbed with you, Thomas, she was younger than you are now. I feared for her life. After I had left her in Granny's care, I climbed the hill to church and prayed for her safe deliverance. Who my darling Mary was mattered not at all to me. Whatever torment was to come, I would never leave her, for I loved her then and love her now and unto all eternity.'

Decimus looked at his sons, staring each one out in turn.

'Not anyone, man nor God, nor the Devil himself, will come between us.'

Thomas, his face drawn and shocked, his eyes filling with tears, did not move. Ella, like a ghost, rose silently from her chair. With her hand on my arm, she bent and kissed me. Ella, that most frigid of women, who for years had rarely concealed her contempt for me, had no words, but in her action gave me the love she could not admit. Touching Harry's sleeve, she asked him to leave. Harry pulled away, shrugging her off, adrift in his own world. Glaring at his father as he passed him, Harry could not bring himself to look at me. I must give him time to come to terms with what he has learned.

I tried to stand, so that I could leave my husband alone with his eldest son, but Decimus held me down, his fingers like pincers digging into my flesh. His harsh words could not disguise his grief.

'Be still, Mary. You will go when I am ready.'

Thomas's eyes were empty, looking straight ahead at nothing. I could not bear to see him so distraught.

'My darling child, I am so sorry.'

Like a cold, wet fog, fear of my son's rejection descended on me.

'Please, Thomas, say something. Do not sit there with your thoughts miles away and your lips sealed so tight.'

I had not noticed before the nerve that twitched in his face. I tried again.

'I understand your pain, Tom, but beg of you, please look at me. I cannot help what I was born to, but your father can vouch that I have paid penance. You have learned from him the truth that we prayed you would never need to know.'

Thomas's eyes travelled slowly up and met mine.

'What do you expect me to say, Mother? Father has ripped my world to shreds. Now I know for certain the rumours I rebutted all my life and closed my ears to are true. My grand-mother was an adulteress who seduced Isobel's grandfather. What does that make me? Am I her cousin or am I too a bastard?'

Decimus shook as he tried to contain himself.

'Thomas, be silent. If you cannot keep a civil tongue in your head, you will say not another word in front of your mother. You are too old for me to use my belt on you, but beware I do not lose my patience. I know full well you have a bitter pill to swallow, but had you not taken up with Squire's daughter in the first place, then we could all have been spared this misery.'

'How can I tell Isobel what I have learned, Father?'

'It's as good a test as any. If you really want this young woman, then I suggest you tell her soon, before her father gets in first. He will delight in any opportunity to drag our name through the mud.'

For a long time Thomas sat with his head in his hands. I dared not touch him, for fear my own dear son would pull away from me and reject me. Though Decimus was usually an impatient man, he understood the trauma he had caused his son and waited quietly for Thomas to recover his composure. Eventually, his patience was rewarded.

'I am determined to marry Isobel, Father; that is, if she will have me. Now it is out, I am glad to learn the truth.'

Decimus's fingers, that still dug into my shoulder, relaxed just a little.

'Some years ago, Thomas, I decided when you reached your majority you should have the old house your mother inherited. Over these past months you have proved to be well fitted to be its master. I have not changed my mind this evening. Take Cloudsmoor Farm now, with my blessing.'

Thomas could not have been more surprised.

'Thank you, Father. I shall try to be a credit to you.'

He leaned forward and, with hands too fine to be a farmer's, ran his fingers down my cheek.

'You will always be welcome in my house, Mother. Pray that Isobel will have me and maybe, by our union, one day the rift which divides our two families will be healed.'

In silent prayer I said 'Amen' to that. When I perceived my eldest child did not, after all, bear his mother a grudge, such was my relief that decorum, so tenuous now, was completely lost. Decimus put his arms about me, drew me into his warm embrace, and let me weep.

As I lie this night next to my lord and listen to him breathe in steady slumber, sleep for me is elusive. My tired brain is lulled into a half-world where my jumbled thoughts mill untrammelled by consciousness.

I should have known Decimus did not love me when he wed me, but then, my love for him was blind. It always has been, even from the very moment I saw him through a haze of withy smoke. I had not noticed when he failed to return my love, but he had not deceived me, for at no time until I gave him Thomas did Decimus tell me he loved me. Thinking back, could he really have loved me when he spread my maiden's limbs in the dirt and, telling me to close my eyes, had forced himself into my unprotesting body? Had he loved me that terrible day when, cold and bleeding, I had stumbled through the mud and darkness, back into his formidable presence? Without compassion Decimus had examined what Mistress Morgan had done to me, then next morning had opened every cut, coating the flesh beneath. Though I thought to die from my pain, even that had not destroyed my love for him. I remember how obsessed by my torn and mutilated belly, with his child active inside me, I had lain in front of the altar and prayed for forgiveness of my mother's and grandmother's sins.

I had begged Almighty God to help me accept this life of subjection to which by the vows I had made on my wedding day I am for ever condemned. God has answered my prayers, for now, safe in my husband's love, I no longer despair. Pictures of the past float before me. I see Decimus, his eyes wet, looking down on me, naked on my child-bed. I remember the cold of his shears when he prepared me to be churched. That day for the very first time, Decimus told me he loved me. In my heart I know that only my lord, above all other men, has the courage to sustain that love. His savage and brutal loving has freed me from my penance and I have found the joy that Granny promised would come of it.

Yet as I watch Decimus sleeping, I cannot sleep for fear of the evil power that will unleash should I dream of my half-brother and wish him ill.

The morning light pushed aside the bleakness of the night. The cockerel in the yard crowed before I gave in to sleep. When the brightness of the day awakened me, Decimus had already left his bed.

The fever that had gripped my mind had not abated. I ran to the window and opened it to the cool autumn air. In the stillness I heard the sound of angry voices drifting up from the yard. One voice belonged to Decimus, the other was Harry's. Dressing in haste, I tried to close my ears to their anger and hurried downstairs, wishing I had not heard their heated conversation.

The parlour was cold, the fire not yet lit, but the smell of beeswax and old leather was familiar and availed me some little comfort. The door opened. I had hoped my husband would be standing there, but it was Harry's frame that filled the doorway. Though he towered over me, Harry was not quite fully grown, yet his look this morning reminded me so much of Decimus. It was as though he saw beyond what others could see and I understood now why Granny had been in awe of her youngest child. Harry would have the stature of his father. One day I might have to make my obeisance to him. What bitterness had come between Decimus and his second son because of my shame?

'Harry, my darling, I could not help but overhear you arguing with your father in the yard.'

Harry's eyes were bright.

'I have no fear of Father's wrath,' he said.

'Oh Harry dear, you know better than to contradict your father, lest you forget he is Master in this house.'

'I won't forgive him, Mother. I hate him. How could he treat you so? He admits he did not love you when he wed you. He took his pleasure being cruel. You were only a maiden when you came to him. How could you resist his strength?'

'My darling, you are so young. Do not try just yet to understand our love. It does not matter that your father did not love me all those years ago. Do not spare me my feelings, Harry. Stop and think for a moment. You will choose the woman you wed with your head and not with your heart.'

Harry was defiant.

'No, Mother, you are wrong. Father has destroyed you. I could never do that.'

He lifted me. His strong and loving arms wrapped themselves about me. My feet hung limp, suspended in the air.

'Harry, my darling, your father has not destroyed me. You are not yet seventeen. When you are older you will understand. Now please, put me down.'

'Do not treat me like a child, Mother. I am not at school now. Am I supposed to believe you came to Father with a spirit as strong as his?'

Harry dropped me. Holding me at arm's length, his expression was withering.

'Just look at you, Mother. You can hardly raise your eyes to him. You spend half your time on your knees in obeisance. For what? Father has given you nothing!'

Holding Harry's hands in mine, I tried to console him.

'You cannot change what your father has done to me, Harry. Nor would I permit you to try.'

Harry had not the quicksilver brain of Thomas who, if truth were out, would acknowledge that had fate placed him otherwise he would not have been a farmer's son. This second son was loving and easy in his manner. Men looked to him for guidance, ignoring his immaturity. Though he was so like his father, at this moment he would have denied it. Harry was far too young to understand that a woman could be happy with a harsh and brutal man, so long as she loved him.

'You do not hate your father, Harry. Though you cannot admit to it, your conscience lies heavy. You do not understand the passion his confession has released in you. When you are fully grown you will seek a woman who will satisfy your need. You will not afford her your pity when you do to her what your father has done to me.

'Now, go seek out your father and take your punishment. He will forgive you your impertinence.'

Harry left me then and I prayed that Decimus would not chastise him, but would try to remember his own youth when he too railed against his father's rule.

And what of Richard, would Decimus have to bare his soul again to his youngest child? Those thoughts must wait for another time. Little Lydia, too, would have to know. Cousin Hector's house had become her home, but one day Decimus would take her back. How could she be told that she must try to love a man of her father's choosing or perhaps, God forbid, finding she could not love him, submit to him in terror? My heart ached for my lord in his onerous duty.

CHAPTER XIX

The Confrontation

Not a week had gone by when Thomas presented Isobel to his father. She is tall, her skin very fair and her crowning glory, the auburn hair that is untamed by a bonnet. Her disposition, though, reminds me so much of Cousin Hector's wife whose nervous hands would not be still. Isobel, when called upon to talk to me, turns her head and mumbles, trying to hide her face behind the handkerchief she twiddles between her fingers. I know she fears me in much the same way as did Grace who, on the only occasion on which I met her, could not control her agitation.

Strangely Isobel's father has welcomed her betrothal. Of course Thomas is pleased and surprised by his reaction, but Decimus is cynical, having anticipated what would happen. In his opinion, my half-brother will do anything to get back the house his father was born in, even sacrificing his daughter, that his seed may return. It makes me sad for Isobel that her father cares so little for her.

I am afraid she will prove to be a disappointment to my lord. Isobel is not the woman he would have had his eldest son wed. He is irritated by her nervousness and abhors her narrow, slender body. For Isobel, childbirth will be an unending torment. Decimus wonders what attracted Thomas in the first place, but I see why he loves her, for she has a brain that matches his own. Yet I cannot help but wonder if Thomas will still want her once the prettiness of her youth has faded and her spirit, broken by childbearing, has made her into a brittle and forbidding woman.

Thomas and Isobel are to be married during this time of Advent, but as the day approaches I cannot control my fear. I try to visualise the confrontation when, in church and face to face with Jacob Thwaite, he recognises me as the woman he addressed with such contrived respect at the Inn. Again and again, on my knees I have begged my husband to let me stay at home, yet no matter what my pleading, it makes no difference. He will not listen to my entreaties.

Tonight is the eve of Thomas and Isobel's wedding and Ella has gone to church to pray for God's blessing on their union. Thomas and Harry are making merry with their friends and as Annie helps me get ready to join Decimus in the parlour overwhelming nausea grips me.

Alone with my lord, I sat at his feet as I was wont to do. Absent-mindedly he stroked my hair, then took out the pins, letting the tresses fall. His kisses, which had always warmed me, somehow left me cold, my heart frozen and unyielding.

He whispered, concern in his voice, 'Mary, I know how afraid you are, but I promise you I will not allow Squire to hurt you. No man that lives, including your half-brother, will dare within my earshot say ill of you.'

'I know all you say to be true, lord, but he is tainted by the Devil. I heard him say aloud at the Inn in Veston that he will drive me out, just as he drove out my mother before me. I think constantly of his words and am so frightened. Can you fight Satan, lord?'

Decimus pulled me into his arms.

'Do you not know, Mary, no matter who he be, I will fight anyone who touches you? Long ago when I burned your flesh for the first time, you were brave, my darling, and trusted me, surrendering yourself into my hands. I promised you then I would always look after you. My dear, nothing can change that.'

Decimus continued and the sickness that had plagued me slowly abated as I relaxed, acknowledging the truth of his words.

'Had I loved you when I wed you, Mary, I should not have worked you in so cruel a way as I very nearly killed you. Looking back on those early days, I have to believe it was your Jesse who guided my hand. No one but he could have stilled it. I thank God my mother was kind to you, for I had no compassion in my heart then. I could not love you until you gave me Thomas.'

Kissing his hands, I sought, if need be, to reassure him of my love.

'My heart does not bear a grudge against you, lord. From the moment I saw you, I loved you whatever the man you were and, even had I guessed you did not love me, could have given myself to no one but you. I remember you were unkind to me, but those days have grown misty with their passing and now they are easy to forget. Perhaps you would never have grown to love me had you not seen, in spite of your discipline, the depth of my love for you. When you took Thomas away, had I resisted and not borne with love the pain you inflicted on me I should not have found the paradise you intended me to find. No, lord, only the severity of your loving could have lifted the penance that my forebears forced upon me. I have no regrets.'

Decimus, affected by my confession, stood up and rummaged in the cupboard that was set into an alcove beside the hearth. From the topmost shelf he took down a small silken bundle and shook it. It was the gossamer gown I had worn for the very first time that wondrous night when he had turned a key in me, unlocking a new world where, from that moment on, I had lived safe and happy under his protection.

'Lord, I had thought the gown lost. Shall I leave you while I put it on?'

'No, Mary, you must let me do it.'

He freed my body of its covering and thinking of the loving to come I tingled all over. Standing naked, I did not feel old, though within a few months I should be forty years of age and deemed a matron. He pulled me down on to his lap, so that I sat with him in Granny's chair and, as we had done so many times before, together we watched the flames leaping from the fire. Placing my legs apart, he was smiling. Did he think Annie

199

might have neglected her duties? The fire warmed me, its heat concentrated on my smooth and shaven skin. As he touched me, I closed my eyes, my heart throbbing with love for him.

'You have always closed your eyes whenever you have been in fear of me, my darling. Do you fear me now?'

'Yes, my love, of course I do, a little.'

'I've no wish to change that, Mary.'

His hands caressed me. As though half asleep, I imagined he held his taper before me. Over and over again the flame in my mind multiplied until, such was my contentment, his voice came from far away.

'Are you happy now, my darling?'

Knowing always when his flame burned me Decimus did not need an answer.

'There is something, Mary, that I have to tell you tonight. I cannot keep it any longer from you and pray what I have to say will not prove unbearable for you, my dear.'

Wrapped in his love, what could possibly be so important?

'When I was just a lad, Mary, maybe eleven or twelve years of age, I watched as the men of the village drove a young woman to her death. Jacob Thwaite was only a boy, little older than I, but it was he who held her, like an animal, on a length of chain. Round her neck, the chain suspended from it, she carried the outsized collar of a ploughing horse. She could not stand upright for the weight of it. The bodice of her gown was ripped and stained with blood from the beating she had taken. Calling her a whore, they led her to the Pound and threw her in with the strays. When they grew tired of scorning her, they dragged her out and a couple of the men cut off her hair and shaved her head.

'I did nothing to stop them. The rector came and took her away. Shortly afterwards, she died and was buried in an unmarked grave.'

Decimus paused.

'She was your mother, Mary . . .'

Gone for ever, paradise was lost. The fire still leapt up the chimney. Nothing, yet everything, had changed. Pulling away from him, suddenly I was screaming with terror. Decimus had to hold me and, crushed against him, my body shook so hard even his great hands must struggle to restrain me. When at last I was still, my strength spent, I turned to him, the only man who could love me.

'Lord, I beg of you, when they come for me, do not let them take me as they took my mother. Dear God, have mercy on her soul.'

Decimus was weeping, his remorse too much for him to bear.

'That I promise they will not do, Mary, so long as I still live.'

I cleaved to my husband. The only place on earth where peace was not denied me was within the circle of his arms. I saw now why, had he known who I was, he would not have wed me. My heart went out to my love in his anguish.

'Do not torment yourself further, lord. You were only a boy at the time, how could you have helped her? She will have forgiven you. I beg of you, though, please do not make me attend Thomas's wedding tomorrow. I know now what Jacob Thwaite meant when he said he had driven out my mother before me and I cannot withstand seeing him again. Please, let me stay here where I am safe. You will not force me to face that evil man, will you, lord? What if he were to turn Thomas away from me?'

'My darling, you must see Thomas wed. He will not be so easily swayed. Have confidence in my son. Jacob Thwaite and his kind will not turn him from his mother.'

He released his hold on me and I slipped from his lap, falling at his feet. Frantic now, I pleaded with him to shut me away.

'Lord, please, please help me. Though your loving has shown me paradise, I fear all of that is lost now. How can I live with my terror? I would rather die.'

In anguish I begged my husband to take my life, yet still my dying heart lived. He bent over me and through my tears I saw the bleakness of his countenance.

'Mary dear, I cannot see you stricken so. I had to tell you about your mother or risk Jacob Thwaite telling you himself. You have travelled such a hard and dangerous road with me, my dear. I prayed your sorrowing was at an end. Maybe I should have known, though, that you could never be free once the men of the village found out who you were. I am only mortal, Mary, but, if I cannot prevent your sorrowing, then you will sorrow only in my loving hands. With God's grace, I shall restore to you the peace you crave and will not let you leave again the haven I have made for you. Be still for me now and don't take your eyes from mine. I must know how far you have travelled and how much farther I can permit you to go. Always remember that we are one, my darling, and that I love you.'

Dawn had broken. Decimus was already up and dressed. Today he would take me to see Thomas and Isobel wed. Annie attended me. Gently, she brushed my hair until it shone like a blackbird's wing, a few silver threads sparkling in the morning light. She wound the heavy tresses around my head and made them secure with long, pearl-tipped pins. Raising my arms and holding tight to the end of the bedpost, I made myself tall while she locked my corset. Lastly she dressed me, looping each tiny button that ran down the back of my finest black silk gown.

Decimus and Harry were still milking when I entered the kitchen on Annie's arm. Breakfast was laid. Ella glanced up, took off her apron and held out her hands to me. Gratefully, I clasped them. Her eyes that had lost their prejudice scanned me.

'You are a credit to my brother, Mary. You are still beautiful and will put the lot of them to shame. Oh, do not cry, my dear, or I shall wish I had not said a word.'

Decimus was watching us from the doorway. When he spoke, his voice was hoarse, the dialect undisguised.

'Aye, Mary, my sister is right.'

He took Granny's pearls from their case and fastened them at my neck.

Thomas and Harry were the first to go. Ella allowed herself a tear, for Thomas had been her first love and now he was lost to her. Seeing Richard, my little boy, spruced up in his Sunday best, I had to smile. Today, his father had given him a man's role and he would escort Ella. Noting we were all ready, Decimus brought the trap round to the yard. Perry, his heavy coat glowing with health, stood between the shafts, his harness polished, his brasses gleaming. Decimus still found it amusing that he looked like a gypsy horse. The incessant wind dragged at my bonnet, the cold of early December striking damp. Shivering, I pulled my cloak tighter about me and buttoned it to the neck. Ella huddled close to Richard. My lord had decided that Lydia should not come home, but stay in Hartley with his cousin. Though he kept it to himself, I imagined Decimus was worried that Jacob Thwaite might harangue his daughter.

Leaving Perry hitched to the railings, Decimus put chocks under the wheels of the trap to stop it from running away. This path to church was gentle, unlike the steps on the other side of the hill that I had climbed all those years previously when Decimus had brought me here to be cleansed of my labours.

A hush greeted us as Decimus opened the door and ushered us inside. Sitting in the front pew, Thomas, his head bowed, was lost in his thoughts. Harry, ramrod straight, groomsman to his elder brother, looked straight ahead. Decimus held my hand and together we walked down the aisle. How full the church was, a sea of faces turning to watch us. Filling the right-hand pews were my husband's brothers and their families. We slipped into our places and sat behind our two full-grown sons.

I could not help but let my eyes stray to the other side of church to where the Thwaite family was assembled, patiently waiting for Isobel and her father. A woman I guessed was Isobel's mother sat alone, a rather forlorn lady who today would lose her daughter, yet, playing no part, must watch her husband give her child away. In silent prayer, I knelt and asked of Almighty God that Isobel be happy with my eldest son and that Thomas should find it in his heart to love her when she had grown old and tired.

Suddenly the chords of the harmonium came to life. Isobel, heavily veiled and holding her father's arm, passed by. Overcome with emotion, I wanted to weep. Since my own, I had not been to a wedding. Decimus had attended those of many of his nephews and nieces, yet not one had been wed since my confinement had ended. How young Isobel looked, standing between her father and my eldest son. What a momentous day this was for her, when for better or worse her life from this moment on would belong to her husband and she must pray he would be kind to her.

Squire Thwaite's head came from the recess of his shoulders, without benefit of neck. He was just as repulsive as I remembered him. Seeing that I was looking at him, Decimus held me lest I faint, yet he need not have worried. The flame of his love burned brightly and, holding my head high, I cared not that I feared my half-brother.

The beauty of the service enfolded me in its power and almost to myself, I mouthed the words as Isobel took her vows, once more giving myself, body and soul, to my own dear lord. His hand squeezed mine as he listened while I renewed my vows of obedience and love.

The rector was not ignorant of our circumstances. The sins I had inherited would not in my lifetime be forgiven. Within these hallowed walls I should always be accepted on sufferance and hoped for nothing better. During the sermon, I felt my husband stiffen with rage that for my shame his son should be lectured. I wondered how Decimus could go on loving me and feared he might comment, yet not wishing to embarrass Thomas my lord kept his own counsel. When the ceremony was over, Thomas, with Isobel on his arm, walked slowly down the aisle. Isobel, her veil drawn back from her face, was radiant in her love for him. Her hair, a rich copper halo about her head, was dotted with the whitest of Christmas roses. Her gown swept the floor. It too was white and fashionable. Tight lace sleeves extended to her wrists; the bodice of lace-covered satin was edged with tiny seed pearls that fell at random to the hem. The veil of net and fine lace almost covered her shoulders, enhancing the milky white of her skin. Yet even her beautiful gown could not disguise Isobel's lack of nourishment. Perhaps marriage would be good for her and my lord's reservations prove unfounded. His face wreathed in smiles, Thomas stood tall in his black suit. Seeing them so happy together, I prayed that one day Tom's wish would come true and that by their union our two families should indeed be reconciled. Decimus, his hand in mine, released me, pushing me forward.

Evil confronted me. His eyes swept over me and as I took my half-brother's outstretched arm, to walk with him down the aisle, I dared not look up. This man was my kin, yet my husband dared not let me go free, for fear he would see me dead. When we reached the door I gulped in the fresh cold air that smelt of the ocean. It helped me to breathe.

This wind was the wind that blew all the way from the Americas, a place I should never see. Why were the Americas so often inexplicably in my thoughts? The eyes that stared down at me could not long be avoided. I looked up. They protruded from his pock-marked flesh and, like a bird of prey, flickered. But the lids to his eyes seemed not to move. He pushed his face into mine as he addressed me and I smelt his breath that was warm and fetid. I had smelt it before when, on the road to Bristol, Satan had waylaid me.

'I have seen you somewhere, whore's daughter. Just now, you have the advantage of me, but I shall remember soon.'

'Oh Decimus,' I thought, 'pray do not leave me too long in the company of this horrible man.'

Suddenly, recognition crossed his face. 'Ah yes, of course, now I remember: you were sitting in the corner, breakfasting alone that day at the Ship. What a jest that I should apologise to you of all people for my robust language! So, you knew who I was and, come to think of it, my intentions, before I had the dubious pleasure of making your acquaintance. I assure you, Madam, that advantage will not fall to you again. You may tell your husband, if you have not already done so, that I shall hound you as I hounded your gypsy whore of a mother before you. Have you asked him about that little incident? I am sure he will not have forgotten. Perhaps he will tell you about it. Your husband is sadistic, my dear. He enjoyed it as much as the rest of us.'

He pushed his face even closer to mine.

'Not for one minute consider yourself of my line. Your rope

gets shorter every day, Mary Cheyne, or whatever you call yourself. I swear I will be rid of you. You cannot hide from me for ever. Tell that to your arrogant husband too!'

His voice was contemptuous and he mocked me with an exaggerated gesture: wiping his nose on a large pocket handkerchief, as if to free himself of my scent.

But my husband had given me courage and despite my physical frailty which mattered not at all to me, no longer fearing my half-brother, I asked of him, 'Sir, pray tell me, where was my father, that he allowed you to shame my mother? I know you tormented her even unto her death. Had you no pity?'

The hawk-like eyes flashed and I saw the hate he made no effort to conceal. I had dared to call his father mine.

'Madam, my father was so concerned that his bastard was safe, that he left his whore to her fate. You may blame yourself for your mother's death, for my father was with you!'

His finger jabbed at me, viciously prodding my breast. I was mortified by his cruel words and almost lost my balance as the ground seemed to rock under my feet. Now I knew for certain why my father had given me the house where he was born, snubbing his legitimate heir. He could not disown his son, but had not forgiven Jacob for driving my mother to her death.

In a moment Decimus stood beside me, putting his arm around my waist to steady me. My lord was taller than Jacob Thwaite. I saw the clash between them that must always have been there yet which my presence had made so much worse. Without respect, he addressed the squire.

'I will not strike a man here on sacred ground, but I swear, Jacob Thwaite, if ever you touch my wife again I shall kill you, as I would a mad dog, for that it what you are.'

Turning to me, my husband was brusque.

'Come, Mary, there will be plenty of time to see Thomas and Isobel. We shall be neighbours. Now we are going home.'

Isobel conceived that Christmas. When, towards the end of the following September, the child lay low in her belly and her time drew near, Isobel insisted her mother attend her, not allowing me to help. Despite her love for my son, Isobel still feared the curse in me and would not allow me to blow into her face the smoke that might have calmed her. For two whole days her poor body was ravished before a son was delivered of her. When Decimus took me to see the tiny babe, I prayed that he, with his wizened little face, would grow strong in the likeness of his father. Perhaps, as Thomas still hoped, the child would be a bridge and the evil my half-brother bore me would be assuaged by this new life.

Hand in hand, atop the huge Sea Bank of the Great River, Decimus and I walked home. In the lazy stillness of a September afternoon, bees still gathered honey, their steady drone breaking the silence. Picked out in the haze that hung over the land, on the hill St Allwen's shimmered like a mirage, almost a ship, that sailed in the distance. Across the rhenes, but two fields away, stood Jacob Thwaite's house. I shivered, despite the bright sun that should have warmed me.

Decimus looked down.

'You are very quiet, Mary. God knows, I give you little opportunity to converse, my love. Tell me you are happy to be silent.'

'You know I am always happy, lord, when I am with you.'

Decimus was not oblivious to my unease, understanding it was more than I could do to bring myself to question him without his permission.

'Something is worrying you, Mary. Tell me what it is.'

'May I ask about my father, lord? What sort of man was he, who could leave my mother to die, humiliated and alone?'

'He was a quiet man, Mary. His wife was very like Isobel. Maybe in her youth she was pretty, but I remember her as a sour and bitter woman. Perhaps she had good reason, for though the village people lowered their eyes and paid their respects to her we all knew that the old squire kept a woman down the Marsh and he had sired her daughter.'

'Jacob Thwaite repels me, my love. My memory of a time before you wed me is so difficult to recall and I only saw my father once, even then not knowing who he was. But I still remember his kind face. Tell me he was not like his son.'

Decimus though for a moment.

'Harry looks more like your father than does Jacob. Jacob's likeness is that seen in a mirror at the fairground which turns beauty into ugliness and we laugh.'

Since Thomas had been wed the imposition of my lord's discipline was so strict that even speaking to him caused me trepidation. Trusting he would indulge me just a little longer, I asked him what I ached to know.

'Please, lord, may I have just one more question? Did my mother look anything like me?'

'I was only a lad, Mary. I remember nothing of her before seeing her in her shame, yoked and chained that terrible day. Your father had taken you away and I bless him for it. You have brought me great joy, Mary. Do not forget, my darling, that your father loved you. He gave you the house that meant so much to him. Think well of him when Cloudsmoor Farm echoes to the sound of our grandchildren's happy laughter.'

CHAPTER XX

Cornelius

That Indian summer of 1881 warmed us almost through to November. In the October, Richard was ten years old. He still had the faraway look in his eyes, reminding me of those blissful days when my lord had delivered him of my womb. On my childbed, I had thought my destiny fulfilled, needing nothing more from life than to bear my husband his sons. But that has proved not to be.

Winter is giving way to spring. The season has been short, but bitterly cold. For nearly six weeks frost has crackled underfoot, the rhenes freezing solid. The hay is almost gone and but a month ago we feared for the animals' lives. At last crocuses raise their brave heads to the sun and the clear air is warmed by a westerly breeze. The smell of the sea draws me back to a hazy time when I first saw this magical Vale and met my love. I seldom leave home now, except for those occasions when I walk alone on the Sea Bank with just Annie for company. Should Decimus require me to venture farther, then he is always at my side, protecting me. Sometimes he worries for me and wonders, if I had not come here, would I have been happy in some other place where no one knows of my past. But he understands that I belong nowhere else and imagining me somewhere different is a pointless exercise.

I am much relieved to see Harry and his father reconciled. As he has gained in maturity, Harry has lost his hostility, comprehending better his father's love for me. Without his criticism, my subjection is made easier. Unlike Thomas and Isobel who are of much the same age, I suspect the girl Harry will wed is as yet still a child. Though I am not supposed to notice, Harry is often away from his bed.

Lydia has not been home at all since before Thomas was wed. In two years, neither Ella nor I have seen her, though as he enjoys his cousin's company Decimus travels regularly to Hartley, sometimes staying for several days. Lydia has lived with Cousin Hector and Grace for six years and in June will be fourteen years old. She has reached maidenhood and Decimus has intimated that this summer, if he judges her disposition to be to his liking, he will bring her home for good. I am worried, wondering if she can find a place within the family after such a long absence. Trying to visualise my daughter and her reaction to her mother fills me with apprehension.

The July morning was bathed in brilliant sunshine. Decimus waited in the yard and I hurried, suppressing my excitement, anxious not to delay him. As always when he visited his cousin, he left Perry at home. Seeing my husband's pretty chestnut mare standing between the shafts of the trap served to heighten my anticipation. At last we were going together to fetch Lydia.

What happy memories I let flit across my mind as Decimus followed the road that led to Hartley. When we were nearer the town would be quite soon enough to examine my worries. I thought instead of the day he had taken me to Rockingham and I had first met his acquaintances. He had bought Perry, my winged horse of the gods. But the freedom my husband had allowed me could not be sustained. My mood changed and gloomily I wondered how long my lord would wait before telling Lydia all that she must know. The lovely morning, filled with birdsong, the air heavy with the scent of grass and dog roses, was suddenly gone. For a moment I was unaware of Decimus's hand on mine.

'We must discuss Lydia's homecoming, my darling,' he said.

Uninvited into my mind had come a vision of Lydia, an old

woman, lost and in torment alone on the ridge looking toward the distant Estuary. Seeing my grief, my lord encouraged me to tell him again of that terrible day when Satan had waylaid me. When I had finished my tale, his admonition was gentle.

'Mary dear, you must put aside your nightmare. You should be more concerned for the present. Lydia will need your help. She has been away a long time and Hector's family probably means more to her than we do. When you see her, try to remember our daughter's spirit had to be tamed and now we must all make the best of it.'

So my lord was preparing me for even greater changes I should see in our daughter. Decimus looked to say more, but stopped himself.

'My love, do not spare me your thoughts. I feel something else is on your mind.'

'Aye, Mary, it is. I fear Lydia will reject you when she hears from me – for I cannot risk others telling her – that your father was the old squire and your mother, his gypsy whore.'

'Though it be the truth, I grieve when you say such dreadful things, lord. Please, do you have to tell her just yet?'

For several minutes Decimus did not speak to me, his mood introspective, as though he might have regretted his choice of words.

'For all these years my cousin has made Lydia welcome in his house, educating her with his own daughters. You must ready yourself, Mary, for the changes that have been wrought in her.'

Dear God, what was my husband preparing me for?

With adoring eyes she looked up at her father, but scarcely had time for me. Meek and unassuming, old beyond her years, Lydia greeted us. Picking her up, a helpless, submissive little bird, Decimus held her to his breast and I saw, from the way he touched her, my husband's love for his daughter. What had become of the child I remembered, her spirit truly broken now, her large trusting eyes revealing her unprotected soul? Hector had performed his task to perfection. One day Lydia would grow into a beautiful woman, but my heart cried out in anguish to see her so transformed.

Lydia introduced me to Hector's children. Only two remained at home, Lucy and Amelia. Kate, the eldest, was married to a doctor in London. Martha too lived in London, training to be a nurse at the Nightingale School. Lucy, her flaxen hair hidden under her sun bonnet, was two years younger than Lydia. Her laughter infectious, she was a confident child. Amelia though, was obviously Lydia's special friend. Unlike Lydia, she appeared quite forceful, her hand on Lydia's arm, as if she perceived how much my daughter needed her protection. I wondered how Hector's children could be so different in temperament from my child when it had been my understanding that they had all been educated together. Lydia would miss Amelia in the months to come.

Hector was not at home but Grace, her hair whiter than when I had seen her previously, though otherwise little changed, seemed more tolerant and was genuinely pleased to see us. Her fondness for Lydia was obvious and I was grateful, for, whatever had happened to her in this house, at least my daughter had not been deprived of love.

On the journey home I was reminded, if I needed reminding, that I hardly knew my child. She sat next to her father, his hand in hers, my attendance superfluous. Nevertheless, however harsh the decision had been to educate her in Hartley, I knew I should never have courage to comment, for my lord as always was above censure.

Ella was overjoyed to have Lydia home, especially now that Richard was at school in Milbury. Decimus allowed Lydia little freedom, not permitting her to go into the village, except when accompanied by Ella. He was anxious to protect his daughter, if he could, from the jibes of wicked men.

One evening, just as the season was drawing to a close, Lydia chose to walk with me to meet her father and Harry as they came up from the fishing. She loved to wander on the Sea Bank and watch the Great River flowing towards the sea. I guessed she found solace in the wide sweeping majesty that unfolded before her. The tide was way out and against the sun two small figures, like black dots, trudged slowly through the silt and mud back to the shore. As they came closer, Lydia waved and her father and Harry, seeing her, each raised an arm in greeting. Bowed from the weight on their backs they carried salmon. When they joined us, I sensed Lydia's relief that her time alone with me was over. Harry took his father's catch from him and bade us farewell. Suddenly the meeting seemed contrived and I knew the time had come when Decimus would tell Lydia of her mother's past.

His voice was soft as he addressed his daughter.

'Shall we three sit a while and watch the sun disappear?'

He drew her down beside him on to the short, hard grass of the bank. She was nearly fully grown, the olive skin inherited from her gypsy forebears glowing in the golden light of evening. Ella had coaxed her hair, darker than it used to be, into ringlets that framed her oval face. The hazel eyes that looked up at her father were light and unexpected, but deep-set and intense. She lowered them as the rays of the setting sun were cast full upon her, hiding from her the anguish on Decimus's face. Having to squint, with her hand shading her eyes, she tried to look up at him. Holding my arm, Decimus pulled me down so that I sat on his other side and could not from there watch Lydia's face.

In a daze, staring far out into the Estuary, I listened to my husband's words. Mercifully he spared her, not telling Lydia that he had not loved me when he wed me. He talked instead of Granny, his mother, who could trace her line back to a time when a young maiden was stolen by gypsies. He told Lydia about the mother of that poor child; of the sons who had died and her shame when she was unable to give her husband an heir. After the gypsies had taken her daughter, she herself died of a broken heart.

'Her name was Lydia, my darling, and I named you Lydia in memory of her.'

Decimus's hand that lay in mine held on to me as he continued, his voice even quieter now.

'On your mother's side, you are descended from that same fair-haired maiden the gypsies stole. They say she was a Daughter of Satan and put her spell on them. Of the sons she bore, many were cursed and died. My darling, I tell you all of this, for I must try if I can, to protect you.'

Involuntarily Lydia sat forward and I could see her face. Slowly she began to crumple. Again and again, she shook her head as her father spelt out the truth.

'You frighten me, Papa.'

Decimus leaned over and with his free hand, to keep them from trembling, held both of hers.

'Lydia, my little one, you must hear me out.'

He told her of the bad blood and sorcery which had come down through countless years to her great grandmother, who was whipped and drowned as a witch. Then, his voice no more than a whisper, he spoke of her grandmother, an adulteress, who was humbled and beaten and now lay buried in an unmarked grave in the churchyard.

Lydia pulled free and, covering her face with her hands, turned away from me, not bearing to look at me. Then she jumped up and ran away towards the Great River that still flowed on relentlessly into the sea. When she stopped short where the mud line joined the grass, her little shoulders heaved with her sobbing.

Decimus restrained me.

'Let her go, Mary. She will come back when she is ready.'

Hopelessly, I kissed my lord's hand that still rested on mine. Stupefied, I doubted not, Lydia was lost to me for ever. To my daughter, her mother was even less to her than a stranger would be. How could she come to me for love? Decimus, his voice steady now, called her back and slowly she turned and came to him. Holding her hands, he pulled her down again, making her listen once more.

'Your mother, my darling, is the love child your grandmother bore the old squire, Jacob Thwaite's father.'

In disbelief, the sun full on her, not bothering to shade her eyes, she stared at her father.

'Oh Papa, why do you have to tell me that?'

Weeping, she clung to him.

'So, my mother was a bastard, born in sin, her mother a common gypsy woman. How can I bear the shame? To think I lived all those years with Aunt Grace and Cousin Hector and they knew but did not tell me. I shall never be able to speak to Amelia again. Every day I rubbed lemon juice into my skin, trying to make it lighter, when all the time I was a gypsy. How Cousin Hector must have laughed when you gave him the task of turning a sow's ear into a silk purse. No wonder he gave me special lessons in rectitude, making me so tired I knew not what day it was. Why did you send me there, Papa?'

Almost as an afterthought, Lydia added.

'Tell me, am I too a Daughter of Satan?'

Decimus found it difficult to answer her.

'Lydia, my dear, your mother has carried that burden for most of her life. But I love her and with me she is safe.'

Gulls calling overhead broke the silence and in the distance a lone cow bellowed after its absent calf. Lydia, her voice small and anxious, appealed to my lord.

'What must I do, Papa, that I may be safe?'

'My dear daughter, it saddens me to have to tell you what the gypsies say. There is only one way you will find peace.'

Decimus got up and stood over her, taking the light.

'You must love your husband enough, Lydia, that you have the courage to let him take your soul from you.'

His words trailed away. Lydia sat and stared up at him, her lips noiselessly mouthing words. Suddenly she jumped to her feet as if to flee, but Decimus caught her and held her to him.

'Oh no, Papa, not that. Do not ask it of me. How could I let any man deprive me of my very being? It is too much, just too much to ask of me.'

Decimus tried to hold her, but she shook free, her voice grown hard, the submission it had taken Hector years to instil thrown aside.

'Now I understand why you sent me to Cousin Hector for all those years. Why should you care that I was lonely without my family? All you sought to do was train me to be quiet as my mother is quiet, who serves you and calls you lord.'

Then, her mouth twisted and cruel, Lydia turned on me, pointing her finger. My heart reeled from the blow.

'Father has taken your soul, Mother!'

Lydia looked down on me, utter contempt written on her face, horror in her eyes. I could not bear to look at her as the tears ran cold down my cheeks. Then she turned to her father and for the first time in all her life, I knew she feared him. He held her close, her little body just reaching his chest, her ringlets shaking. Decimus, almost beside himself, pleaded with her.

'Lydia, please, let me finish. I would have spared you this ordeal, but dared not take a chance that you learn who you are from someone other than me.'

Sinking to her knees, she submitted to her father's rule. He caught her, not letting her demean herself, and in a small desperate voice, no longer calling him Papa, Lydia begged her father to help her.

'With God's grace, child, when the time comes, I shall try with all my heart to seek a husband for you who will love you. That I promise.'

Gathering his daughter into his arms, he kissed her, then, hand-in-hand, they went home together. Dejected, I walked unnoticed behind them.

In the months that followed I often felt Lydia watching me. Sometimes she hid a smile behind her hand when she witnessed my submissions. Though Decimus could not have doubted my distress, he said nothing to Lydia, just telling me I must accept her scorn. In the very meekness she mocked, by my example she was shown the path she must tread from the day my lord committed her to the care of a husband.

For more than two years Lydia observed my life of contemplation and toil. When sometimes her mockery became too much to bear and I wept, she would laugh out loud. I despaired for her. Ella, her strongest of supporters, was concerned that Lydia enjoyed setting the fox among the chickens. When on Sundays Decimus read to his family from the Bible, he would draw Lydia's attention to the Gospels from where she would learn of her duties as a wife. I too had learned, when my lord had placed the Book into my hands, as a young wife, not knowing yet the role my husband had determined for me.

As time passed, on those occasions when Lydia was left alone in my company, though it could not fail to have been in her mind, she tried always to avoid mention of the conversation she had had that day with her father on the Sea Bank of the Great River. Some days Lydia would be kind to me. It was almost as though she were two different people trapped in one body. When my lord called me, at the end of a long and exhausting day, and I was weary from the tasks he had set my hands, Lydia would put her arm about me and offer me her sympathy. Perhaps after she was wed she might understand how much, in spite of my fatigue, I needed my lord's loving, for only the joy of his love could sustain me.

Harvest had been gathered and Decimus could relax before the rigours of winter. The nights had drawn in and that October evening, warmed by the fire, I lay at the feet of my love. The door was locked; the wings of Granny's chair curved above us. Decimus loosened my hair, letting it fall free.

'We have such little time together, my darling. Almost from the moment she returned from Hartley, Lydia has taunted you. I am not unaware of your pain, Mary.'

'Our daughter can be so cruel, lord.'

'I know that, my dear, but I have had to show her, by your example, the unremitting servitude of the life that is ahead of her. If she is to find peace, there will be no other way for Lydia.'

'I fear for her, lord. My heart withers under her gaze and some days I am almost beyond my wits. She makes me feel like a freak that is tethered at a peep show.'

'I have news for you, Mary, and hope soon your torment can be over, my darling. I think I have found a husband for Lydia.'

Startled, I looked up at him, opening my mouth to speak, but stopped, his fingers against my lips preventing my question.

'Hush, my sweet wife, you know better than to ask my intentions.'

Leaning over me, he threw more logs on to the fire that would keep out the chill of the autumn evening. When he was good and ready, and not before, he would tell me what he deemed I should know.

As I waited with Lydia for Decimus to return from his brother Luke's house at Wytherington, voices and the sound of well-shod horses came from the yard. Decimus was back. Glancing at Lydia, I saw her face was impassive, yet she must have been nervous. The door opened and dropping to my knees, in the presence of my lord, I bowed my head. Raising me, he introduced me to the gentleman who accompanied him.

'Mary, I want you to meet Cornelius Shepherd. By marriage he is a kinsman of my brother.'

The young man was as tall as Decimus, but a lot thinner. The breeches he wore were of the finest skin, his boots cleaned and polished. His jacket was well cut and at his neck the stock was freshly laundered. Atop his head were yellow curls, their colour yet to fade. His bright blue eyes that held mine were confident and he smiled.

I imagined Decimus had already informed him of his requirement in a husband for Lydia. For a moment, I wondered if Lydia would have been happier following Martha, turning her back on marriage and becoming a nurse instead. But I dismissed the thought: such decisions were not mine to make. Upon dropping Cornelius a curtsy, Lydia was raised from her obeisance and a ripple of awareness passed between them.

Cornelius Shepherd had a mild and gentle manner that belied his thirty-two years, but I guessed there was more to him than that and did not doubt my lord had chosen him wisely. I worried, though, that he was almost old enough to be Lydia's father, being double her age, yet Decimus considered that an advantage, believing Lydia would find it easier to give herself to an older man who would understand her needs. Cornelius was a gentleman farmer and a nephew by marriage of my dear husband's brother. The family owned a coal mine and land in Somerset. I contemplated how far away Lydia would be if she were wed to him, much farther than Hartley. I could not afford to own such thoughts, accepting that Decimus knew better than I, that Lydia would earn scant respect from a man in these parts.

Lydia was betrothed to Cornelius on her seventeenth birthday. Over the following year she spent many weeks with Cornelius's parents, getting to know his family. Sometimes Cornelius stayed with Luke and rode over from Wytherington on a fine black horse, to see Lydia. All the while, we watched their love grow. The wedding was set for the first Saturday in August of the year 1886. By the time she was wed, Lydia would be well past her eighteenth birthday.

On the first Sunday morning in July, Decimus and I climbed the hill together to the church that a thousand years before had been dedicated to St Allwen, a local maiden who had thwarted a wicked tyrant. The church had stood guard over the village for centuries, providing succour for the poor, the dispossessed and the despairing. For the first time, the rector intoned the timeless words.

'I publish the Banns of Marriage between Cornelius Shepherd, Bachelor of the Parish of Innslow in the County of Somerset, and Lydia Ellen Hillyer, Spinster of this Tithing. If any of you know cause, or just impediment, why these two persons should not be joined together in holy Matrimony, ye are to declare it. This is the first time of asking.'

The silence that followed was unbroken except for my beating heart. Holding Decimus's fingers tight in my hand, I did not let go until the rector continued the service.

Convention dictated I should take Lydia aside and talk to her, but my lord doubted she would listen to me even though of late she had seemed more tolerant of my position. Instead, on the eve of her wedding, with the sun setting on her last full day in his house, Decimus called Lydia to the parlour. On this occasion, Ella was not invited to attend. I stood with my lord as impatiently he paced the floor, waiting for Lydia to obey what would be his last command of her.

She appeared in the doorway, blinking in the rays of the setting sun. Instantly I thought of the maiden who had squinted in the same golden light when on the River Bank she had looked up at her father and he had told her of the curse she had inherited and could not avoid. Lydia's beauty had matured and the hazel eyes, set in a flawless skin, scanned the room. I sat down, the stool beside my husband's chair reserved for me. Her smile was controlled and serene as she observed my status. Even now, after watching me for four years or so, in my heart I doubted if Lydia truly understood how much she must love Cornelius in order that he purge her of her sins, to keep her safe from the Devil. Decimus sat down, but indicated Lydia should stand before him, a chair denied her.

'My darling, I have but one duty left as your father.'

Lydia's face clouded, but she looked straight at him.

'Do you wish to be wed to Cornelius Shepherd?'

'Yes, Papa, I do. I love Cornelius, as I could not love any other man and want to be his wife.'

'It is necessary, my dear, that you fully understand your duties as a wife. Whatever your husband asks of you, without exception you will obey him, as your mother obeys me. You will at all times humble yourself before him, as your mother humbles herself to me. If you feel anger towards your husband, you will turn it away and will snuff it out. Do you understand what I am saying to you, Lydia?'

Lydia, her eyes lowered, following her father's words, spoke in barely a whisper.

'Yes, Father, I understand that I must obey Cornelius even if at times it distresses me to do so.'

'Are you absolutely sure you wish to be wed, Lydia? This is your very last chance to change your mind.'

'I love him. My love is so strong it hurts.'

'Then, God be with you, my child. We will all look forward to tomorrow when I shall give you to Cornelius. From the day you are wed, my support and my house must be refused you. May God send you strength and by your labours give Cornelius many fine sons.

'Now, Lydia, go to your room and, until the sun has finally gone down, prostrate yourself and pray to God for the courage to give yourself to your husband.'

Lydia left us then and Decimus raised me from my stool.

'Our task is finished, Mary. We can do no more to help her. Lydia is in God's hands now. When you watch me give her away, remember the day Jesse gave you to me and pray that Lydia will find fulfilment with Cornelius as you have been fulfilled in my care.'

CHAPTER XXI

The Wedding

Dawn broke over Thorn End Farm, but I was wide awake long before the first cockerel crowed. Leaving Decimus still asleep, in my nightgown I crept downstairs and wandered out into the deserted yard. Soon it would be a hive of activity, the cows waiting patiently to be milked, the clatter of milk churns disturbing the peace. High thin clouds told me that later it might rain, but Lydia would be wed in the brightness of an August sun and nothing must mar this day.

I thought of my dear lord's brother at Wytherington, where Cornelius and his family were staying overnight. I wondered, was Cornelius still in his bed? Perhaps his mother was awake. Was she, too, watching the high clouds move imperceptibly to the east? I prayed she would be gentle with Lydia as Granny had been gentle with me when I had wed her youngest son. I had never been to Innslow and my heart was knotted with fear for my child. If she were unhappy, there was nothing we could do to help her.

The appointed hour was almost upon us. Amelia, Lydia's bridesmaid, had already arrived, having driven down this morning from Milbury where she was staying with her parents, guests of Hector's elder brother at the Castle. She and Ella were helping Lydia with her gown. Decimus, stern in his sombre suit, summoned his family. Thomas and Isobel, the glow of their love undimmed, Harry, Richard and I waited for Ella to bring Lydia down from her room. The air was charged with excitement.

Lydia, veiled, with eyes downcast, stood before my lord.

'I have called you before the family, Lydia, so we may all say our farewells.'

From his pocket he drew out the oval brooch with a circlet of old gold. My father had given it to me, now Decimus was passing it on to yet another generation of women.

'Your mother and I want you to have this. We hope it will bring you good luck, Lydia.'

Decimus pinned the brooch to her wedding dress. To my lord it was a symbol of the blood we shared, for the maiden whose flaxen hair adorned it had been his kin too. Then, kissing his daughter on both her cheeks, he caught hold of the veil and, lifting it, brought it forward, dropping it over her face. The layers of net fell, the lacy edges dipping towards the floor. My breath was trapped, tears not far away, for we could no longer see her. Hidden by the folds of the heavy veil, Lydia was lost to us and I was not prepared. The glorious gown of the palest ivory satin, which Ella's loving fingers had taken months to make, was hidden too. Lydia found her father's hand; an anonymous little soul, just another woman, who today would exchange her father's name for that of her new husband. We had to leave them then, mourning the last of their love as they waited together for the carriage to take Lydia away.

A hush hung over the aisle and I held tight to Harry's arm. The church was full. My lord's kin spilled into pews left vacant by Cornelius's family. Only his parents and a sister sat waiting behind him. In the front pew, Cornelius was alone with his friend, neither of them turning their heads. I thought of Thomas's wedding when with his brother Harry escorting him he had sat bolt upright, waiting for Isobel and her father. How beautiful the church was now, pristine, its restoration, which had taken so long, complete. The new organ was muted, bathing us in its gentle, mellow tones. Posies of flowers decorated the pew ends, their motif repeated in the blooms that fell in profusion at the altar steps. In my place, feeling the presence of the Blessed Saint, I knelt in prayer. Comforted, my mind could drift away.

Suddenly the organ came to life and I jumped. Harry touched me and in gratitude I held his hand. Together we stood. Lydia, full of grace, glided past us on her father's arm. She was the same age as I had been when at the altar rail I had given my love and my life to Decimus. In his black suit, gold watch chain drawn across his breast, my husband was still a handsome man.

Cornelius and Lydia faced the rector. The ceremony had begun. Cornelius's voice, strong and steady, answered: 'I will'. Then Lydia, in tones that were soft and reverent, made her reply. I heard the words: 'Who giveth this woman'. Decimus placed his daughter's hand into the waiting hands of the rector and I watched as my lord gave Lydia away. A shiver so tiny I could have imagined it was but a feather drifting past me. Decimus joined Harry and me in the pew, Lydia no longer his responsibility.

The rector, holding Lydia's hand, pressed it into Cornelius's and Cornelius took his gift of him. As they made their vows, I observed the look of love which passed between them, but my undisciplined mind had wandered away from the beautiful service, thinking instead of my poor unwed mother. Could she, lying in her unmarked grave, see her granddaughter wed today? Silently I prayed for my mother's Soul.

With the sliding of the ring on to her finger, Cornelius and Lydia were wed. The rector looked up. In thunderous tones, he addressed the congregation. For any who might seek to meddle and defy the Will of Almighty God, he intoned the unforgettable words.

'Those whom God hath joined together let no man put asunder.'

Holding tight to my lord's hand, I murmured, 'Amen'.

Decimus, not releasing me, led me to the vestry, where together with Cornelius's parents we witnessed the signing of the Marriage Register. Then, in procession, walking behind Amelia and Cornelius's friend, Decimus with Cornelius's mother and I on the arm of his father, we followed the bride and groom out into the sunlight.

Rose petals covered the ground. The gypsies had strewn them, so that Lydia, their daughter too, should walk through a fragrant carpet. In a colourful throng, the gypsies waved us on our way.

By the time we reached home, soft white clouds had rolled in from the sea. Decimus's kin filled the house and I had not known such contentment, for our dear daughter was happy. Fearing it might rain before they boarded their train in Milbury, we hurried the newly weds on their way. Decimus had helped me to dress their trap with ribbons and flowers. Also, he had made an arch of willow, which, too, we covered in flowers, that they might ride in a sweet-smelling chariot. Ella cried to see Lydia go, for she was so young and took nothing with her save her love for her husband.

Until they were well out of sight, we called after them. It was only then that Harry told me Perry was lame.

'He'll be all right, Mother, but he's getting old and it will happen again.'

Was it wrong that I be concerned for the welfare of a horse? But dear Perry was more than a horse to me. My love had tried to set me free and, while Peregrine the Wanderer still lived, that freedom was not yet dead. When all the guests had gone home, in the silence of a velvety night I crept out through the yard and up into the first field. Perry heard me. The grass was wet from recent rain and the dust had settled. From the west, pale light on the ocean was reflected by lazy, slow-moving clouds.

Perry, my winged Pegasus, my inspiration and joy, came to me. When he pushed his soft warm muzzle into my hand, I thought of the first time he had come to me that morning after we had brought him home from Rockingham. There was nothing but grass to give him then, but Perry had not minded and had willingly taken it. Brushing my face against the strong thick neck, I let him nibble at the edge of my gown. I had never disappointed him again. He took from me the carrot I brought him, the grinding of his teeth sounding hollow against my cheek.

I dreamed of the day when, like Boadicea in her chariot, I had taken Perry's reins for the very first time and felt his strength. But I had loved him from the very moment his great feathered feet had danced for me at Rockingham Fair. After Satan had lain in wait for me on the long road to Bristol, Perry had brought me safely home again. Hearing a sound behind me, I turned as Decimus touched my shoulder. In the darkness, I looked up, straining to see into his face.

'I notice Harry has told you, Perry is lame.'

'I cannot help but fear for him, lord. What will you do?'

'I know you love the horse, Mary, but I will not keep an animal through the winter that cannot earn its keep.'

His words chilled me to the marrow. Pent-up tears overflowed. My knees buckled from under me.

'I beg of you, lord. Please, not yet!'

For a moment, Decimus said nothing. Then, as though he wearied of explanations, he spoke to me.

'You learned a harsh lesson long ago, Mary, when I took Thomas from you. Do you really need to learn that lesson again?'

I could not reply. Words that might have made him change his mind were trapped in my throat.

He took my arm. 'Come away now, lest we forget this happy day.'

A whole week had gone by. I could not bring myself to see Perry again, lest he should guess from my demeanour my lord's intentions. Sitting astride his horse, Harry passed the scullery window. Tethered behind, his feathered feet hesitant now, was the old Welsh Cob. Soon Perry's spirit would be free to roam at will the hills of his native land. But my spirit was destined to be captive and doomed to dwell in servitude. I was numbed; tears would not come. Ella led me away from the window and putting her arms around me, my head finding her hard, bony breast, she gave me her love. After all, she was Granny's daughter and I loved her too. When at last my tears flowed, I wept for the beauty that was gone for ever.

Later that night after Harry had returned home alone, my lord took me to the barn. Remains of a withy fire glowed in the darkness.

'I've brought you here, Mary, that you should remember the first time you heard the willow's song that took your spirit to paradise.'

'How can I forget, lord, when even now after all this time my body bears its imprint. I recall afterwards lying in the Garden of Eden, my skin burning, the fire cooled by the dew you had gathered.'

Decimus drew me down and, warmed by the embers, we sat side by side. He stoked the fire and it burst into life, throwing long flickering shadows on to the walls.

'You didn't dream of freedom then, did you, Mary?'

'No, lord, I dreamed of the many sons I should give you and that, like Granny, rarely would be without a child in my womb. But that was yesterday's dream. The freedom you allowed me and your faith in me, that I worked so hard to earn, is finally dead now.'

Stroking my hair, my husband comforted me.

'Do not mourn, Mary. Your freedom was dead long before I took Perry from you. I know the chains that imprison your heart are heavy just now, but they were not always heavy, were they, my darling? How often have you pleaded with me to confine you as I used to?'

I kissed his hand, desperate that he might understand the quandary in my mind.

'I know it, lord, but I have been such a disappointment to you.'

He cradled me in his arms.

'No, Mary, you are my love. For as long as the spirit of your forebears invades this village, I cannot set you free. I was a fool to have thought I could and should have known better.'

With his loving arms blotting out the world, I found solace.

'I have something to tell you, Mary, and hope it will make you happy. I have decided that Richard shall stay at school and in time will enter him for university. We could do with a scholar in the family.'

'We have always known Richard was different, lord. When you took him from my womb, I dwelt in Arcadia.'

'Richard has not the temperament to be a farmer. He will not waste his life pitting his energies against ignorant men with their mindless superstition. I pray to God he will grasp the opportunity I intend for him.'

The ferocity in my love's eyes reminded me of another time when I had seen that look of fury and was taken back over the years to the day he had walked me into the Great River. Because the men of the village had mocked me, Decimus had shown me my father's house.

I stroked my husband's face. What a price he had paid for marrying me. Richard, his youngest son, would be spared the pain that Decimus still endured. Now there was just one son left at home and he was fully grown.

'My love, I feel I know your mind and imagine Harry will inherit the farm when you die.'

Decimus looked down on me and I knew in spite of everything, he loved me. For a moment he said nothing.

'You are right, Mary. I have already told Harry the farm will be his one day.'

'I see compassion in Harry's eyes when he observes my supplication. I believe he has grown to understand our love, but fear he may be like you and will not let compassion stop him doing to a woman what you have done to me.'

'No, Mary, I don't suppose he will. We Hillyers don't know the meaning of the word compromise.'

In his arms, I did not care.

'I know you are not as other men, my love. Not for a moment have I regretted the suffering you have brought me. Better I should live just one more day in your loving hands, lord, than spend a lifetime with some other man.'

Decimus shook his head. His look of love transported me and I dared not break his mood.

'Truly, Mary, I have given you a strange life. I doubt if Harry will find a woman who will let him love her as I have loved you.'

'No matter, lord, so long as she gives him sons to carry on your name.'

How strange was my lord's countenance.

'Come, Mary, the embers of the fire are burned low and you are far too old to let me love you in the dirt.'

Should I ask him now why he sorrowed for a past that was buried before he knew me? Fearing to anger him, my courage deserted me and meekly I followed him to bed.

CHAPTER XXII

Charlotte

S
ummers have turned to autumn and winters given way to spring again. Inexorably our lives are passing. Decimus has more time for me and it seems the vows we made all those years previously are renewed. He and I have never been so happy together as we are now. His dark, coarse hair has turned to grey and the damp has penetrated his bones. My lord is no longer young and God has not seen fit to return to him the immense strength he enjoyed before his accident. That event proved to be a turning point and, though I still remember it well, it occurred more than nine years ago. But Decimus's presence still towers over us all and there is no doubting he is master of his household.

Harry, made serious by the duties he has inherited, stands as tall as his father. I am comforted to know that, should I outlive my own dear husband, as his widow I shall stay in this house and make my obeisance to Harry. Ella looks to the day when Harry will be wed and a younger woman can help her with her chores. Her strong hands that have turned butter and held aloft heavy golden cheeses are gnarled and tired.

Thomas and Isobel at Cloudsmoor Farm now have three small children. William, approaching eight years old, will soon go away to school. In the intervening years, Isobel has given Thomas two daughters. Her hair no longer flaming, Isobel is withdrawn and dutiful, her pale skin fragile, like old porcelain.

Sometimes I receive letters from Lydia, but mostly they are

addressed to Ella, who always lets me read them. Decimus and I had hoped before too long we should receive an invitation from Cornelius to visit Lydia in her new home, but strangely in all this time it has not been forthcoming. In nearly three years of marriage, Lydia has not conceived and, though her love for Cornelius appears undiminished, in the lines she writes, Ella and I sense her anxiety. On more than one occasion Decimus has written to Cornelius inviting them to stay, but each time Cornelius in the politest way has declined and we wonder when we shall see our daughter again.

Hidden between the letters the postman left on the mat, and addressed to Decimus, protruded a postcard. The lazy, almost illegible scrawl was Cornelius's hand. He and Lydia, at the end of July, would be staying for a week at the Swan Inn in Milbury. There was business to which he must attend. He invited us to take tea with them. My poor Decimus, he still mourned the loss of his daughter and was bitterly affronted. Why stay at the Inn when they would be so much more comfortable with us? Convinced now that our daughter was not happy, none the less I longed for the day in July when we should see her.

Ella, looking more like Granny every day, sat in the trap, a large black umbrella shading her face from the sun. Decimus helped me up, then took his place beside me. None of us spoke very much, each contemplating how we should cope with Lydia's changed circumstances. Why should unhappy memories crowd my mind? I thought of the time once before when Ella had accompanied us to Milbury. That day Granny had been buried in her family's vault.

To the rear of the Inn was a pretty garden and, leaving us there, Decimus went inside. Looking up at the open windows, where lace curtains ballooned outwards, I saw a movement. The lace, quickly raised, just as quickly was lowered. I knew Lydia was watching us. Why should she be so hesitant? On a wobbly little table, a maid laid tea for five.

Lydia, on the arm of Cornelius, with Decimus following behind, appeared in the doorway – my first sight of our daughter since her wedding day. Now I was sure; something was wrong; but what? Cornelius, his charm intact, greeted us as though it were the most natural thing in the world that we take tea in such a public place. Lydia's eyes were filled with tears; she had not instigated this formal meeting. Decimus, looking as though he would burst, somehow for Lydia's sake contained himself, though I wondered the handle of his cup did not snap in two, for his knuckles showed white as he gripped it.

Lydia had lost weight. The dress she wore was too large. Could it be a hand-me-down? Her shoes were scuffed, the edges of her petticoat frayed a little. I could not understand. Cornelius was not short of money. She still looked up at her husband with the soft, hopeless look of love, yet when Cornelius raised his arm merely to flick away a wasp Lydia flinched as if expecting him to strike her. She was frightened of him, but why should that surprise me? Did I not fear my husband too?

But Cornelius did not return her secret looks and I guessed he could not love her as Decimus loved me. We had intruded and I wondered, would it have been better had we not come? I recalled old Queenie's warning and terrible thoughts threatened to overwhelm me. As soon as tea was over, stiffly Decimus took his leave of them and, glad to be going home, sadly we left Lydia behind.

Ella kissed her niece goodbye and my cheek in turn for a moment brushed Lydia's.

'I love you, Lydia.'

'Do you, Mother? How can you when for years I was so unkind to you?'

'My little one, one day if God looks kindly on you and you bear your husband a child, then you will understand. I shall always love you, Lydia. I am your mother.'

Five months have gone by since we saw Lydia and we are looking forward to Christmastide of this year 1889 when Richard will come home from school, not to return there. Ella and I have made plum puddings and Decimus has let us burn the lamps right into the night so that all will be ready for the Festival of

232

the Nativity. Guinea fowl hang by their feet maturing in the pantry and Ella has made furmity, for which I confess I have not acquired a taste.

On the eve of Christmas, surrounded by feathers, my fingers raw and my nose tickling, for I had just finished plucking the birds, Richard took me by the hand and led me to the parlour. The son who was still my babe had not lost the far-away look in his eyes. Gently, he was laughing at me.

'Close your eyes, Mother, and do not open them again until I tell you.'

Laughing too, I did as he asked, stumbling over the doorsill as he led me, blind, into the room. When he bade me, I opened my eyes and, looking up in wonderment, could not believe what I saw.

'Richard, my darling, what is this?'

'It's a Christmas Tree, Mother. The Queen has one, so why should not we?'

In the corner, bathed in its own light, was a fir tree. It was our very first Christmas Tree. It stood all of six feet high. Thin red, green and white candles, perched on the end of every branch, flickered. Tiny balls of wax spilled over so that the lower branches were made pendulous with stalactites. Gaily-coloured streamers shimmered in the draught. Boxes, wrapped in pretty paper, balanced precariously between the spiky branches. Atop the tree, Richard had set an angel. Her white muslin wings had silver tips and a golden halo was suspended over her waxen head. Her eyes were downcast in humility, but her mouth wore a beatific smile. Reaching up to my youngest child, I held his dear sweet face between my hands.

'How did I not know of this, my darling? Are my eyes always closed?'

Richard could not conceal his smile, but it was fond and I knew he loved me.

'You dream, Mother. It was not difficult to keep you away, but truly, I brought you into the parlour for another reason. I want to talk to you quietly while you are on your own.'

I shook my head, lest he, like his brother Thomas once before, should wish to take me into his confidence. I could keep nothing from his father and had failed Thomas that day. This son, though in some ways so young, had a maturity about him, an air which was hard to describe.

'No, Mother. There is nothing I am to tell you which Father does not already know.'

Dear Richard had guessed my dilemma.

'I shall be here on the farm for a while helping Harry and Father. But come next harvest, I shall leave and go up to Oxford.'

'My darling boy, your father has told me. It is his dearest wish that you become a scholar.'

Richard set me down in Granny's chair, a position that was always denied me; but not listening to my protestations and imploring me to be quiet, Richard sat on the stool that was my usual place and, holding my hands in his, told me of his plans.

'I have chosen to read Theology, Mother. God has called me and I am destined for the priesthood.'

The voice in my head screamed. 'Dear God, they will not have you.' Aloud the words could not form. Richard held tight to both my hands that had started to tremble.

'Tell me what is in your heart, Mother.'

'My child, I cannot.'

How could I sit at the feet of my lord yet again and listen as he told Richard the awful truth?

'Look at me, Mother.'

I could not look up. He would see my shame. Staring at his hands that still held mine, at last I found my voice.

'You cannot be a priest, Richard. Your Mother is tainted. The Devil has touched me with his hoof.'

Through my tears, I looked up at my youngest son. His eyes no longer laughed at me, but held mine steady. He was not shocked.

'Hush, Mother dear, your secrets do not frighten me.'

'My little one, you cannot possibly understand the evil in me, for I am called a Daughter of Satan. But for your father, who has purged me of the sins I inherited, I am without redemption.'

Richard's hands, cupped around mine, warmed and soothed me, but he had to know.

'I am damned, Richard.'

'No, Mother. Harry and Father have told me what you cannot. You are as pure as is the angel I placed on the tree. Her smile makes me think of you. You have not sinned, Mother, yet even if you had you will be forgiven. Our Lord tells us that a sinner, if he repenteth, shall not be denied the Kingdom of Heaven.'

How long had Richard known about me? Had I been foolish not to see it before now?

'The men of the village have not forgiven me, Richard. For fear of Jacob Thwaite's vengeance I rarely leave the confines of this house without your father's protection.'

'I know that too, Mother. But you have learned to accept what you cannot change.'

I was bewildered.

'Richard, my darling, your love gives me great comfort. Go, study and, with God's grace, one day I pray you will become a priest.'

My beloved Decimus was standing in the doorway. He was watching me and, fearing he might upbraid me for my familiarity, I jumped from his chair and ran to him. I kissed his hand and he held me, making it easier for me to lower myself before him. From my knees, I looked up at our youngest son, anxious that he might laugh at me in my subjection, just as Lydia had so often done. But Richard, bending over me, kissed my forehead. In a voice barely above a whisper, he murmured his approval.

'God bless you, Mother,' he said.

Isobel is more frail each time we see her at the old house that had been my inheritance, and it seems she is sustained only by her love for Thomas. With time we have become used to her indisposition and no longer comment on her frailty. Richard writes long enthusiastic letters to his father from Oxford. But Lydia's letters to Ella have become shorter and she writes more often to me. In two more years Lydia has still not conceived and from reading between her lines we realise she knows now, as we had already guessed, that Cornelius's love has turned from her. But Decimus can do nothing to help Lydia, for having given his daughter away he will not defy the will of Almighty God.

Harry has found himself an attractive girl to wed. Her name is Charlotte Watkins. She is daughter of a master mariner who has recently retired to the Vale. Her mother is long dead and Charlotte keeps house for her father. She is just eighteen years old, while Harry is ten years her senior.

The snow, which usually went as quickly as it came, was fearsomely deep and all but the track through the village was impassable for wheels. It was early in February when Harry saddled his horse and set off for Captain Watkins's house. Decimus laughed when he observed my preparations for Harry's return with Charlotte and her father.

'Mary, my love, it is not you who is the lamb going to slaughter.'

'I should not be shocked by anything you say, lord, but Charlotte is very young and I fear Harry is much too old for her.'

Though my cheeks burned deepest red, Decimus was amused by my boldness.

'No, Mary, you were only eighteen when I wed you. Charlotte is not too young to learn to be Harry's wife. From what I have seen of her, she has good full breasts and hips wide enough for childbearing.'

I did not know whether to laugh or cry. Decimus would not take me seriously and I was shamed by his calculated appraisal of a woman. It came as no surprise, though, that Harry was like his father. I had guessed a long time ago that he would be just as objective as Decimus had been when he came to choose himself a wife.

'You make fun of me, lord.'

'That I do, Mary. You have no defence either, but in truth I hope she likes you, my dear, for there is much that you can teach her. Harry will not make Thomas's mistake. He will wed a woman whose body is made for loving.'

'I will do whatever you ask of me, lord. I shall not forget the love your mother gave me. She helped me during those early months when I feared you terribly.'

Decimus opened his arms to me, and Ella, who was busying herself almost unnoticed, left us alone. He drew me safe against the rough tweed of his jacket and my face found the warmth beneath. How lucky indeed would Charlotte be should she find a love like ours.

'Mary, my darling, when Charlotte meets you, she will see a mirror image of the woman she must become, if she is to make a man like Harry happy.'

It was almost three in the afternoon when Annie woke me. I rarely slept during the day, but Decimus had insisted I rest before I meet Charlotte and her father. Annie brushed my hair, more silver now than black, setting it high on my head in a complicated knot. The gown I wore was simple, the black wool was thin, like nun's veiling, the neck cut a little too low for modesty. Slowly I descended the flight of stairs and, hearing voices in the reception room, I knocked before entering, then at my husband's command I opened the door.

Harry took my arm and guided me. Decimus stood beside his tasselled chair. I kissed my lord's hand, bowed my head and sank at his feet.

'Mary, I want you to meet Captain Watkins and his daughter Charlotte, who is to be betrothed to Harry.'

Smiling gently, Decimus helped me regain my balance and Charlotte, startled by my submission, in turn bent her knee. Flushed with confusion, she was small and dainty. Light brown hair was swept off her face in a bun. Her complexion was fair, but she was not as pale as was Isobel before Thomas married her. With steady green eyes, she held my gaze and my heart went out to her for her courage, imagining only too well the fear she tried to hide. No doubt she had heard the lurid tales that were told about me.

Captain Watkins looked down on me. He was as big as Decimus, with the same worldly air. Dropping him a curtsy, I lowered my eyes lest he should think me forward.

'My dear Mrs Hillyer, I am delighted to make your acquaintance,' he said.

His tone was warm and he was not contemptuous of me as others had so often been. He seemed not about to ridicule me for my position and I felt our family at last had a friend. I guessed he could see farther than the village boundary and sensed my husband's delight in his company. Though I could not quite put my finger on what it was about Captain Watkins that was so familiar, there was something. Maybe it was his bearing, for he carried an authority very similar to that of my own dear husband, yet, as far as I knew, their paths had not crossed.

When Captain Watkins and his daughter took their leave of us, the light had already gone. Captain Watkins's horse was strong, with feathered feet, and for a moment I wanted to weep, such was his likeness to Perry. Decimus lifted Charlotte up to Harry, who, sitting back in his saddle, clasped her in front of him. Outlined against the snow, their shadowy figures disappeared into the night.

Decimus pronounced himself well pleased. Charlotte's betrothal had her father's blessing. Captain Watkins had witnessed my subjection and could not doubt his daughter would in time learn to love Harry as I loved his father. The wedding was set for Easter and I was content, knowing instinctively that Charlotte would have the strength to give her life to my son.

CHAPTER XXIII

Decimus

Later that night I lay in bed with my lord and he held me in his arms. In the flickering glow of a single candle, we talked of when we met and were betrothed in a springtime I could scarcely remember, that was so long ago. Just a little hesitantly, I confided to Decimus my worries.

'My love, I cannot help but fear for Charlotte. I seek not to question you, for you have already impressed on me that she is not too young for Harry, but please can you ask him to be gentle with her?'

Decimus's eyebrows shot up. He was not pleased by my interjection.

'No, Mary. I certainly cannot do that and I caution you to say nothing to Harry.'

'I would not dream of talking to Harry of such things, lord. But I had hoped you might.'

'Was I not gentle enough with you then, my dear sweet wife?'

'It seemed so at the time, but no, lord, you did not love me and were cruel when you broke my maidenhead and lay me in the dirt.'

'Aye, Mary, that's true. I was brutal with you, but, looking back, would you have wished it otherwise?'

'I should do, lord, but no, your harshness awakened a passion in me I could not have guessed I owned.'

'Do not fear for Charlotte, then, Mary. Harry is his own man, as was my father. My mother loved him much as you love me. I am convinced of that, Mary. Though they rarely left the village, they fought convention together. Adversity sealed their love. Harry is like my father and will not hurt Charlotte as I hurt you. Thank God he has not suffered the burden of my experience.'

'Lord, whatever do you mean?'

I felt his body grow tense.

'Nothing Mary, my tongue is loosened. I have imbibed too much fine wine with Captain Watkins. Now go to sleep.'

He had closed the conversation. Something had happened and he had withdrawn from me, yet I could not let him go.

'My love, one day you will tell me what you have avoided these past thirty years or more. Do you not love me enough to trust me with your secrets?'

There, it was out. Never before had I dared. Looking up into his face, I put my arms around him that he should know that, whatever he had withheld from me, I loved him. He seemed to dream but I was not a part of his dream. Fearing terribly that even now I might lose him, and regretting my impulsiveness, I stroked his chest; the tension in his body seemed to ease just a little.

'At last you have trapped me, Mary, and I have no choice but to tell you of the years I spent at sea.'

I could scarce draw breath; the shock of his confession falling on me like a stone. His words, festering inside him for so long, came forth in a pent-up torrent and I could not interrupt.

'I was just sixteen years old when in Bristol Docks I signed ship's articles and was taken on as an apprentice. Life was merciless beyond your imagining. The sea was my cruel and unforgiving master for seven years before I returned to my father's house.'

Oh dear God, what had I done? I still lay in his arms, but, in disbelief, was mute. Granny had not mentioned a life at sea.

'You wonder why I could not tell you, Mary?'

His voice had hardened so that I hardly recognised its tone. I felt so cold. Seven whole years was such a long time.

'In all the years I loved her, lord, why did Granny not speak of it, for surely you had nothing to hide?'

Decimus had stiffened again and I could not hold back my tears.

'You will never countenance what I have had to hide, Mary. My mother feared my past so much, for the sake of her sanity she banished it from her mind. To preserve my sanity, I too drove my past from my thoughts. I had intended to take my secret to the grave and not to yoke you, my love, with the burden of my guilt. No one who still lives knows the remorse that haunts me. I cannot be rid of it.'

A nerve twitched in his face. Avoiding the confrontation, for a moment my mind recalled that night when Decimus had told Thomas about me and the self-same nerve had twitched in Thomas's face. Yet I could not move my hand to touch my husband now.

'Does Ella know of those years, lord?'

'No, Mary. A young man is allowed to sow his wild oats. My sister would have been the last to ask questions of me.'

'But, lord, what made you leave this beautiful Vale?'

'I owed my grandfather at the Castle a favour.'

The deep-set lines in his face I knew so well and which had been there when he courted me were set even deeper. What revelation was coming now?

'There was little I could expect to inherit as my father's youngest son. Grandfather knew that and paid for me to go away to school. He was a merchant venturer with investments in shipping. He suggested that, if I were to serve on one of his ships, I could be of use to him by reporting back on his captains. The morality of it didn't worry me and I jumped at the opportunity to travel and see the world.

'Grandfather also had a liking for the pipe, which incidentally my cousin shares. That gave me an advantage.'

'Do you mean Cousin Hector, lord? And what pipe?'

'The opium pipe, Mary. When he was learning to be a doctor, Hector cultivated a liking for the stuff. Why do you think he took Lydia into his house for all those years? Did you really imagine it stemmed from the kindness of his heart?'

241

I did not know what to think. My world had been turned upside down.

'Yes, lord. Why should I think otherwise? Does Hector know of your time at sea?'

Decimus, his voice rasping as he tried to maintain control, weighed what he said.

'Only that bit I wished to tell him.'

'I am covered in confusion, lord. Please say no more. I wish with all my heart I had not started this.'

'Well you did, Mary, and now you will know the whole story, for I have kept it from you too long.'

A strange voice that belonged to another man came from his lips.

'And my payment for services rendered? For generations Hillyers have lived here and worked this land as tenant farmers, paying their dues to the FitzWarrens. My grandfather and I grew to understand one another and I was rewarded for my efforts with the freehold.'

'But is that so terrible that you had to keep it secret all these years? I fear, lord, it cannot be all you have concealed.'

He drew breath and spat out his words.

'No, now I have started you will have to learn the rest of it. I was Third Mate by the time I was nineteen. I've always been ambitious, Mary. Then the Captain found out what I was up to and picked an argument, paying me off in some godforsaken, stinking, rat-infested port.'

I was mesmerised by my husband's words. There was no stopping him now.

'You have heard tales of slave ships, Mary. They were pariahs of the sea, but there was a good living to be made from slavery long after the trade was officially banned. I was greedy, but then I've always been greedy, and for my sins signed on as Mate. I wouldn't have been Mate on any other ship. Then for three brutal years, a fugitive from the law, I served on a slaver!'

My heart cried out in anguish.

'But the trade in slaves was abolished before you were even born,' I said.

Ignoring me, he was weeping, but he could not stop now.

'They were herded into pens, whole families at a time. We bartered for them, Mary. Sometimes we had to make a run for it, but to begin with it was easy enough to evade patrols sent out by the British and French garrisons. It was only later that it got more difficult, until eventually we had to sail right round the Cape and back, picking them up from the east coast. But it was a lucrative business and at the time I didn't give a damn.

'Do you have any idea what it was like, months at a time at sea with a human cargo? The stench of rotting flesh is still in my nostrils and the degradation I was accomplice to will live with me until my dying day. The cruelty we inflicted on those poor wretches did not matter to me then. I shall rot in Hell for it.'

My heart, battered by the enormity of his crime, was numb. Slowly, realisation of what he had done came to me. His bitterness and recrimination swept over me. Even now, he had not finished.

'My God, Mary, it should have taught me a lesson, but it didn't. My greed was not sated or how could I have married you for your money?'

I could not stop him even had I wished to.

'You've never seen the fury of a hurricane. The wind and the waves . . . the ship thrown about, the wind ripping through us, as it carried us along. Below, they'd set up a wail that rose and fell as she shuddered in a mountainous sea to maintain her way. Day after day it would go on and we prayed, God knows we prayed, that we puny men, engaged in a disgusting trade, should survive.

'Then, Mary, when at last the seas grew calm, we would throw the dead over the side. There was no Christian burial for them, poor souls. In the Americas, for good money, we handed over as many as remained alive. Then, we turned her round and the whole bloody voyage started again.'

Holding him close, I wept for him. No wonder Granny had not told me. I remembered now how she had cried each time she talked of her youngest son. She dared not risk telling me all of this and destroying my love for him, ruin his only chance of happiness. Knowing, too, that he did not love me when he wed me, she would have condemned him to a life of misery, while I, broken and in servitude, fearing him, would have surrendered without love. As he opened his mouth to speak, I touched his face. I still loved him.

'We covered up her name, flew no flag and our motley crew, of all nations and none, could not go home.'

My penance was paid, but there was nothing I could do to ease his agony. Still he unburdened himself on me.

'From my wanderings, Mary, I embraced strange ideas and brought them home with me. I saw women in bondage serving their masters. You had no chance of a normal life in my accursed hands.'

His voice was vicious.

'Do you want me to release you from your vows, Mary?'

Suddenly I needed to take no more of his bitterness. My courage had not failed me.

'I will not allow your conscience to drive out my love, Decimus. In the sight of God you are my husband and always will be. You have shown me the Garden of Eden and purged my sins as no other man could have done. You have fathered my children. I will not let you extinguish that which is beautiful.'

He laughed and a savageness came from his throat. Still he dwelt in the past and I was powerless to stop him. To myself I vowed he would not again bear his guilt alone.

'I do not care what you have kept from me, lord, and forgive you whatever evil you have done. If the dreadful fires of Hell lay claim to you, then I will follow wherever you go.'

The candle was throwing long shadows across the wall. My own words had frightened me and I was shaking, terrified by my commitment. On the wall, the distorted image I saw was not my husband's face, but the face that had leered at me on the road when I had travelled alone to Bristol. My courage nearly deserting me, I beseeched my husband to blow out the light.

As I lay shivering in the cold and the dark, though, I knew I did not really fear Satan. Before God I had but one master and he lay, his head in my arms, his mind in mortal torment. A thought so cruel I should not have expressed it came to me.

'Was Captain Watkins also a slaver, my love?'

'No, Mary. He is an honourable man.'

The comparison was more than my love could bear. In the intimacy of his bed, where none but I could hear his weakness, as I cradled him in my arms, his body shook with great rending sobs.

'I thank God your Jesse brought you to me, Mary. He knew, but for you, I was a doomed man. Without your love, I should not have been turned from my wickedness.'

'Hush, my love, do not torment yourself further.'

But Decimus had to go on.

'After I guessed who you were, Mary, each time you looked at me I saw the face of your poor mother and thought I felt her curse on me. Fearing you, I sent you to Mistress Morgan, telling her to cut my mark deep into your flesh. Yet as I hurt you more and watched your pain, I saw by your devotions that you atoned for the sins you had inherited. By your sorrows, I too hoped to be purged and forgiven. I shaved your head and gave you a scourge, yet it was not you, but I, who had sinned and was beyond redemption. No matter how badly I treated you, you still loved me. I even saw your love grow as your sorrowing increased. When I took Thomas from you, I knew I must leave you with nothing in this world, for it was the only way I could see of releasing you from the terrible burden of your birth and I could take you to a place where I hoped you would be happy. Can God forgive me the evil that I have done, Mary?'

'My love, I do not know. All I can repeat is my conversation with Richard. If a sinner repenteth, then the Lord will not deny him the Kingdom of Heaven. That is my hope too.

'But before God, you will always be my lord, no matter who or what you are. Whether we enter Heaven or Hell, we shall do it together. I shall never leave you and swear you will not sorrow alone again. I pray that, by my sorrowing, your sins will be purged, lord. Otherwise, of all men, why did Jesse choose to give me to you?

'You will not remember the occasion, my love, It was my first harvest supper and Jesse sat beside me. He knew I was carrying Thomas, though I was scarcely sure of it myself. He advised me then and I have not forgotten his words. That day, my soul would not lie still within me and I despaired for the future. Jesse admonished me and told me I must have faith, to give you my will and to obey you above all things. He said I was to keep nothing from you and joy would come of it . . . Do not imagine for one moment that the old man was ignorant of your past, lord.'

For a long while, we lay together in the blackness of the winter night and Decimus said nothing. When at last he spoke to me again, he did not mince his words.

'I am a hard, cruel man, Mary, made so by the life I have chosen to lead. I cannot change what I am, nor would your Jesse expect it of me. You will not benefit, because you have seen me in my weakness.'

Weeping with relief, I found his hands, drew them to me and kissed them. Nothing had changed between us. There was no need for words. The chasm that had yawned before me was closed and slowly, with truth shared, we drifted into sleep.

Mary Cheyne Hillyer,
1892.

CHAPTER XXIV

Innslow

We welcomed Charlotte into the family as Harry's bride. What a dear, sweet child she is. Charlotte, so anxious to learn, has been taken under Ella's wing. They spend rapturous hours together discussing recipes. No longer fearing to lose her position within her brother's household, Ella is only too pleased that in time Charlotte will take over the duties her hands have grown too tired to perform. I am often excluded from their conversations, yet try not to be envious that Charlotte will become mistress of this house. From the very first day Decimus brought me here, I have accepted my role will never be that, and my strange situation is unlikely to be repeated. I hope that soon Charlotte may take me into her confidence. Acknowledging that she will find it difficult to understand my unusual position, Decimus has cautioned me to wait, thinking it better that Harry's new wife adjust more slowly to the special circumstances in which she finds herself. Charlotte is getting over the embarrassment she experienced when first she faced the family each morning, though as the weeks pass I notice the increasing severity of Harry's manner and doubt if he truly loves her. I believe he has quite forgotten that day when almost in tears he lifted me in his arms and railed against his father. Sometimes I catch Decimus's eye and he will slowly smile, shaking his head, as if he too remembers the occasion, though by his look he cautions me lest by some carelessness I speak of it. I find myself longing for Harry to see Charlotte's loyalty and the transparency of her love for him.

Decimus allows Annie, who is well schooled in the ways of love, to attend Charlotte, though Charlotte is repelled by her ugliness. Poor Annie has aged prematurely and I can understand Charlotte's reluctance to allow Annie to touch her. I am sure, though, that when Charlotte comes to know Annie she will see, hidden behind the mask, a pure and gentle heart. I pray in a little while trust will grow between them.

Each morning during this long hot summer, when I am left to toil alone, as is still my husband's insistence, and in the hours I spend in quiet contemplation, I pray that Almighty God may one day forgive my beloved Decimus and release him from his dreadful burden. Often he and I walk together on the Sea Bank. Sometimes I wait for him to return from the fishing. We are closer now, though a while ago I should not have thought that possible. Over the years there have been so many things about Decimus that seemed odd at the time. Now I know he was a seafaring man, they begin to make sense. His countenance too – that strange look as he stares into the middle distance, not noticing irritating trivia – now I understand.

All the while in those happy summer months, though we did not realise it at the time, storm clouds had been gathering. Charlotte was heavy with her first child when the old year of 1892 gave way to a new. On a cold, bleak day in early January the postman came, delivering a letter from Lydia. The envelope, addressed to Decimus, smudged and barely legible, had not been stained by the rain. Lydia's tears had fallen unhindered and her script was difficult to read. After first scanning the letter himself, Decimus placed it into my hands, his arm around me, drawing me close. My heart fluttered, guessing her lines boded ill, for Decimus was rarely tender unless his thoughts had turned to love.

Lydia told us she was barren and Cornelius no more made pretence at love. She begged us to travel to Innslow to see her, desperate that her father should persuade Cornelius to care for her again. Laying the letter on the table, I looked up at my lord. Pain was chiselled deep into his face. He had promised Lydia to seek a husband who would love her, yet I knew well it was not Decimus's fault but mine that Cornelius's love had turned from her. Now, by her vows, she was locked into a loveless union. What could her father do to help her? I thought of her happiness the day she was wed and my shiver, almost imagined, when Decimus had given her away. But worst of all, I remembered those awesome words of the marriage service: 'Those whom God hath joined together let no man put asunder.'

Decimus determined that as soon as the weather improved, notwithstanding Cornelius's reluctance to see us, we should travel to Innslow. With that in mind he wrote to his son-in-law.

But I must not look too far ahead, for to do so would be to deny a pleasure that for Decimus and me was very sweet. At the end of February, not a year after they were wed, Charlotte gave birth to a son and for a little while we were able to put aside Lydia's troubles. With Annie to guide me, I delivered my grand-son of Charlotte. Harry had chosen his wife wisely, for, though I wept with her in her pain, her body gave up the child with ease. Taking the babe from her, as my children had been taken from me, I did not let her touch him, understanding now how Harry would come to love his wife. Leaving Charlotte in Annie's care, I swaddled the infant and carried him to the parlour where his father waited. Placing him in Harry's arms, he knew his son. There was wetness in Harry's eyes as he looked down at the tiny form, the child grasping his finger so tightly. Harry left me then with Decimus and returned to Charlotte, that his son might suckle from her. Harry would see by her recent suffering the depth of Charlotte's love for him and I knew he would not be unaffected. I prayed that she would, in the timespan God allowed her, give Harry many fine sons to bear the name of Hillyer.

The journey to Innslow opened my eyes to a different world, remote from the slow, ordered pace of life beside the Great River. I had not boarded a train before and I held tightly to Decimus's hand as we walked past the great hissing locomotive, to find our carriage. Decimus laughed, telling me my nervousness reminded him of the day he took me to Rockingham Fair, my new life ahead of me. But seeing my distress, he bit his lip, regretting he had mentioned it, and changed the subject. Though Perry had been dead these past six years, I could not recall that time without in my mind seeing him, his mane and his tail flying in the wind, his feathered feet dancing for me.

The long journey took its toll and I was tired by the time we reached our destination. My ankles had swollen and my corset hurt. My husband had not seen fit to compromise on the austerity of my apparel. Decimus lifted me down on to the platform, then called a porter to carry our bags. The station above Kenford was the nearest to Innslow and, dreading I might have to walk, though it was only a mile or so, I was much relieved to see Cornelius had come to meet us.

He seemed but a shadow of the young man who had courted Lydia. How Cornelius had changed since we last saw him at the Inn in Milbury. With his tow hair matted and the bright blue of his eyes washed out, there was no charm to him now and I wondered what ill health had befallen him in the intervening years. Lydia had not mentioned her husband was sick. The trap he had brought for us to ride in was old and worn out and I doubted had seen polish in many a long day. What sort of reception was this? Cornelius made no effort to make us feel welcome and my unease intensified.

Though my memory of a life before I knew my husband had been almost obliterated, none the less, looking around me, my thoughts returned to Kingswood. All about us, coating the railings and the branches of stunted trees, trapped in the ruts of the road, even clinging to the grass itself, lay a thin layer of coal dust. Disturbed by those half-forgotten memories, I watched the train disappear over a viaduct and steam on, into the coalfields of Somerset. The emotions of a young girl with no one to love came pouring back with a vengeance. In those far-off days, how desperately I had longed to be free. Now I held on to Decimus and he clasped my hands, even unto eternity imprisoning me within his love. The poor, dirty little pony was urged on.

Between high hawthorn hedges, the lane before us wound its way downwards. In some parts it was so overgrown that the hedges threatened to engulf the trap. Perhaps the countryside would be pretty come summer, but without leaves on the trees everything was bare. The valley before us was sheltered and the lie of the land inhibited the wind, so that mercifully the coal dust was left behind. Innslow church, not unlike the one so familiar to us, nestled safe in the bend of a river. In fact, compared with the river we knew, it seemed little more than a stream. Crossing it, I noticed how old the bridge was. Every so often were places to stand to let pack horses pass. Frothing and boiling on one side, on the other the river was slowed by a weir I could not quite see. Weeping willows, tipping their long slender branches into the clear water, were reflected in a deep and tranquil pool.

With a perfunctory grunt, Cornelius, his whip in his hand, pointed out his house, then, as he grunted again, the whip found his pony's back. The farmhouse, though large, was run down and had no colour to it. Paint that had once been white peeled from around the windows and on the roof were gaps in the slates. Outbuildings, with doors hanging from their hinges or lost altogether, were untidy and strewn with broken and rusty implements. But for a few chickens, the yard was deserted. Decimus handed me down, yet the door to the house stayed closed. Surely Lydia must have heard us; had not the noise of our approach disturbed her? His face set and impassive, Cornelius opened the door on to a dark, narrow passageway. The air was stale and I shivered as the damp cold crept into me. This place was not as Lydia in her letters had described it. Muttering that she should not be far away and he would summon his wife, Cornelius showed us into a room at the front of the house that looked out over the road by which we had come. I supposed this must be the parlour, yet how cheerless and dilapidated was everything, far removed from what I had anticipated. On the windowsill, taking the light, in an orange lustre bowl, stood a hideous plant with huge, green fronds. There was no fire in the hearth that lay empty and unblacked; the paintwork of the alcoves on either side was a bilious green. On the ceiling were brown rings where the lamp had been left untended and its wick had smoked. Old floral paper that must have been cheerful when it was hung decorated the walls. Where pictures, now gone, had been, we could see the original colour. Cornelius left us and my husband told me to sit down. The chair was unyielding, its grubby lace antimacassar matching those on the over-stuffed black leather sofas. What could I say? Decimus, too, was lost for words. Surely Lydia's love must have blinded her or she would have noticed when first she came here how poverty-stricken her surroundings appeared. Cornelius, we had been assured, was most comfortably placed. It beggared belief that, in not seven years, this much deterioration could have taken place.

The knock on the door was hesitant. Turning swiftly, Decimus lifted the latch. Lydia, our little girl, her hands falling limply at her sides, stood unspeaking, her head bowed as she waited in the unlit doorway. Until I stood up I could not see her properly, for a high-backed sofa was obscuring her slight figure. Kissing his hand, she knelt before her father; then raising her face, she looked up into his.

Our daughter, not yet twenty-five years old, looked nearer forty. I can scarcely describe her, such was our horror. Her dark hair was sparse and stringy. In places she was bald. Her olive skin had a yellow tinge and Lydia's hazel eyes, always unnerving in their intensity, now were downcast in submission, their cat-like lightness dulled to extinction. Lifting her, Decimus held his child to his breast. Even that day when he had told her of her bitter inheritance, he had not allowed her to kneel. I saw he was weeping, for our daughter was no more than skin stretched over bone. Her hands were red and roughened and the gown that hung on her was the self-same gown she had worn when she had left us on her wedding day.

Decimus carried her in his arms, for she was close to fainting, and with loving tenderness laid her on the hard sofa, placing a cushion under her head. From where she lay, her dull eyes looked up at us, yet still she had not spoken a word. Then in a strange monotonous voice, barely loud enough to catch, for she was wary, she told us of her fear of Cornelius. He had ceased to try for a child. He had given up, for she could not conceive. Instead he beat her, her pain and her servitude pleasuring him.

Old Queenie's words, delivered in her odd hypnotic tones, crowded my mind. Decimus, his face like thunder, took his leave of us and, left on my own with our daughter, I cradled the poor child in my arms. But this Lydia was neither the girl who had run free with the gypsy children nor the composed young maiden who had come home from Hartley. I had hardly known her then, for she had not needed me and her love was only for Ella. I recognised this Lydia, though, and so did her father, for she was the young woman who had caught the eye of a lad and begged him for help as Jacob Thwaite, her lover's son, led her, yoked, through the murderous crowd to her death. My heart cried out for Decimus in his anguish, for at last he could see he had nothing to fear from her.

Though I whispered loving words to her, Lydia turned her head away. Then, in the same shadeless whisper I had heard just now, she told me what had happened to her. First, Lydia talked of the happy times before they were wed, when Cornelius had brought her to Innslow to meet his parents. Hand in hand they had walked on the bank of the little river and watched dragonflies darting before them. Bright blue mayflies had circled them and their love had grown. When Cornelius had brought her back as his bride, they had swum together, naked, in the tranquil pool, then in the long fragrant grass he had taken her virginity and loved her. Lydia had been happy and had looked forward to giving her husband a child. But that summer went by and the next and then the one after that had gone. Still Lydia had not conceived and Cornelius had grown impatient, saying she was cursed as was her mother before her, for Lydia hurt him when he loved her. He had sent her from his bed and, locking her in, made her sleep in a separate room. Yet still loving him and hoping even in her agony to please her husband, Lydia had not minded his cruelty, knowing Cornelius must hurt her if he were to take her soul from her and she in turn were to find peace. But after they had returned from the Inn in Milbury where we had taken tea with them in the garden, Cornelius had rarely loved Lydia again.

Often with her clothes soiled and her hair unkempt, he had left her imprisoned alone for days. Denying her food, he had suggested fasting was good for her soul. Waiting first for her strength to ebb, Cornelius then had taken her out and beaten her. Almost in a dream, Lydia spoke again in that strange, vacant voice. Knowing I should always remember her terrible words, I pitied her.

'The curse of our forebears is truly upon me now, Mother. My husband has taken my spirit, yet he does not love me. Nor any more can I love him. My soul is quite beyond redemption.'

The words of the old Gypsy Queen rang in my head, her warning as clear as the day she had uttered it. Cornelius had taken Lydia and destroyed her, though not in love as my beloved Decimus had bound me to him, but with malice in his heart. While Cornelius lived, Lydia would never be free.

As the evil thought seeped into my mind, I saw and smelt the empty shroud of a chimera that had waylaid me on the road to Bristol. Fear gripped me and I prayed, 'Oh dear God, do not abandon my child.' What further penance must Lydia pay to atone for the sins we had inherited? With all my heart I prayed that God should let me take the burden from my daughter. Closing my eyes, I held her poor wasted hands in mine and together we prayed that her suffering might end and the curse be lifted, that there might be no more generations of women to nurture it.

A commotion had broken out somewhere in the house and I heard Decimus shout. Then there was a thud. Leaving Lydia on the sofa, I ran to the door and opened it. Decimus, dishevelled, strode towards me down the passageway and brushed past me as I held the door for him. Kneeling at the side of the sofa, he clasped his daughter in his arms and turned her face so that she should watch his lips. Such was his remorse, he could scarcely speak.

'I do not expect your forgiveness, Lydia. I promised to give

254

you to a man who would love you. I have broken my promise and can do nothing to help you, my darling. I have spoken to Cornelius, though I fear that has done you more harm than good. You are his chattel as your mother is mine and that cannot be changed. I am so sorry, Lydia, but there is no choice for you. It is not for me to meddle with the will of Almighty God. I pray He will give you strength to keep the vows you made when you were wed.'

Lydia did not weep. As though in a trance, she rose from where she had lain and glided, sylph-like, to the door. Without a backward glance and not a word, she left us.

I saw then that Decimus was hurt. His face was cut and blood coated the knuckles of one hand; though as he got up from his knees, he seemed not to notice.

'We have no further business here, Mary.'

Propelling me, his hand gripping my elbow, he frog-marched me back through the hall and out into the deserted yard. How could my lord leave his daughter in this dreadful place? Wanting to protest, yet seeing his countenance and fearing him, I dared not seek his indulgence. Leaving me for a moment, he went back inside to fetch our bags. Then, finding the dirty little pony, he backed it once more between the shafts of the worn-out trap. When he had loaded our bags and all was secure, Decimus handed me up. Making haste to the station, I was glad in spite of my fatigue that he had decided we should not stay in Innslow. Leaving the pony and trap in the care of the stationmaster, we crossed the line and waited for the train to take us back to Bristol.

It had started to rain and soon the light would fade. The stones on the track, covered in coal dust, were washed and black, treacly water lay in puddles between them. From where we were standing the viaduct was lost to our sight and I wondered how long we should have to wait, cold and wet, with only a flimsy roof for shelter. The rails began to sing and, blessed relief, in the distance rose puffs of white smoke. The train was coming and we were going home.

Decimus found an empty compartment. Unseeing, he stared

out of the window, watching the darkening sky. With his arm about my shoulders, he let me weep. I hurt so much, the vice around my waist bit into me, its satin long since worn away, the uncovered metal making sore my skin. Yet the pain of it being the least of my concerns, I repeated to my lord the conversation I had had with Lydia. I told him of the happy times before she knew she was barren and of how Cornelius turned from her because she hurt him when he loved her.

All of a sudden, I felt my lord grow tense. He shook his head in disbelief. What had I said that had angered him so? I felt my mouth run dry. It was as though I had been struck by a thunderbolt. He jumped from his seat. I had never seen Decimus so distraught and, fearing him, I held his hands to my lips, seeking forgiveness for whatever bad news I had inadvertently brought him.

'I will not believe my daughter is barren, Mary. From what you tell me, it is Cornelius who is to blame. That man will never father a child!'

Though he was deeply angered and shouted at me, at first I failed to understand Decimus's reasoning. Then gradually he calmed sufficiently to explain what, as a woman, I could not know and I came to understand his fury.

I drew him back into his seat, took out my handkerchief and, wetting it with spit, wiped away the blood that had congealed on his face and his poor bruised hand.

'He'll not forget my visit in a hurry, Mary. But I fear he provoked me and Lydia will suffer for my temper. We should not have gone to her. We raised her hopes and now her anguish will be greater than ever.'

Though I was hesitant, I could not let Decimus have the last word, for his sadness threatened to overwhelm him.

'I am glad we went to Innslow, lord. Now Lydia knows we have not forgotten her.'

It was dark and rain was falling steadily as the train drew into Temple Meads. The gas lamps were lit and their light spread across the cobbles. It seemed as if the stars had come down from a blue-black sky, reminding me of happy days gone by, when my

256

lord had first instructed me in the life I must accept if I were to please him. Decimus called a cab, for we could not complete our journey home this night. Snug inside, with the doors enclosing us, and looking out at the broad back of the cabbie with his collar pulled up against the rain, we set off down the incline and into the winking lights of Bristol that beckoned us.

The hotel Decimus ordered the cabbie to take us to was grand and I hung back, but with my husband beside me I need not have worried. Even here he was comfortable in his surroundings, his authority respected. Mr Hillyer was known to them, he had stayed there before. The room Decimus chose was hung with the finest striped silk fabric, and had lamps set into the walls, blazing like day. I shielded my eyes from their mirrored brightness, and Decimus, seeing how bemused I was, turned them down. In the privacy of a strange room, he took me in his arms, holding me secure. Telling me to unpack just sufficient for our needs, he left me then. Not since we had stayed with Cousin Hector had I slept in such a grand room. There were so many mirrors, no matter in which direction I looked I could see my reflection. Enclosed within its canopy, the bed was sumptuous, the feathers puffed high. Opening it, I touched the silken sheets. Inspecting the room more carefully, I saw there were two doors, one by which we had entered and another I had not noticed until now. I wondered what lay behind it and whether it was the door Decimus had used when he had left me. I had not long to wait to find out.

The door opened. Smiling broadly, Decimus stood, almost filling the space, his arms akimbo. Behind him, steam rose from an ornate bath. Over his shoulder I could see that room, too, was full of mirrors. Helping me, for I was too weary to manage on my own, Decimus undressed me. Standing before him, naked but for my corset, I did not expect him to release me, for since his confession he made no secret that my imprisonment pleasured him. Without comment, taking the key from his watch chain, he unlocked me, removing my encumbrance.

The water was hot and soothed my aching bones. Left to soak, I lay back, even now seeing a blurred reflection of myself. A large mirror was suspended from the ceiling. By pulling a cord it tilted so that through the steam I could see all of me. Satisfied with my fuzzy image, I blew the reflection a kiss. Abashed, I averted my eyes. Decimus had witnessed my vanity. Holding a huge pink towel in front of him, he was laughing fit to burst. With a flourish, he dropped the towel. He was naked.

'Hurry up, Mary. You're not dirty and we can't waste that lovely water,' he said.

When I had dried, I attended Decimus, soaping him all over. Though he would be sixty next birthday, to me he was still handsome. There was no flabbiness to him; his body was firm, his muscles hard. I kissed him, and he protested, pushing me away, though not as to be unkind. In truth I was so fatigued I knew not how to stand. Perhaps we were both too tired for love.

Behind the door was a dressing robe which Decimus bade me wear. When I wrapped it about me, its red satin was cool against my skin. Still wet, my love was standing behind me and in the many mirrors that reflected our images I looked at myself again. In countless years until this special moment I had worn only black, yet, even as my heart leapt, my joy was tinged with guilt. Understanding my sorrow, my husband was insistent.

'While it is right we remember Lydia's torment, we must not forget our own love, my darling.'

Letting the wrapper fall from my shoulders, I knelt, so that he should not doubt that I was, as he had told Lydia, his chattel to do with as he pleased. Whatever must happen to me in order that I pleasure him, I did not care. Though convention might condemn him, to me he was my love. Safe in his hands, no matter what he asked of me, I knew that nothing in this world could destroy my trust in him. Acknowledging my obeisance, Decimus was kind, knowing as well as I that without him I should not live.

He ordered food. I had not realised how famished I was, for we had not eaten since noon. A table was laid with sparkling glass and silver. Though I was embarrassed, the maids seemed unconcerned, waiting on us as if dining in nothing more than a dressing robe were not in the slightest unusual.

When we had eaten, despite the comfortable bed I could not sleep. Decimus slumbered beside me, but my brain would not lie still. Lulled by his gentle snoring, at last I dreamed of long ago before I was born. Walking on the Sea Bank I came upon a young maiden. Her hair was dark and her olive skin pale. She had been paddling. Her feet and legs were covered in fine grey silt. Looking up at me, her light hazel eyes were shining in innocence. A tall reed-thin man stood beside her. With his hand on her head, he told me her name; was it Dorrie? The sound was caught by the wind and I barely heard. Then the dream was gone, but I had dreamed it before and knew I would again.

Slowly I opened my eyes and blinked. Light poured into the room. Already dressed, Decimus was sitting on the bed beside me. For a moment I wondered where I was and tried to raise myself. He restrained me; his speech, no more a farmer's, was clipped. He told me to be still and I sensed his excitement at being in the city. He had removed the covers, and I closed my eyes again, knowing he enjoyed my passivity. I lay back on my pillows, resigned to his critical appraisal. Though I still wore the red satin wrapper, it was undone and the cold morning air cooled my skin. I sighed, his gentle fingers touching me, he and not I determining their travel. Opening my eyes, I looked up at my lord. Now I had woken, his voice was urgent, his intention not in doubt. His question, though, was unexpected.

'Tell me, Mary. There must be something you would like me to do to make you happy?'

'No, lord, there is nothing. You must do with me whatever is your will. So long as I please you, then I am content. I need no more.'

'My darling, you would have disappointed me had your answer been otherwise. Now do not wake too quickly, Mary, for I cannot prepare you for what is to come and maybe if you can sleep for just a little while longer I shall not hurt you too much. Before I begin, though, you must understand the pleasure your body will give me, when I love you this way.'

Taking the wrapper away, Decimus faced me to the bed so

that to breathe I must turn my head. Pushing my knees up under me, he touched me and my sleepy body was suffused with love for him. Faint with joy, I ached and, at his mercy, waited on his pleasure. Holding me so tight that I could not move, without warning he thrust himself into me.

Gasping with shock, I cried out and gripping the sheet, that I should not flinch and obstruct his enjoyment, my nails drove into my palms. The pain of his love searing me, in my heart silently I begged him to stop. Yet even as he ravished me, perceiving his pleasure, I wept, and my deprivation could gain no importance.

When at last it was over and my sorrowing could end, I was thankful that my body had pleased him. Decimus raised my arms and bid me hold fast to the bedpost. Striking cold, his heavy iron corset encircled my waist and, my tears not warranting his compassion, he squeezed it shut and clicked the key in the lock. His dominion undisputed, my imprisonment was complete.

Brusquely, he turned from me, telling me to make haste with my toilet. He advised me that when I was dressed I was to join him in the breakfast room.

Stepping cautiously, making not a sound, my feet sank into the carpet's deep velvet pile. Faint from my ordeal, I still shook. Descending the wide, opulent staircase, to steady me I gripped the banister rail with both my hands. Heavy brass rods held the carpet in place and I tried to avoid them lest my heels catch. My hands began to perspire, their wetness squeaking on the polish. I dared not let go, lest I should fall. Fearful without Decimus, I dreaded that someone might see me and, guessing the fate that had befallen me, pity me in my degradation.

As I entered the breakfast room heads turned and I could not look up. Decimus rose from his table, but did not come for me. With my feet like lead, I approached him. Setting me in my place, his quiet words were as balm, soothing my apprehension.

'You are beautiful, my darling.'

Then, a little mischievously, he added, 'See, Mary, the men can't keep their eyes off you.'

My cheeks on fire, I looked up at him. Did he not care that

others should observe the woman he had made me? He was enjoying my discomfort, his eyes laughing at my confusion. I stared down at my plate but still forgave him his impropriety, because I loved him.

'Lord, you shame me. Do you forget how old I am?'

'I care nothing for your age, Mary.'

Leaning forward so that the other gentlemen should not hear my question, I asked of him, my curiosity getting the better of me, 'I do not understand, lord. Why are there no ladies to accompany those gentlemen, that they must breakfast alone?'

Making no effort to conceal his merriment, Decimus sat back, his eyes twinkling.

'My dear, sweet, innocent wife, I am not about to instruct you further in the ways of the world. But we are in no hurry this morning and when you are feeling better, Mary, I had thought to show you the docks. Maybe you will learn even more about your husband.'

Having arranged for our bags to be sent on to the station, we left the hotel. I held my husband's arm, for the cobbles were uneven and I was nervous I might trip, as we walked in the direction of the City Gate. Once through the archway, for as far as we could see, stretching ahead of us was the Quay. Ships, often three abreast, filled St Augustine's basin. Some were grace-ful, their tall masts inclining with the gentle motion of the water, but many were ugly, their dirty smoke-stacks smeared with soot. Decimus pointed out the house near St Stephen's church where I had rested on my journey so many years previously. How much of the past I had forgotten and, though its loss had long since ceased to bother me, how anxious I had been when first my lord had set out to destroy my memory. Days would pass when in a dream I would try, yet fail, to remember who I was. Surely when I had been here before there was not then a forest of smoke-stacks? Seeming to guess my thoughts, Decimus, lamenting the demise of the beautiful, high-masted sailing ships, commented that this was progress, though he did not see it as such. Maybe one day he would take me to the new port at Avonmouth, for now mostly only steamers came up the river on the tide. Linking his arm tightly through mine to support me, he helped me to step over ropes securing ships alongside. Some, stretched and taut, were knee high and he had to lift me over them. He seemed to dream.

'I still love the sea, Mary.'

I saw the look in his eyes as he stared straight ahead of him and thoughts of Granny came back to me. Dear Granny, if she could have seen, with truth laid bare, how happy we were, the turmoil in her heart would have been eased. How well she would have known the countenance her youngest son bore.

'My love, you said the sea was a cruel and unforgiving master, so how can you profess to still love it and hanker after those days?'

'Do you not love a cruel master, Mary?'

My lord's look was mocking and, remembering my deprivation, nodding, I could not converse. I had no secrets from my husband; even those I had not known I possessed were no longer mine. Though no matter how cruel a master, he was sure of the depth of my love for him, and he spoke only the truth.

The scene I had first encountered more than thirty years before was spread out before me. The noise and the smell had not changed. Tar, molasses, tobacco; all mingled with the smell of the sea, bringing back lost memories. But I was alone then and my eyes had been closed. Without Decimus to guide me, would they have opened? My love had shown me so many things; secrets of the quiet countryside; species of migrating birds as they swept across the wide flat lands of the Estuary. Now he talked about ships, whence they had come and where they were going. I knew in my heart that the sea would always be his first love.

As though his soul dwelt in some other land, he spoke to me: 'I am sorry, Mary, but I will always remember with joy those distant days, with a deck beneath my feet and a fair wind in our sails. Sometimes in stormy weather, St Elmo's fire glowed blue around our spars. In the tropics the sea at night was magical. The water was luminous, crested by phosphorous waves. And the air was warm. Illuminating the far horizon, lights would flash around invisible clouds. The sunsets and the dawns, they humbled me, Mary.'

My lord knew every inch of me. He owned me, body and soul, yet from the very beginning I had guessed there was much about my husband I would never share. So long as he let me be with him, not leaving me alone, that was all I would ever ask of him. He continued to reminisce.

'No man forced me, Mary. I followed a wicked, evil trade and should have perished. But I didn't.'

His voice had hardened.

'The Devil looks after his own, Mary.'

'Oh no, my love, please do not say that. You were humbled by the beauty of God and I believe you to be truly penitent.'

On the Narrow Quay, Decimus hailed a cab to take us to the railway station at Temple Meads. The driver's look was a little odd when he was asked to lower the hood, for the weather was still quite inclement. We followed the road round a beautiful square that boasted fine, tall houses. Crossing a bridge that opened to admit ships, on the farther side, splendid before us, rose the timeless church of St Mary's at Redcliffe. Soon the station would be in sight and my stomach knotted with excitement. Now, we really were going home.

'Dear God, please let Lydia come home one day.'

Even as I uttered that hopeless prayer, I shuddered.

On the train Decimus let me sit by the window. From here I could see another city. The grand buildings and merchants' fine houses had gone. Mean, narrow streets were faced with terraces that stood back-to-back in rows. Tiny yards abutted the railway embankment, allowing a fleeting glimpse of other people's lives. By the time we had changed trains at the junction, it was late in the afternoon before we reached Milbury. I wondered how we should get home, for Harry was not expecting us back for a week.

The journey had tired me out and while Decimus went in search of someone who, for a consideration, would take us the rest of the way, he left me at the Swan for a while.

Lydia's nightmare seemed of another world, for nothing had changed back at Thorn End Farm. Yet I had only to close my eyes for a vision of Lydia, humbled in her servitude, beseeching her father to help her, to float before me.

CHAPTER XXV

Lydia's Sorrow

We pray the weather will improve soon, for Decimus is in constant fear the harvest may fail and the root crops this year will rot in the ground. Our unhappy spring has been followed by a wet, dismal summer. Only with God's blessing have we made any hay at all.

Still the cattle are up to their knees in mud and we are nearing September. The land is too heavy to work and we dread a severe winter such as we experienced two years ago. Decimus fears that although he may salvage something there will be insufficient to feed the livestock through to the spring.

Decimus has learned from his eldest brother Luke in Wytherington that Cornelius is sick. My husband has professed no surprise, confiding that his son-in-law, when we saw him, was even then ravaged by drink. We have received no word from Lydia, for since our visit, compounding our despair, her writing has all but ceased. Strangely, the only information we have comes indirectly from Hector, for in all these years since Lydia left Hartley Amelia has not lost touch with her friend and occasionally they correspond. Richard is due home in November and we are looking forward to seeing him and learning of his plans.

Annie opened the door to the yard. A tall young man, every inch a Hillyer, stood in the porchway. He was laughing. To surprise us, he had begged a ride with the carrier. He was dressed in black and about his neck was a clerical collar. A bulging canvas bag was his only luggage.

My sleeves rolled back, up to my elbows in soapsuds, I leaned on my brush. Where I had just scrubbed it, the scullery floor lay wet and shining. Deep in contemplation and lost in the task I had been set, in disbelief, from my knees, I stared at my youngest son. Richard, his expression as unworldly as ever, poked his head round the door.

'Aren't you going to invite me in, Mother?'

His voice was deep and resonant. During these past three years when we had not seen him, it had matured. He held out his hands to me and I dried my arms on my pinafore, my trance broken, and ran to him, weeping with joy. I clasped my hands about his neck. The son I would always think of as my babe was home. He picked me up and swung me round, his young arms not noticing my weight. Smothering him with kisses, then standing back, I held him away from me, evaluating how much he had grown. Behind him stood Decimus. As they embraced one another, I saw how proud my lord was of this youngest son. Suddenly everyone was talking at once. Ella, with Charlotte in tow, introduced her new charge. Charlotte was younger than Richard. She dropped her new brother-in-law a curtsy, with eyes downcast, and seeing her modesty, aware of his brother's needs, Richard smiled.

That whole week I could not catch my breath, time flew so fast. Thomas and Isobel invited us all to Cloudsmoor Farm; then, not two days later, everyone came to us. Ella and I laboured into the small hours, preparing food. All in one, we celebrated Richard's and Harry's birthdays and the house fairly bulged with family. Charlotte played the piano and, with Thomas's children in front, we all gathered round and sang. What a happy time we had. Even Decimus for a while forgot his woes, for he still worried about the winter to come.

But the very next day, Harry took me aside. He and his father had been talking to Richard and Decimus wished me to join them. Dreading the meeting, yet doubting if Richard could stay much longer, I had guessed this day would not be put off for long.

In the reception room, Decimus, Harry and Richard pored over maps laid out on the table. My heart thudded. Dear God, had Decimus told his sons what it had taken him more than thirty years to tell me?

One look at my lord's face showed me the pain in his eyes that I doubted his sons could see. The maps belonged to Richard; Decimus had not told them his secrets. Richard was determined to go abroad, advising me he was on his way to join a mission.

'I am going to Africa, Mother!' he said.

Fearing I should faint, swaying, I held to the edge of the table. 'Oh dear God, no.' Looking at Decimus, I saw he had already been told.

To protest would have been useless. Richard's mind was made up. Yet burdened by my husband's conscience, how could I not try to dissuade him?

'Richard, my darling, whatever has persuaded you to go there? Do you have to be so far away from us?'

Richard's look was kind and, almost as though speaking to a child, he assured me, 'Mother, I have no choice. God has called me and I must go where I am sent.'

My poor Decimus, how I wished I had not spoken.

'When will you leave us, Richard?' I asked.

'First thing tomorrow morning, Mother. I have to travel to London to board a ship for Mombasa. She sails at the end of the week.'

In a strange, sad way his departure reminded me of the day Lydia had left us. Richard, too, took nothing with him save the clothes he stood in and his canvas bag. Harry brought round the trap to take his brother to Milbury. He would see him off on the train to London. How quickly the trap was lost to our sight. In my heart, I doubted if I would see Richard again.

That night, I lay in my love's arms and we wept for our son who was lost to us. Decimus's conscience would not let him sleep and I prayed that Almighty God should see fit to ease his pain.

'The Lord has taken my son and is punishing me for my wickedness, Mary.'

Trying to comfort him, I cradled his head in my arms.

'Richard has been called, my love. It is not for us to reason why. I know you fear for him as I do, but you must accept God's will, even as I accept yours. Richard is happy and, knowing that, cast out your bitterness, lest it destroy you. Let us pray to God that Richard has inherited your strength.'

Christmas came and my heart was heavy as I secured Richard's angel to the top of the fir tree. Yet despite our grief we could not be miserable for long, for Daniel, the child Charlotte had given Harry, was ten months old and he took his first steps that Christmastide. Amazed, Harry watched his father play with Daniel. Decimus doted on his grandchildren and I marvelled that he could be so patient, for with his own children he could not have been a sterner father.

We ushered in the new year of 1894 and with Ella, Decimus and I went to church, attending the Watch Night service. Kneeling beside my husband, I prayed for him in his torment, for barely a day could pass when his conscience did not trouble him.

It was Twelfth Night when Decimus received a letter from Lydia. The envelope was ringed with black. Cornelius was dead and Lydia begged her father to come at once to support her. Early in the afternoon of the same day, Decimus, dressed in mourning, left us for the long journey by train to Innslow. He would leave his horse at livery in Milbury until he returned. When I asked if I might accompany him, he refused me, saying the weather was bad and he feared that if he took the trap he would get bogged down. But perhaps the weather was only an excuse and in truth Decimus foresaw the reception that awaited him.

For two bitterly cold nights I lay in a bed empty of my love with only my dreams for company. Late in the afternoon of the following day, in the teeth of a gale, my beloved Decimus rode into the yard, but he was not alone. Crouched in the saddle in front of him, her head lowered against the wind and muffled from the cold, was Lydia.

Dismounting, Decimus held her in the saddle to stop her from falling, then lifted her down. Her slight body like a misshapen sack folding against him, he carried her through the scullery into the warmth and light of the kitchen. At first, without moving, Lydia sat where my lord had placed her. The dirty tattered shawl fell from her, and she lifted vacant eyes.

Pressing my hands to my lips, I stifled an involuntary cry. I hardly dared look at her. Stretched, sallow skin covered her high cheekbones. Her eyes, sunk so deep they were but shadows, were devoid of colour. Her mouth had withered and the sinews in her neck stood out. The black gown she wore had not been made for her. It fell about her in folds drawn in by the belt at her waist.

Comforting her niece, an arm around Lydia's shoulders, Ella, wounded and shocked by her appearance, kissed her. Yet Lydia seemed not to notice her aunt's affection and made no response. In horror, Harry's wife watched. Many months had elapsed before Charlotte had gained confidence in this house. What terror must this scene have aroused in her?

Decimus was exhausted, strain written on his face.

'Let Lydia rest, Mary. Tomorrow will be soon enough for questions.'

Leaving Lydia in Ella's care, Decimus went out to attend to his horse. Annie was told to heat water for the bath. Taking down a warming pan, I filled it with glowing charcoal still hot from the fire. I followed Ella upstairs, where we retrieved from the linen press clean, sweet-smelling sheets for Lydia's bed. Charlotte, left alone with her sister-in-law, had to come to terms with her emotions as best she could.

While she lit the fire that was laid in the grate, Ella bade me make up the bed. Though it was always kept aired for guests who arrived unannounced, the bed was cold. I slid the warming pan between the sheets and slowly swept it from side to side. Once the curtains were drawn the room was inviting, and was much as Lydia would have remembered it. Satisfied we could do no more, I asked Ella if I might be excused.

In the kitchen, Charlotte and Annie had dragged the heavy table back from the fire, leaving room by the hearth for the bath. Asking Charlotte to leave us, Annie and I took off the widow's gown. Old darned underwear hung on my child's limp, emaciated body. She still bore the imprint of her beatings and, sickened, I looked up at Annie. She knew as well as I did that Lydia's bruising was not borne with love but had been inflicted on her with hatred. When Lydia was bathed, her hair, what was left of it, was washed. Annie's gentle hands dried her and we dressed her in a warm, woollen nightgown. Sitting in the rocking chair next to the fire, Lydia was not really there. We gave her bread soaked in hot, sweet milk, yet as she ate it she neither wept nor spoke. I stroked her head; her straw-like hair, though washed, was brittle.

I took her to bed and, tucking her in, welcomed her home. Kissing her on the cheek, I left her in Annie's care. Annie would watch over Lydia that night for I could not forget, whatever my daughter's plight, that attendance upon my husband came first and my duty could not be conceded.

Listening to the wind howling outside, and watching the candle flickering in the draught, I lay in bed with my lord. With his arm resting across my belly, as was so familiar, our bodies warmed one another. Starting at the beginning, he told me all that had happened.

The afternoon he had left us, Decimus had taken the train to Bristol, staying there overnight before setting off first thing the next morning for Innslow. From the station above Kenford he had walked to Cornelius's house, to be met in the yard by a stony-faced sister. The funeral was to be held that day and Decimus was made no more welcome than on the last occasion when he had stood in that desolate yard. He guessed very soon that the family held Lydia, and her inability to conceive, responsible for her husband's drunkenness, that had remorselessly led to his demise. Cornelius had died following delirium tremens.

Begging my husband's indulgence, I asked him what that was. As he informed me, his voice was scathing.

'The man was fighting mad, Mary. That madness was brought about by hallucinations and they in turn were caused by excessive drinking. In the end, the drink poisoned him.'

Decimus continued with his story. Lydia was nowhere to be found and he was told in an offhand way that she was somewhere about. Eventually he had found her in a corner of an upstairs room, with the same ragged shawl she had worn home pulled about her shoulders. Dry-eyed, she sat on the floor mourning her husband. With her arms holding tight to her knees and seeming oblivious to the cold and the starkness of her surroundings, Lydia was beside herself with grief. Until he spoke to her, she had not realised her father had come to her. Then, as though her life depended upon his protection, she had clung to him.

My love's voice almost broke as he recalled her anguish. With his own hands he had washed her and for her husband's funeral begged the black, shapeless gown from the hard-faced sister-in-law. Lydia was deprived of clothes and wore only cast-offs. Decimus had had to carry his daughter to church, she was so near to fainting. Cutting a pathetic little figure, she received no sympathy as Cornelius's widow, and only when his body was laid to rest and Lydia threw the first sod on to the coffin did she weep.

Supporting his daughter, he had taken her back to the house that had seen her betrayal and her husband's Will was read.

Cornelius Shepherd had been a gentleman of some substance, though his financial standing was reflected in neither his abode nor the wellbeing of his wife. He had died a bitter, vindictive man. Lydia was left nothing. In the Will, Cornelius ordered that she should ask humbly for charity of his family, or otherwise be cast out to throw herself on the mercy of the Poor Law Commissioners. Decimus had brought her home.

He seemed to have finished his tale and I was numbed by his revelation.

'I cannot bear it when I think how Lydia has suffered, lord. When you dressed her in her widow's weeds, you must have seen her poor broken body, battered from its beatings. Yet I also bear such weals and am uplifted when I see the marks of your love on me. How can it be, when for Lydia they are the most terrible affliction?'

Decimus leaned over me and when he kissed me his lips were gentle.

'Cornelius did not love Lydia. Do not try to compare what I have done to you, Mary, with what has happened to our daughter. Have I not told you many times; there are few women who would let a man love them as I have loved you.'

'Lord, I have no regrets.'

Sometime in the deepest darkness of the night I heard a lost soul cry out in torment. Creeping from my lord's bed, I went to my daughter and, holding her close, let Annie sleep for a while.

Though the winter was milder than we had dared to hope, a cold snap at the beginning of March proved too much for Luke, and it was with sadness that we attended his funeral in Wytherington. Having for most of his life not known a day's illness, when at over eighty years of age the end came, it was swift and merciful. Now there were only five of Granny's ten children remaining alive. Besides Ella, another sister, already widowed, lived in Milbury. Two brothers, whom we rarely saw, farmed some miles down river. Decimus, though he should not have been surprised by the loss of his eldest brother, none the less was morose and introspective, and for several days confronted his own mortality.

In June, we celebrated Lydia's twenty-sixth birthday, though at the time she seemed unaware of its passing. Almost six months have gone by since Decimus brought her home. Still she speaks little of her ordeal. In fact she rarely speaks at all and we fear her mind may have been seduced, though Decimus hesitates to take her to a doctor, having a healthy scepticism when it comes to head doctors. I dread her being committed to an asylum and pray her indisposition is only temporary. Lydia wakes most nights, calling out for me, so that I sleep more lightly now, as I did in those halcyon days after I had given birth and before my children were taken from me. Lydia was not three months old the day Decimus gave her to a wet nurse.

Her bruising has faded and only fine white lines criss-cross her back, stomach and thighs. I fear they will not disappear and will be for ever a reminder of her marriage to Cornelius. Her hair has begun to grow again and gradually her skin has lost its crêpe-like texture. Her eyes appear less sunken, though their cat-like lightness has not returned. The gaunt, thin frailty of her body has almost gone, for the good country food and the fresh air will not be denied their effect.

Unlike last year when the harvest came close to failure, this year God looked kindly on us and we gathered in bumper crops. The farmers' wives had prepared a communal supper to celebrate and afterwards there would be dancing and the gypsies would play their fiddles as they had done for as long as I could remember.

We were all ready and anxious to leave for church to thank God for his bounty. Lydia begged us to go without her, for she said her head ached. But Decimus would not permit her to stay at home when all the family would be brought together under God's roof. We were perplexed by her anxiety. In church Lydia shook, her body racked by uncontrollable sobbing. We had no choice but to take her home, leaving Thomas and Isobel, Harry and Charlotte and all the children to go with Ella to harvest supper. I had looked forward to the occasion in the hope that Yasmin might be there and together we could sit quietly remi-niscing and talk about the days when we were young.

Decimus was impatient. Being determined not to neglect the men who had worked so hard for him to bring in the harvest, he could not stay long with us. As soon as Lydia was sufficiently calmed he returned to enjoy the festivities. In the quiet and safety of home, Lydia ceased her weeping. As we sat in the parlour together, the setting sun casting its dying rays on my daughter, I was reminded of the eve of her wedding and our happiness that her life would be safe with Cornelius. It had all gone so terribly wrong. Now, as gradually she overcame her unreasoning fear and I held her hands in mine, more composed, she opened her heart to me.

'Mother, I have to tell you something which will be for ever on my conscience, but I can keep it to myself no longer.'

Instantly, Lydia's voice had reverted to a monotone.

'I have sinned against Almighty God. I killed my husband. I wished him dead and now he is dead. Nothing can change what I have done. No matter what happens to me, wherever I go, my sin will never be forgiven. There is no place to hide to let me forget.'

Panic reared in my stomach. The hairs on my neck began to rise and the palms of my hands perspired. But I had to listen.

Falling to her knees as she heard her own voice acknowledge what she had done, Lydia wept again. She had feared to enter the House of God, terrified she would be struck down for her wickedness. As her tragedy unfolded, desperately I wished that Decimus had not left us. I could not help it, but as my mind recoiled from her confession the superstition my lord had tried so hard to free me of reared its ugly head. All the while I held her hands, her face close to mine, and waited on her words.

After our ill-fated visit, Lydia had known for certain that she was truly alone. Even her father could do nothing to help her. He had only caused her to be reminded that she had taken her marriage vows in the presence of Almighty God and was until death wedded to Cornelius.

'Pray, Mother, please love me, for in its telling my story will set you against me.'

'No, Lydia, I am your mother. Whatever you have done, I will always love you.'

In the warm, still evening, my daughter unburdened her soul to me.

'It was only a week or so after your visit, Mother. I had been setting dough to prove. Though it was not yet noon, Cornelius was already drunk. He lurched in from the yard and stood over me. I tried to run away, but could not move for fear of him.

Knowing the beating that was to come, I prayed that the Lord might take my life and spare me.

'Cornelius shook me until my teeth rattled, then dragged me out of the scullery towards the cider store where none could witness his brutality. I begged him for mercy, Mother, but it was to no avail. He called me a cursed whore, born of a whore.

'Pray believe me when I tell you what came next, Mother, for what happened to me is unbelievable.'

In her torment, Lydia had prayed aloud to Almighty God to save her. With the first blow, she had fallen and hit her head. Into her mind had come a vision. An old man stood beside her, light radiating from him. He folded his cloak over her poor defenceless body, shielding her from the blows. Yet when Cornelius had finished with her and she had looked up, the old man had gone.

Though Lydia received many more beatings, every time the old man was at her side protecting her. Then one day, Cornelius had come for her, but on this occasion she had not prayed to Almighty God to help her, but instead, hating her husband, silently she had cursed him, wishing him dead. Cornelius's blows had fallen without hindrance on her poor, rent body and nothing had protected her.

'I knew without doubt, Mother, by wishing the death of my husband, the curse of our forebears was stirring within me and for my wickedness I must suffer in my husband's hands.'

So Jesse had protected Lydia too. I thought of the terrible day when Satan had come for me. How could Lydia know that Jesse would always be there to protect her, forgiving her her sins, so long as he saw her to be penitent. Now she had confessed, in my heart I prayed Jesse would protect her again.

Lydia seemed to dream.

'You will not have known of it, Mother, but one day when I had been home from Hartley for maybe two years or so and had tormented you beyond your endurance, Father took me aside and put the Bible into my hands, drawing my attention to the story of Adam and Eve. I read again of the wicked serpent that beguiled Eve. Father showed me a small black brooch, the hideous snake about to devour the heart which hung suspended from its mouth. He said you had inherited the brooch from your mother and one day it must be mine. He told me too of the still child you had borne and the umbilical cord that, like an evil serpent, was wrapped around her neck, killing her.

'Father frightened me, Mother, and from then on I tried not to mock you in your servitude, though sometimes, I admit, I could not help myself. I see that even today you wear the iron corset around your waist that Father said was to restrict you and not let you forget your subjection. I tried, Mother, but I have not the courage to seek salvation as you have done.'

My child had lost her train of thought and gently I drew her back, asking her what she had done that had killed her husband.

'Cornelius was rarely sober, Mother, and soon after I had cursed him he had to take to his bed. He lay there shaking and in torment, screaming that his body was consumed by vipers. He said they crawled over him, leaving their slough on his skin. In terror he tried to escape them, but to no profit. Monsters were constantly in his company and he told his family that I had put my curse on him.'

Lydia had ceased to weep and her dulled eyes met mine.

'I knew, Mother, because I had wished him ill, the serpent in my heart was sucking the life from my husband.'

My poor, dear child. Thank God Decimus had explained to me how Cornelius had met his demise. But I could not interrupt Lydia, for fear she would not complete her tale.

It had been the end of November before Cornelius had truly weakened but even then he had found the strength to beat his wife. He lingered for yet a while longer. The doctor was with him when he died, but Lydia, in her husband's final hours, could not go near him for fear of his blasphemy.

The doctor, full of sympathy, came down to her, waiting while she settled herself before informing her that Cornelius was dead. But he really need not have bothered, for in her heart Lydia knew it already.

'He said, Mother, that Cornelius's passing was a happy release, for my husband had a death wish once he was told he could not

276

father children. He said Cornelius was maddened by drink and would have been certified had he not died. The doctor was so kind to me, Mother. He waited while I wrote to Father and posted my letter for me. Yet I did not deserve his pity for he could not know it was by my hand that Cornelius was dead.'

Lydia was silent for a moment before she continued.

'When we were wed, I loved him and I know he loved me. He did not drink then. I am sure Cornelius did not know he could not father a son. His love turned from me only when I failed to conceive.'

I held her close, for after all he had done to her my poor grown-up child felt compassion for her dead husband. Trying to comfort her, I longed for Decimus to return home. Only he could convince his daughter she was not to blame. As superstition threatened to engulf me, with all my heart I tried to believe what I was telling her. 'Lydia, my dear, you did not kill Cornelius. It was his drinking which killed him. Though it is wicked to speak ill of the dead, the truth must be faced. He was a wicked man, who hated you when he was told he was impotent and he knew you were not.'

I wished with all my heart we had never set eyes on Cornelius Shepherd and prayed Lydia would not descend into damnation where Cornelius, by his bitter hatred of her, had consigned her.

The sun had set and Lydia had tired herself. I lit the lamp and in its golden light together we waited for her father to return. Not until Decimus knew the whole truth and had given her his love and support, as I knew he would, would Lydia accept that she had not killed her husband. Only then would she have the strength to lift up her head and live again.

277

CHAPTER XXVI

Storm Clouds

Lydia may never forget her ordeal at the hands of Cornelius Shepherd, but over the months that led up to Christmas she recovered her looks and occasionally her eyes regained their old cat-like colour.

This new year of 1895 has brought changes in me which I do not welcome, for I have to face that time of life women dread the most. My womb no longer bleeds each month. At night I wake breathless from heat, yet cold, with sweat running wet between my breasts. My head aches and my arms and legs are wooden, my ankles swollen by the end of each day. Often I am irritable and dread that I may inadvertently offend my husband. When going about the daily tasks he sets, confusion will suddenly overtake me. Toil that in the past freed my mind to wander leaves me exhausted from its discipline. Since I was a young wife I have accepted my husband will not be lenient with me and do not ask it of him now. Yet I pray my indisposition will not last long and he will not be inconvenienced by my condition. I am totally unprepared for what is happening to me. Ella's temper had not altered at all when the moon no longer claimed her. Much of the time existence is an unending struggle as I try to wrestle with my loss of confidence brought about by the havoc that is wrought in me.

But in all the years we have been wed, I should know by now that my beloved husband will not desert me in this time of fear and apprehension. In spite of my embarrassment, he does not appear to care that my breasts, once so full and heavy, have begun to sag and are soft. I fear terribly that my ageing body will not please him and he may no longer want to love me. Sometimes he has to struggle to enter me and I dread he will not bother and will take his pleasure elsewhere.

He is patient with me, though, and seems to understand the trauma that tears me apart. He gives me time so that, when he loves me, my mind has already overcome the difficulties my alien body has in accepting him and I can welcome him with joy. Often he will laugh when I try to cover my nakedness in front of him as I have never done before. At others, though, he will gauge my mood and, opening his arms, will hold me secure in his love and then the world that is outside ceases to matter.

Some mornings, safe in the knowledge that Harry can manage without him, Decimus will lie abed late and gently run his fingers over my breasts. In his great hands they become alive again and my nipples stand erect and ready, straining to be loved, as though this watershed had not occurred. My husband's loving has become more tender and he likes to feel my kisses. He has shown me how my hands can ease the tension in the muscles of his back and, as I sit astride him, he will feign sleep until my arms nearly drop off with fatigue. Silver hairs grow in profusion across his shoulders and his body is covered with down. He is pleasured when I run my fingers through the soft grey mat. With my love's support I am coming not to mind that I am growing old. So long as he takes me with him, that is all I will ever need.

Lydia has been offered a teaching post in Milbury. Her father has urged her to grasp the opportunity to use the education she acquired with Cousin Hector. Decimus hopes, through her independence, she may look forward to the future instead of perpetually reliving her past. After Easter she is to leave us to stay with Decimus's widowed sister on the Hartley Road in Milbury. At last Lydia seems happy.

During the late summer Charlotte gave Harry another child and I helped to deliver their first daughter, giving us, in all, seven grandchildren. Though Charlotte seems very susceptible to pain and wept profusely on her childbed, her body, unlike Isobel's, is designed for childbearing. As the new-born babe cried in my arms, I wondered how many more children Charlotte would carry.

Decimus and I talk often of the days when we looked forward to our grandchildren's laughter breathing new life into the walls of Cloudsmoor Farm. Now, however, I find myself hoping, though I know it to be of little worth, that Isobel may bear no more infants. After giving Thomas two sons and three daughters, she is worn out from her labours. I wonder how much longer her body can be sustained by her sense of duty and love for Thomas. To those who do not know her, Isobel appears a cold, sharp-tongued woman. Though she does not complain, Isobel cannot fail to have recognised that her constitution will not survive such constant childbearing. Thomas still loves her, yet my eldest son, in spite of the sensitivity he showed in his youth and his continuing thirst for reading, is a vigorous man, upholding traditional values. He has matured into a disciplinarian like his father, enough of a Hillyer not to compromise in his expectations.

The countryside was waking again. Migrating swans and geese had returned to their breeding grounds. The bare willow trees were a hazy green, their buds bursting, and spring laid down a carpet of flowers. For nearly a year, Lydia had been a teacher. She had renewed her friendship with Amelia, now married to Dr Mac's son, a solicitor practising in Milbury. With her aunt as chaperon, Lydia seemed to enjoy the social round of Milbury.

At the end of term Lydia brought home a gentleman friend to stay with us over Easter. Samuel Tyler was a school master. He had probably not seen forty years, though his manner and his looks belied his age, making him appear much older. He was tall and thin, his chest a little concave, his dark curly hair thinning somewhat. I could not quite place him, yet when I asked Decimus where I had met Sam previously my husband assured me I had not. Before his family had fallen on hard times they were well to do. Lydia told us that Sam's forebears were buried under the nave of St Mark's and not in the churchyard. Supporting his mother after his father died, Sam had not married. With his fine hands and elegant ways, he would not have made a farmer. I hoped he was tougher than he looked, but feared Sam might have inherited the consumption that Lydia had said killed his father. Yet when I saw the way he treated my daughter, as though he cherished her, I could not doubt Sam was kind and generous. What he lacked in physical strength was compensated for by his intellect and his progressive socialist ideals.

Confounding their differences, Decimus and Sam enjoyed one another's company. On the subject of politics they would argue for hours. Much to my surprise Lydia shared many of Sam's beliefs, some of which seemed quite bizarre if not, to my ears, a little laughable. Sam thought himself a stoic, insisting he be allowed to bathe each morning in cold water. Splashing about, he considered his harsh regime beneficial to his wellbeing. My husband joked to me that perhaps the treatment might be good for my condition, yet thankfully he did not pursue it.

Witnessing the reverence with which Charlotte addressed her husband, Sam made plain his views to Decimus. He did not seek obedience in a wife. He expected the woman he married to enjoy a life of her own and stand by his side as his equal. Yet when I watched Charlotte, who, as Decimus had once observed, must become a mirror image of me, I could not see in her conduct that she was unhappy.

During the late spring and summer we saw much of Sam. Lydia's personality changed, her school-teaching giving her new confidence. In some ways the restrained young maiden who had come home from Cousin Hector's house in Hartley was with us again. Sam admired composure in a woman and did not mind that Lydia had been married before. I cannot tell what she advised Sam with regard to Cornelius.

Borrowing Decimus's waders, Sam would accompany Harry, even in the dead of night, to help him bring back the salmon. Though his physique was against him, Sam seemed to enjoy manual labour and as autumn set in, with lots of laughter, would try to plough a straight furrow. Sam spent Christmas with us and the gathering was easy and informal. Remembering he had failed Lydia when he introduced her to Cornelius, Decimus said nothing this time which might assist in her choice. None the less we saw the love between Sam and Lydia grow.

The evenings were drawing out and Charlotte was heavy with her third child. While Isobel's spirit was depleted by childbearing, Charlotte's thrived on it and we wondered whether the house might one day not be large enough to accommodate them all, for Charlotte was still not yet twenty-four years old. With barely two years between them, she gave Harry another daughter. We guessed Harry was a little disappointed, for he had wanted a son, but Charlotte was still fertile and, God willing, would conceive again soon.

My womb had not bled for nearly two years, though still my body resented the changes that had come upon it. Yet the days when Decimus must heed the passing phases of the moon were over and I could rejoice, for now his passion need know no restriction and he could take when he wanted it the love that was his by right.

Lydia was betrothed to Samuel on Midsummer's Day of this year of 1897. To mark the occasion, he gave her a ring, a lone diamond surrounded by tiny seed pearls. The wedding was planned for November. Sam was now headmaster of the County School and, after they were wed, Lydia would join him in the schoolhouse in Milbury. But Cornelius's death still haunted Lydia and it seemed she could not suppress a desperate compulsion. Before taking her marriage vows again, she needed in the sight of God to confess her sins. Only after she had asked for and received forgiveness would she request the rector to marry her to Sam.

It was the morning of the penultimate day of October. Full of foreboding and against his better judgement, for Lydia was adamant she must face her trial without him, Decimus allowed her to go to church alone. When morning had become afternoon and Lydia had not returned, with each passing hour I became more sick with fear. Decimus was anxious too, wishing with all his heart he had stopped her. When at four o'clock Lydia had still not come home, Decimus ordered me to dress, determined we should set out to look for her. Glowering at me, for my fingers trembled so, he bade Annie fasten the buttons of my boots. Fearing to be left behind, I pulled my shawl up over my head, not really caring if I should be cold.

In the grip of a wind that blew up the Estuary, my shawl quite inadequate, I clung to Decimus. Fallen leaves swirled in eddies at our feet. Great black clouds rolled in from the Atlantic, bringing premature dusk, and the rumble of distant thunder made taut my fraying nerves. How much more light had we before darkness made useless our search? Decimus, his face set and gaunt, urged me forward. Dread gnawed at my insides as I prayed our child still lived.

On the hill, the House of Our Lord, a bastion against evil, consecrated a thousand years ago and dedicated to the Blessed Saint Allwen, stood like a rock defying the storm. A circle of elms bowing, acknowledging the force of the wind, protected the churchyard. Taking my hand, Decimus led me between gravestones to where the ground fell away and steps rose steeply from the lane beyond. He put his arm about my waist and our thoughts were as one. I needed no reminding of the day we set out from his father's house. Near to fainting, weary from giving birth, I had been exhausted from my penance. But for my lord's persuasion, the priest would have denied me sanctuary. His harsh words that I had never forgotten, even now, rang in my ears.

'. . . by the sins you have inherited, you have fallen into transgression. The salvation you seek will be afforded you only if you obey God's law. Through your love and your sorrowing you may yet atone for the sins of your forebears. Remember, without love your soul will be lost . . .'

The priest had forewarned me of what was to come. As he prophesied, in my husband's hands I had sorrowed indeed and without exception Decimus had ruled over me. But I had striven to obey God's law, hoping now that one day, with my beloved Decimus beside me, we should find salvation together.

Decimus opened the heavy door and disappeared into the gloom of the nave. Left outside with just gravestones for company, I searched for our daughter. Tearing at me, the wind became a living thing. Like a sprite, first it was here and then there. But this wind was not the gentle breeze from heaven that had blown into my soul. Singing a wheedling song, the pitch rising higher and higher, like a whirlpool it twisted about me, invading me, my shawl blown clear away. Screaming, the wind seemed to laugh and, though standing on hallowed ground, I shuddered. Spying an old man, a gravedigger by trade, I walked over to him and asked whether or not he had seen Lydia. But lowering his eyes and turning his back on me, not answering me, he made the Sign of the Cross. I had lived among them for all these years, yet the village people still reviled and feared me. The dreadful sense of impending doom that had been with me all day deepened, and I prayed Decimus would not leave me here too long.

Hailing the old gravedigger, Decimus hurried back to me and the man, his cap clutched in his hand, fawning, under his breath muttered something. In melancholy, we retraced our steps, for Lydia was not here. By the time we reached home, darkness had fallen and lightning was forking across the sky, illuminating the yard. Yet still the clouds had not dropped their rain.

It had turned seven o'clock before Lydia came home. Motionless, she stood in the doorway. Decimus, leaping to her side, caught her before she fell. Cold as death, her lips moved, though we could not catch what she said. Her father scooped her up in his arms and carried her into the warmth and light of the parlour. Decimus poured her some brandy and held the glass in both hands to warm the liquid. Urging her to drink, he held the glass to her lips. Then, in the voice we had first heard in Innslow, Lydia told us what had happened to her; and, my flesh creeping, I begged not to hear.

'Forgive me, Papa, for I have sinned against Almighty God. For me there is no salvation. Before the altar I prostrated myself and a priest heard my confession. I told him what I had done to Cornelius, but when I tried to tell him what Cornelius had done to me he closed his heart and would not listen.

'He called me a true Daughter of Satan and told me God

would not forgive me for killing my husband. Then he raised his Cross in front of his face and through the Cross he looked at me and, cursing the Devil in me, drove me out, telling me even in death hallowed ground would be denied me.

'I cannot marry Samuel in the presence of Almighty God. I am a sinner, Father, born of a line of sinners. My grandmother was an adulteress and my great-grandmother a witch. The iniquities of my forebears have been visited on me and my iniquities will be visited upon my children and my children's children, even unto the third and fourth generations . . .'

Numbed with grief, her voice died away. Lydia, our dearest daughter, gazed into eternity. In the few hours since she had left us, her eyes had sunk deep into their sockets. As she lay, silent in her torment, my beloved lord stood over her, protecting her; then, gathering her in his arms, he wept for her and, through his tears, I saw fury in his eyes. He told her God would forgive her, for she had repented of her sins, that she had not killed Cornelius Shepherd, who, sodden with drink, had died by his own hand.

Then, confronting his own iniquities which he saw visited upon his daughter, Decimus cursed the man who dared to call himself a priest and vowed he would destroy him, for by such ignorance was echoed generations of hatred that had poisoned the hearts and minds of the people of this land. I could not believe my lord's blasphemy and, though I marvelled at the depth of his love for Lydia, despairing for my husband I shook with fear. Lydia was beyond weeping. She was back in the half-world it had taken her so long to escape. I prayed that her new life was not destroyed and Samuel Tyler would not reject our precious child in her unmitigated despair.

Suddenly there was an almighty bludgeoning on the door to the yard. Harry, hurrying to open it, held the lamp high and in its gentle light Captain Watkins stood clasping his chest and fighting for breath. Staggering through the doorway, such was his exhaustion, he nearly knocked the lamp from Harry's hand. Charlotte ran to her father's side, but shaking her off he had no time to regain his composure.

285

'Decimus, my friend, I have woeful news. The church of the Blessed St Allwen is ablaze and, for all to see, glows like a beacon on the hill. The gale that blows up the Estuary fans the flames and not a soul can go near. Only the walls contain the inferno, but not for long, for heat melts the lead in the windows and flares, like great flaming torches, light up the heavens. From the bottom of the hill, the noise of splintering glass and the roar of the fire as the roof caved in was deafening.'

My mind, immobile with shock, was too slow to accept his awesome words. But Decimus was not in shock and made haste to see for himself.

Catching hold of his arm, Captain Watkins restrained him.

'That is not all, my friend, for there is muttering in the village that the fire is the work of the Devil. They are frightened men and know of only one they call the Devil's Daughter. This afternoon, your wife was seen near the church. You must get her out of here, Decimus.'

Paralysed with fear, I looked at Lydia. Her face was blank. Battered by the news, she could only shake her head. Could it possibly be that Lydia had wreaked an appalling revenge on those who sought to cast her out? Even as I set the thought aside, sanity would not let me dwell on it. I knew the evil could not be true, for had not my own dear Decimus searched for Lydia in the church, but found she had already left? Had there been burning then, would he not have discovered it? My thoughts unmarshalled, my mind was in turmoil. Seeing it was Decimus's decision that I should stay, Captain Watkins, always so formal, bent over me, kissing my cheek.

'Mary, I shall pray for you, my dear,' he said.

Charlotte did not wish to leave without me, but Harry insisted she go with her father, ordering her to take the children to safety with his brother at Cloudsmoor Farm. Lydia, uncomprehending, her mind befuddled, held Ella's hand as she had done when she was a child and gently, for Ella must go with the others, Decimus prised her fingers from her aunt's.

Kneeling down, he lifted his daughter's face until it was level with his.

'My darling daughter, you will never forget this terrible day, for now I must send you away to a place where you will be safe. If I do not, then they will surely come for you too.'

As we opened the door to the yard, the smell of burning assailed our nostrils and Decimus cursed. Broken clouds that raced overhead to the south almost like a sunset glowed pink through to orange. Even as we watched, sparks exploded into the night sky. Fear as I had never known engulfed me and I knew my mother had felt like this when the crowd had come for her. Holding me close, Decimus sheltered me. Captain Watkins, shepherding Charlotte and Ella with the children in their arms, said goodbye. The moon, casting its uncertain light, flitted in and out of the clouds and soon our dear ones were lost to our sight.

Harry had saddled our strongest horse, for to smuggle his sister away he must first ride through the fields behind the gypsy encampment and then, in a headlong dash, would take the road to Hartley. Anxious to be going, Harry sat back in his saddle and Decimus, lifting Lydia in front of him, sent them on their way.

CHAPTER XXVII

The Inevitable

We heard them first, their chant rising and falling on the wind. Then, through the bedroom window, we saw them; maybe two dozen men, each holding aloft a torch of flaming pitch, the scene reminding me of pictures of some other time that I had seen only in history books.

Decimus opened the window and, leaning out, unhooked the shutters and closed them. Since I had come here as a young wife he had not in all these years secured the shutters. Entombed, my husband did not intend I should escape. As the men of the village had come for my mother and her mother before her, now they were coming for me and my fear was such that my mind was nearly deranged. Yet as Decimus drew the curtains and lit the lamp, in its warm glow my terror seemed strangely misplaced. With the shutters closed, we could no longer hear their chant and, looking about the familiar room, I prayed I might wake soon and my terrible dream could be forgotten.

But Decimus was not persuaded. He was busying himself. From the keys hanging at his waist, he selected one and opened the old chest which stood at the end of the bed and had always been locked from me. He threw back the lid. I had not seen inside it before and I sat, my arms pulled tight about my knees to stop them from trembling, and watched as Decimus with abandon threw the contents on to the floor.

A faded picture of a ship lay before me, quickly covered by

strings of shells. Next, shields with strange-looking motifs were thrown on top. Out came odd-shaped animals, some carved from wood, others of bone. A parchment, curled and browned at the edges with a huge wax seal; nothing was hidden from me. A wide leather belt, a pocket hanging from it, the buckle green with age, was followed by a seaman's cap, stiff with old grease and musty, all were thrown on to the pile. A knife with an ornate ivory handle was taken from a worn leather sheath and set aside.

My husband's past was laid out for my inspection. In his hand, yet trying to hide it behind his back, he held a battered black leather whip, much used. I think my love might have spared me the shock had I not already seen it, but it was too late now.

His tone was dismissive.

'A tool of my trade, Mary. I'm not proud of it.'

Then he came to what he was seeking. I gasped, for he drew out the old gossamer gown I had not seen for so long and had almost forgotten. Concealed in its folds, wrapped in tarred paper, lay a pistol. Next to it, separately wrapped, was a box of ammunition. My lord, triumph written on his face, weighed the gun in his hand.

I wanted to touch him, but could not move.

'Please, I beg of you, lord, do not kill for me.'

His voice was strangely flat.

'If there is no other way, Mary, than to kill a man, then so be it.'

'Have you had to kill a man, lord?'

With his fingers he revolved the chamber, pointedly ignoring my question. I had not seen a revolver before and though my voice quaked I dared to question my husband again.

'It's a Colt, Mary. I bought it in the Americas.'

He shrugged as if it were of little consequence.

'Like the rest of this stuff, it had its use. And the bullets? After your trip round the docks, you don't need explanations. You can buy most things if you know where to go.'

Casting my eyes over my husband's mementoes, I looked into the open chest. Sovereigns in their hundreds lined the floor, but I hardly cared, for lying in the corner, its tiny red eyes just catching the light, the serpent was watching me and he seemed to smile. Crying out, I bit my lip, yet felt no pain. Decimus, seeing where my eyes had alighted, threw the gossamer gown back into the chest, smothering the malevolence.

'Forget it, Mary. It's only a gewgaw. I should have thrown it out years ago.'

But that would have changed nothing, for had not the old Gypsy Queen told me the brooch was merely a symbol of the curse I carried in my veins? At last, that curse had turned full circle and, like my mother and women through so many generations before me, now I must face my accusers.

I thought of Richard, a missionary. If only he were here to speak for me, but his duties had taken him to a far-away place called Africa; memories of that land for my own dear husband were his own peculiar penance.

With a thud, the first stone hit the shutter. The crowd had seen the light through a crack. Hysteria welled in me. My whole being beat to the rhythm of my heart and the walls came closer as sweat ran in rivulets between my breasts. Yet even now, my mind sought refuge and wandered. Memories so dear, yet of little relevance, bubbled up into my consciousness and all the while my body trembled and my teeth chattered in my head, as only one half of me watched my lord prepare for what he must do. But I had not mistaken his triumph. Decimus was as a man possessed.

He swung the wide leather belt around his waist. It was too big and hung on his hips, but it seemed not to matter and he fastened the buckle. Then, taking his knife, carefully he drew the blade across his thumb and, satisfied it was sharp, with a grunt pushed it through a loop in the belt. Loaded with bullets, the gun that he called a Colt found a place in the holster. Then, with remembered skill, Decimus wound the old whip about his shoulders and twisted it around his body. Wondering how many backs had forfeited their skin to it, I shuddered.

In awe, I stared at this man who was my master. While I had shrunk, he, comfortable in his fearsome attire, had grown. Cringing, my head bowed, and kneeling at his feet, I whispered, 'Dear God. I hardly know you, Sir.'

I feared this frightful stranger who stood over me and shrank from him.

'My dear, sweet wife, do you truly not know me? You are my life, Mary.'

His voice was unchanged. His lips brushed my forehead and, taking me in his arms, he held me, and the naked fear that had threatened to stifle me was dispelled. My dear Decimus was not a stranger and I loved him with all my heart. But he was anxious to make haste and his tone was abrupt.

'Come, Mary, we can't leave Annie alone for much longer.'

How selfish I had shown myself to be! For a moment I had quite forgotten dear Annie. Always loyal, she loved her master, maybe as much as I did, and whatever the consequences she would not leave him now.

Decimus turned down the lamp, lit a candle and took me downstairs. The men were closer, their chant reverberating through the house. In the scullery, with only the yard door between us, the noise of the crowd deafened me and my head felt fit to burst. Annie already sat in the shadow and Decimus bade me stay with her. Huddled against me, her eyes revealing her terror, she wept. The door shook with the blows that hammered in time with the chanting and, stricken, I looked up at Decimus. From his face, I could see the crowd spoke the truth. Kneeling, he drew me into his arms and covered my ears, trying to blot out the noise. They were calling for me, the daughter of Hannah Smith!

So now I knew why Decimus had been unkind to me in those early days. Had I borne my poor mother's true name from the beginning, he would have guessed who I was and not for a king's ransom would Decimus have wed me. I had sorely deceived him. Why, had my father misled me?

I had brought shame on my husband. Riven with guilt and sick with panic, I tore myself away and ran headlong to the door. It was me they wanted, not him. I pulled back the bolt and with both my hands I fought to turn the key.

Suddenly Decimus held my arm in a vice. Crying out from

the pain, I struggled, screaming at him, my fists beating at his chest.

'Lord, I beg of you, please, you must let me go.'

He held me, his hand like a manacle gripping my arm. With his other hand, he slammed the bolt home; then all in one sweep, my husband struck me, my head rocked back, his hold on me so tight I did not fall. Limp now, my body could shake no more with fear. Blood tasted in my mouth. My lip had split and, defeated, I wept from the stinging pain of his blow.

Beside himself with fury, his brutal words beat a path to my brain.

'Don't you ever do that to me!'

Shaking me, he threw me into a chair. All was lost now and I did not care if he struck me again. Instead, lifting me, he cradled me in his great strong arms.

His eyes were brimming with tears.

'You little fool, Mary. Do you think I give a damn by what name they call you?'

I kissed his dear sweet hand, cool against the fire that raged in my face.

'Lord, I am so sorry to have angered you, but I fear they will kill you too and I am not worth that. Please, I beg of you, you must let me go.'

I looked up at him and saw his eyes glittered, hard, like steel.

'I promise you, Mary, they will not kill me and I will let no man take you from me.'

Helping me to my feet, he bid me sit with Annie. The harshness of his blow had induced a calm, so that now my fate did not really matter. My destiny was not in my hands, but then it never had been. My lord addressed me again.

'They are not evil men, Mary. I have lived among them for most of my life. But their church has burned down and they fear it is the work of the Devil. I cannot delay, but must talk to them now, before their fear is inflamed to madness.'

Drawing back the bolt, Decimus turned the key in the lock. The cold night air invaded us as he opened the door, the lamp above our heads swaying gently in the draught. I held my breath.

292

Making a perfect target, he stood in the doorway and seconds seemed like minutes. The chanting died away and, as though it were one man, the crowd breathed. In the light of their torches, the knife at his waist glinted and in his hand he held the gun. In the quiet, Decimus stood motionless, staring them down.

A voice called out.

''Tis not you we want, Sir, 'tis woman we call the Devil's Daughter. Now you send 'er out and no 'arm 'll come to 'ee.'

Decimus sounded amused.

'Come forward and let me see you in the light, or are you afraid to be identified?'

Another voice spoke up, not so respectful.

'We want the woman who come 'ere callin' 'erself Mary Cheyne.'

The crowd was jeering. The man continued.

'She were offspring of 'annah Smith from down the Marsh.'

There was a ripple of approval. Another voice among them shouted.

'Aye, spawned by the bloody Devil, too. She can go back to 'im an all.'

I heard the click as Decimus cocked his gun. But so did the crowd and the uproar that threatened faded away.

I had been wed to my beloved lord for close on forty years and in all that time had not seen him as I saw him now, for captured in this moment, I knew he had faced down a mob before and sensed his excitement as he held them, frightened to move against him. Not a man among them, young or old, would look up at Decimus and not know fear in his heart.

Slowly he walked towards them, testing them, and they retreated, their stillness that of a wild animal about to steal its prey. Deliberately he engaged my accusers in quiet conversation.

A man shouted over the heads of the others.

'You can't fool us. I saw 'er pokin' round the graveyard. Wind were whinin' like the Devil 'is self was keepin' 'er company.'

'Did you not also see me? Am I accused of consorting with the Devil?'

Decimus was contemptuous. The man fell silent and the crowd shifted allegiance.

Another man yelled out.

'Tha's as maybe, but they d' say she spoke all weird over poor Gabriel Meredith. She stitched 'im up an' 'e be a cripple now.'

Decimus's voice was steady.

'But for my wife's ministerings, Gabriel Meredith would be dead. Don't you forget, I was there!'

Then in subdued tones, carried to them on the wind, he captured their fear and slowly dissipated it. Decimus reminded the men old enough to remember of the terrible day my mother was led to her death. My lord was not the only man present whose conscience would not lie still within him. Then he talked of the day when he had taken me from his father's house with Thomas in my arms. He had brought me here to Thorn End Farm, my feet bare, my head shaven and without covering so that all who looked upon me should know I was penitent.

Remembering my humiliation, through my tears I could see there were fewer men now. Some were leaving, their torches held less high. Dear God, could it really be over? Suddenly there was a diversion, the remaining crowd separating.

A man, different from the others, thick-set, with an intimidating presence, strode through them. The crowd fell back as the single figure confronted my husband.

My half-brother, Squire Jacob Thwaite, his contorted face illuminated by the hurricane lamp his bailiff held, had come for me as he had come for my mother before me. All passion spent, hopeless for reprieve, I crept back into the shadow and watched while my beloved husband negotiated for my life with the man who had vowed he would destroy me.

He had waited a long time for this opportunity, but had I not also waited, knowing in my heart of its inevitability? A lifetime of devotion, obedient to my lord, had prepared me and I knew now that whatever decision he made I had the courage to accept my fate. The terror that had smitten me when first I saw their torches had left me and my soul was at peace.

But Decimus was not defeated. Jacob Thwaite's voice rose

in his excitement. Decimus's stayed level. The crowd's loyalty fluctuated as they listened to my lord fight Squire Thwaite, not with force of arms, but with words, clearly spoken.

Suddenly Squire Thwaite's voice had modified. I was bemused when he spoke to Decimus as though he were a friend.

'Cast out the canker from your heart, man. The woman who came here calling herself Mary Cheyne beguiled you and has brought you nothing but misfortune. Did you not have her attend old Mistress Morgan, to have your mark cut into her flesh? No one will hold that against you, Decimus. How else could you protect yourself and your son from the curse she carried? Was not your second son born with a caul, protecting him from his mother? And your third; did he not take Holy Orders to cleanse himself of her?'

I could not credit my half-brother's wickedness. The veneer of friendship slipped as, relentless in his attack, he turned to the subject of Lydia.

'Now the daughter she bore you is a very different matter. You should beware of her. I watched her prostrate herself today before the altar. Thank God, Rector drove her out.'

Squire Thwaite waved at the crowd standing behind him, his gesture thrown away.

'It's high time these good people knew about Lydia. She's tarred with the same brush as the rest of her ilk and put a spell on her husband. She killed him!'

The crowd had grown again and I heard it gasp. They knew nothing of this and, fearing for my daughter, I prayed she was safe in Harry's care with Cousin Hector in Hartley. Jacob Thwaite looked to say more. Was there nothing this man would not stoop to? What else did he know about our family? My stomach lurched; he knew nothing of Decimus's past and never would. No one but I would share those secrets.

'And the last child that woman carried in her womb; was she not born dead, strangled by her own cord? I tell you, your woman is cursed, Hillyer, as was her mother before her.'

At first my lord did not answer. Could he possibly accept such a brutal indictment of his family?

But no, Decimus was not deceived. I could scarcely believe what he was doing, for he played a perilous game and I feared for his life. Laughing, he had returned the gun to his belt. Ignoring my half-brother's wicked taunts, lest those at the back might be hard of hearing my lord's words carried into the crowd.

'Your father sired my wife, Squire, and to protect her from you he gave her her name and that sticks in your craw.'

Decimus's words had the ring of truth and had found their mark. Squire Thwaite drew himself up to his full height. My half-brother was a big man, rotund and going to seed, but Decimus looked down on him. He would not yield to Squire's authority.

A scene as though on a stage was being played out before me. It hardly mattered if I were there or not. A hush had fallen over the crowd as they tried to catch each word. Their numbers had grown yet again. There was menace in Squire Thwaite's voice as he ignored my husband's censure. He had not yet concluded his condemnation and his utterance pierced my heart.

'We are civilised men, Hillyer. Unless you want to watch her die as her wretched mother died, then I recommend you accept my proposal.'

Nothing moved in that smoke-laden night. The wind had momentarily died away and even the lamp in the scullery no longer swayed in the draught.

'I offer you and your woman safe passage, but on two conditions. One, neither of you ever returns to this County.'

Squire Thwaite could not control his venom as he spat out his second condition.

'And two, you will restore to me, his rightful heir, the title to land and property belonging to my father, that was lost through spellwork to his bastard.'

The men began to mutter to themselves. This was not what they had come to hear. In his hatred for me, the Squire had forgotten them. They had come out this cold October night in blind and unreasoning terror of Satan. Jacob Thwaite had played on those terrors. Now they saw themselves manipulated, for he did not care for their fear. Callously he had used them for his own gain. The crowd seethed with hatred for their betters. Not party to a feud over property rights, they threatened to turn on him. Squire, guessing he was losing them, like a viper hissed at Decimus.

Decimus did not flinch, but walked past him towards the men. I could almost smell their fear as they edged away. Turning, confident of his hold over them, Decimus stood with his back to the crowd, leaving Jacob Thwaite alone with only his bailiff to defend him.

My lord had always been a man apart. Now, sensing the mood had changed, he spoke calmly to my half-brother.

'Your father rejected you, Jacob. How you must have hurt him, for I remember him as a gentle man. He was flawed, but are not we all?'

Despite his indiscretions, the old squire, unlike his son, had been much respected. The crowd murmured to itself and Decimus continued.

'For his sins, the woman he loved was not his wife, but a young gypsy. By your actions, you condemned her to death. She did not deserve that. Your father could not forgive you, Jacob, and left Cloudsmoor Farm, the house where he was born, to the love child that poor woman gave him: Mary Cheyne, my wife!'

For a moment I thought Decimus would strike the Squire, but he managed to contain himself.

'From the day you came home from the colonies you have wanted to be rid of her, but you will have to kill me first.'

Decimus was scathing.

'Through Thomas and Isobel your seed and mine will inherit the land you so covet. Be satisfied with that.'

Decimus was unwinding his whip. I could not believe his ferocity as he addressed his adversary.

'As for your second suggestion, the sweat and blood of generations of my kin for a thousand years and more are soaked in this land. No man, not even you, Squire, will drive me out.'

The crowd was restless, caught up in an argument they wanted no part of. Squire Thwaite, desperate now, denounced Decimus, saying he would arrest him and deliver him to the magistrates, for my lord was as guilty of witchcraft as I. But the men whose fear he had incited scoffed at the Squire and quietly walked away. By his example this night, he had forfeited whatever respect remained.

As he left with his man, Jacob cursed my husband and vowed he would take his revenge. With a flick of his wrist, my lord uncoiled the whip. Suddenly its crack split the air. With words that only a man could repeat, Decimus promised my half-brother that if ever he dared trespass on our land again my lord would kill him. With a mighty crash, Decimus closed the door, shutting out the night and restoring our sanctuary.

He opened his arms to me.

'It's all over, Mary. They will not come back.'

Sick and faint with fear for my own dear lord, my tears had run dry and I had no words. Despairing, I had looked into the abyss. In gratitude, I ran to my love and fell into his arms, my hands tight about his neck.

Hushed and reverent, Annie walked ahead of us, carrying a candle. In the parlour, my lord put down the whip and unbuckling his belt, set it aside. Adjusting the wick, he lit the lamp, bathing the room in its light. Annie, with tears running down her cheeks, her head bowed, knelt in homage to her master. Touched by her loyalty, Decimus kissed her forehead before gently dismissing her.

'Go to bed, Annie. There is nothing more to fear.'

He poured himself a drink and gave me brandy.

'You will keep me company, Mary. I am much too wide awake to sleep just yet.'

Startled, I took the golden liquid from him. The near-empty glass that had been Lydia's was still on the cabinet where it had rested since Captain Watkins had stumbled out of the darkness with his terrible tidings. Tonight Decimus had twice broken his rule, for only the men of his household were allowed to drink alcohol. Not daring to believe my trial could be over, I sat at his feet and had but one question to ask of my husband.

'What will happen now, my love? I fear the constables will come to arrest you. Will we ever be free of Jacob's spite?'

'He is a spent force here, Mary. A man like Jacob Thwaite rules by fear and tonight he was robbed of his dignity. He has no evidence to set before the magistrate. Mark my words, within a short while he'll be back in the colonies and good riddance to him.'

Decimus thought for a moment.

'You know, Mary, Jacob could easily have started the fire himself. It wouldn't have mattered to him whether you or Lydia were blamed. How easy it was to inflame the passions of those poor souls tonight. I am afraid that after today I cannot let Lydia come home again.'

'My love, I know my half-brother is an evil man, but I cannot forget we share the same father. He gave me my name and I love him for it. For my father's sake, I do not wish Jacob harm. But, lord, what will happen to Lydia now?'

Decimus leaned forward and threw more logs on to the fire. It crackled into life and sparks flew up the chimney.

'With Hector, Lydia is in safe hands, but, lest trouble follows her, Harry will not come home before morning. Sam Tyler is not the strong man I would have chosen for Lydia, but I have failed the child once. This time she will choose a husband for herself. We must thank God Sam is not a superstitious man.'

For a while Decimus and I sat together, not needing conversation. Seeking the pins in my hair, he laughed, for his hands were so calloused and rough they caught on the strands.

'You do it, Mary. You cannot see for yourself, my darling, but flushed from the brandy you are still a most beautiful woman.'

There was no mistaking my lord's persuasion. Whatever our fears for her future, there was nothing more we could do to help Lydia tonight. My head swam. I had not eaten. Was I intoxicated? Did it matter, so long as my husband was pleased with me? He had saved me from my mother's terrible fate and there could be no restriction upon my gratitude.

'Lord, you have set at peace my troubled soul. I was ready to die.'

'I know, Mary. When I stood in front of that crowd, I thought constantly of your mother. I have never forgotten her pleading and I too hope some day for peace. Maybe in a small way I have avenged her death. But to save you, I would have killed a man and without regret.'

Decimus looked pensive.

'I'm still the same brute I always was. I've a long way to go.'

With my hair falling about my shoulders, I shook my head to release the tresses. Undoing the buttons of my blouse, I freed my breasts. Perhaps with my body I could assuage my husband's torment. Standing, I took off all that I could, until but for my corset I was naked. Long used to the sparsity of my clothing, I did not feel cold.

His voice had lowered a pitch.

'Come sit with me a while longer, Mary.'

The corset that gripped my waist had alarmed me when my lord had introduced me to it. In my mind's eye, I remembered that day when Decimus had taken me to Milbury, my hands for the first time on Perry's reins. Perry's unbroken spirit had been synonymous with the freedom my husband had sought for me. But my freedom had always been at Decimus's discretion.

My lord's thoughts were also drawn to the corset that imprisoned me.

'I knew how much you hated whalebone, Mary, and I was cruel to make you wear this thing, but in truth confess I do not regret the decision. Perhaps its imposition tells you more about me than I have admitted.'

My lord seemed weighed down by his thoughts and, reaching up, I put my fingers to his lips.

'Hush, my love, you do not need to explain your actions to me. From the day you broke my maidenhead, I knew I should always be in subjection to you, as was Sarah to Abraham, who feared him and called him lord.'

Decimus's countenance had the distant look that Granny would have known so well.

'You must wonder why such little persuasion was needed, Mary, for me to go to sea. But after being away at school, village life suffocated me and I could not fit in. To come to terms with the hybrid I was, I had to leave this beautiful Vale. My grand-father, the old lord, treated my mother abominably but he was fond of me and that pleased her. He was an astute old man and though I earned my reward I've always been grateful to him for setting me up and giving me the manners of a gentleman. On my father's side, my kin toiled all their lives as tenants, liegemen to the FitzWarrens. Grandfather Hillyer has a special place in my heart. It was he who showed me the secrets of the countryside and gave me a love of the soil. You see, Mary, even now I am neither fish nor fowl.'

Decimus continued to stare into the past. What a strange mood he was in.

'One day at sea, I looked at myself in a mirror and saw the man I had become. Tired of my wanderings, I came home.'

With his handkerchief, he wiped the blood that still seeped from the corner of my mouth, then ran his hands over the smooth rigid surface that constrained me. He put his hands about my waist, lifted me from the floor and placed me on his lap. His face against mine was wet.

'I am sorry I struck you, Mary. I thought I was about to lose you and pray I never strike you in anger again.'

'It does not matter, lord. Nothing you could do to me would rob you of my love.'

Decimus seemed determined to chastise himself with his con-science.

'I had to enslave you, Mary. At first you were no different from the other women I imprisoned. I could only be aroused by a woman if she were in chains.'

His voice had broken.

'God knows, I didn't deserve your love, but you gave it to me and you gave me my family too. I thank you for that.'

'I would not change you, lord.'

Decimus wrapped his arms around me, seeming glad I had heard his confession. Burying my head in the warm leather of his jerkin, I asked a favour of him.

'I beg of you, lord, just this once, please do not send me to that special land you made just for me. I fear I may be there already, but long to stay here with you.'

'Don't you want me to love you, Mary?'

'Oh yes, my love, but more than anything in the whole world I need so much to give you my love and for you to know that, however cruel, your loving does not distress me.'

For a moment, fearing I had been familiar, my heart raced, but I need not have worried.

'When I created your paradise, it was to ease your pain when I loved you, Mary. That you may be purged of the sins you inherited, it was God's will you should sorrow in my hands, but, Lord help me, I am the man my experience has made me and I cannot change. Do you not care I should hurt you, my dear?'

'No, lord. I care not at all, for my heart views dispassionately the suffering my body endures. Nothing matters now, save the joy we share. All my illusions are gone. Now I know for certain there is nowhere I belong other than in your loving hands.'

With fingers that shook I undid the buttons of his shirt, while his eyes studied me. Smiling, he held my hands, stopping me.

'Enough, Mary.'

For a moment I feared I might have broken his mood, but had not. Unlocking my corset, he released me from bondage and I could breathe more easily. Gently he placed me ready for his loving. The rough serge of his trousers scraped me, harsh against my skin, but it mattered not.

He ran his fingers over the many scars my body bore. His mark, still bright, raised and sensitive to his touch, was spread across my belly. Decimus's voice could not hide his emotions.

'You are mine, Mary. Had I done to those slave women what you have allowed me do to you, not one of them would have loved me. Before I wed you, I knew nothing of love.'

Happier than I could remember, I looked up at Decimus

'I cannot know or care for other women, lord. Your loving has kindled a passion in me that will burn for ever. My soul will never leave you.'

Pressing his fingers firmly against my lips, he silenced me. With his teeth barely sheathed, he covered my body with kisses.

We had aged together, my love and I. His harsh, cruel hands that seemed not cruel to me held me still, my body contorted to his need.

Tenderly, Decimus lifted me and, content I had not failed my lord, I cleaved to him as he carried me to bed. Happy, I watched as he placed back into the chest his terrible whip, the knife and all that had lain on the floor. As he unloaded the gun, I heard his heartfelt prayer.

'I pray to God, Mary, I shall never need to hold a gun in anger again.'

Through sleepy eyes, I saw Decimus put it away, then I held out my arms to my husband, who came to me and, as one, we slept. Some time in the quiet of the night, my lord had need of me. More gently now, his passion measured, he took his pleasure. When he had done he let me rest, lying beside him, safe and happy.

I hardly heard him remind me; he must be up when the cockerel crowed, for Harry was not here to milk the cows.

I had fallen asleep.

With God's grace, I shall finish my story.
Mary Cheyne Hillyer,
1897.

CHAPTER XXVIII

The Reckoning

Waking, I reached out to touch him, but Decimus had gone and I shivered as memories of yesterday came flooding back. The shutters that had protected us overnight were open now and this morning the wind that had fanned the flames had returned to rattle the windows in their casements.

Putting my feet to the floor, I was weak and my legs quaked under me. Every bone in my body ached from the violence of my husband's passion and, steadying myself, I shuffled to the window and drew back the curtains. The yard was deserted. The house had never been so quiet and in the silence it seemed to brood. If only Harry would return soon and tell us Lydia was safe.

I looked out over the familiar fields, where a line of pollarded willows, gaunt and leafless now, marked the rhene as it ran, its tiny waters searching for the sea. I prayed that in a place far from here Lydia might find with Samuel the happiness denied her with Cornelius. Yet with my prayers came doubts, knowing in my heart Samuel would not have the courage to love her as Decimus loved me.

Why should I remember Queenie? It was such a long time ago when, in her strange compelling lingo, she had warned me against my daughter. I recalled the time before Lydia was wed, when some days it was as if she were two people trapped in one.

What foolish thoughts were these? Though she loved Samuel, even with him I doubted she would find peace, for he was a quiet man, his head filled with ideas, kind, unlikely to perceive her needs.

My heart sank as I contemplated the children Lydia would bear. I saw there was one who would carry the curse in her veins. Silt clinging to her feet and legs, her eyes shining in innocence, she looked up at me. A tall, reed-thin man stood beside her and I knew now where I had seen Samuel Tyler before. I had dreamed of the future and not of the past.

Shaken by my vision and unable to dress on my own, I called Annie to assist me. Her hands were gentle as she helped me into my corset and prepared me to greet my lord. She guided me down the stairs, then led me through the empty hall and into the warmth of the kitchen beyond.

This was not to be a normal day, though, when happy and lost in a world of my husband's creation I toiled at the tasks he set. On my knees, the scrubbing brush heavy in my hand, my mind could not break free. Something was wrong. When one hour had become two, I went in search of my love. Even the animals seemed subdued. The cows had been milked and were back in their field. Decimus was not in the barn. Retracing my steps, I found Annie and asked her where was her master.

In all her life dear Annie had been dumb and until this moment it had not mattered. She seemed not at all concerned for his safety, yet as I tried to understand her signs my apprehension grew. She took my hand and led me to where Decimus kept his waders. Then she opened the cupboard and pointed. The waders were not there.

'But, Annie dear, the fishing season is well over, why should he need them?'

Annie shrugged; she had not considered it strange.

Why had my love gone to the river? Perplexed, I closed the cupboard door; then, as the air moved and the latch fell, that same foul stench of rot I had smelt on the road to Bristol wafted over me. Last night my love and I had thought to postpone our fate, yet now I prayed to Almighty God that He would let us meet our destiny together. The road on which Decimus and I had travelled was ended and the dreadful Day of Judgement was upon us.

Holding to Annie for support, my body trembled with fear.

'Your master needs me, Annie, and I must go to him, for wherever his journey takes him I have to follow.'

Harry would be home soon, God willing. Guessing she would not see her master again, Annie's eyes had filled with tears. Holding her in my arms, I kissed her sweet face and bade her goodbye.

'Let my children know I love them, Annie.'

I picked up my skirts and, so they would not impede my progress, I held them high. My fatigue of no importance now, I ran up the stairs. With one last look I scanned this special place, where Decimus had loved me; where he had taken my will and given me his. My soul had found peace here, but without my lord I could not live. Frantically, for I had little time, I opened the old sea chest, which was no longer locked against me, and without fuss, threw my love's mementoes on to the bed. Seeing the picture of his terrible ship, I shuddered at the ill my husband had done, but nothing could stop me now. His faded indentures were swept aside. Fear of the knife in its sheath was lost. Even his dreadful whip had no power to frighten me. Under the gossamer gown, made heavy by his gun and hidden from me, I found my mother's brooch. Though it was only a symbol of the evil power of its curse, as I grabbed it I vowed no granddaughter of mine would hold the gew-gaw in her hand. Burning me, it seared my flesh, and when I rammed it into the bodice of my gown the pin pierced my breast. I wept but heeded not its stab.

All that was most dear and would soon be lost to me I left in this room. Stumbling, blindly I ran, down the stairs and out into the windswept yard. The cold wind slapped at my face and pulled at my hair. I was cold, but what need had I of a cloak? Aloud I called out, the wind carrying my words away.

Wait for me, lord.'

'Oh dear God, please let him wait for me.'

On and on I ran, not caring for the stitch in my side. My

lungs could not fill, for my breath was trapped by the iron girdle that controlled me, but I was used to its pain and ran on. Ever on, I ran towards the Sea Bank of the Great River. No obstacle would stand in my way. My skirt caught on brambles. I pulled at it, hearing it tear, but what did that matter? Again and again, for fear he might not hear me, I called out to my love.

'Wait for me, lord. Please, please wait for me.'

The church of the Blessed Saint Allwen, standing on the hill like a sentinel, its blackened walls forsaken, was open to the skies. Sadness overwhelmed me, and with my hands locked together, in my torment I prayed for deliverance.

'Dear God, forgive me my sins and guide me safe through the purgatory to come.'

It had begun to rain. Suddenly, barring my way, was a man. Battered by the wind, my head bent in prayer, I had not seen him coming.

''Tis no good, missus, tide's comin' in. Yer man 'll be covered by time you get down there.'

The man's eyes lolled in his head.

'He were standin' there in the mud, dead, 'alf 'is 'ead eaten by som'at.'

The man was gloating, relishing my terror.

''Twere terrible fight. Them tracks like, all round 'im. Reckon 'e were a sea serpent, like whale who come up a few year back, not five mile down river.'

Why listen? I ran on.

'Dear God, I beg of you: deliver my lord from evil.'

Marking the fishing, a line of wooden stakes led far out into the river to where I must find Decimus. I thought of the secret paths he used, but I had no need of them. I should not survive. The grass beneath my feet was soft and springy, the safety of the bank left behind. Soon the grass too was gone and mud oozed over my boots. Ignoring my feet, I raised my head and, looking far out into the Great River, cast my eyes to the distant horizon. I thought of the day I had gazed on this scene for the very first time. Jesse had been with me then. Now I understood what Jesse had meant, for no man would rob me of this wondrous land.

Since the day I laboured with Thomas and saw him delivered of me, I had known in my heart that in our children our eternal spirit will live for ever. In a hundred years and more, men who are born of Decimus's seed will tread this land and there will be women like me to love them. And one day the curse will be lifted when there are no more daughters left to inherit its torment.

In my mind I pictured a distant daughter and reached out to her; for what is time? She could not deny the pull of her roots and from wherever fate had taken her she had returned to this land. Behind her, rebuilt, was the church of the Blessed Saint Allwen. As she looked down across the flat, quiet countryside towards the Great River, with his arm about her, her husband supported her. He loved her as my lord loves me and, as a gentle wind from the sea blew right through her, this daughter of mine knew she had found the place where she truly belonged.

The curse had come to an end, for she had borne no daughters to continue it and her soul was at peace.

In the river was a boat. Her long black hull lay low in the water, a foresail set on her bowsprit, her mast pointing to the heavens. The men on her deck called out to me to go back, but I did not heed them. I thought only of Decimus and prayed for his soul to live. The words of St Paul were in my head. 'Love suffereth long and is kind. Love never faileth.'

Following the line of stakes, I clung to each one, the mud sucking me down. Dragging myself ever deeper, I crawled into the Great River. Geese, crying in despair, flew overhead and still I went on to where I must find my love. Then I could go no further, my skirts held fast by thick grey silt. Falling prostrate into the oozing slime, I lifted my head and stared at the waters rising before me. Praying to Almighty God, I begged Him to restore me to my beloved lord.

My hair was wet, my hands and body so cold they screamed at me. Coughing, I tore the evil serpent from my breast and threw it way out above the seething waters. I saw it writhe, caught in a shaft of light that crept between the clouds. Then it fell and its maleficence disappeared beneath the waves.

Cold, mud-soaked water lapped at my face and, drawing it

deep into my lungs, I pleaded for salvation. I could not see, nor could I breathe. My head was bursting with noise, but I made no sound. Now choking in agony, in terror and convulsion, clasping my hands together I prayed that God would take me soon.

In my delirium, Decimus came to me. His eyes laughed gently as his steady gaze held mine. Taking me in his arms, my pain belonging to another world, he turned me to face the heavens.

There in the sky, transcending the sun, glowed a great golden light and Jesse, bathed in its brilliance, was waiting for us. Placing my hand in his, I am not afraid. With Jesse on one side of me and my beloved Decimus on the other, I pray that, by my sorrowing and by my infinite love for my husband, Almighty God may forgive Decimus his sins and together in humility we shall enter the Kingdom of Heaven.

'And now Lord, what is our Hope?
Truly, our Hope is in Thee.'

Amen.

Epilogue

And what of the serpent? He lay on his belly in the river, eating dirt, until, in the dying days of 1940, when Hitler's bombs rained their terror on Bristol, he stirred again.

In peace, far from the Blitz she had fled, Jane walked with Lydia, her grandmother, on the Sea Bank of the great River Severn. The tide was full.

Jane's eyes, nearer green than hazel and set in an oval face that was paler than those of her Romany forebears, beseeched her Nana as she asked if she might paddle. Nana laughed to herself. What would Dorrie say if she could see little Jane paddling in the mud in the middle of winter?

'Nana, Nana, look what I've found!'

Suddenly startled, Lydia looked up.

Clasped in Jane's hand was a brooch. Slippery with slime and ugly in the extreme, a heart suspended from its smiling mouth, its red eyes glinted in the sun.

Lydia, her face ashen, took the brooch and, in greeting, the long silver pin pierced her hand.

'Dear God, I thought never to see this thing again.'

To be continued . . .